I0741344

Memoir of a Death Angel:

The Seven Lives of Persephone

By Aphrodite Anagnost

Chapter 1

1980

Sand and seaweed grated like bits of broken glass in the seat of my pink gingham swimsuit. I rubbed coconut tanning oil from greasy hands onto my ruffled bottoms, then peeled strips of sea lettuce from my belly and feet.

Smiling, gazing at me through Chanel sunglasses, Auntie Georgie sat on a gold tablecloth borrowed from her coffee shop, the Fairway Diner. She took a drag off a lipstick-stained menthol cigarette. Digging with her feet, toenails painted strawberry-red, she probed straight down through wet sand. "Aha!" She said, and washed the quahog free of muck in the receding surf, then dropped it into a wooden peck basket with a spool handle.

"A bushel and a peck and a hug around the neck," chirped my auntie, who once made a fair living as a zarzuela singer in Del Rio, Texas.

Yiayia Friday waved from the jetty. Balanced on two boulders, my grandmother swayed in a brisk salty wind that was driving two

1

white sailboats further from shore. I squirmed closer to my aunt, aching to crawl into a lap already occupied by the basket of clams. Yiayia was my grandmother, but she scared me.

From the day of her precipitous birth attended by a goatherd on the Ionian Isle of Paxos, in an olive plantation beneath a towering thirteenth century Venetian fortress built by our ancestors, my yiayia had always been suspected by everyone—peasants, priests, even her own mother and daughters—of being a witch.

Auntie Georgie put aside the basket. "Go ahead. Climb up."

I crawled over her crossed thighs and curled myself into a ball. "I don't want to wait for Yiayia," I cried. "Can't we go home now?"

Embracing me, Georgie kissed the pale pink shadow of a hemangioma, a birthmark that started on my palm and scuttled like a crab a quarter-inch up my wrist. My grandmother had one just like it. Last week my parents had boarded a plane for Gaios, leaving me at Yiayia's beach house. She'd told me how she'd been birthed at twilight to the clanging of copper goat bells, their notes carried by summer wind beneath the shadow of a ruined windmill under our family's villa, the Frangopanagioti Castro.

"Don't be scared of your grandmother," said my aunt, urging me forward with a warm palm against my back. "I'll take care of you."

I looked back toward the water. Yiayia was still waving. Her head bobbed above the turbulent surf. She was like a duck, never sinking, never completely wet. "But I have to go," I told Georgie. "Right now!"

My auntie rolled her eyes. "Of course you do." We crossed the dunes, blackberry brambles scratching our legs. I picked the biggest, most bloated berry and let its sour juice flood my mouth. I smiled up at Aunt Georgie.

"I thought you had to go to the bathroom. Now hurry up, Persephone."

I ran behind my aunt, then beyond her toward the asphalt.

"Persephone! Stay on the sidewalk." Auntie Georgie stood on tiptoes, calling me.

A hubcap lay on the tarred road in the shadow of a towering pine. A red windsock at a nearby cottage billowed in the breeze, carrying the wrackline scent of low tide. A screen door slammed.

Overhead a cloud like a dirty camel wandered over the dunes.

"Persephone, move," Auntie said, her tone tough and urgent. "Get out of the street this minute!"

I took three steps further and bent to pick up the gleaming platter. Georgie screamed. I straightened and looked back at her, hubcap in hand, ignoring the huge black sedan hurling toward me.

Thunder crashed and the wind kissed my eyes, drying, almost burning them, as Georgie gripped the pink ruffled straps that held my top on and flung me to the sidewalk like a goose with clipped wings.

I clapped, laughed, and began to crawl to the grass where the shining disc with the Mercedes triskelion lay. Lightning struck the beach behind us. A thunderous crack severed the air.

"Persephone!" Auntie Georgie shouted. "You could've been killed by that car! Or worse, turned into a vegetable or a cripple."

The tears streaming below her sunglasses seemed strange, as did the notion that I could've been transformed into eggplant—or worse yet, slimy okra.

"Let go of that nasty hubcap." She knelt to collect me out of the dandelions. I dried her cheeks with the back of one hand, then engulfed her neck with my arms, comforted by her camphorated breath.

Fog camped over us. Flash lightning lit up the sky.

"Are you hurt?"

"No."

"We have to go back for Yiayia. Can't leave her out in a storm."

Why not? I thought. Yiayia's magic caused storms. Maybe even this one. Her magic could summon the ancient magus. My mother had told me she had called him to my baptism and chrismation by throwing a handful of salt into her cooking fire every Monday for seven weeks. I rubbed the pale mark on my wrist that prickled now. Evaporating water left tingly, salty patches all over my skin.

"Persephone!" Georgie said, shaking my shoulder. "You're daydreaming again."

I woke from my recall of last week's spinning lesson. I'd agreed to let Yiayia teach me how to use a drop spindle and wheel. I appreciated its meditative qualities. I was craftsy, and it beat paint-by-numbers sets and papier maché. I loved the wild colors we used to dye the yarns—the indigos, alum, madderoot, copper, red sandalwood, and chromium.

"Let's cross the street. Don't forget to look both ways, and hurry up. Get in there and use the bathroom. Quick!"

We crossed and stepped onto the crabgrass and pinecone lawn that cut into a stand of loblollies surrounding our gingerbread cottage. Weeping willows flanked the screened porch. My grandmother had planted them the first year after she'd given birth to Auntie Georgie, and the second a year later, when my mother Medea had been born. No men had been allowed near her during labor. She avoided hospitals, and prided herself on never needing the help of "American medicines."

"Dr. Porter's Purple Pills for Pallid People, bah!" Yiayia'd said.

She'd buried the placentas under those willows. I believed she told me the story to keep me from climbing her precious trees.

"Why isn't yours bigger? You're older." I pointed at my auntie's tree. "Not that it isn't a good tree. It's bushier than Medea's."

She turned her body into the wind, as if lining herself up with some magnetic force I couldn't yet feel. "Your mother's tree is taller because it faces south. Or it might be over the septic field."

At the outdoor shower, Georgie leaned over and rubbed the sand from my bare feet and legs under the cool spigot. "Is something wrong?" She peered over her sunglasses.

"No," I lied.

"Then go." She patted my pink bottom.

Oh, how I hated that suit. I'd wondered if my grandmother had spent the early summer making me hideous outfits out of an old checkered table cloth to punish me for sins I had yet to commit.

I ran into the open cottage, a stray gust pushing me like a shotgun blast through the living room and into the parlor where Yiayia's three-legged Saxony spinning wheel sat, skeins of blue yarn bursting from a wicker basket. Past the four closets that masqueraded as bedrooms, and into the tiny iron-stained bathroom in the back of the house. The heavy sky descended, darkening every window. My eyes filled with tears. My mother was absent, as usual. Scanning the bathroom shelves while I peed, I counted six dark brown bottles

4

of liquids decorated with skulls and crossbones, like pirate's flags. I recognized the corroded jar labeled *Chrome Mordant: Danger. If ingested contact Poison Control Center immediately.* Yiayia and I'd used it to stabilize bright yellow mohair just last week.

I squeezed a stiff grass-green plastic bottle of chlorhexidine. Glistening white cream streamed out like toothpaste. I sang, "You Are My Sunshine" really fast while washing my hands. My elbow knocked a bottle of Pine-Sol off the counter onto the asbestos tile. I picked up the glass and threw a blue and white towel, crossed and striped like a Greek flag, over the mess.

"Persephone, hurry. We've got to go back for Yiayia," called Auntie Georgie, rapping on the bathroom door.

I flung it open and grabbed my Duncan Butterfly yo-yo off the Formica-topped sideboard in the narrow hall. "Why won't she come by herself?"

"Because she doesn't think she has to come in."

"Well maybe she doesn't," I said.

Georgie frowned. "Humph," she said, and pulled me out the door.

We held hands as we flew through the saw grass, ducking from the thunder and the hard-falling rain. My yo-yo smacked my kneecap as I swung it around the world.

Yiayia's head buoyed as she toiled between the rocks. "Mama!" shrieked Auntie Georgie.

Yiayia waved, raised herself out of the warm foamy surf, dragging a large hemp sack.

She hunched and limped against the weight of her get, hair stringy with strands of sea greens, skirted blue bathing suit stained with algae. Lightning flashed behind her.

"*Ti ehees?*" said Auntie Georgie.

Yiayia knelt on the beach, cackling, gums studded with a few gold teeth. She opened her bag, revealing a collection of mussels tangled with trapped starfish, tiny hermit crabs, sea horses, and periwinkles.

"Plenty of mussels, Mama." Georgie nodded in approval. "Good work."

"Later we roast them." Yiayia smacked her lips. "Then I make a stew."

I thought of my grandmother's big, black cauldron, always smelling of oregano from her garden, and the meals that emerged: okra and garlic fritters in egg and lemon sauce, whole astonished-looking fish staring skyward. My pet lamb, Hedwig, stewed with celery. And all manner of recipes involving the hens that ran amuck in the back yard under her sun-bleached laundry billowing like ghosts that hung from a clothesline strung between trees.

Yiayia's violet eyes twinkled. Dug into the sand with both hands and pulled up a dense malleable patty. She molded it into a ball the size of a fist. She reached into her bag, and like a drunk picking Taurus out of the night sky, she found a blue-and-white-banded shell. She held it up. An inch long, balanced and symmetrical, spiraling as it narrowed to a pointed spire.

"Let's go, Mama," said Georgie.

"Atlantic Dogwinkle," Yiayia said, smiling as she rotated it between two fingers. She pressed the perfect shell into the sphere of sand in her other hand, pointed end first.

"Once a living animal, now dead." She placed the ball just out of reach of the high-tide wrack line, upon a dried horseshoe crab shell. She crossed herself three times right over left and mumbled a prayer in Katharevouse, high-Greek spoken only by monks and scholars. Yiayia staggered back onto her feet, knees reluctantly straightening. "The Dogwinkle is a predatory sea snail, a carnivorous gastropod."

"Let me help you with that, Mama," said Georgie, reaching for the bag of mollusks.

"*Oyhee*. No. I've got it." My grandmother heaved the sack like Santa's bag of toys and dropped it into the half-filled basket of clams. She lifted the bushel, balanced it on her head, and trudged over the dunes, in front of us, just the way she liked it.

"What's with the ball of sand?" I said. "And why did she put the blue and white shell in the middle of it?"

Auntie Georgie, silent, adjusted her breasts in her bathing suit.

"And why did she whisper all those prayers?"

"To make a poppet," answered Georgie at last.

"Oh." I ducked behind my auntie's thigh, barnacled to her leg all the way home.

"Good night, Auntie," I said. "Good night, Yiayia."

Yiayia Friday peered up from her coffee ice cream. Her face twisted into a new expression, as if the spirit of some dead fortune teller had suddenly possessed her, and with a Romani accent said, "Vant some? What about a nice cup-a-cakey?"

Her witchy ways reminded me of what an oddball I was. My class-mates in second grade were real Americans. From normal families. I eyed the talisman that hung from her neck fastened by a leather shoelace—a chamois pouch bound by locks of human hair.

Yiayia smacked her lips and gummed her dessert, offering me a spoonful straight out of the carton.

"No, thanks." I squirmed in my chair as the beige paste melted to liquid in her mouth.

"Give me a kiss," said Yiayia, offering a pocked cheek. Cream ran into the creases at the corners of her mouth and collected in her mustache. From where I sat, charcoal lace curtains framed her face like a shroud. Her crooked finger tapped where the kiss was to be planted, directly adjacent to a hairy brown mole. I stared at the bump and thought of Hansel and Gretel.

Yiayia leaned back in her chair, overturned her demitasse, and presented it to me. My turn. I reached out and rotated the cup three times counterclockwise with my finger against its tiny handle.

"No," She shook her head and wagged her finger. "Clockwise to tell the future."

I spotted glints of violet in her eyes, like flowers. Elizabeth Taylor was supposed to have violet eyes, but they couldn't be as purple as Yiayia's. Turning the cup three times to the right, I crossed myself thrice, right over left.

Across the kitchen Auntie Georgie knelt on the lima bean linoleum, scrubbing a spot of blood off the floor in front of the fridge.

"Why are you squatting in front of the icebox like a gypsy?" said Yiayia Friday.

Auntie Georgie shook her canary latex-gloved hands over the bucket of carbon tetrachloride and vinegar, then pushed her sunglasses up the bridge of her nose with the uppermost part of her arm. Her cheeks were flushed from holding her breath.

"Can I help, Auntie? I like that smell."

"No, Persephone. It's poisonous."

"Why are you using it then?"

"To kill the germs," Georgie said. "They're everywhere. You can't be too careful."

"Pay attention to the cup." Yiayia tapped a bent finger on the table. "Never mind her. Do you see these brown stains? They're called 'dregs.' Soften your eyes. Look into the shapes behind the grounds. What image comes?"

"Nothing. I don't see anything."

"No! Don't look with your eyes, look with your mind. Don't you see anything dripping into the bottom of the cup?"

"A brown streak."

"Is there more than one?"

"Yes."

"Do they cross, or run parallel?"

"They cross."

"Do you see that triangular shape gathering in the bottom?"

"No. I don't see anything."

"Yes, you do! You see the box and the stem coming up from the triangle, the thorn coming out of the stem, and the crust covering the top…" Yiayia's neck sank into her shoulders. She peered out the window with a cross-eyed stare at doves on a clothesline. "… Like a murder of crows."

"No, I don't see it, Yiayia," I said, eyes misting.

Auntie Georgie stood with a sigh. Her shades flashed like shiny black saucers.

"The child says she can't see it, Mama." Georgie laid the gloves on the edge of the pail of poison. "I need to take a shower."

"But she can see it," said Yiayia Friday, face souring like bad goat milk, hair clumped like asparagus stalks seeped in rancid olive oil.

I ran to my bedroom and hugged Fred, my giant stuffed frog. Yiayia's thumping missteps followed me to the door. Her fingernails drummed on the painted knob. I switched off my night light and lay down on the covers, holding my breath.

"Persephone?" Yiayia called. "Don't hold your breath, sweetheart. Let the doorknob turn."

I said nothing.

"Don't hold your breath against me. I invented that breath-holding trick, you know." Yiayia rattled the door again. "I could teach you other things. Let me in."

I took a gulp of air. The knob began to turn, and then stuck fast.

"Hellia!" said Yiayia.

I held my breath as long as I could, then exhaled and gasped as Yiayia's heels clopped back into the kitchen.

"You can let your breath out, now, Persephone," said Yiayia's voice in my head. "I won't try to get in again. I love you."

I listened to the night rain, and when I finally slept, I dreamed of sweet, luscious blackberries and thorns, ripe in the sun. Within a triangular garden of tiger lilies grew a square cluster of antique roses. In the middle stood a splintered wooden cross. Above it hovered a murder of crows.

Chapter 2

I awoke to the clamor of Yiayia in the kitchen. I felt hot, unable to take a deep breath, my head reeling and throbbing as if balls of hail made of fire were pounding my skull. Was this doom? Terror? I smelled something burning, so it occurred to me to call the fire department. I looked under my bed and found only dust bunnies, nothing scary like a dead mouse, a snake, or a troll eyeing my ankle. I snuck out of bed and cracked open the door, checking the hall for smoke. Yiayia had the stove on, scorching residue of old sugar off a burner grate. She didn't seem alarmed. So I pressed the door closed and tiptoed to my bedroom window, and slid it open.

I snuggled back into bed and wrapped myself around Fred, sinking my nose into his soft, green polyester fur. I played with his little plastic cherry-red tongue. Oh, where was Auntie? Whenever I stayed at the beach house when my parents were on holiday, Georgie had been my constant companion, chatting me up by the time Yiayia started her morning rituals. Why, oh, why had my parents left me here? I would've rather been in Paxos, in the shadows of the Venetian Castro of Frangopanagioti, watching from the beach as my mother, Medea, hunted for sponges in the blue and white Ionian Sea.

Yiayia was grinding coffee beans with a mortar and pestle, singing the Greek national anthem. She belted *Elevtheria Y Thanatos*, "Freedom or Death," every morning.

A brika bubbled on the stove, shaking the mud brewing within. Yiayia had a special way of making coffee, just as she had a special way of reading the grounds, the *kafeomatea*. After the birth of the poppet with the dogwinkle heart, the tasseomancy session the night before, followed by the breath-holding trick, I wasn't really in the mood for any more of Yiayia's fortune-telling or spells. But now she was on her second boiling of the brika. The copper rattled and released fumes of cardamom.

She sang the refrain of "Freedom or Death" three times, as was customary.

> *Ke san prota andreomeni*
> *Haire o haire Elevtheria!*
> As we greet thee again
> Hail oh hail, Freedom!

Her alto voice cracked in her ultimate call to freedom as the brika bubbled its third and final time. "Persephone!" she called. "Time for coffee!"

Auntie Georgie normally would've had something planned, and we'd be out of the house before Yiayia's morning rituals had even begun. We'd often go to Georgie's Fairway Diner, and then check her vending machines in town. It was Thursday, the day we visited Vince, Georgie's tobacco supplier. He ran The Uptown Cigarette Company out of an old clam-packing house in Jamestown. He and the guys would fill her pick-up with crates of cigarettes. Then Georgie and I would travel to all the restaurants and shopping centers in Newport, fill up the machines, and collect kilos of coins into gray sacks.

"Persephone!" called my grandmother again. "Time is killing us!"

I emerged from my bedroom, still in lady bug pajamas. I rubbed the sleep out of my eyes with one hand. The other dragged Fred along. I found Yiayia bent over the stove, whispering in Greek, casting handfuls of salt onto the fire.

"Get some clothes on. We have a big day. We need to cook the mussels and spin some yarn. And I'm expecting a guest." She poured a glass of milk out of a fresh bottle, then stirred a few tablespoons of Eclipse coffee syrup into it and pushed it in front of me.

I dropped Fred and took a sweet sip, then licked the extract-covered spoon. Yiayia set a plate of toasted English muffins on the table. I dribbled syrup into the nooks and crannies of the bread. Eclipse was great on pancakes, milkshakes, and gave ice cream an extra kick.

"This kitchen is like camping," she said, sneering at the two-burner enamel stove. "I'm used to better."

Yiayia had hosted my baptismal reception and all my name days in the private medieval-style banquet hall at her winter home, the Hill House, which she almost never visited anymore. She preferred vagrancy to her mansion in Barrington, to which she would only return to throw parties. For most functions, she'd invite the usual guests—our local friends and relatives, visitors from the old country, professional black-veiled mourners, and entertainers on tour at Medea's theatre—and have their spirits "fixed" on gold-embossed name cards. She'd serve *koliva*, a memorial wheat; *psaraki*, tiny fish served whole; *horta*, wild hillside greens crisped in olive oil. And many pitas, flaky pastries stuffed with sheep cheese, spinach, squash, honey-sweetened pumpkin, and truffles she'd gathered herself with the help of her beloved mushroom-hunting pig, Sassoon, who also answered to "The Boar of Everholt."

She'd provided an identical feast for my great-grandmother Penelope's passing, the memorial service for my great-great-grandfather Capitan Cleitis—leader of the rebels who relieved Mani of Turkish domination in the Balkan War of 1812—and at the baptisms of my two cousins, Christy and Calliope. Also for Medea's wedding, for all four of Georgie's weddings, and on everyone's saints' days … and for Christmas and Easter.

I took a crunch of the English muffin and downed the coffee milk. "Why did you summon Father Stavros when I was little?"

She frowned, eyebrows like sideways question marks. "When…?" pretending she couldn't read my mind. She peered into my near-empty tumbler, then poured real, grown-up coffee into two demitasse and slid one towards me across the blue plastic padded table cloth. I stared for a moment into the cup—no message, only foam. Finally Yiayia answered. "For the sacred chrism, the blessed oil, made by the synod of bishops. For peace, pardon, and protection by the Holy Mother."

I pushed the coffee away and shook my head.

"Drink it."

"But I don't want it. I feel sick."

"Come on. First, we have to start the stew. Then I'll fix those marks on your skin. And I need Eucharist and unction. The Holy Father is coming." She hunched at the table, body slumped potato-like as a hag's, then stood with a groan. "Youth was never for me. I don't think it's for you, either." She held out a gnarled hand, glaring.

My head was already spinning. My heart beat like a blacksmith's hammer against my ribs. The room swirled when I stood. A flash of warmth made me unbutton the top of my crimson one-piece. My feet felt trapped. I couldn't wait to chuck that get-up.

"Go to your room and change. It's a hot one today."

I tried to hurry, but stopped to steady myself in the doorway of my room. I slipped out of the combed-cotton ladybugs into a pink seersucker romper, then collapsed onto my bed in a flush of heat.

Yiayia was in the kitchen, washing mussels. The shells clattered and water swished against the sides of her cast-iron pot as she dropped them in. Then she began rinsing and chopping vegetables with a fury, plopping them into the now-simmering concoction. Clouds of tomatoey clam broth and onions expanded into every room. I hoped that in her madness she'd forget the eels. And prayed she'd forget I was there until Georgie got back. My eyes throbbed; my chest felt tight. I was tired of the breath-holding trick, and besides, I couldn't keep it up all day.

"Get up," called Yiayia's hoarse voice. Her face lighted. "We don't have any time for turmoil. Let's fix those marks."

I had no choice. I hauled myself out of bed, neck sweating. I had about as much motivation as a brick.

"Let's go see Sassoon." Yiayia cackled like an egg-laying hen as she gimped her way back to the kitchen. "He can help you." She leaned over the range and turned the mussel stew with a big wooden spoon, both fists clenched around the handle.

I stood beside her, mouth watering. Little splashes sizzled as they dripped off her spoon and onto the hot surface of the stove. "You ready?" she said, her aquiline nose sniffing the rising steam. She turned the flame down to simmer. "The Boar of Everholt is waiting."

#   #   #

Her garden was hidden behind the bungalow. A line of lilac bushes, five feet tall, rimmed her tomato stakes and climbing peas. Beyond them rose the miniature pet mansion where her truffle sniffer, Sassoon, and his goose Betty lived, two animals enjoying the American dream. The Amish-built cedar shake two-room cottage had a little fake chimney and large windows for cross-ventilation.

Sassoon was sunning himself on the open-air lattice porch while Betty wandered the picketed yard behind their abode, rooting through weeds and sucking up worms.

"Sassoon! Here boy!" Yiayia put two fingers in her mouth and whistled like a drunken fan at a baseball game.

Sassoon's tail twitched. His sniffed and lifted his head, then plopped it back down with a grunt.

Yiayia was still in her bibbed apron, one hand in a pocket, carrying a galvanized cinder bucket by the crook of her elbow. She took out a hand stuffed with potato chip crumbles. "The Boar of Everholt awakens," she said, dropping the chips over the picket.

Betty let out a rusty honk. Her fat gray body swayed from side to side as she ran for chips, abandoning grubs and weeds.

Yiayia lifted the latch and let the boar out of his yard, trapping Betty behind the gate to scarf-up his left-overs.

The goose curved her long slender neck into half a heart, like a swan, cocked her head, and gazed at me with a golden-rimmed coal black eye. She let out a nasal *Haaahnnn*!

"Give her a biscuit," said Yiayia, handing me a dry black disc, like a hockey puck. She slid between the picnic bench and table. "Sassoon! Sit!" She tossed a cookie and patted the coarse topknot that crowned the bump on his head like a bad toupee.

Yiayia leaned over Sassoon and positioned the bucket beneath his phallus, then pressed his lower abdomen with balled-up knuckles until the pig released a golden stream. "Good boy."

14

He let out two short squeals. He squirmed on his back, little cloven hooves kicking at air until he managed to roll over and stand up. She offered another biscuit and led him back into his enclosure, bribing him.

"Tell no one of this."

No way, I thought. Yiayia slipped into the front yard and stooped beneath my mother's willow. She reached into her apron pocket and took out a triskelion tool, each blade both knife and spoon. She dug into the earth, torso thrusting with each stab. Her metal tub rattled as she mixed pig pee with dirt.

Georgie's fourth husband had been an obstetrician, and I liked to sneak into his library and peep at anatomy atlases. I could imagine the ruby placenta from my mother's birth with its three-pronged cord buried there under the tree.

Yiayia mumbled an *aitesis* for peace, pardon, and protection of the Holy Mother, and crossed herself three times right over left. "Holy Basil grew on the spot where Saint Helen found the Holy Cross, therefore I have prayed." Then she planted a handful of seeds in the small depression under the tree, muttering curses under her breath. "*Skordia*! Cursed foul dirt stinks like garlic!"

She patted the ground. "Always remember. You must rant and rave. *Semer le baslic.* To sow a good crop of basil. Otherwise it just won't grow. It'll drive you crazy."

I felt suddenly restless, robbed that Auntie Georgie had been gone so long, that I was stuck out here with Yiayia not knowing what was next.

"Come here," she said.

She gimped to the back yard and dropped onto a bench. "Sit." I slipped in next to her, as obedient as Sassoon, though less vocal. She stirred the dirt and pig pee with a wooden spoon, identical to the utensil she'd used for the mussels. Was it the same one? I suppressed a gag. She turned my wrist over and stroked my hemangioma with light fingertips, then slathered the warm paste onto my wrist. "I was born with the same mark," she said.

I pulled back. "Ew! But Yiayia. That's just gross. It stinks."

She grabbed my hand and returned it to the table, wrist up. "You must leave it on and let it dry. The marks will disappear. Let me see your neck."

I lifted my ponytail up and dropped my head forward.

She tied my hair into a bun and spread putty onto what my mother called my stork bite. "Now let down your top."

I gasped. "But…Yiayia."

"No one can see. I've made us invisible."

I stared up into her violet eyes.

"No one will know what we've done. I'll erase those marks. But we haven't much time."

At that moment a lavender breeze swept across the yard. I took it as an omen I should obey. So I unbuttoned the straps and dropped the top of my romper.

She squinted, looked down and mumbled into her vessel. "*Catharee*. Clean." She scooped up a dollop of mud in the crook of one bent finger and smeared some on my beauty marks, as Medea had called them. She covered the large one below my left nipple, which always looked swollen, like a little ant hill. She lowered her head into a shadow cast by the lilacs, and said, "Holy Mother, you are the hope and protection of the faithful. Do not despise my petition. *Doxa si*."

I didn't know until years later that these "witches' marks" identified me with a certain spiritual inheritance. The ritual was a protective rubric. But I was baffled by Yiayia's odd choice of dirt and pig piss, which together smelled like steamed broccoli.

I squinted into the glaring sunlight. "How long do I need to leave it on?"

"Until tomorrow." She dropped the spoon back into the pail with a clank. "Put your shirt back on, my little Dogwinkle."

Her eyes could hurt you, almost burn you, if you looked at them too long. I looked down, dog prints in a patch of dried mud. Buttercups poked through the crabgrass.

"Pray," she said. "It can only help."

Yiayia collected her triskelion and a few sprigs of oregano she'd picked from the pots outside the back door. I slipped back into my top, then got another whiff of that lavender breeze.

A faint voice on the wind was calling my name. "Persephone, Persephone."

"No," I whispered. "Go away."

Chapter 3

Back under the hood over the stove, Yiayia Friday hovered over the pot and poured vermouth into the mussel stew. "You're tired. Go take a nap. Want some Absorbine Junior?"

"No thanks." When I'd had strep throat, she made me gargle with it. I'd coughed and sputtered, then finally vomited, dazed for hours.

I wandered to my room, through the shotgun hallway linking the kitchen to the rest of the house, past daguerreotypes of stiff, dark-haired relatives from Paxos. Flow Blue plates were mounted on walls of the narrow hallway. Saints Paraskevi, George, Athanassios, Helen, Evangelos, Mary, and scenes from the life of Jesus hung from rusty nails that had cracked the plaster.

I dropped into bed feeling like I'd like to remain cocooned for a week, just me and Fred, my ladybug comforter twisted around us. At least, until Auntie Georgie got home. The air had become suddenly still. It felt hard to breathe in the pervasive miasma of shellfish. I thought of fire trucks, sirens blaring, and men in yellow suits holding vibrating hoses squirming wild as giant serpents.

For a while, I lay awake, seeing visions in the shadows, colors swirling like oil and vinegar in a cruet. The darkness deepened, and I imagined dusk falling on a field of scarlet poppies.

\#   \#   \#

In my recurring dream came Yiayia Paraskevi—which means Friday, or day of preparation. She was twelve, running through a stone castle just before dawn, and dressed in a ceremonial white nightie, an *aspro poukameso*, the simple rectangle of combed cotton worn by virgins. Until their marriage night, that is; when their dresses would be stained pink, then be given to the grooms' eager parents. So real she appeared, yet I knew I was dreaming, Yiayia carried a linen bundle of bloody rags. She crept down a stair and onto a marble floor made bright by warm rays shining through massive open double oak doors.

A butler was afoot, shuffling around the parlor from window to window, pulling open heavy curtains with a whoosh. Paraskevi held her breath to freeze his movement, then darted through the front doorway and sprinted across a stone terrace engulfed by yawning pale yellow primroses twisting to gaze at the rising sun. Reaching the end of an open field of winter rye sparkling with poppies, she darted behind a hedgerow of yews, and plunged into a fringe of forest still lost in long slivers of night.

Friday's cheeks were sanded rosy by traces of salt left by drying tears. She crossed herself right over left, and knelt before the wet shadow of an enormous fir, a tree that spoke to her with the thick heaving tongues of animals lost in its branches.

I tried to help her, to change the dream and make it better, but couldn't. Furiously she dug a hole with only fingernails and broken sticks. I dreamt of hungry worms squirming in the porridge of dirt, sand, nibbles of pine cones, and patches of leaves that lined the bottom of the earthy basin. At last she covered over the bloody rags and patted the mound. A light rain pattered on the grave of rags and washed all traces of blood and sweat away.

In the next dream, back at the *castro*, Paraskevi sat at a large banquet table swaybacked under platters of pastries, cheeses, grapes, and goblets of wine in honor of her name day. *Chronia Pola*. Many years, many years. Mandolins and bouzouki struck the first notes of "The Butcher's Dance."

Guests rushed to the terrace to join a ribbon of dancers as the mandolins' notes plucked at the languid summer air. Servers carried new platters of olives, and flaky pitas in the shape of moons and stars. Amphorae of wines poured like an endless dark sea through punctured hulls into the glasses of the celebrants. Through the veranda, Paraskevi watched coaches drawn by bay horses pull up at the *castro* after the bell had tolled, after the singing of the fourth hour following the liturgy and devotions to Agia Paraskevi Saint Friday. In her vague smile I saw a strange mixture of dread and joy.

A single crow glided over the terrace and disappeared into the hot ball the sun.

Notes from the bouzouki tumbled from the air and sunk onto the stone path below. The mandolins fell silent. Dancers one by one dropped their hands and broke from the line.

A black dog stood in the middle of the terrace, sides heaving, eyes joyful, clutching Paraskevi's earth-stained, bloody linens in its jaws.

#   #   #

I awoke and repeated the dream to myself. So compelling and vivid, it demanded my memory. Yet what did it mean?

I clung to Fred, and pulled the comforter to my chin. In a dream-fall of colors—the purple-hued light filtering through the violet Roman shade, the slice of daybreak that peeked from behind it, the hovering gray cloud of Yiayia's mussel stew, the dried mud that cracked and pulled at my skin—I lingered in a fugue state, in a world between sleep and wake, under a long finger of terminal daylight.

Then, I heard the three-beat waltz of a cantering horse. I jumped out of bed and looked around a corner of blue cotton ticking. A monk in a dusty black cape, face hooded, leapt silently off an ebony horse. Windswept and chafed, he had the leathery look of a desert father. He loosened the saddle, removed the bridle, then left the mare untied to graze in the back yard. I'd never seen a real live horse before. We only traveled in cars. I wanted to feed her and rub her coat.

The floor moaned as the priest crossed the threshold.

I froze, listening for footsteps, but heard only Yiayia puttering about in the kitchen. A deep-throated sequence of invocations—first, the communion prayer, then, readings from the Pauline Epistles and the Gospel of Luke, and next, a plea for intercession from the most holy, pure and ever-virgin, Mary—slipped through the space under my door like musical notes from the plucked mandolins of my dream freed from their pages.

I tiptoed out of the purple darkness of my room into the hallway illuminated by horizontal rays. I peered around the corner into Yiayia's room. She was kneeling before her *candeli*—altar of candles, crucifix, oil lamp, and icons of Saint Paraskevi and Christos Kai Maria. Her incense and censers were pushed into a corner to accommodate the priest's Pix. I was drawn to the pressed-gold-leaf and sapphire pectoral cross that swung below his heart from a plaited strand of horse tail and gold thread around his neck.

Dark eyebrows curved over black eyes. His neck was slightly inclined, and it struck me that this man's features lacked any trace of anger or arrogance. His straight nose turned a bit downwards like a foxglove, and high cheekbones framed his face. His skin was covered with shallow wrinkles. Topping his broad straight forehead, a thick crop of wavy gray hair ended in wide curls above his shoulders.

The monk dipped his thumb into the oil from a lamp burning on the table and made a cross on Yiayia's forehead. "And He anointed many that were sick and healed them. And the anointing ye have received abideth in you."

Ashamed that I'd intruded on something so personal—as though I'd witnessed my grandmother undressing for bed—I crept back to my room. But I knew they'd sensed my presence. He wasn't an ordinary priest. He was a Magus.

"When she is of age she will study with me, just as you and your mother did. I will teach her as the holy line of Fathers taught your ancestors, even before the birth of Christ."

I pulled the duvet over my head. My mind had gone blank, shocked into silence. Eyes moist, hair on my arms rising, I inhaled the scent of lavender from the robes of the Magus as he mounted outside my window. The hollow triplets of steel horseshoes on turf faded in seconds.

Yiayia shouldered the door open, letting in the last beams of afternoon light.

"*Kali nichta*, my little Dogwinkle. It's been a big day."

"Where's Auntie Georgie? When is she coming home?"

"Soon. She had a little fire at The Fairway. From the lightning storm. But it's okay now."

I sighed. "Good night, Yiayia."

I fought the reflex to cringe as she kissed my forehead with her hair-crowned lip. She made the sign of the cross over me, then lumbered down the hall back to the kitchen.

I stroked the dried mud on my wrist, careful not to disturb the plaster, fearing her spooky ways were terribly important, but having no clue what it all meant.

Chapter 4

Three days later, I rode, cold, wrapped in the arms of my mother, Medea, in a funeral limousine scented with Imperial Violet, by Prince Matchabelli, Yiayia's favorite. Next to me sat Auntie Georgie, spitting on my black patent leather shoes as she held them in her lap, then rubbing them with a lace hankie. On her other side, my cousin Calliope slumped, half-asleep, leaning against the padded shoulder of Georgie's coal-black suit.

My mother's blazer was powdered with crocus pollen from her trip to Gaios, a fishing village on the island of Paxos—Yiayia's birthplace, the birthplace of Circe. In the shadows of the family Castro, an islet boulder, *Grias Pidimas*—Old Ladies' Leap—jutted out past the terraced green hillside. Every summer at the beach blackened by volcanic ash, my parents, Medea and Angelo, would dive for sponges and sift the sand for treasures of ancient sunken ships.

Now Medea popped open her satin pocket book and rummaged, elbow-deep, as if the tiny purse were bottomless. She retrieved a wad of lipstick-stained Kleenex, and peeled it like an onion until she reached two delicate pieces of brown coral shaped like perfect eggs. She dabbed her eyes with an edge of the wrinkled tissue, then polished each piece with her tears.

"Give one to Calliope," she whispered, placing a coral egg in each of my palms and closing my fingers around them. Auntie Georgie turned to me and I passed one to her.

"From *Grias Pidimas*," Medea said. "Natural. Made smooth by the sea."

Georgie leaned forward and mouthed, "Thank you, Medea." My auntie dropped the egg into Calliope's white-gloved hand.

My mother coughed and cried, rubbing my back through my black-velvet dress. The collar tugged and scratched. Auntie Georgie's eyes, only half-hidden by sunglasses, lost their dark cast in half-light. I turned to look back out the rear window of the hearse, where Yiayia bounced with the dull thump of every pothole on the coastal road, her casket jumping in its velveteen compartment.

Calliope's lips were moving, as if counting. She rolled the coral egg in her hand. I knew she was praying.

I straightened and spoke into my mother's ear, each lobe heavy with long strands of black pearls. "Why is Yiayia riding in the back?"

"Hush, *agapemou*," said Medea, whose blessed name was Panagiota. "Yiayia's body is sleeping in the casket. She won't get up. Don't worry."

I frowned at Medea's pretense of normalcy. "Who made her sleep?"

No answer. The adults in my family felt better if they thought the things that frightened most people would scare me, too.

On the coast road, beneath an overcast sky, ripples tossed their froth across the flood-tide of an otherwise ashen sea. I turned my eyes toward the sheets of clouds blowing apart in the darkening sky.

Medea's clothes whispered above the purr of the engine as she moved. Gulls swooping over the high cliffs of Newport, Rhode Island crooned their matins cries, inaudible to everyone but the four of us.

I looked to my mother and Auntie, and to Calliope, our tetrad like a black shamrock lost in the requiem of seabirds. My father and two uncles sat opposite in somber silent study of their programs while the Matepas women talked.

"How did you know to leave Paxos so quickly, before I had a chance to call?" Auntie Georgie asked Medea.

My mother snapped, "How d'ya think?"

"Don't get angry with me, Medea! Someone could've called. I don't know."

"Well, they didn't."

"I don't want to argue about it." Georgie slid a cigarette halfway out of a silver case, then returned it to its tight soldierly rank.

"Fine," said my mother, lips tight. Her fingers, glistening with gold bands, came to rest on my own.

The driver slowed and turned up a fin-backed ridge which swung around a cove. Here shingle met sand and salt-watery fingers rose and poked into hollows of rock, like Grecian horses galloping in from the foam.

The men sat, pretending to hear nothing of the conversation as the long car accelerated onto a smoother road. They only looked up from their programs now and then to gaze at one another and flip strings of blue-eyed worry beads.

Medea crossed herself three times, right over left.

The car hit a pothole and jolted my cousin Calliope, one year older than me, from her fugue. "No one can do anything for Yiayia now but bury her," she said. "And pray, I guess." She sounded exhausted.

Medea nodded. "Her body will become permanently incorruptible, yes. But we'll have to pray for forty days, until the memorial service."

"Pah! Nonsense," said Auntie Georgie. "Dust to dust."

"*Skata*!" said my mother. "Her body will sleep during the intermediate stage of partial blessedness. We'll pray and help her along."

Calliope closed her eyes, lips still moving. She appeared to have resumed praying, but I knew better. She was counting backwards by sevens from one-hundred, something she did when people fought.

"Medea, Mama's spiritual transformation is between her and God," said Georgie.

The hearse flew over a speed bump and the casket hit the ceiling with a thud.

"Then why do we light candles for our grandparents, who died spiritual fighters during the Balkan War of 1912?" ranted my mother. "Why burn incense if not to reach the nose of Heaven?" She threw a fist into the air. "Why do we make a ceremonial wheat-berry cake with pomegranates and raisins and cover it in a white shroud of powdered sugar on the fortieth day, if not to seek the resurrection of the spirit and the body? Once I saw the soul—"

"Oh, leave me alone," sighed Auntie Georgie. "And don't talk that way when little ears are listening."

My mother picked up my hand that held the coral egg and raised it briefly to her lips. "They don't have little ears in every way, or little eyes, either. Pray they'll always be happy girls."

"Stop it," said my aunt. "I want to think of other things. About my taxes, and the fire marshal's investigation at the Fairway, and will the black-eyed Susans get rain."

"The black-eyed Susans don't need rain. They're wild. They can walk to the sea," I said. Yiayia had told me that.

My father met my gaze and winked and we both struggled to stop giggling. He fiddled with his black silk armband, then resumed studying his program, again picking up the beat of the worry beads' clicking.

"That's right, honey," said Auntie Georgie, reaching over and straightening the silver satin bow that clung to my hair like a caterpillar.

"Ha," said my mother. "Look who teaches me how to talk to children. Now raggedy wildflowers can grow feet and walk to the sea."

#   #   #

The driver slowed and turned right, up the oak-canopied driveway that rose from the coastal road and ended at The Church of the Annunciation. My cousin Christy, Georgie's eldest by her first husband, had been following us in his new tangerine Corvette convertible. He speeded up and passed us by cutting through the lawn of the church, then screeched to a stop. "The Ride of the Valkyries" wailed to an end on the stereo. He popped out of a flung-open door in his Navy dress whites.

Our chauffeur, chuckling, pulled up in the lot next to him and straightened his black-billed cap. Christy sprang to our side door and opened it before the driver could get there. "Baby sister!" He leaned over and wrapped his arms around Calliope, kissing her neck until she snorted. He kissed each of us first on the right, then on the left cheek as we disembarked.

The church's gold dome billowed like a swan above us, centered by a gleaming crucifix. Below the dome, the great quarried stone walls were veined with darkened streaks of minerals.

"Nice day for a funeral, if there can be such a thing," said Christy, pointing to a streak of light that had broken through a cloud and caught the dome napping.

A phalanx of pallbearers headed toward the casket and stopped to greet us. They looked like secret agents. Women in black garments made splendid by gold brooches kissed our faces and walked us to the book-matched mahogany doors.

"*Agia steen mimni.* May her memory be eternal," said Father Athanassios.

The Presbytera greeted us from the narthex and kissed each of us—right cheek, then left—and guided us to the vestibule candles. I lit a white one that smelled like honeybees and planted it in the sand urn. Then crossed myself and prayed Yiayia Friday's journey to Paradise would be free from potholes and policemen. Walking to the iconostasis, I kissed Jesus, Mary, and Agia Paraskevi, the namesake of Friday, planting my lips on the painted folds of her robe.

I inhaled with all the strength of my ribs. Incense carried my prayers to God. The words seemed to flow like Eclipse coffee syrup from the center of my chest. Then, as if in a dream, I lit another candle that misted my eyes.

I walked to the first pew, my mother guiding me from behind with gentle touches. In the corner of an eye, I caught Yiayia's shadow as it rose from the polished cherry coffin resting before the altar.

For the first time that day, my fear of the body of Yiayia Friday lifted, and I prayed hard for her soul's ascension through the oculus at the apex of the dome.

The eight rounded soprano tones soared from the canticle, from low sorrow to the highest joy of the freed spirit. Sitting between my aunt and mother, I scanned the church to see the shadow of Yiayia again, but she was gone.

"I'm sorry I was afraid of you, Yiayia Friday," I whispered into the scented air.

The sallow, clenched forehead of Father Athanassios reflected the rumpled light of the paraffin candles that illuminated a path for my grandmother's shadow to follow. We prayed and crossed ourselves as the censer swung toward us and Father Athanassios prepared Yiayia's body to receive our lamentations, and the casting of holy water.

We lined up in the center aisle with dozens of others in black dresses and suits with black armbands to kiss the closed eyes and the cross at her breast.

Father Athanassios glared as I hesitated before kissing her. Somehow, she looked much younger, hair smooth and coiffed.

In death, her features had been augmented by the mortician's cosmetics: her lips parted; face moist with cold cream; dentures installed; cheeks stuffed with cotton batting; mouth and bridge of her nose, pink as if wind-kissed. Even her knuckles looked rosy, as though blood coursed beneath living skin. Her upper eyelids had been shaded with bronzer, and sculpted waves of hair set with spray framed her face. Her cool flesh left a dusting of waxy powder as my lips brushed her cheek. Her neck veins protruded, and I tried pressing one down, but it popped up again. The aromas of strange fluids, cosmetics, and Gardenia by Prince Matchabelli stayed with me as I turned from her casket.

My mother led me back to our row and sat me down beside her, then turned her gaze to an empty seat in the shadows of an enormous basket of white lilies.

I softened my eyes and sighed. My heartbeat slowed and I nestled into the warm wood of the pew and the smooth, soft flesh of my mother's arm. I followed her gaze to the end of the pew. My grandmother smiled at us, her silhouette melting into the clouded air.

"I kissed you," I whispered, finally relieved of any revulsion for Yiayia.

"I love you," her lips said back.

My mother squeezed my hand. Still looking back at the ghost of my grandmother, Medea got up from the pew and began the second procession to the coffin, where we were to toss white roses and look upon the body for the last time. A body that had repulsed me so. I felt ashamed.

My aunt whispered into my ear from behind. "You don't have to look in the casket again. She understands." She patted my shoulder.

I'd never seen a dead person before. Her wrinkles had vanished, perhaps from those hours in the water before—well, Auntie Georgie hadn't found her until noon, the day after the Magus had come and a bolt of lightning had struck the Fairway. Yiayia had never returned to the house. When Georgie went down to call she'd spotted the body floating among the rocks, her sack half-filled with mussels.

I'd woken a few minutes later to the tears and sobs of Auntie Georgie. By then, my parents had already boarded a jet and left Paxos.

#   #   #

In the distance, our chauffeur, in his black-billed cap, stood in the shadow of elm trees beaten by rain. I could see him, darkly, through the leafy wind. Then, in the dip of a sodden branch, he was gone.

Father Athanassios stood over the casket, rain dripping from his jowls. The coffin rested atop a pair of two-by-fours above the grave. We tossed more white roses upon the closed lid. And the priest recited the *troparion*, the requiem for those who have fallen asleep.

"With the spirits of the righteous made perfect, give rest to the soul of your servant, Paraskevi Matepas, O Savior, and preserve it in that life of blessedness which is with You, O You Who Loves Mankind."

"Father Athanassios," said my mother, "Can I see her one last time?"

The priest bit his lip and looked over the drenched congregants crowding the grave. His grip tightened on the worn leather prayer book.

"Please. I have a picture of Mama and Papa on their wedding day. I'd like to put it in with her."

Under his impatient stare, my mother shivered and opened her satin purse, sheltered by Auntie's umbrella. She slipped an old photograph out of an age-darkened envelope, stepped forward, and with trembling fingers held it out to Father Athanassios.

"Certainly," he said. The rain left white spots on the picture, in spite of the canopy, until he shielded it between the leaves of his prayer book.

He motioned to the pallbearers to open the casket once more. My uncle and father snapped open the latches and lifted the lid, spilling roses onto wet grass. The priest stepped forward and held out the photograph, about to drop it in the coffin.

"No! Let me do it," sobbed my mother, the scent of crushed petals rising from the grave.

Over the priest's shoulder, I looked again at the far copse of elms, searching for the chauffeur with his black-billed cap. I saw only a dark shadow in the downpour slowly rising, fashioning itself into a man. Then his wings unfurled. But when the rain swept by, my cousin Christy stood alone, smoking a cigarette, where the chauffeur had just been.

Father Athanassios held the picture out to my mother, who knelt beside the casket and tucked it under the cross in Yiayia's hands. That's when Calliope and I stepped forward together and dropped our eggs into the casket as if we'd practiced it.

Auntie Georgie took the hand Medea had released, and tucked a Jordan almond into my palm. The clacking of worry beads broke through the rain's cacophony.

"Oh, Auntie," I said. "Look. Christy's gone."

"No, he's over there next to the statue of the angel. The one waiting to be set on Yiayia's grave."

I squinted. "No, he's not."

The little forest of elms, over two hundred yards away, was now empty of man, beast, or bird, and the rain had stopped.

Someone stepped up behind us, and startled me. When I turned to look, Cousin Christy gave me a wet wink, unpinned the rose from his lapel, and dropped it onto the pile of flowers. Then he joined the pallbearers with their webbed straps and helped lower Yiayia Friday—with her picture, her cross, dozens of roses, and a pair of coral eggs from the motherland—into the ground.

We stood and watched the men push piles of loose, moist earth with their big flat shovels. At last, Christy planted his like a sapling and raised his face to the last drop of rain.

"Caw," a crow cawed. I looked up. Dozens of black wings banking on a front of fresh wind turned in a wide gyre, then raced across the sky.

I'd learned to sense energy fields when I was a very young child. Not by thought, but by relaxing until I could no longer define the edges of my body. I could swim in the electric field that flowed from my heart out my fingertips. Yet I'd remain perfectly awake.

I was floating now. Heat shot up my spine into my head; my ears buzzed; flows of vibration like tiny bolts of lightning passed though the spaces between my cells. My toes tingled. I heard church bells. I had become the clear sky.

And soon the ghost of Yiayia Friday would rise from the grave and walk the tiny stretch of woods swaying at the edge of the cemetery. By then Medea would be mumbling the last of her forty-day prayers.

And the chauffeur in his black-billed cap would be there too, waiting for my grandmother's spirit. I knew all this quite well. I'd already learned it from Yiayia Friday. But why?

Chapter 5

Newport, Rhode Island

July, 1988

My father waited in the foyer, rattling the blue-eyed *kumboloi* in one hand and his keys in the other to the tune of "Candy Man" coming from the record player in the parlor.

"Persephone!" wailed my mother.

The screech curved up the stairwell and sliced through the yellow-papered walls of my bedroom. I threw my summer party dress with the Peter Pan collar to the floor and jumped onto my goose-down duvet, burying my head under my ragged stuffed frog, Fred.

"Your shoes!" she said. "Your shoes, they're covered in mud."

The clack of her stiletto heels over the throbbing Italian marble of the landing shook the clusters of sunny daisy blooms from the papered walls of my room.

Medea flung her muscled body against my bedroom door. At the splintering crack of wood, I raised my head from Fred's warm, sheltering fur.

The door flew open, and my mother stood erect and furious on the threshold. To her right the glass doorknob had just buried itself into Captain Jean-Luc Picard's belly, where a remnant of the blasted poster hung like entrails, plaster dribbling from his wound.

In the sudden, held breath of the house, my father trotted out the front door, still flipping and agitating the hard storm of blue-eyed worry beads that swarmed like bees in his argentine rattle.

"Give me an explanation," Medea shouted. Two of her long, finicky fingers dangled a pair of muddy black Cappezio's by their straps. "And what were you planning to wear on your feet tonight at the Newport Musical?"

I sighed. "I'll clean them, Mom."

"And how will you do that?" A smirk of disgust lifted one side of her mouth and crossed to the other. "There's the stink of horse in this muddy crust and it won't come out."

She takes so long to dress herself with so little result, I mused, stopping my mouth to preserve a moment of dignified silence. The house held its breath again.

"What did you say?" A flake of mud cracked off and landed on her once-clean shoe.

"Nothing."

The house resumed its natural breathing.

I could wash away the mud and exorcise the smell, but said nothing. I turned instead toward the bright day glowing through the bedroom window.

"Think you can hide your thoughts from me?" said my mother. "Well, you can't. Didn't I give you my breath, bone and blood? Yet you think you own gifts even I don't have. Really, how did you get them?"

"From Yiayia Friday," I said.

"Then why not summon Yiayia and get her to clean these shoes? And while you're at it, have her bake you a lemon poppy-seed cake. You have seven minutes."

Medea yanked the knob from the wall and slammed the door behind her as she left. Plaster snowed onto the olive Berber carpet.

"Witch," I said.

In the bathroom I called Yiayia Friday. "Get to work or else," I told her. Soon the shoes were clean and smelling like a new car's leather interior. A sunny yellow cake dotted with lovely blue seeds and frosted with lemon butter cream was steaming on the kitchen counter.

"I'm not the witch. You are," called Medea from the kitchen. "I chose other things."

#   #   #

The Newport Musical Theater and Country Inn, known affectionately by regular customers as "The Tent," was two miles from our house. It sat at the end of a winding tree-canopied two-lane road past the Phillips mansion, nestled deep within a dark forest. A place where H.P. Lovecraft and his elder paramour, Providence poet and spiritualist Zelia Brown had once plunged with insolence and absinthe into rakish dissipation, inspiring "Medusa's Coil."

My parents had bought the twenty-acre dairy farm in 1970 and renovated the Victorian farmhouse and creamery into a restaurant. It quickly became famous for the continental cuisine preferred by the Newport sailing elite and the local Italian Mafia.

Thus continued a centuries-old tradition of family bravado.

#   #   #

When he was twenty-five years old, my dad had fled for his life from Greece, after being accused of drilling holes in Dr. Mengala's private plane during the Nazi occupation of Athens. He escaped to the U.S. with a press pass provided by his brother, the chief of secret police of Greece, who had achieved his position by befriending Rudolph Hess over cutthroat games of bridge. My father Angelo and his brother Petro were both ringers for Niarchos, the billionaire shipping tycoon.

Dad was an aeronautical engineer by training, but spoke no English. So, after arriving in New York, he'd failed to land a lucrative job.

He enrolled at the language institute and The New York Culinary Academy, his studies funded by uncut emeralds smuggled into America in the hollowed-out heels of his American-made wingtips.

Pumped full of the pure Herculean blood of Sparta, he'd had a mop of auburn hair capacious enough to contain seven ounces of gold dust mixed into his gentleman's pomade. So, the one-hundred-and-fifty stall milking barn that sprawled behind the restaurant had been converted into a summer theater with the money retrieved from his golden locks.

When Medea first saw the interior of the barn she'd thrilled at the sight of the great hooks in the ceiling above the stalls from which dangled huge leather slings. She'd cooed and caressed the leather, longing to use the straps for her Dominatrix act. Later, she cleaned them herself with glycerin soap and treated them with mink oil.

"They were used to support cattle," my father had told her. "Not men. They were held upright by the slings during milking because they were always drunk."

"Drunk?" my mother had said, even happier than before. "The cows?"

"Of course. They were fed on the alcoholic corn mash left over from the stills."

"Funny what a man will do to save a dollar," Medea had mused.

"After the alcohol tainted-milk was stripped from the cattle's teats, it was thinned with water, then laced with chalk for color."

She wrinkled her nose. "Was it good?"

"It was swill." My father shrugged. "That's what they called it. It killed babies."

My mother had broken into wild laughter, which led to uncontrollable hiccupping followed by projectile vomiting. Then she'd attempted to swing from the milking slings and had to be restrained by my father's arms thrown around her shoulders.

# # #

My formerly dirty shoes, once dishonored after helping me muck horse stalls, now shone with a pristine innocence as Dad pulled his Thunderbird into the parking lot of my parent's restaurant/theatre complex, "The Tent."

By then, he hadn't spoken to my mother for two and a half days.

"The Candy Man will be wonderful, tonight. You just wait and see," said Medea.

He exhaled on his sunglasses and cleaned them with his handkerchief, silent.

"Fuck you," said Medea, I think, to both of us. "This is an investment, not a gamble."

"I don't want to go in," I said.

"You don't have a choice."

"I want to go live with Aunt Georgie. And Cousin Calliope."

"You've got Calliope for the rest of the summer. And Georgie! She's with her dreary little gang of Armenians in Brooklyn," said Medea. "That second little business of hers. What is it? Oh yes, manufacturing epaulets for the military. This is how she wishes to spend her life—half her time on earth in the little four-foot wide brownstone with a creaky iron gate. Brooklyn, Ye Gods! Maybe you can visit her when she comes back to Newport to take care of that dreadful shack on the highway."

"The Fairway Diner," I said.

"Golf!" said Medea, "She built a diner beside a golf course. Now, I want you to be the hostess here tonight."

"No."

"Okay. Then you can answer the phone."

"I have a lithp," I said.

Her lip curled. "No problem. Yiayia can speak for you."

"Fine," I said, "I'll have her sit by the phone."

I sat in candlelight at table number one in the Country Inn munching celery hearts and jumbo pimento olives while Medea sipped a Manhattan through a tight red straw. She counted money, ironing out the creases with her palms, arranging the bills so that the faces all pointed in the same direction.

After a few minutes, she hauled up without excusing herself and walked toward the ladies room.

Twilight pushed through the beveled windows. The other tables were still empty. Dad had disappeared into the kitchen to mix sauces and demonstrate the preparation of the night's cider-braised pheasant with pearl onions and apples to the assistant chefs, Graham and Julia.

I opened my signed copy of the autobiography of Sylvia Plath, *The Bell Jar*, and counted metaphors. Page after page—one outrageously lavish metaphor per page—like pearls Plath had hoarded to drop for some dark reason, some act of entrapment.

But Sylvia Plath was dead, her last breath taken in the gas oven into which she had thrust her head. Who had given me the book anyways? Who'd left it on my bed?

My eyelids grew heavy. The black helices on the harvest tablecloth began to spin. The light through the window dimmed to shadows.

Once again, Newport County was adding up its nightly murders, and I could feel the hospital groan with its weight of gurneys.

For the first time I connected the muddy burial of Penelope's placenta with the dream of the forest burial of Yiayia Friday's clothes. It seemed to me then that the blurs of the helices toward which my head drooped had become human souls I would someday hoard and drop, like pearls, one by one, into the earth.

I chuckled.

The vision had been a trick by poetry—I guessed. A gift from Medea, via Sylvia Plath.

#   #   #

About my intelligence at the age of fourteen: It was never tested by any other instrument than my own estimation. That made it a thing of extraordinary beauty, one I could carry with me surreptitiously—its chief charm and value.

For instance, though I guessed it had been she who'd left the book for the purpose of a spell, I would never let Medea know I had also guessed her hand had dropped *The Bell Jar* on my pillow to frighten me away from pursuing the path to … I knew not where.

I laughed. She would be so annoyed to return to the table and find a daughter who was holding her breath.

My cousin Calliope and I were both smart enough to learn the breath-holding trick, the meanings of the Ryder-Waite Deck, how to read the stars, dream interpretation, Romanian sympathetic magic, and the power of prayer. This body of knowledge we often practiced and applied in my attic at 140 Red Chimney Drive.

School was the place where A's were plums I plucked from the air while little boys tried to look up my freshly-ironed dresses. Home was the place my mother did the equivalent to my head. But she would never see my panties, like the little boys did. I kept a diary with a lock on it to hold my secrets.

Truculence and display, truculence and display. The primary nouns of my being as I journeyed the thus-far narrow passages of my life.

\#   \#   \#

By the time my mother and father returned to the table together —an accident not often accomplished unless Medea was giggly with Manhattans and my father in a trance—the light in the dining room had descended to gloaming. Not this time by the agency of a dream, but rather of the sun. Streaks of dust sparkled like powdered jewels on the window glass by its fading orange glare.

First, I heard the excited trill of my mother's voice warbling in mock song. I shook my head to see her approaching with my dark-suited father in tow. He was regarding the two women in black sheaths and pearls beside him, not Medea.

"Now don't you two run away after the show in the barn," she whispered to the two smiling women passing before Dad, too low for him to hear.

"We wouldn't think of missing one of your after-show performances, Medea," said the eldest, a dowager of seventy with a silver pompadour *à la* Liberace. She took my father's arm, though it hadn't been offered.

"Oh, we wouldn't dare miss your show," said the younger woman, whose almond eyes flashed below an inverted peak of black hair that half-covered her forehead.

"I'd have you for breakfast if you did, Angie," my mother said, twittering. Angie smiled back. My father, locked between the three, blanched and stepped away from them to the table, shedding the arm that had captured his. Covering a cough, he pulled out a chair for himself alone.

Mother glared.

"Don't be so old-fashioned, Medea," said the silver-haired woman, aflutter with waving fingers. "We're perfectly able to seat ourselves.

In spite of my father's tightening jaw, we were suddenly a party of five around a centerpiece of pinecones and horseshoe nails, one of Medea's more craftsy creations.

Ms. Wick and Ms. Block were devotees of my mother's cabaret performances in the restaurant's after-hours black box café. Medea's act followed the semi-retired Las Vegas celebrities who strutted their allotted hours on the barn's main stage.

Ms. Wick and Ms. Block were lesbians and therefore fascinating. I enjoyed their false-eyelash batting, winks and sly touches. My father wished both of them dead and mounted; especially when they grew ecstatic, teary-eyed, and leapt to their feet hailing Medea's more ludicrous performances with shouted bravos.

Poor father, a ghost of a child who had only longed to grow up, find a wife who loved him, a noble profession, and a hospitable home. What remained for him now, his dead dreams and his prayer beads? Medea had blown several fortunes on the barn, the creamery, the restaurant, penny stocks, dogs and horses, and blackjack. After emptying a coffer by predicting a black-jack dealer's hole card one after another, she was barred from casinos everywhere, except New Jersey where anyone who isn't drunk and a public nuisance can play. But in Atlantic City, her psychic strategies failed. No longer could she predict the next card to be dealt from a shoe, the next roll of the dice, or where the roulette ball would fall. Atlantic City was cursed to her.

She was a crazy opera-diva with, by my own still-juvenile estimation, misapplied talents. Still, she refused to return to the hereditary arts at which she might have excelled.

Chapter 6

"Persephone!" Medea screeched from the edge of the parking lot, the low-hung sun barely lighting the sequins of her dress.

Calliope and I dove into the field of tall rye behind the barn, as laughter at the Candyman's jokes filtered through the cedar shakes of the theater. We lay still as the dead between stalks of gray moldy grain, happy to have scalped our tickets to the show to a pair of very convincing drag queens. The money was rolled tight into cylinders we used as telescopes to peer through blowing blades of grass.

Nearby, cows lowed goodbye to the departing sun. Night slunk into the lot where Medea roved and cursed, looking into cars and under them, seeking our slaughtered bodies. Calliope giggled and I laughed, wondering what foolish thing I could say to my mother—after she'd given up, when the show was done, when Calliope and I must return to the company of the living.

"Blasted brats," muttered Medea, tugging the elephant knees out of her nylons.

"What'll we say to her when we do turn up?" whispered Calliope.

"We were dragged into the celebrity trailer and force-fed Gobstoppers and Wonka Bars?"

My cousin's gaze suddenly turned toward the woods. *"Tavros,"* she whispered.

Medea disappeared back into the theater. The rank, sweet stench of bull filled my nostrils and I started to rise.

"Get down," Calliope gasped.

I ducked my head. The earth smelled of moss on wet stone, of fermenting rye mold. Ghosts of milkmaids looking for shepherds stirred, twitched, and slipped off into dark. The dampness of shadows held me. I closed my eyes and heard black wings flapping.

"Run!" Calliope cried.

I glanced at the split-rail fence, still green with copper coat, to estimate the distance. Seventy-seven steps. Twenty-three seconds. *Tavros* was behind me at the edge of the woods, stomping a hoof, neck muscles bunched, tilting head and horn to the scrambled sky. Trumpeting, bellowing, filling my head with sound.

I rolled under the bottom rail after Calliope. Tavros' breath scalded my bare legs, his wet muzzle kissed my skin. Then Calliope and I were safe, convulsing with laughter and hot tears.

"Oh, Mother," I shouted. "It was so mean of you to summon the bull."

Calliope scratched her clammy palms. "I'm still sweating."

"We could've been gored."

I hadn't eaten meat since I'd visited my father's *horio* near Sparta, because the village had roasted my friend Achilles, an innocent goat, in celebration of the Feast of Emancipation from the Ottomans. The salty meat had sprung sweet to my tongue, the sauce dripping down my chin. But later, told the slices I'd savored had been carved from Achilles, I gave up flesh then and there.

Calliope and I filed through the theater. The crowd in Brooks Brothers' jackets and summery gowns was still chatting about the antics of the Candyman on the main stage in the concrete barn. Pushing through the swinging double doors, we collided with a waiter carrying a tray of caviar, sour cream, and crisp crackers. He pivoted on the heel of one black patent leather shoe like a tap dancer. "Ooh," he squeaked.

We ran to the warming tables. My father was placing curled lemon rinds on salmon like ribbons on a present.

"We'd like steak, Dad."

"Oh, please," said Calliope. "Very rare, with Lyonaisse potatoes and lots of juice to soak bread in."

My father cupped a hand to one ear. "Hmm?"

"Please. We really do want steak. Honest. Bloody."

"Yes, Uncle. Still mooing," said Calliope. "Gourmet Magazine says yours are the best steaks on the island."

We ate with heads down, avoiding my mother's Medusa stare. When pangs of guilt swept into my feast, I swept them back out. When I soaked the last heel of bread in the last drop of thickened stock, I prayed for the soul of the innocent cow, then left the last bite for the Hungry Ghost.

Ms. Wick and Ms. Block stopped at our table—"the head table" as my mother liked to call it—on their way to the bar.

Medea put her golden napkin to her mouth, just so, concealing the final moments of chewing, as the two women sat down, flanking my mother, their sycophantic lips kissing her cheeks.

"Candyman was su-u-uch a scream," crooned Ms. Wick.

"Oh yes," said Ms. Block. "Will he be here for your performance after dinner? Does he always wear those sunglasses? Can we get an autograph? Just give us his ashtray. He's such a star!"

"He said he wouldn't miss it for all the bumble in the bees," said Medea, slipping her voice into her nasal passages, confirming her pitch.

"How about a Beefeater Martini, extra dry, rocks on the side, extra olives, Ms. Block?" Medea offered.

"Sounds heavenly for you, dear," said Ms. Block kissing the air. "I'd prefer a pink lady, extra sweet, slightly chilled, shaken with rocks, extra creamy."

"Persephone," said Medea. "Please go mix these lovely ladies' cocktails. Then serve the dears at their table with a platter of stuffed mushrooms, compliments of the house."

My bitten tongue panged. "Am I the bartender? Mrs. Hamm didn't teach these recipes in my ninth grade class."

"Sam will give you the manual, as usual. Or you could just ask him to coach you."

Calliope and I slipped through the crowd and under the bar's gate. The varnished oak island glowed with the reflections of cognacs, brandies, whiskeys, gins, and vodkas lined up like medicines in an apothecary's shop. Luminous bottles of candy-colored aperitifs gleamed like stained glass, above canisters of pearl onions, maraschino cherries, limes and lemon wedges, slices of pineapple, mango, and papaya, celery stalks, Spanish olives stuffed with pimentos, almonds, and blue cheese, and fresh herbs.

"Sam, I can mix the martini by myself, but I'll need help with the pink lady."

He reached for the grenadine and vodka and flashed us a shy Haitian smile. His long black fingers set a glass, the cupola shaped like the breast of Marie Antoinette, on the soft towel dressing the mixing ledge.

I received from his warm hands the stainless steel shakers, one alive with ice, as if to summon the spirits into the fellowship circle of Sam, Calliope, and me. And hence, into the glass, producing a seductive pink lady sweet enough to kiss.

"Be fruitful, Ms. Block," I muttered, hands hovering over the glass in prayer. I dropped a cherry into the drink to represent the fetus in her uterus.

After stabbing three olives with a toothpick decked with golden tinsel, I remixed the martini using the same toothpick as a swizzle stick, soaking the olive flesh with gin and a hint of rare estate-bottled Haitian vermouth.

The pimentos bulged like swollen corks. I sucked each red sliver from the olives, careful to keep the fruits intact on their spear.

My cousin giggled with, I think, a semi-awareness of what I was doing.

"I love you, Calliope," I said. "Now, let's deliver these potions together."

I smiled at the bartender whose custom Creole aftershave coated his gleaming skin with a hint of sassafras. "Thanks, Sam."

Having presented the drinks and the stuffed mushrooms while Ms. Wick and Ms. Block looked the other way, Calliope and I returned to Medea's head table, where she waited with narrowed eyes.

"I won't ask what you've done this time," she said. "But you will play the piano tonight for our friends after my rendering of Bizet's *Toreador*."

"I need to use the ladies' room," I said. "Excuse me."

"Oh no, you don't." She clamped a hand around my wrist. "Those bathrooms have had at least fifty customers in them since the cleaning lady left. Too many germs there, Missy. You girls will have to go outside, behind the lilacs. Come on, I'll stand guard."

"No thank you, Auntie," Calliope said sweetly. "We can handle it. Let's go, Persephone."

"If you don't come back afterward, I'll come get you! You will play that piano tonight, Persephone."

"I don't want to, Mother."

"Would you prefer to go to boarding school?"

I considered the offer. "Maybe. If Calliope can come with me."

She leaned back, already in the middle of her second lobster. "I'm through talking to you," Medea huffed. "You'll play tonight, or else."

Pushing back our chairs, Calliope and I left blobs of spumoni melting on our deep dish apple pie. Hand in hand we picked our way like mice through the obstacle-course of tables.

"Where does she put all that food, Persephone?" whispered Calliope, eyes wide in the gloom.

"I can tell you where it's going to end up," I whispered back.

In the empty anteroom of the restaurant, we tipped the cigarette machine first on its left side, then pushed it forward, nearly toppling it onto its face. Calliope pulled the lever under the Newport Lights while I slapped its back a few times, until it spat out a pack.

After peeing in the shrubs, we sat down in a cluster of poppies and smoked.

The minutes flew by as the night grew a cooler, richer black. Calliope and I swore to be dear to one another to the end of our lives. Then so tightly entwined our pinkies that even demons in rages of love for one of us could never sunder our tie. Calliope had been born the daughter of the American ambassador, Georgie's second husband, but soon became, thanks to death and remarriage, the stepdaughter of Senator Ajax Praxos of Rhode Island, who'd killed himself with a small black knife when offended while playing poker.

"I'm a child of death," she said, as the sawing of cicadas quickened around us.

She needed my consolation. "And so you are reborn." It was one of those gloomy evenings when old wounds ached.

The owls sang to us between meals of field mice. Death hung like snakes in the moon-drenched branches of the chestnut trees. Yiayia Friday's black dog sang in my memory as if to recall evening shade and solemn doom.

Medea's mezzo-soprano wafted through the windows, doors, and chimney of the restaurant's black box theater, telling us we were already truant from her show.

Just as we were dusting ourselves off, a car pulled onto the shoulder by the berm at the edge of the property. The grey sedan blended with the night and the gravely voices speaking Italian, as the smoke of the engine mingled with the perfumed wall of lilacs enclosing us. Two men in trench coats and fedoras climbed up the rise of low hill between parking lot and barn.

We peeked through the crinkly red petals of poppies, our breathing silenced. The pockets of their black coats sagged with some hidden weight. They walked the perimeter of the restaurant and black-box theater. One crouched at a window, testing the sash. The other crept to a back door, twisted a knob that refused to turn, then ducked away from a shaft of moonlight as he bent, head level with the keyhole.

I murdered the flaming ash of the cigarette between forefinger and thumb wetted with spit. We knelt lower in the circle of poppies, behind the row of lilacs heavy with panicles, not breathing. Hands covered our mouths lest we make a sound.

"*Andiamo*," said the broad-shouldered shadow.

"*Piu tarde*," said the other, sounding disgusted. They headed back over the hill.

Chapter 7

We stood on the wide brick stair at the front door of the Country Inn and Newport Musical Theatre picking sticks and leaves out of each other's hair. Menthol smoke trailed us like Pigpen and his dust cloud. The massive white door was stuck so tight, it took two arms to fling it open, as though a vacuum had sucked it shut. We rushed through the golden-carpeted aisle of the restaurant, empty except for busboys carrying trays bearing the remains of lobsters and crabs, potatoes and wilted radish garnishes, the empty shells of pecan pie and lonely maraschino cherries on melting spumoni swamps.

"Whom should we tell?" I muttered. We passed through the open French doorway and waved to Sam, who was sorting cocktail glasses behind the bar, trying to close up. Two drunken blonds, assets propped high with state-of-the-art push-up bras, slouched low on stools, blowing smoke rings, sucking at the dregs of pink frozen drinks, the kind festooned with umbrellas and pineapple chunks.

"We can't just tell Dad," I muttered. "It'll have to be Medea. Dad's stopped talking."

"Should we wait until she's finished singing?"

I stared at her. "Are you kidding? She'll kill us if we get between her and her song."

"*Toreador en guarde! Toreador! Toreador!*" Calliope chirped. "Medea sings *'L'amour t'attend!'* like a screeching guinea hen."

We walked through three great rooms of tables and chairs, newly dressed with golden tablecloths and yellow beeswax candlesticks, toward the back of the restaurant.

"Wow. Medea loves to pitch that 'head voice,' as those in-the-opera-know call it," said Calliope with her best Katherine Hepburn voice. "Right through the unfortunate ceiling."

The poor song climbed its way out of Medea's throat like a man from a mine.

"Shhh," I swallowed my laugh, dabbing streaming tears with a long lock of hair. "Wait. Please. Those Colombo-looking guys were scoping the place for a break-in. Would you stop, so I can think?"

"You're right. Medea will be in no mood to talk right now."

Her voice bled under the door to the theater, a renovated storeroom with black-painted walls and a pipe grid overhead. Medea regarded this space as ultra-chic, a sacred artistic berth where she could explore her version of "pure performance." We listened and waited under a quaking chandelier. Fingerprint- and lipstick-stained flutes on rows of trays against a cherry-paneled wall resonated like a hand-bell choir. The windowpanes vibrated in their frames. An almond Roca rolled on top of one half-eaten peppermint parfait, then off the tray, and plopped on the terracotta and midnight checkerboard floor.

"Got to figure out how to get her attention without pissing her off," I said.

We took turns staring hard at my mother through the astragal of the massive green door to the theater. Under a spinning disco ball she invoked Carmen, white-gloved hands lifted as if angels were swooping toward her from the rafters. She buzzed and swayed, contralto reverberating through her thick trunk sheathed in emerald taffeta, her boosted cleavage pulsing pizzicato. The recorded accompaniment seemed to oscillate up through her muscular calves to boom through the top of her head. Her bouffant wig bobbed. The bangles around her wrists glittered in rhinestone rainbows, trapped in the folds of her elbow-length gloves.

"Maybe we could pull the fire alarm?" Calliope suggested.

"Or get *Tavros* the Bull to run through the building."

"Maybe we should charm some bees to swarm the hollows of her wig and deposit pollen."

I cracked the great green door open. Three dozen sets of eyes widened as Medea's mouth stretched wide, uvula shaking under the spotlight, all her weight shifting forward in chartreuse pumps. After the final high F, we slipped in, still reeking of Newport Lights. Smoothing our grass-stained skirts under us, we scooted into a pair of armchairs around a small table in the back. I licked my fingers and snuffed out the candle that lit our faces, inhaling burnt paraffin.

Medea blew kisses to the Candyman, dodging the crimson roses Haitian Sam threw, thorns and all, as he did at the end of every performance. She smiled and waited, bowing again and again at each lull in the applause.

"Encore, encore!" called the Candyman from his seat, smoke circling upward from his extra-long flapper-style cigarette holder to where angels floated.

"*Grazie, grazie,*" said Medea. "But we still have a special treat tonight. My daughter, Persephone, will play the *Pathetique*. Enjoy!"

The clapping swelled. My moist armpits stuck to the fabric of my dress. "No, Mom," I mouthed. I moved my lips and pointed to my chest. Need to talk, I mimed, holding up my right thumb and tapping my second and third digits, producing the universal sign for speech. "I need to talk to you." I pointed to my mouth, but my mother only shrugged.

I shook my head. I need you now. I pointed at my heart, then my mouth, then to her.

She frowned, shook her head, and pointed at the piano.

"No, Mom," I mouthed, head wagging. "Now! It's important!" I said, really fast, hands flying.

"Thank you, everyone. And now, the *Pathetique*."

I swallowed pooled saliva. She wants me to play the *Pathetique* while Mafia guys with guns are scoping out the restaurant?

"Go tell Sam and my dad," I told Calliope. "Maybe they'll call the police now."

"Okay," she said. "But it's too late to save you from the stage. Tonight."

I regarded the rebuilt Victorian Grand with a sneer. Clouds of cigar smoke swirled with steaming wax in the humid air.

The sense of my own greatness as a pianist lay monstrously heavy on my shoulders, as if some deranged, toothless seaman rode upon me piggyback, grotesque legs wrapped around my neck. When I sat at the piano, fingers finding the several hearts of each key, I entered a world into which not even Calliope could travel with me. Though the applause could take me to a peak of *evforia*, I always consequently found myself alone, insufferably, with only little insensate birds of imagination to which I could speak my love.

My cousin squeezed my hand, leaving blue-eyed worry beads on a braid of horsehair in my palm. Not looking at the audience, I carried it to the piano and hung it from one stag horn of the piano's candelabra, so that it cast a sapphire glimmer across the keys of the upper register.

I crossed myself three times, right over left, with diminutive motions, trying to appear secular, nonchalant. I looked at the sheet music in front of me. It was the *Apassionata*, not the *Pathetique*. I gasped. My fingers fell from the keys, waiting pointlessly for the *Pathetique* to appear. I summoned Yiayia Friday. Coughs and varied rustlings assaulted my ears. Yiayia not answering, I prayed to the Holy Virgin, eyes tightly closed.

"Persephone," hissed my mother from the first row. "Go on."

I stood, opened the piano bench, and waded through portfolios of sonatas, pages scattering to lie flat out like white corpses. Through the lens of tears glazing my eyes, I found the first movement of the *Pathetique* and placed it over the *Apassionata*.

I cupped my hands over the keys and waited for my fingers to begin. But the ivory was cold. The ice of it streamed into my fingertips. Then, out of the corner of my eye, I could see a waiter's tray, sloppy with a mountain of discarded desserts, glowing in a corner. The remains of cakes with sprinkles floated in melting heaps of ice cream, coffee ice cream. As the liquid pooled and oozed off edges of tipped saucers, it coalesced, then took the wraithlike form of Yiayia Friday. She flung her head back and laughed. The air was thick with spirits. I glanced at the audience, careful to avoid Medea's glare. The spectators were oblivious to the fact that a ghost was materializing out of melted coffee ice cream.

I shrugged, looked down at the keys, then scaled up and down in e minor. The ebony A, B, and E keys seemed inflated compared with the other black keys. My fingers quaked and flattened, despite the fact that Yiayia was there, presumably to help me. At home Medea balanced quarters on my knuckles to stop their shaking and maintain the cups.

I slid out of e minor and into e flat. The second movement, *adagio contabile*, burst from my hands. My anger at Medea sent the invisible quarters flying from the stage and into the first row. Tink… tink … tink… they sounded in tintabulation.

I stopped and looked out. Yiayia swam in a haze of shadow at the back of the room. Her hands worked as if she were packing a snowball. She formed a sphere of light the colors of cupcake sprinkles, then flung it over the crowd at Medea. Like a comet trail, sprays of electricity blew through the room. The Candyman slapped his neck as if swatting a mosquito.

Lifting hands high, I hurled my fingers down onto the keys and started over with the first movement in front of me: *Grave: Allegro dis molto con brio*.

My fingers grew colder. I studied the keyboard as the A, B, and E grew larger. The clanking of cups, the creaking of chairs, the twang of the plumbing in the walls swelled. My fingers raced toward the end of the first movement in spite of the sluggish keys.

The notes of "The Candyman" became distinct within the flurry of notes.

"Who can take a sunrise, sprinkle it with dew. Cover it with chocolate and make the world seem new?" played simultaneously in my head.

"That was wonderful, Persephone." Medea stood from her chair.

"The candy man can, we know that he can," sang Yiayia.

"All right, Persephone. Terrific," said Medea with a sneer.

The Candyman shouted a "*Bravo*." He stood and clapped like a seal with limp wrists.

The whole room was vibrating. A pencil bounced off the music stand and onto the floor. Medea flung her own envy-green ball of light back at Yiayia, who vanished. The top-heavy candelabra collapsed on the piano, bulbs exploding over the edge of the shiny mahogany, slick with polish. When I lunged to catch the flying candelabra, the crystal chandelier pieces soaring like bullets, I knocked the keyboard lid down onto my left hand. A blast of pain was crushing the tips of my fingers.

#   #   #

I woke behind a white plastic curtain in the Newport Hospital Emergency Department. The room turned around me like a pinwheel. The fluorescent lights on polished tile glared the sour colors of bile, puke, bilirubin, and urine, a grab bag of biological waste. Coughs and moans of children rose from the cubicles and resolved into clouds of phlegm.

My father sat beside me, stroking my face. Medea stood at the foot of my bed. Someone put a grape lollipop in my mouth. Behind my mother, against the curtain, a burly form in a chauffeur's cap floated beyond my view with wings trailing like a bridal train.

"Code blue, Pediatric Emergency, Code Blue Pediatric Emergency," blared a female voice over the loudspeaker.

Summoning all my strength, I fought to keep my eyelids open. Then, cries of children fell over the ward in granolithic layers from the depths of time as if penetrating the present with Neanderthal grief and Antediluvian woe. Chief Miontonomo of the Narragansett tribe had lain stricken in Mohegan captivity, bleeding from multiple wounds inflicted by tomahawk blows.

When I woke again I felt confused, and wondered a moment where I was, what century I had landed in, how I got there.

"Are you… are you awake, Persephone." My father's words were hesitant, almost stuttering. The first time I'd heard his weakened voice in days. "How…does your hand….ffffeel. *Ponai*?" He'd had spells like this before. Each time I'd worried if he'd recover. I was worried now.

"I'm okay, I guess." I wiggled my fingers. "Oh. The fingertips of my left hand hurt."

And then I remembered the flying candelabra, the fireball battle between Yiayia and Medea that'd seemed to go unnoticed, the shards of glass piercing my face, the crashing piano lid, the crushed chandelier crystals, the wild night ride in my father's T-bird, and

50

someone—a nurse?—putting to my lips another purple sucker that made me feel strangely happy.

And then, the dark.

"Feel for a pulse," a male voice said, waking me from my lollipop narcosis.

"None," said a woman from the curtained cubicle beside mine.

"Start CPR. You! Clear the airway and get ready to intubate."

"*Ponai?*" said my father again. Any pain? It was still easier for him to speak in his native tongue. "*O iatros eene etho.*" The doctor is here.

The lined, mustached face of a doctor in a long white coat broke through the haze like a sun. "Persephone. You had an accident with a piano."

"I was playing a song from 'Charlie and the Chocolate Factory.'"

"You've got glass in your face. It won't hurt when I take it out. That lollipop has pain medicine in it. Keep licking. The tips of the fingers on your left hand were crushed, but they'll heal. It might hurt to bend them for a while. You won't be able to use that hand for at least four weeks. They'll be sore."

I looked at my hand. Its fingertips were blue and swollen, widened like a tree frog's.

"You won't need bandages," he said. Just tincture of time."

Yiayia would say, What about Dr. William's purple pills for perpetually pallid people?

"When will she be able to play again?" Medea shuddered. "And what about her face?"

The doctor turned to her. "Volar fractures heal fine on their own. We'll have her lick that lollipop some more, then I'll give her some Valium. I'll have to pick the glass out with tweezers under a magnifier."

"But will she have scars? What if you leave a piece in?" Another spasm shook Medea's emerald green frame. A bobby pin fell to the ground. Her wig drooped. "Oh! Angelo, I hate glass!" she sobbed.

"No worries," the doctor shook his head. "The splinters haven't penetrated very far."

He patted my shoulder, whispered something to Medea, then left, shoes squeaking on the bleach-streaked linoleum tiles.

My mother leaned over, bulky in taffeta. "And we will schedule a piano lesson with Magda as soon as possible."

"And how am I supposed to play, with my feet?"

"Plenty of pain pills at home."

"Mom, the men outside the restaurant. Did Calliope tell you?"

Her eyes grew hard as nuggets of jade. "Tell me what?"

"About the Mafia guys checking the locks on the back doors and windows at the Newport Musical."

She gasped. "What the…?"

"We know," said my father, nodding.

Medea spun on her heels waving her arms like a lunatic. "Know what? I don't know. When is 'I' the same as 'we?' I'll tell you: never! What guys? Where were you? Did you talk to them? How do you know anything about this? How do you know anything about anything?"

My father stroked my face, kissed me, and reached into his pocket for his *kumboloi*. He began rattling.

"You told us to go pee in the lilacs, so we did. That's when we heard them checking windows and doors, speaking Italian."

"What! Why didn't you tell me?"

"I tried to. Calliope tried. Shit, Ma¸ Yiayia tried! You made me play, then you made the candelabra fall and the glass break, and the lid crush my fingers. Now you tell me there's drugs for this? Well I don't want pain killers, I don't want Magda. I don't want you nagging me to play the piano because you wanted to be Miss America and an opera star and swim in the Olympics, but Yiayia Friday wouldn't let you. You need a psychiatrist."

Medea's cheeks flushed the hue of rhubarb. The taffeta dress clung to her armpits, green as a murky sea. Her mouth twisted as though she'd swallowed sour wine from the bottom of Yiayia's bathtub.

"Witch!" she spat.

Chapter 8

Thus ended the first period of my life, which I have chosen to call my Time of Intimations. And so began, on a summer Sunday of Our Lord, my Time of Painful Fingers.

That night, Calliope had pulled up our shared satin sheet, her Yorkshire terrier Matty peeking from her tennis bag. We talked of the martyrdom of saints until the copper face of the grandfather clock on the landing released its chimes at the hour of three and I lapsed into a drugged sleep.

Yiayia Friday ushered in a breeze that rustled the triple pinch-pleat of my bedroom window. Pain dripped from the tips of my fingers into bright bottles of *toksinee* lined in a row.

The unyielding archers of Mani, the undefeated middle finger of the Peloponnesos, dipped their arrows in Spider Berry, Fever Honey, Hack Lemon, Bore weed, Mineral Salt, Silent Death, Blood Vinegar.

Smiling faces trapped within the bottles were battered by baseballs. Half filled, the syrupy dark liquid of Lung Burn with Yiayia's face locked within ascended to its cap and the voice of Candy Man sang its song, *askema*, badly.

"Kewpie dolls," I said. I was a sleep talker.

Calliope's soft hand nudged me awake. "Carnival," she said, "It's late afternoon."

Over Medea's objections, my father had left two tickets to the carnival on the polished leather seat of his worn black leather, tulip-embossed "King of the Vampires" chair in the entry hall of our house on 140 Red Chimney Drive.

What I loved most about having little cuts on my face, and my fingertips crushed, was that I got to say *"adio"* to the Newport Musical Theater and Country Inn Restaurant for the rest of the summer. Calliope and I were free, and half-dressed in minutes before running down the stairs.

At the carnival, we stood in line for cotton candy. Watching Auntie Georgie's chauffeur in his black-billed cap cross in front of the merry-go-round and return to the limo for a snooze in the parking lot, I held the crumpled dollar, creased and sticky in my hand.

"One blue cotton candy."

"I like blue the best because it's so unnatural," said Calliope. "Do you want to ride the pink teacups?"

"Teacups? That's for little girls. What about the Whip 'n Skid?"

Within five minutes, I had my head hanging over the edge of our pink teacup, vomiting blue syrup. Calliope held my hair back, flying wild in the popcorn wind, and when the swirling stopped, dragged me off the ride and half-carried me toward the lavatory.

"Stop," I said, in front of a trash can reeking of grease and dirty socks. "I'm gonna be sick again."

I barfed three more times, head inside the trash can ten inches from the front page of the local newspaper. Between heaves I tried to get the whole cover story.

Judge Ray Petrucci allows race for Mayor, Cianci wins from Jail. And under it, *Claus von Bulow suspect in murder of socialite and philanthropist wife, Sunny von Bulow.* "Calliope, don't you know Claus von Bulow?"

"Yeah," she said, turning up her nose. "Before we lost our father, the ambassador, to the horns of a rhinoceros while on safari, we dined and parleyed with the von Bulows when the Kennedys were using Rosecliff."

"Well, they think old Claus killed his wife, Sunny. I'm trying not to puke on the paper. Oh—and Mayor Cianci got reelected from jail."

Calliope unzipped her backpack and handed me a wet nap. "Use this," she said. "Still think the pink teacups are for babies?"

I lifted my head from the trash can and wiped my lips with the lemon glycerin towellette.

"I feel better now."

We sat on a wrought-iron bench loud with lions in arabesque swirlies and watched the lights of the Ferris wheel crest against the dimming sky to mix with early stars.

"Let's get a Pepsi to calm your stomach," Calliope said, getting up.

At the soda stand, Calliope grimaced to see kewpie dolls knocked from their shelf. A vendor in white shirt and visor handed her a tall sticky cup of ice and cola.

Click, click!

A man in plaid Bermuda shorts and a T-shirt that said *Frodo's Photo Studio Aargh!* repeatedly snapped the shutter of his Nikon camera right in our faces, as if we were Mary-Kate and Ashley.

The flashes lit the dark, now quickly falling, and I felt a chill rip up my spine. The brightly burning face of a child with wings materialized above Calliope's head. The cherub held out her little hands to stop the photographer from approaching us on shaky legs.

Then darkness was complete over the tiny village of cheesy snack bars. White-capped barkers shouted invitations to break balloons with darts and shoot ducks with a Rimfire 22 for stuffed animal prizes. And above the park the pale red and blue lights at the top of the speeding Ferris wheel were beacons for the lost.

"Oh Calliope, did you see the angel?"

"What angel? Where? Did I miss it?"

"She was hovering over your head, Calliope, protecting you."

"From what?"

"From the crippled photographer. Or from his flash."

"Maybe I didn't see her because she was over my head." Calliope handed me the cup, foaming and overflowing.

"Let's go on the Ferris wheel," I said, to drop the subject.

"Are you sure? You were just sick."

"That was from the teacups spinning in circles. I want to soar in the sky. And, besides, we'll have the angel as a protector … well, maybe. I don't know where she went. But she looked friendly, not like the soul of some angry ghost."

"Have you ever seen an angry ghost?"

"No, only Yiayia. But an angry ghost would be ugly or scary, and she wasn't like that. Besides, she was an angel, not a ghost, I think."

Round and round, we soared and dove, Calliope and I, holding hands, squealing. At our greatest height, we looked down at the carnival lights disappearing and re-appearing, fading and igniting in the dark. On the horizon, the lights of the Gatsbyesque mansions and Regatta boats strung with pollen-yellow bulbs dipped and levitated as if we were jumping rope without tripping, dying and resurrecting.

I stood up, kissed my cross, and then I was falling. Calliope's screams from above descending in an avalanche of sound.

The warm air tunneled over me, resinous and floral, with aromas of mastika and anise, cedar wood, neroli and helichrism—all in the dark roiling wind stinging me with raindrops rushing towards the small fires of Earth.

And then a thrust of soft cloth rose up against my body, and swooped me through the perfumed air before setting me softly down. "Seven hundred years of this" I heard the voice of Yiayia whisper inside my head. "Seven hundred years."

I fainted, I think.

When I awoke again to the living, the sound of bees stirred all around me … bees intent for the hive, not paying attention, fumbling over me as they flew. My head was cushioned in Calliope's lap, my cheek pressed against her blue-jeans. Blood dripped from my mouth onto the coal-black Marino fabric of the coat that enfolded me. My tongue was bleeding.

The flash of a camera shut my eyes.

"I can't take anymore," I said, breathless. "I want to go home. Did you see what happened?"

"No," said Calliope. "You—just you stood up in the cab. When the Ferris wheel headed down, we lurched forward and you disappeared over the bar."

Auntie's limo purred like a car down a smooth stretch of road and I put my head on Calliope's shoulder as if I were her child. The chauffeur, coatless, sleeves rolled up, sang *"Danke schoen"* with Wayne Newton on the eight-track. I vaguely remembered his act from summers before at the Newport Musical. I cried all the way from Rocky Point Park to Cowesett.

"When I looked down I saw only a cloud," said Calliope. "A downy, silvery-black cloud that shone in the lights."

I stopped crying. Something hard shot from my heart to my sleeve.

"Medea did this," I said, pain rushing to the tips of my fingers, "Medea did this to me. It wasn't Yiayia Friday. It was my mother."

"No, she didn't. And nobody forced you to stand up. Besides, Medea couldn't do this."

"Maybe you're right," I said. "Maybe this is something Medea could never do." That would be a first.

Chapter 9

The next morning, Calliope sat at the money counting table in the kitchen, picking mold from the cracks between the table and its leaf with a nail file.

Sequestered in her racket bag, Matty was napping, stomach filled with leftover oyster-stuffed quail in Béarnaise sauce from the Country Inn.

I stood at the shabby counter, the doors to the cabinets spotted with fingerprints and stained with cooking grime. The smell of old grease rising from the burner pans of Medea's stove lifted to my objecting nose.

"Your Miracle Shake tastes like old shoelaces," I said, dropping ice cubes into the blender. "How about some extra chocolate and saccharin?"

I shuffled through the semi-bare cabinet looking for chocolate powder and vanilla extract, anything to make the Shaklee soy shake taste better than predigested cardboard.

The loose assemblage of spices and fly traps, flour and cornstarch, leaking syrup bottles and cans of Raid stood amidst Oreo crumbs and ants, expired, with their legs pointing upward. A mouse trap laced with stale Stilton cheese had trapped a furry head, its spring set by Medea.

"Here, behind the chandelier spray… the triple fat burner carbo-blocker vitamin pills we lost."

"Oh, good," said Calliope, looking up from a small ball of mold she had fashioned out of the crud from the crack in the laminate.

Pushing aside the spray, I grasped a milky blue bottle and held its label to a strand of morning light.

"Syrup of Ipecac," I said "Medea's latest emetic. My mother hides it here."

"Emetic?"

"To induce vomiting, I said.

Calliope's eyes widened. Her mother, Georgie, was so normal.

I put the bottle back and threw a shot of Eclipse coffee syrup into the blender, then pushed the start button. The whirring filled the kitchen. When it died, Medea's footfalls punctuated the brief silence. I sat down at the table in a scrolled Windsor chair with a cracked back, leaving the brew unpoured.

Her steps made a right turn in the dining room and pirouetted toward the sliding French door, which she wrenched open with a metallic click and whoosh. The clacking disappeared into the backyard flower garden of wilting tiger lilies. Calliope covered her mouth with her hand as Medea released the uncounted consumables she'd stuffed into her stomach in the wee hours of the morning at Newport's greatest epicurean gambling hole, Davey Jones' Supper Club.

"You made her do that!" Calliope squealed.

I shrugged. "Didn't need to."

The sliding glass door closed with a thud. Medea crossed the dining room and approached the kitchen door.

It flew open, and she appeared at the threshold, face plastered in a thick green facial paste. Posed like an angry Colossus, she glared at me, looked to the blender, and then stared at the sink piled high with pieces of bridles and bits covered in soapy bubbles.

"*Kalimera*," I said in my best sarcastic Greek. Good day.

"*Kal-i-mera*," she said, drawing out the syllables.

She stared into Calliope, who looked down at her knapsack where Matty rested in ignorant peace at her feet.

"What's that smell?" said Medea, sniffing the air. "It's in your bedroom too."

"What's that little blue bottle in your pocket, Mama?"

Ignoring my question, she dragged her feet across the kitchen floor, toes exploding with bunions that poked through incisions she made with a steak knife in her canvas sneakers.

"And what's this?" she said, picking a hair off my shoulder.

"This is my barn coat, Mi Madre. Of course it has hair on it."

Her mask began to crack, plankton paste flaking onto her shoulders. She picked another hair from my coat.

"This is not from a horse." She held the strand of dog hair up to the Tiffany dragonfly pendant light, her youth-promoting facial mask and bold scarlet eyes reflected on the floating sheen of laminate on the money counting table. "This is too long to be a horse hair, now that it's summer."

"I don't know, *mitera*. Maybe it's left over from winter."

"Only mother in Nigerian will save you," Medea said, waiting, arms folded under her bosoms.

I prayed silently to Yiayia to send me the Nigerian word for mother but was disappointed.

"I thought not," said Medea. "Your great grandmother, Penelope, could speak twenty-four languages, but not you. So, I'll ask again. "What is that smell?"

Calliope squirmed behind me.

Medea smiled. My father's athletic socks with red stripes on the top were pulled half-way over her beige hose too short for stockings, too long for anklets. The nylons were secured in Gordian knots at the front of her shins. Varicose conduits, like snakes scarred from saline injections, crawled across her skin in coiled lumps up a pock-marked thigh that flashed from her robe.

"It could be a bunny hair. You know I'm taking care of the Caperosi's rabbit hutch. They also have cats, two gerbils, and a very cute lovable Yorkie that I cuddle with. They pay cash."

"That horrible smell is in your room, too." Medea sniffed the air then presented chestnut hair she'd picked off my shoulder.

"This is my barn coat, Mama. Of course it has hair on it."

"Oh, well. Good," she said. "Pour me a cup of coffee, please. No, I'll make it."

Still waiting for an answer to her Nigerian quiz-show question, Medea filled the *brika* three quarters with water, added seven tablespoons of coffee grounds, and slid it onto the stove.

"I would have done it for you, Mama."

Medea sat at the table and stared at Calliope without saying anything while the coffee boiled. Still steaming, I poured the boiling liquid into the cup set before her.

"That's a nice house dress," said Calliope. She bit her lip and looked down at the worn, scuffed, cigarette-burnt table and studied the crud stuck between the leaves of plastic laminate.

Medea wore a cotton paramecium-print wash dress barely visible beneath her loosely belted robe. From the robe's hem dragged the torn lace trim of a polyester slip from Filenes's basement store.

Making no reply, she stood long enough to slip off the top of her robe and let it fall behind her across the back of the chair.

"Thank you," Medea said at last. "Nothing but the finest."

Calliope had been snacking on her cuticles. She felt Medea's gaze, and looked up.

Through her threadbare dress, Medea's pearly pink trousseau sagged with the weight of heavy pendulous bosoms. The right breast listed starboard. The stiffened aroma of mothballs jiggled from her outfit as she moved, even as she breathed.

Medea banged on the table with the palm of one open hand, whipping up waves in her coffee cup.

She reached into the pocket of her robe, extracted a handful of wadded-up facial tissue and empty baggies, and slammed them down on the table.

"Damn." She thrust an angry hand into the robe's other bulging pocket and jerked out the rolled-up newspaper. "And what's this?"

She emptied her coffee cup, still steaming and turned it over in its saucer, rotating it three times counterclockwise. Then she stood and headed towards the living room, dimming the lights of the pendant dragonfly and orange butterfly lamps. She paused a moment and smiled, admiring the diffused patterns of colored light on the walls. She turned on the hi-fi and piped Liszt's "Mephisto Waltz" into every room of the house.

I saw her dance a few steps with an imaginary partner before she came back and sat down at the table, unfolded the Providence Journal, opened to page four, and spread the article between the demitasse so both Calliope and I could read it. We sat in shocked silence.

Angel Saves Child

The fifteen-year-old daughter of theatrical entrepreneur and socialite Medea Matepas, Persephone Matepas-Vican, was found last night by authorities lying at the bottom of a Ferris wheel at J.J. Delaney's Traveling Carnival at Rocky Point Park in Newport at 8 p.m. The prone but conscious teenager told Sheriff Guy Pappas and policemen that she had fallen from the top of the Ferris wheel, but was caught and brought to the ground by an angel. The police did report she was wrapped in a large black coat, which contained blood stains. The coat has been taken in as evidence.

Though the carnival grounds had been crowded no witness to the event could be found except her cousin, sixteen-year-old Calliope Matepas, who was in the Ferris wheel cab with her. Calliope said that Persephone had fallen but that she saw no angel, but

"—only a black cloud" catch Persephone.

A spokesman for Newport Memorial hospital said Persephone had been released to a family chauffeur after close examination showed no physical trauma except a bloody nose.

Neither of the girl's parents could be reached for comment.

"Section B, page four." I shrugged. I could see my mother was about to erupt into Mrs. Volcano, so I used the best Valium voice I could muster. "No one will read it."

"Are you trying to ruin me?" screamed Medea. "Of course someone will read it. It only takes one. I'll be a laughingstock. Your father will have another stroke. After all I've done to build the business, promote culture…presented the best talent and served the best wine and food, prepared by the world's best chefs. After all the sweat and blood, am I to be made a mockery of and my theatre destroyed? All because of a little—"

"Say it, Mother. I know what you're going to say."

"You lied, you lied!"

"I told the truth," I said.

"The truth would shrivel your tongue!"

"I told the truth. I was caught by an angel and he smelled like ambrosia. It laid me down…he laid me down in the middle of a crowd and wrapped me in his cloak and he whispered my name—'Persephone, Persephone.'"

"Witch, witch, witch!" screamed Medea. "Not like your great grandmother Penelope. Not like Yiayia or the others, either. No, you will never be one of them. Not a real one. You're going to be a musician. A musician! Even if I have to half kill you and tie you to the hitching post."

I held up the five fingers of my left hand, swollen and blue. Dried blood framed the crescents of my nails. The cuticles started to ooze. Blood dripped onto the floor.

Medea screamed. Backing up, she stumbled away from me, tears flooding her cheeks.

"Mama!" she shouted, her face a ghostly white. The strands of her wild hair shot up from her head like electrified snakes vibrating in death throes in poisonous air.

"Mama's Nigerian for 'mother'," she wailed. "Mama, Mama! It was a trick question, you dim-witted, ignorant, little witch. I'll cleanse you. I'll tame you. I'll drown you in holy water. I'll call in an exorcist and the Archbishop Iakovos, himself. God damn your little sanctimonious ass."

A fury welled up in me. It rose from my feet and burned hot in my head. I grabbed a fly swatter and lunged for her as she cried out in anger and grief and slithered toward the door.

I drew back and swung with all my might, but she was gone.

#   #   #

Calliope lay sobbing on her pillow. She wouldn't look up when I spoke and stroked her curls, all damp with tears.

"Please, Calliope. Please."

It was the first time I felt true spiritual separation from someone I loved.

St. Augustine wrote that separation from God caused anguish, and that anguish caused hatred of God so black that one felt distanced from God by ever-widening gulfs. Each chasm caused greater anguish and consequent hatred, hence greater anguish in a widening and eternal gyre, never to be pardoned or assuaged.

So I fought against the void between us when Calliope turned away. I begged and pulled the duvet from her face. Bathed in tears, she soon fell asleep.

Crows' wings beat at my window beneath the swooning willow that always welcomed with open arms gusts of wind blowing in from the ocean.

Medea had already fled the house. My father was gone. I searched our Sears suburban split level, Medea's headquarters, where my lot had been cast. Nothing stirred, except the swinging chimes of the grandfather clock on whose face the early afternoon wore weary. Rain pattered on the roof. In the distance feathered tribes hued and cried.

When the front doorknob of tarnished brass turned slowly, its faint squeaks echoing in the soul of the near empty house, I held my breath until its movement silenced. Then came scratching and rapping on the doors and windows.

Afraid I would be unable to hold my breath forever to keep whomever or whatever out, I rushed into the basement cedar closet, shut the door tight behind me, and prayed in pitch dark. In my mind I held Calliope in white light to protect her. My fatigue from nonstop talking, pleading and praying slipped into the depths of my lungs. I moved little air and squeezed myself in a tiny corner of the cedar closet, fitting myself between mountains of hat boxes behind rows of ladies suits with fur collars, whose mated pill hats occupied boxes that comprised my walls of defense.

The chimes on the landing struck twice, like sledge hammer strikes to my ears. And a time of sounds began.

Chapter 10

There were worse places to be than wedged between stacks of boxes behind old mothball-infused fur collars, all stuffed into the back of Medea's cedar closet. But, dizzy from the mix of mothballs and Chanel Number Seven, I couldn't think of any just then.

I pressed my face against the cedar wall to clear my mind. Who or what was scratching at the basement window? I took six slow deep breaths, then held the seventh, as Yiayia had taught me. I heard a formless body of mercurial air flooding around me and saw generations of stars. The scratching dissolved. Wind swept through the catacombs of our basement and slipped under the closet door. I released my breath, inhaled a deep chest full of air, and held onto it like water in a desert.

The voice of a half-remembered priest in a brown dusty cape reached me in a flash, redeemed from oblivion. "Behold the *tôledôt* of the heavens and the earth when they sprang to life between the week of creation and the germination of the holy garden."

The fingers at the window were those of shadows doing dirty work for someone else. Noisy and sloppy, fumbling at various latches. I counted to seven and held my breath at intervals to stop the rattling of the latch, the scratching at the sill.

"May Calliope sleep like the dead," I prayed.

"This damned thing's got some kinda special lock," said a hoarse voice.

"Yeah, Rocco. A fuckin' double latch. You pop it open, there's another one right behind it. They got some kind of rod-thing holding the freaking windows down."

"Why don't we just break a window?"

"Boss told us not to make no mess. I dunno. Maybe we could break something small. But you're pretty fat."

"Yeah? Well, you ain't so small yourself."

"Shut up and check the back for a way in."

Imagine a garden soaked with spring rain. I took in a deep breath and steadied my head against a cedar post still oozing with life, sticky with pitch. A faint haze of star and moonlight passed under the door and enveloped my pounding heart in its warming gauze. "Angels protect and shield me."

Crash! The cellar window fell in. I knew that sound well, because I'd once broken it with a nice blond boy from Raven Street who'd found me locked out of my house, in tears, sitting on my front step, back when I was eight. We'd cleaned the sill of shards, then he'd lowered me in through the tiny rectangular hole without severing an artery.

Medea had screamed about it for weeks. She had a broken-glass phobia, always felt the rims of cups before she took a sip. She checked all the windows of the house, the car, and the dinner theatre for cracks several times a day, and preferred unbreakable plastic everything.

"Lower me in, Rocco." Maybe the intruder had gone so hoarse from screaming a lot, like when Medea lost her voice after Matty chewed her best pair of fashion boots.

I pressed my ear to the closet's cedar wall.

"I'm stuck," one man groaned. "Shouldn't 'a eaten those gaggers for lunch. Think I'm gonna hurl."

"How 'bout if I push you through?"

"You'll squash my chest! First I'll ralf. Then I'll die."

#　　#　　#

The fat shadow must've hung pinioned in the window for a minute or two. The shark teeth of the frame clamped on his bulky flesh until I finally blew my breath out. Then the house rattled and creaked and groaned with the bump of his falling. A nauseous green light glowed under each step of the intruders' squeaky creeper shoes. Beams poked through the astragal of the closet door. I held my sleeping cousin in the light, calling angelic guardians to shield her. Angels, like vampires, must be invited, Yiayia had taught me.

When I pressed an eye to the keyhole the verdant luminosities shook my brain. Winged creatures flitted in the auras surrounding the two burglars, and I remembered how the horizon had dipped and risen and swung in scarlet waves during my ride in the Ferris wheel car.

Two stealthing shadows shambled through the cellar door and crept up the basement stair. Towards my room, where my cousin lay sleeping. "Calliope, wake up," I whispered, but she slept through the commotion of images in my head. Fireflies, like miniscule fairies carved on a Grecian frieze, slipped in though the cracked window of my bedroom, swirling over the bed. The phosphorescent glimmers coalesced into a cloud, like blind creatures at the bottom of a cold, sulfuric sea.

I fell back into the black compress of my father's suits, draped behind me, and fainted with grief.

Dreamless, I slept for hours curled in the arms of my great grandmother Penelope while my grandmother spun wool and sang a Greek cradlesong.

"*Nani, nanaiki,*" sang Yiayia. "Sleep, sleep."

#　　#　　#

"Persephone," hollered Calliope from upstairs, her voice muffled by the walls of my cedar prison. "Where are you?"

"Here, in the basement closet. Trapped behind Medea's shoes. Dozens of pairs." I shoved at the door, slamming my bruised hand and tumbled out, limbs all pins and needles. Struggling to my feet, I wove through the corridor of boxes, swatting at flying bugs streaming through the broken cellar window.

67

"I can barely hear you," shouted Calliope.

I crunched across a glass carpet, gift of the break-in, my paddock boots crushing the blood-speckled spicules. Medea would be hysterical. Two of her most nightmarish phobias in one: blood and broken glass. I bolted up the stairs, slamming the cellar door behind me, flipping light switches as I passed. At the main stair of the house, I looked up and saw Calliope on the landing like a wraith, miraculously raised, still in white bedclothes.

"I found this under my pillow," she said, holding out a large manila envelope. "What were you doing in the cellar?"

"You didn't hear those guys carrying on like a pair of fat New Jersey roosters?"

She frowned. "Who? Why are you still in your barn jacket? Your hair is standing on end."

"Burglars came in through the basement window. You know, like at the restaurant? I held them back as long as I could, until I fell asleep, or passed out, or something. They never found me. Have you looked in that envelope yet?"

She shook her head. "I found it under my pillow. When I woke up I just knew it was there."

I bounded up the steps. "Let me see." I reached for the envelope.

"Oh no, you don't." She held it behind her. "The angel gave it to me for a reason. We'll open it together."

We sat on my bed cross-legged, on top of the down comforter, and gave each other a good-luck cheek kiss. A breeze wafted through an open window, flapping the curtains, carrying the scent and hue of night-darkened wisteria blooms from the garden. Swallows nesting in the eaves outside my window chirped premature greetings to the sun as it rose and warmed the dew-soaked hills behind our house.

The envelope was stainless, creaseless, unmarked by address or postage stamp. Calliope opened it without ripping the seal and removed a stack of photographs.

"Don't smudge them with your thumb," I said.

"I'm not." She glared at me through a lock of hair, then set the stack face-up between us on the comforter.

"The carnival." I took long breaths to still my heart and slow my lungs. "Okay," I said. "Stop sniffling."

Calliope wiped her cheeks on one sleeve. She lit a votive candle, and we were ready.

"Okay," I said. My left hand throbbed with each beat of my heart.

The first photograph was flawed by a dark, cloud-like mass floating in from the left-hand side. To the right, carnival tents fluttered banners from a distance. The Ferris wheel rose like a rotund colossus above everything.

"The photographer from Frodo's photo's. The one in the Bermuda shorts," I said.

Calliope flipped aside the second, third, fourth, and fifth photographs. Boys and balloons and games and rides. A carnival barker laying down his spiel. The smells of caramel apples and cotton candy seemed to thicken the air and wrap the bedroom like the swaddling clothes of baby Jesus in the arms of his holy mother.

"Whoa," I said. "Stop."

The next picture was of Calliope standing in front of the kewpie kiosk, a hundred rotund pink dolls lined up behind her.

She drew in a breath. "That's scary."

I nodded. "Even for a witch."

We sat for a few moments in silence, studying the astonishment on each other's faces. Then I looked down at the photographs again.

I uncovered the next one. "What's this?"

"Holy Mary," Calliope breathed, the blood draining from her cheeks.

The photograph seemed an enlargement of the one taken at the kewpie doll kiosk. In it, the dolls had been replaced by bottles with labels: red algae, ricin, quarter evil, quarter ill, charbon, anthrax, blackwater, murrain, milzbrand, splenic fever, quick rot, blackrot, sheep death.

"More poisons," said Calliope. "I've had enough of poisons."

"Yiayia used to say, 'Have patience with poisons.'" I giggled.

She shook her head, rolled her eyes, and sighed. "Whatever."

The sweet breath of morning blew once more through the room, then came to a halt. The air staled.

"What's this?" I pointed to the muck that had settled in the bottle of murrain. Above its label, thickened ribbons of precipitated chemicals curved and coalesced into shaded and sculpted shadows.

"It's Yiayia," said Calliope, "inside the bottle, like a genie."

I tore the photo from her hands and threw it on the floor. Matty woke from his slumber and gave a troubled yip.

"It's not her." I shook my head. "No way. Anyhow, we have other photos to look at."

Calliope scowled. "I know it's her."

I ignored her. The next photo showed a hand reaching down from the sky to grip my ponytail, jerking me from the cab at the top of the Ferris wheel.

Calliope peeked through outspread fingers she'd clamped over her face. I squinted at the photo. The hand was skeletal, disembodied from the thickened night air above it. Tendons and muscles bulged like marbles from its fingers and gripping knuckles. The hand seemed held together by a tight glove of ancient spotted vellum, streaked by blue meandering veins. As I stared, it faded, turning wispy, then emerged in sharp focus again. Matty released a long wailing howl that frizzed the split ends of Calliope's soft, wavy hair.

"Looks like a real hand to me," I said in a weak voice that tiptoed as if frightened of being heard. I held my bruised fingers in the palm of my uninjured hand. "Wish I knew who it belonged to."

"It's Yiayia's, you moron. That was her face in the poison."

"But she wouldn't want to kill me. She loves me… I…"

Calliope had tears in her eyes. "I need a hug. I'm really scared."

"Well, maybe these aren't real photographs?" I said, trying to scoff. "Fakes."

"You know they're real." She slapped away my proffered fingers. Uncrossing her legs, she slid to the floor to retrieve the kewpie doll photo. "All real."

She scrambled back onto the bed and studied the photo where Yiayia's face had appeared in the medicine bottle. She stared again at the hand reaching down from the sky, then leaned over to pull an entomologist's magnifier out of the junk drawer in the bedside table.

"Don't you see? This proves what happened at the carnival was real," she said. "You had a bloody nose. Blood was on the coat you were wrapped in. I saw a dark cloud save you. It happened so fast. My mom's chauffeur caught you in his coat. That's why he didn't have one on when he drove us home from the hospital—and I saw his wings. And here's the proof!"

She reached into the pile and withdrew a new one. She dropped the other two photos.

"Oh my God." I leaned close. A familiar figure was cushioning my fall, enfolding me within the fabric of a chauffeur's coat.

The fingers of my left hand ached in bruised throbs. I sniffed back the hot blood that began to run from my nose.

"You're bleeding." Calliope jerked a Kleenex from the box on the bedside table and pushed it into my free hand. "We need help. We've got to ask the police to find your parents. We should call my mother."

A long worm of chill wound around my spine and head, then floated toward the opened window I'd like to have escaped through myself. "Okay. But let's only tell Georgie about the pictures."

"Why?"

"Why?" My far-away voice coming back with a bang and clatter. "Why? It's obvious why," I muttered. " I…I don't know why. It doesn't matter why!"

I leaned over Calliope and grabbed the receiver, pulling the ebony phone base off the table. Its edge of high impact plastic hit the howling Matty between the eyes. The little terrier whimpered out a feeble grunt and scrambled to safety under the bed.

# # #

"How long have your parents been gone?" Sheriff Guy Pappas whispered in a deep baritone. A one-eyed Cyclops of a man. It was his day off. He'd been out working on his alpaca farm. The oily scent of unwashed wool clung to his Levi's. He could've bridged two rivers with his long legs and workman's boots of white leather. He jotted down phrases in a flip-top notebook as he stood in the living room framed by the casement of the bay window, his slight belly outlined by a monogrammed polo shirt.

I stared, mesmerized. The smell of sheep coated but did not disguise the pheromones underneath.

Calliope nudged me with a pointy elbow. Her shivering ended, having become unthinkable under the hawkish gaze of the sheriff's one good eye, which turned toward me, staring, and seemed to be thinking, You are no man. No man.

"They never came back home from the theater," my cousin blurted out. "Since yesterday afternoon we haven't heard a word. Medea was really pissed when they left."

"Which was when, exactly?"

"Noon thirty–ish."

I stared at the sheriff's eye when he looked down at his notebook. Two younger policemen were rummaging through the compartments of the plantation desk by the fireplace. One, under the weight of a sagging pistol and gun-belt, excused himself and climbed the main stair to search the landing and upper floor. Outside the window, flashing lights revolved ceaselessly, throwing their red glare into a mirror high on the living room wall.

"I'm gonna get the basement," said a police photographer, crossing in front of us on his way to find the cellar door.

"Do your parents normally stay in touch when they leave?" said Pappas, voice resonating in e, teasing the strings of the piano.

Calliope dug in harder with the elbow this time, in my liver. I suppressed a grunt, and kept silent.

"They didn't say where they were going after work and they haven't called," she said, against my wishes. They were, after all, my parents, not hers.

The sheriff whistled long and deep through capped teeth as if he'd recognized a lie when he heard one. "First the carnival, now this." He looked hard at Calliope, who'd only been speaking the truth.

The sheriff's one good eye shifted sideways, as he listened to something. A sound, not in this room, which was overwhelmed by the discordant ticking of Medea's collection of cuckoo clocks. He ambled over to the sofa and took a seat between Calliope and me, stretching out his long legs, large hazel-grey eye scanning the *étagère* covered with painted pots glowing amber each time the squad car light came around full circle.

"Now, I want you young ladies to take a close look at these photographs." His long, thick fingers pulling mug shots from an envelope on the inlaid tulipwood table around which Medea's living room had been designed. No one was even allowed to touch that table, never mind set something on it. She'd said in her Audrey Hepburn voice, "It's Louis the Fourteenth, don't you know."

Calliope and I leaned close, holding our breaths, and stared at two rows of faces with numbers written under them.

"We actually didn't see the burglars tonight," she said. "But I know they're the same guys that were hanging around outside the Newport Musical the other night, trying to open the doors and windows of the restaurant. I'll never forget their voices. Isn't this one, Persephone?"

"Yes. That's one of them." My fingertips still ached.

Sheriff Pappas stopped sucking a peppermint held in his cheek and blew out a heavy breath. Seven painted birds excited by the changing of the hour started their digital cuckooing on the wall clocks. On the sofa, Pappas was no longer a Cyclops, but a half-blind Tiresias with a black eye patch. No matter. He could see more with one eye than other men could see with two.

As Calliope moved closer to him her shivering lessened. He wasn't bad looking. In fact, the hazel eye was beautiful. She seemed to have forgotten about the concealed one that had caught my wonder. Was it blind or just—gone? Was the seriously interesting patch only a disguise?

Calliope pointed to one mug shot as the grandfather clocks all sprang to cranky life and hailed the dying of the cuckoos.

"What's the matter, sheriff?" said the remaining policeman, turning toward us from the mess of the plantation desk.

"Look at this," said Pappas. "This is the one she recognizes. The one they call 'Capitan'."

"Holy cow." The policeman's eyes widened.

"We'll talk about it outside. Later." The sheriff focused on a daguerreotype of a young magus perched on the mantle. A heavily jeweled bar cross rested on the magus' priestly surplice. Without looking away, Pappas slid all the photos back into their envelope.

"You sure they didn't take anything?" the policeman asked us, tapping one foot.

"Positive," blurted my cousin. "We checked the entire house."

"They didn't take anything," the sheriff confirmed, as if she hadn't spoken.

He sat on the sofa, quiet, for several minutes through the ticking of the clocks, gazing into thin air. The shallow lines of his forehead became deeply furrowed; his eye grew a blander grey.

Sweat sheened on his throat. He slid a hand-rolled cigarette from
a silver box in his jeans' pocket, held it for a moment, then put it
back, shaking his head. "Anything else you want to tell me?"

Across from the sofa, the rotating lights flung blood-red
shadows on the wall, which was lined with gilded images of the
seven labors of Hercules, on Franklin Mint display plates.

"We do have something to show you," I said. "About the
carnival."

#   #   #

Pappas stood at the doorway as Calliope reached into the
drawer of my bedside table. I scooped the phone from the floor and
replaced it on its base. Matty crawled out from under the bed and
sat on a down pillow, a stunted sheik on a paillasse. He forced a
growl at the sheriff, brief enough to be cute.

The breeze carried spicy fumes from the garden, of the mint
and wild cinnamon that grew beneath my window.

Calliope found the envelope and handed it to the sheriff. Still
standing in the doorway, he inspected the photos, sighed heavily,
and looked at us again with that dilated eye.

"Excuse me, ladies." He walked over to the phone. "May I?"

He dialed and tapped one foot, sighing, while he waited for
someone on the other end to pick up.

"I need twenty four hour surveillance on the girls and the
house," he said. "Never mind who's the Police Chief of this town,
and who isn't. I'm the sheriff. I want a squad car parked outside
in the driveway with two cops in it. Two in the house, and another
cruiser circling the block every five minutes. Tell everyone to bring
breakfast, lunch—and supper."

He turned to me. "What relative do we call to tuck you into
bed tonight?"

"Not necessary," I said.

His eyebrow lifted.

"Okay," I said. "Auntie Georgie. Calliope's mom."

"Okay. Sure. Fine. This will all be over tomorrow morning.
Jesus, what is it with you Greeks?"

He dropped a business card in the center of Medea's Louis the Fourteenth table. "Call. If you need me. Anytime. Okay?" He stared at me for a moment, then spread his grin into a wide and gleaming thing.

I closed the door behind him and watched him through the sidelight until he disappeared. If he'd been a kid, his walk would have been a skip.

Chapter 11

"He said 'you Greeks,' not 'us Greeks,' Auntie Georgie. He's as Greek as we are. Right?"

She was sitting across from Calliope and me at Medea's piled-high kitchen table, burnished hands folded in her lap, topaz eyes moving slowly, behind dark glasses, back and forth from her daughter to me.

"So," she said quietly. "Is that the whole story? You've told me absolutely every detail? "

"Everything," I said. Calliope nodded, turned to the window and make a rapid-fire gesture of crossing herself as if it were a secret habit.

Auntie Georgie had been supervising the pouring of liquefied metals into molds at her Brooklyn epaulette factory when Sheriff Pappas called her back to Newport. A half hour later she was on Amtrak to Kingston, then home in three hours with a shop apron still tied around her neck.

"Sheriff Pappas is right," she said. "This will all be over by tomorrow morning."

"How do you know that, Mother?" Calliope looked up from the invisible tracings she had been making on the table with one finger.

"Guy Pappas has been a member of our church all his life, but rarely comes since his wife died ten years ago." Auntie Georgie paused for a long five seconds. I looked into her eyes and knew she'd been praying for the soul of her departed husband, the ambassador, who'd shot himself. "While his wife was alive Pappas put on a good show of belonging. But then her car swerved off Highway 95, and she died in a snow bank. Now, he only comes to weddings and funerals. And he sits alone."

"He seems… intelligent," I said, avoiding her face.

"Listen." My aunt looked over dark glasses and made me shiver with her sharp gaze. "That break-in attempt at the theatre was not for money, but all about Medea and what certain people fear she will become." Her eyebrows rose, and her face pinched when she repeated, 'certain people.' "The break-in was all about those pictures. Sheriff Pappas has linked it to your parents in the only possible way. They've not been kidnapped for ransom, but to be questioned. Matters like this are soon resolved by Greek expatriates. A swift intercession and your Medea and Angelo will be home by tomorrow morning."

"I…I don't understand." I said. Forming those words felt foreign to teeth and tongue.

Auntie Georgie turned away. Calliope stared at her with the wide eyes of a child, gaping. "That's all I can tell you," said my aunt. "All I can say and, really, all that I know."

I tried to hide the disappointment that flooded me. The realm of shadows that had hung over me almost all my life had a too-familiar, bitter taste of rust. Auntie Georgie seemed to know this.

"You think Medea doesn't love you," she said, suddenly turning toward me. "But she does. Why do you think she bought that grand piano?"

The kitchen door banged open. A tall policeman assigned to the house stalked in, in search of coffee. Having poured a cup, he excused himself and ambled out, his gun-belt slipping below his hips.

"Well, what shall we do with the rest of the day?" Georgie feigned a chipper English spirit that almost made me laugh because of the dark shades, the mocking eyes hidden behind them. "The bugs are out, the birds are hopping. It seems a very good day for horseback riding. I can almost hear the hounds."

"Oh, good!" squealed Calliope, bouncing in her seat.

I felt instantly happier. I'd started riding seriously at seven, then following the hounds since the age of ten. My stallion, Agrippa the Ingrate, trained to the highest level by Georgie's former paramour, the Marquis Andrade of Portugal, was stabled at Drum Rock Hunt Club, ten miles from our house, outside the realm of Medea's Domain.

Agrippa hadn't seen me in weeks. He'd probably begun expressing anguish by wolfing hay and splashing water all over his stall. I longed to be with him, to hug his strong neck, and spit in his nostrils so he'd continue to love me alone.

"Okay," I said. "If you say my parents will be home in the morning, I believe you. Let's go hill topping."

#   #   #

I sat deep in the saddle on Agrippa the Ingrate, imagining myself naked, my most beloved state. The wind from the pass between high evergreen hills rushed through my prep-school bob, whipping my hair back.

Georgie and Calliope galloped ahead, on bay thoroughbreds across a firm dirt track that hugged a hedge of yews. Fir trees filled the air with resinous memory: church, the bloom of mid-summer, the diligent honeybee. The retired horses galloped too slowly for the racetrack, but too quick for careful people. The thrill-seeking hearts of Calliope and Georgie throbbed with Spartan heat.

I cantered a quarter of a league behind on Agrippa, a coal Hungarian, whose blood descended from the sturdy and sane Norman Nonius. His ancestor, Nonius Senior, had been Napoleon's horse, left in Budapest during the conquest of the Balkan lands.

Agrippa sustained the cadence of the Blue Danube. I clenched his mane. For a horse in wide-open country, he cantered in slow motion. Energy throbbed from his tucked haunches through my pelvic bones as I held my torso upright and still. My legs melted into his flesh. We were one animal with four legs.

The meadow breezed by in fragrant shades of mesquite grass and clover, their blossoms like emerald water lilies on Monet's forest pond.

I touched the top of Agrippa's arched neck, yielding both fists, closed but soft, every third stride. And every third step his back would rise, his croup would sink, and his neck would swell from his withers with thunderous power and the softness of a baby seal. He snorted, then relaxed, sprouting wings, suspended above the blue earth, his back a living spring.

The day's unlooked-for, sinister twist came out of nowhere.

A branch drew blood from my cheek before I could duck. I bent and wrapped my arms around Agrippa's neck, dodging more coming branches, face buried deep in the musk of his mane.

We rushed through an overhand of maple leaves, down game trails too small for deer or even a big dog. Shifting starboard, I pressed the horse away from my left leg, staying low, the angry trees striking at my thighs.

"Agrippa, you ingrate!" My loose whip gave him a kiss of leather. Agrippa's sweat misted my face, gluing dust to my skin. Wild honeysuckle poured into green bowls of ancient leaves. Bees swarmed as if to presage the birth of the dense forest behind, where wizened oak had grown thick and dark since the *tôledôt*. The rhythm of four foreign hooves suddenly overlapped our own.

A long bony face suddenly poked out of the trees. A heaving, henna-brown torso emerged, a flying tail flashing behind.

Debouching from an island of maples, hickory, and ash, the mare stood motionless, skened by a chorus of sycamore trees. Waxy leaves caressed her flanks with flat, green hands. Her flaring nostrils exhaled a scent from deep within her chest, a single beckoning call to Agrippa to come.

Blood dripped as dew from my sliced cheekbone and touched my lips with the flat hard taste of iron. "Relax, Agrippa." I offered a reassuring touch, fingers stroking his moist, quivering withers.

Sunlight refracted shiny leaves, dressing her flanks and withers in metallic vestments. She lifted her tail and turned to face us, coat oiled mahogany, nearly black. Beneath her forelock bloomed a six pointed star. Her haunches crouched, her hind legs braced, and she struck off at a dead run along the tree line.

Spasm exploded in Agrippa's flanks as his body flew into a capriole—first a leap, then both hind legs kicked out. A snap ripped the fabric of the air. The deep-throated cry of an arrow-ridden war horse tore from his lungs.

I fastened myself tighter to Agrippa's deep-bolted body, no cleft between us, lest he become a weapon against my throbbing brain. My cheek adhered to his neck, my chest to his withers.

As we followed the star-horse into a forest bower of sun-spread irises, her voice rose to a wild bellow. She flew down a game trail, jumped a fallen pine, then disappeared behind a tapestry of leaves.

Agrippa humped his back, lunged, then stopped. My feet flew from the stirrups; my body rocketed out of the saddle.

I dropped the reins. The slightest pull would've made him run or stand on his hind legs like a man. Instead I lay forward and wrapped my arms around his rippling chest. The fascicles beneath his skin shook as if to repel the stings of bees swarming from a secret hive deep in the woods.

I slid over his wet skin, making a bridge with my hands, clasping them around his slippery thorax, and inhaling his deep savage salty scent. I spat onto his upside-down question mark ears, so my scent would pump into his veins. Then he would recognize me, and know my name.

"Persephone," I whispered. "Persephone, Persephone."

Agrippa crouched and lifted himself again, hovering over a patch of wild poppies. The birds stopped singing. The clouds halted in their stasis. The rustling leaves quieted and the vault of sky stood still. I took in a breath, rolled my tongue and formed a string of rrrrrs, calling to him.

Agrippa lowered his head to the ground, his sniffs dusting the skin of my arm. I lay back and watched the broad, overlapping leaves above me form pinhole images of a solar crescent between the parting clouds.

A voice whispered to me. His breath warmed my ear. "Saul, Saul, why persecutest thou me? I am Jesus whom thou persecutest: it is hard for thee to kick against the pricks."

I shook my head. My name's not Saul. What pricks? I closed my eyes against the hot bright beams. Who was that? Gabriel? Michael? God?

The blaze spoke again. "It is hard for thee to kick against the goad. Rise and I shall take you to your destination."

My ears buzzed and rang. A reddish glow scratched my eyes like sandpaper. The pain had a soporific effect until finally I became saturated with sleep, dreaming of Yiayia's black dog carrying the rags in his mouth.

Chapter 12

When my eyes opened again I was lying on my back on a bed of pine needles. Pressing the heel of one hand against my bleeding cheek, I yanked rubbery legs together, throwing my weight onto stunned knees.

A green and yellow, fluffy centipede the length of my nose crawled across my arm. I flicked it onto a nearby cactus whose prickly three-pronged tree swarmed with hummingbirds and lizards. I studied an expanding hole in the blanket of clouds as my fatigued legs failed and I wobbled and fell back again.

The noon sun spun upside down. The sky rotated ninety degrees and darkened as it cooled like pumice. Now I reclined not on pine shats, but on a bed of prickly Astroturf.

The air was warm with *mole* chocolate. Fat tree frogs chirped like crickets. My mind grabbed at an iguana as it slithered under a hot flat rock. Where was I? Nearby, Echinacea flowers waved. In the distance a mission bell rang twelve times from its stucco chamber.

A whoosh interrupted the song of the frogs as drops from a sprinkler arced like rain across my torn face. My arms spread like those of a snow angel until one hand found a hole in the ground with a green glow-in-the-dark golf ball resting inside it. I sat up and in the distance spied straw sombreros, tour busses, and camera equipment on tripods surrounding a vast quiet pond by the seventh hole. The golf course sat in the middle of a ridge encircled by leagues of flat desert.

The sun's reflection in the water cooled as the moon took its first bite from the sun's head. On the surface of the pond, bands of light and shadow streamed and merged like reflective shimmers on the bottom of a swimming pool.

Moments later, the ridge before me was inky black. At its foot, light mellowed through an aperture in thin high clouds that collected and held their position. The cooling air kissed my nose. I turned my head eastward toward a sky now enveloped in rose and purple glare.

"Agrippa!" I called. There was no answer. "Auntie Georgie? Calliope!" But I knew there were no Agrippa, no Georgie and no Calliope in Mexico.

It was then that I understood what was happening in the sky.

The moon's dark shadow raced across the heavens and hesitated. The bite taken from the sun had widened as if it were being eaten by the black jaws of an invisible fish.

"Eclipse," I muttered. "Eclipse in Mexico." Then, forgetting the blood on my cheek and my impossible transport to a foreign country, I sat up and threw my head back in wonder.

I remembered what I'd learned in middle school earth science and turned away to find the faces of the moon and the half-eaten sun reflected on the still water of the pond. Behind the moon, the western sky brightened. Lunar mountains peaked into the sun's dwindling crescent, ripping it into long beads of sunlight. For a few seconds, there was an arc of pink.

Short polar brushes were bending by the weight of the moon's wicked gravity. I could feel it.

Only then, when the moon froze on the sun's face, did I marvel at my sudden removal from Newport, my arrival south of the border. No explanation, no ticket, no train, no runway, no car with its engine running waiting for my return. Not even a horse.

"Agrippa, Agrippa," I called. But there was no warming snort, no reassuring hooves beating time, closing in behind me.

The earth felt firm, alive, and real. I could hear its breathing. I dug my fingers into the matted web of grass, sandy crystals clotting under my nails.

In the pond's sky, Venus flashed, lit only by the sun's single reddened limb.

A moment later, the sky's spell began to disperse. As the moon passed its phase of shrouding, the sun appeared in one lunar valley and presented a pink diamond ring. For me? The bright inner corona lingered a few more seconds and the perfectly cut ring of sunlight swelled. Then, the distant rumbles of motorcycles rippled through the pond's surface and shook loose the sun's emerging face.

I looked up as the sun hung for a moment at its highest niche. But then the sight rumpled into velvet. And when I bolted to Newport through the wormhole, it was as painful as being born—my eyes burning and my ears buzzing with the hooting of nighthawks. So I lay there thinking.

Chapter 13

I keep my secrets secret. All Matepas woman do. We've been rowled by the spurs of duty to protect the sacred Paxos scrolls, both a pain in our royal asses and an honor. We have hidden the holy artifacts from the eyes of Ottoman, Persian, Visigoth, Hun, and Venetian raiders who've tried to mount the crenulated parapets of the Frangopanagioti Castro without success. We have concealed the scrolls, sentried by bats in secret chambers, in caves on the island for centuries.

I'd shrunk from Yiayia Friday because she was old, smelled like mothballs, and had missing teeth. The ones she'd managed to keep were cracked and grey at their mercury cores. She gummed her ice cream and scared me when I was small because she was yellowed with age like the curled and wrinkled pages of a musty old book, dry to the touch and ready to crumble to dust. I couldn't stand to be close to anyone so ready to die. I was afraid of endless grief and my own salt tears never stopping.

I couldn't bear the knowledge that I would outlive my half-tamed pet squirrel, Merrill. I wept for months when my poor red cardinal from Brazil, Elpino, dipped his beak into his feeder, choked on boiled white rice, and died. It's not fair gerbils have such short brutish lives. Death had always been my enemy.

So I buried my affection for Yiayia—until now.

The scrolls whisper, "The resurrection of the dead is one of the most important dogmas of our holy faith and is confirmed in many passages throughout Holy Scripture: 'For the hour is coming in which all that are in the graves shall hear his voice and come forth….Behold I show you a mystery; We shall not all sleep, but we shall all be changed in a moment, in the twinkling of an eye, at the last trump.'"

I didn't ever try to memorize these scriptures, or any holy words. I read over them once, and remembered. Another sign I'd changed.

This didn't happen with secular books. I read the first sentence of Pride and Prejudice seven times before I gleaned a clear conception of what Jane Austen was talking about when she said, "It is a truth universally acknowledged that a single man in possession of good fortune must be in want of a wife."

It seemed to be the other way around, especially in Victorian England. A single man flaunting his wealth in society might be looking for a wife, or a strumpet. A single woman, whose options, unlike those of a man, were so limited, was absolutely in desperate want of a husband.

"Are you all right? How's your head? Is there something wrong with your eyes?" said Georgie's voice.

At first it seemed I had seraphim eyes. But the eyes on my scapulas faded first. Then the eyes on my hands closed their hooded lids. My palms itched and sweated.

"Are you still here?" said the blurred figure of Georgie.

"Of course. Where else? I'm right here like I'm supposed to be, with my pillows and girly bolster. Wanna play canasta?"

"Why are you fiddling with those sunglasses under your duvet?"

"I was planning on dressing up as Jackie O at the Tent tonight."

"I think you look good as Jackie O" said Calliope's voice. "Let me see those sunglasses."

"No, they're mine," I said, pushing the faux tortoise shell oversized bug eyes up the bridge of my nose.

"Well, that's what I meant," said Calliope, pulling down the covers again. "I wasn't going to take them from you. I wanted to see Jackie O in sunglasses. Hey-you're a dish."

"Thank you."

Calliope's sweet voice resonated. I looked for her but she was gone. I could only find a single dark shape standing by my open bedroom door.

"Is anything at all bothering you?" said Aunt Georgie. "And cut the wisecracks."

"Nothing whatsoever," I lied. "Stop hovering. Please leave me in peace. I just want to lie around, and enjoy my day. Maybe I'll finish the book I'm reading, The Exorcist. I'm at the part where the girl throws the priest down the stairs and the bed levitates. I want to find out what happens to her mother."

The grind of tires splattered pebbles against the undercarriages of at least two cars pulling up in our driveway. Auntie Georgie rose from the chair beside my bed and hurried to the window.

"It's them," she said.

"Who?"

Two doors opened and slammed, and then, two more.

Calliope sighed. "Holy shit," she said.

"Watch your mouth," said Georgie. "They're back."

"I don't need any help," said Medea's voice from outside. "Will you p-l-lease get away from me. If I need to take your arm, I'll ask. I'm trying to keep my dignity, if you don't mind."

"All right, Medea," said Sheriff Pappas. "You're in charge. Just trying to help."

The front door creaked open.

"Oh, shit," said the cop who was supposed to be standing guard at the front door. Instead, he had stationed himself in the kitchen, drinking coffee and noshing on crispy delicacies from my mother's freezer, baked in the toaster oven.

A cup shattered on the tile floor. I hoped it wasn't Medea's Limoges with the tulips.

"Shit," he said again, above the clatter of hunks of broken china dropping into the enameled touch-free trash can.

Heavy footsteps hurried to the front door to meet the cacophony of men's voices, over which Medea's shrill mezzo rose. "Where's my daughter?"

I held my breath for a moment, out of habit. Locking doors was better than a trick. It had become a life strategy.

"Where is she?"

I climbed out of bed and smoothed my crumpled cotton blouse with chains of violets, eyelet trim, and a Peter Pan collar. I checked the zipper of my Levis. I took seven big steps to the top of the stairs.

Below me were the blurred forms of men in brown uniforms from the sheriff's department commingled with men in blue uniforms from the police department. Among them, Sheriff Pappas stood like a patch-eyed colossus, one muscular hand steadying Medea's shoulder.

"Pur-r-rsephone! Come down here." My mother's eyes bored into mine in an electric stare that buzzed me like a shock collar. I could feel it better than I could see it. She was fuzzy, but huge, her shape like the cloaked Virgin Mary herself hovering above the hall carpet. The rug was all the shades of cinnamon, with tiny red hearts woven in by little Iranian rug weavers. They looked like drops of blood to me now.

Medea stood on one scuffed black stiletto. The heel of the other shoe had broken off. Her milk-chocolate wig had slipped catawampus from her loosened bun, her messy hair falling in strands to her shoulders streaked with chestnut and grey. The hair under her wig didn't look bad, even in her disheveled state. An ample Morticia Addams, with a mushroom on top. All in all, Medea's form was not altogether unbeautiful, especially when seen with impaired vision through dark glasses.

She looked like she'd had some wild sexual experience in a garage with a diesel mechanic. Of course, I knew she hadn't. Mom's left arm wore a bright new cast. Her gold lame cocktail gown was torn, the various slits revealed hard, knotted thighs. Her skin smelled of engine oil and dried blood.

"Persephone," said Medea. "What have you gotten into now?"

"Nothing, Mother. We went riding. I'm reading the book you gave me. You know, 'The Exorcist'."

"Look in the junk drawer and find a five dollar bill. Go to Vendetto's Market and pick up a paper, a book of matches, and a cigar. Talk to Guido and make him give you a real Cuban cigar."

"Anything else, Mom?" I said as I descended the middle of the stair, counting each step as I used to do in the pitch dark when I was a small child.

"And take off those glasses. They look ridiculous."

"I regret to inform you that I have a headache and I don't want to talk about my outfit. What happened to you?"

"Regrets? At your age? Ridiculous! And don't pay for the cigar," said Medea, hugging me.

I counted my five steps from the plinth to the pier table and looked where the mirror hung. I saw a dark ghost with bug eyes approaching me from the shadows in the glass.

Maintain. That's what loaded people say when they're trying to act straight. Okay. Fix lip gloss. Fine. Fluff hair. Okay. Money in top right hand drawer. Not there. Look with your fingers. Okay. Must be on right. No money in top. Okay. Feel where you're rummaging. Behind the carpet tacks. Ouch. Under the old Hershey's kisses, squishy in their foil jackets. Gross. Here it is. Cash.

Where was Dad? I hadn't seen him.

"Where's my father?" I said, turning to the policemen.

"He's fine," said Sheriff Pappas. Don't worry, Persephone."

"He's in the hospital," said Medea.

"He's getting checked out, but he's absolutely okay," said the sheriff, his strong fingers gentling my shoulder.

"What happened?" I squinted behind my sunglasses, trying to search the faces that were beginning to disappear in the failing light.

"Angelo and I were robbed. The police escort didn't show up when the Tent closed. After those shit-heads took the sack of money they crammed us into the trunk of the T-bird. They shot your father in the temple because he wouldn't talk. He bled all over me. They left us for dead."

I felt my forehead spasm with worry. "I'm so sorry, Mom. I want to see Dad."

"He's fine. The bullet lodged in the bone in his temple. Nowhere near the brain. That big, thick, Spartan skull, thank God, saved him. He woke up after about five minutes. You can't see him yet. He's at the trauma center in Providence. They're taking the bullet out now. Thank God!"

"But Mom, I want—"

"Go to Vendetto's, now," Medea interrupted. "Get me that newspaper. And don't forget the cigar."

I regained my composure, trying to act as casual as possible. "I didn't think you still smoked."

"I smoke like the Minoan eruption of the Santorini crater," said Medea, her chin thrust out on a quest to the tip of her upturned nose.

I counted five bills, not sure if they were ones, thrust the tidy stack deep into the darkness of my right jeans pocket, and left.

#   #   #

Hold it together. Act normal. Remember the way. You've counted these steps before. Dr. Franek had told me compulsions like step counting and religious prostrations were normal for a teenager dealing with my eccentric family. To relieve anxiety about the latchkey around my neck. I told him the Matepases were lunatics. He had reminded me they were smart and loved me.

I blew kisses towards the voices, their bodies dissolving like icing on Pasta Flora melting in the sun. I turned on my heel, one-hundred eighty degrees, perfectly. My fingers found the doorknob from memory.

Confidence. Head up. No hesitation. No quick jerky steps, and for God's sakes, don't stumble. They're watching me. Take it easy. My steps cross the concrete footers at a perfect right angle to the street. I turn right and stay in the center of sidewalk, finding the seams to keep me straight—perfectly straight. Dog barks. A fringe of grass compresses under the schnauzer's feet as he gallops towards me. He sniffs my knees. I pat his head. He lets me go without eating my calves. Seven-hundred and seventy-seven steps and I am to Main Street. Engines roar. Feet thump all around me like wild camels stumbling in the dark. Not like horses or elephants, with heavy four-beat tread. But camels are slouchy and cautionary. Their walk is lateral and two beat, like mine. One two…one two.

Tracking the left sidewalk edge like a Great Wallenda and catching the joints between the concrete pads with the tip of my left toe. My toes are sensitized like fingers, or lips. I could play the piano with them. Something easy, like the score Bergman used for

'The Seventh Seal.' That was just weird. Medea's idea of a family movie. And the porcelain monk, Death playing chess.

Something, some force seems to be holding me back, like old stiff sticky gum on the bottom of my shoe. Or a bungee cord pulling me back home from my waist. I march on.

I reach a confluence of roars, and stop. Suntan-oiled skin brushes my arm. I hear shadows breathing. Five of them, one wearing Opium. Patchouli. Old Spice. Ivory soap. Mushroom Pizza on a smoker's breath. A car, like a Minotaur screeches to a hulking halt. Doors open, then swing shut, the Minotaur bellows on.

I progress with the hoard across the street surrounded by the roars of traffic. The man-eating mares of Diomedes slide to the edge of the crosswalk pulling Thracian chariots behind them. I huddle in the migrating pack, sticking close to the smell of Old Spice and lemon rind. Coffee breath. I reach the corner. I sense within fifty yards, the newsstand.

The bank was in front of me. A heavy four-door sedan slides to a stop. The blob parked in front of me blended with the anonymous honking shadows that came barreling down Main Street, burning rubber. A man, overdressed in a tropical-wool suit, suddenly grabbed me from behind and pointed the blur of gun—long and fat, an automatic—at the tumble of security guards flooding from the revolving doors of Citizen's Bank.

"It's Okay, Missy. Just shut up and I'll let you go," he said, holding me before him like a shield, folding himself into the back seat of the car before he pulled me in, my legs kicking like a Rockette's.

"I have to take you to Green Falls and tie you to a tree so the police can't question you about my face."

"But what about the security cameras?" I said, the scald of tears sliding down my cheeks, stomach jumping with every punch of the gas pedal to the floor.

"Dismantled them before the job," he said with a laugh. He paused. "Hey, aren't you a smart one?"

"Did you remember to dismantle the alarms?"

"Baby Boy did it," said the bank robber.

"Shit. I forgot. Sorry, boss," said Baby Boy.

The flood of alarm bells followed us down Main Street.

"Everybody, stay cool. Shut up and think," said the bank robber. "Baby Boy, chill, maintain. Keep driving."

"How the fuck did she know that?" said the accomplice in the front passenger seat.

I took off my glasses and let the bank robber look into my eyes. I blinked. My corneas felt rough and thick, and opaque with swelling, as if covered with scales.

He placed a pressed cotton handkerchief in my hand.

"You can't see me," said the bank robber. "Poor girl." His voice was soft as a whisper and flowed in a serpentine curl of sound that lingered, hesitated, withdrew, and recessed in my ear like the velvety touch of a butterfly's wing.

He brushed slow tears from my lips. His soft fingers absorbed each drop. My tears melted into his tender skin. Then he lifted the hand, held the tears to his tongue, and tasted them.

I felt naked before him.

"Holy God, Baby Boy, we've got to take her back."

"You crazy? Fuck you, man," said the driver. "We can't go back. If you don't want to leave the little bitch tied to a tree, let's kick her ass outa' the car now. Fuck you, Boss. I'm slowing down, asshole. Open that door."

"I said we're taking her back. Hang a right, cocksucker, and shut your mouth."

Baby Boy slammed his elbow against the door, striking the button and driving the window open.

"*Vaffanculo*" Baby Boy exploded.

"Watch your driving. Do what I tell ya," said the bank robber.

A pistol barrel thwacked up against the back of Baby Boy's skull.

"Boss!"

"That was a love tap, asshole," he hissed. "Drive. Watch the road."

The gentle man beside me pulled his free hand from his pocket and plucked out a crumpled handkerchief wrapped in the arsenical scent of dried apricot seeds. A moment later, the sound of crunching pits percolated from his mouth.

Baby Boy swerved to the right, the engine roaring and brakes screaming like a hell-roasted devil.

"Where would you like me to leave you, Miss?" asked the bank robber, touching my hand with a slight press.

"Vendetto's, please."

Baby Boy pulled up to the curb. Flashing lights and sirens tore at the air. Motors roared and died over the sound of cawing of crows from the rooftops of Vendetto's. The bank robber with the soft voice reached over my lap, pulled the handle, and pushed open the door.

At his urging I put one foot out onto the street.

"Wait," he said, touching my hip through my jeans.

I half turned.

"I've done a lot of bad things," he said. "Would you bless me? Please."

"I can give you a minute and a half," I offered. "Go. And remember, tomorrow, there will be apricots."

The door shut, and the car slid away. I waved, then inhaled and held my breath hard. The breeze was tinged with juniper from a clay pot on the sidewalk. The sharp edge of singed brake fumes smashed with gas fumes, fusing with desperate shouts, and frantic jigglings of tight locks. The eye-watering, oniony stench of allium from the vendors' carts permeated my sinuses from both sides of the door of Vendetto's.

I stood in front of the door, still holding my breath. The blessing of a minute and a half. On the other side of the glass, a man in floral California surfer-boy shorts had lifted a Nikon held to his neck by a dangling cord and was struggling to snap a frozen shutter. He mouthed curses as the car sped away.

His yellow T-shirt struck a familiar cord. I squinted to read its fuzzy declaration in bold print: "Frodo's Photo Studio. Aargh!"

He lowered his camera and stared at me while my lungs strained to hold onto their remaining air.

Past the masses of pansies, policemen were trapped within their cars, the locks jammed. A sergeant was shouting to his partner and growing red-faced while twisting pliers around the waist of the manual police-car door lock.

Muffled yells and shouts seeped from cars up and down the block.

When my breath was gone the locks began to move. I groped for the door handle and pulled, letting myself into the store.

The Nikon guy from Frodo's ceased fighting with his camera and backed away.

Though I could see little detail of the photographer's face, I felt the burning stare of his wide unshuttered eyes. Like Medea's stare. Like shocks from a collar.

"Excuse me," I said, passing him, and retracing the steps of my many visits to the newsstand at Vendetto's.

I can give you more than a minute and a half.

I inhaled again and held my breath. I took the paper from the top left corner of the rack, where the Providence Journal had resided since my mother was a girl. I turned exactly ninety degrees and walked to the counter.

"Trouble with the door?"

"No, Guido," I said, exhaling. "Can I have three cigars, please? You know, the kind my mother likes?"

"That's funny," said Guido. "Now customers are piling in here like lemmings. Ya'd think we were selling Red Sox tickets. What's up with all the cop cars?"

"False alarm at the bank, I think. Do you have any Visine? Got something in my eyes. Need to get the red out."

"Visine? Yeah, yeah," said Guido. "Hey, Joey! Go get a box of Visine from row thirteen for Persephone here. She's got mud in 'er eye."

"Thanks, Guido."

"You should get those peepers looked at, honey. Once I had a piece of steel stuck in my eye for two weeks, back in Nam. Was dodging bullets and couldn't see worth a damn. I learned to feel the air in front of the slugs as they sped by. I think I learned to smell land mines. In fact, I'll wager I could teach it. My eye hurt like hell. Had to have the shard dug out by a flight surgeon with a missing pinkie. Hey—want a donut? Gotcher favorite, Boston Cream. Fresh from Allie's."

"No thanks, Guido. I'm trying to quit sweets. Medea says that sweets and pent-up anger ooze out of your face and give you pimples."

Guido chuckled. "Cohiba, yes? I think she switched from Magicos to the Exquisitos Secretos, if I remember right."

"Three Exquisitos Secretos, then," I said.

He squatted, groaning, knees popping, and stuck his golden-ringed fingers into the cool glass case below the cash register into an unmarked cigar box. He tossed a handful of cigars onto the counter.

He leaned over and whispered, "Three Cubans."

I picked one up and squinted tight to read the writing. One dropped onto the floor. I knelt and slid my hand under the cabinet, searching for the Cohiba that rolled the fastest. I fingered around under the counter's edge and found dead insect parts dusted with *schmutz*, the cigar, and a clunky mass of cold metal.

I returned the cigar to the counter and offered the cold chunk to Guido.

"My keys. Ya found 'em," said Guido, in a stunned voice. "Thought they were lost forever." He reached over the counter and whispered, "These aren't just any keys. They open every door at the Cave Monastery outside Rome. My brother is the current caretaker. Job's been in my family for generations. St. Luke the Evangelist carved a Madonna icon of wax and left it in the cave. The monastery built around it burned down seven times, but the icon survived." Guido shook the keys and squinted at them. "Ah, man. I'll have to soak 'em in rancid wine. They're full of rust."

"I hadn't noticed," I said quite honestly, reaching into my pocket for the cash.

"Put that away right now," said Guido.

"I have the money," I said.

"No, I insist," he said as he assembled a box of donuts. "What'll it be?"

"No, thank you," I said. "Really."

"If you don't tell me what you want, they'll all be Boston Cream."

"Okay, then. If you insist. Three Boston Cream. Two all chocolate, whipped cream filled. You know, the kind without a hole. Oh, and for Medea, well, she likes the cinnamon cake crullers. So, seven of those."

Guido assembled the box, wrapping each piece in crisp waxed paper. I inhaled deeply. The cinnamon hovering over the box reminded me of the wild garden beneath my bedroom window.

"I can't help it, Guido." I reached in and wrapped my fingers around the perimeter of a random donut, careful not to smash any icing.

I knew this one had to be a chocolate cream filled. The smooth chocolate powder dusted my fingertips like talc. The soft scent reached my nose and I prepared myself for a flood of cocoa-infused flavor.

I closed my eyes and sank my teeth into the ball of chocolate, mouth watering, tongue smeared with cream filling, the sweetness almost painful.

The cadence of his walk said he was fifty feet behind me.

I smelled the musk and oak leaves and lingering gunpowder before his long, thick fingers touched my shoulder.

"Persephone, I got a message from the Chief that there was a robbery. You look fine, though. If you saw anything I need to hand you over to the investigator on duty."

I chewed quickly, pushed the masticated donut to the back of my throat so I wouldn't choke. Tough choice, chocolate or the luscious sheriff. One thing that really embarrassed this teenage woman was getting caught red-handed by a handsome man with my mouth stuffed with junk food.

Sheriff Pappas licked his thumb and rubbed my upper lip.

That was almost a kiss. The only things missing were lips and tongues.

"You've got a chocolate mustache," he said. "So did you see anything?"

"No."

"You sure?"

"Quite sure."

"What's wrong with your eyes?" He held my chin in his hands, tipping my face up to the light.

"I got some dust in them out riding, and I'm allergic," I said. "Don't worry, I'm getting better."

Well, my eyes weren't really getting better. But I couldn't say to this normal guy, "Woe is me. For I am lost and have unclean lips and I dwell in the midst of people of unclean lips. For my eyes have seen the King, the Lord of Hosts." And watched an eclipse. And probably burned my retinas. After I teleported through a wormhole and back again.

"I'm taking you to the doctor," said the sheriff.

At that moment, I realized my mind was a sponge for thoughts that could enter into my head from without. They didn't even have to be my own thoughts. How would I know? What troubled me were the bad ones. Jealousy. Wanting to look like Sharon Stone. Wanting to be as rich as Warren Buffet. Wanting to be a Hollywood daughter, like Liza Minnelli, but without having to struggle with my crazy family. I went from being nobody to being the most important person on the planet. Then, I was bitch-slapped by guilt because of my cockiness. The good thoughts didn't trouble me, and I didn't care if those were mine or not. What bothered me were fragments like "for men, self-improvement stops at toilet training." That could've easily been someone else's thought. Like Medea's. Maybe.

"Hey, Pappas." Guido posed over the counter, his arm masking the keys. "I think you should take her to the doctor. But let her finish her donut. What'll you have?"

"Coffee, black. Thanks."

Guido dragged his cupped fingers over the keys and slipped them into the pocket of his stained white apron without even the hint of a clang. I was good at keeping secrets, and Guido Vendetto knew it.

"Thank you, Guido," I said, balancing the tower of donuts, the newspaper, and the bag of Medea's smokes and my Visine. Blurrily, I counted my steps to the door.

"We're taking you to Dr. Barrett," said Sheriff Pappas, following behind. He blew at the lid of his plastic cup, slurped, then gulped. "Shall I call your mother first?"

"It's okay. She went to see Dad. I'll let you take me to Dr. Barrett, but can we stop first at the Annunciation Cathedral? I need to talk to Father Stavros."

"Is there a problem?" he asked, stopping to look at me.

"No problems. Only solutions," I said, standing as tall as I could, my face level with his neck.

His veins were visible beneath the angle of his jaw, as if his tie were too tightly strapped to his collar. His skin was tan against his white shirt. It was the color of acorns.

I heard a distant hissing. The sheriff was holding the door for me. I stood and listened to the sizzling serpent sound that buzzed in from the street.

Pappas suddenly released his grip on the door and ran toward me, throwing his massive six and a half foot frame over my thin teenage body. The boom of the explosion shook the walls. We slid across the slippery polished oak floor and under a table of Famous Amos cookies, boxes of Panettone, anise pizzelles and canisters of biscotti blanketed in pyrotechnic powder.

Coruscating angel dust from the explosion floated in the air surrounding our boxed-in hovel. Main St. streamed with the fire consuming the remains of the sheriff's car. Blades of flame ran together like eels out the windows and beneath the frame, peaking into hollows that moments ago had been a sedan. Eels of fire slithered and clumped together in a massive burning ball.

Sheriff Pappas rolled off but still held me tight from behind. I pushed against his strong arms, soft with golden hair, and my backside collapsed into him as if there were elastic pulling us together to form loving spoons, fitting each other, clattering without space.

Soon, the street outside was a busy blur with those who, like my hot sheriff, serve and protect: a few firemen, policemen, EMTs, all decked out in heavy protective garments the colors of traffic lights and crime scene tape.

Sheriff Pappas didn't get up. He moved, all right, but stayed with me, his nose in my hair, his heavy oak leaf breath warming the crook of my neck. He held me like the outer petal cradles the inside of a smaller, younger, more delicate rose.

I pushed against his embrace again.

"You insolent young cub, hold still," he muttered.

I pushed my young ass into him. "I'm like Mama," I mumbled. "I can't help liking you."

"What?" he said.

The worst he could suspect was the only truth for him. I would be a fog, then a ghost in the fog.

"I'm too old for you," I said.

"Glad you told me. The joy of being alive is in the poetry," he whispered, filling my head with his spirit.

"If I could only find what it is I'm looking for. Something I lost. Something I need terribly. If I lost it forever, then there'd be no hope."

"Whatever you dropped, we'll find it."

"That's not what I meant. And I know," I said, tipping my head to feel his warm breath against my cheek. My hands relaxed on his arms and I felt the beat of his heart, which seemed to alter slightly with the phases of his breathing.

I released my sobriety, determined to be fully conscious of this rapture, to bear all things, and endure all things.

I'd had a few make-out sessions at school dances, surprised at my own disgust at the way sweaty awkward paws groped at my breasts like chikan on a Japanese train. It had been the same with their slimy kissing methods. One cute boy, my homecoming dance date from geometry class, had slithered his tongue through my mouth like a homeless escargot searching for its shell: all drooly and mechanical, without sensitivity, just wet and hard and brutal.

I really didn't belong at school functions, but I still spent a fair amount of effort trying to blend. This meant putting up with a certain amount of normal teen stuff. To fuck one of them would be to go to one of the dark gods, though, so I avoided it.

Now, I allowed myself to tremble. He stroked the length of my arm, as if he relished the softness of my skin against the calloused pads of his fingers. His hand descended to my wrists, lightly touching them, before his fingertips glided back up my arm, savoring each curve. His fingers climbed back up my neck, moving a stray lock of hair, and slid over my throat.

I loved the risk; my throat so bare, so vulnerable. His lips on my neck sent a shudder and a bolt of heat straight to my crotch, where the warm wetness eased from my body. His tongue barely grazed my neck, warm, soft, unlike the bulge I felt pressing against the crack of my buttocks through my tight Levis.

He turned me over like a chef rolling sushi in a snug seaweed wrapper. He looked into my eyes, still dim with film. Objects continued to plunk onto the table above us. Smash. Glass shards fell to the ground. A bottle of Pine-Sol cracked and splattered. We were spared by our shelter beneath the table.

I reached up and moved his eye patch over.

The eye was almost all pupil, with a wedge of grey iris like a piece of pie. We were so close our eyelashes touched.

"A shard of lead. Bomb squad."

"It's so beautiful. You should keep the patch off all the time."

"Too much light. Messes up depth perception."

"Everyone stay down!" ordered a rough voice from the doorway. "Nobody move. It's gonna take some time. Is anyone hurt? You're going to be okay."

"Breathe," commanded the sheriff. I felt him whisper in my ear more than I heard the words. "Don't cork up any locks, please."

I obeyed. I was so new to this. To the utter joy I felt in the arms of someone else. I parted my lips to invite his kiss. Warm acorn breath filled my mouth. He held me and kissed me like a poet, dipping and pausing, by instinct and empathy. It was I who entered his mouth with my tongue. Still, I was passive, awaiting an invitation. My tongue lay on his, and we lay breathing, looking into each other's injured eyes, knowing this altered vision was special. He had the mesmerizing quality of Mesmer.

I closed my eyes and pressed my pelvis into his hard root, moving in a small slow dance under the table, the only safe place in a mad scene of explosions, sirens, falling chandeliers, and broken cookies on the floor around us.

He kissed me under the hollow of my right ear, then between my brows. As the rush of fire blasted throughout me for the first time ever, I realized, at this moment I could feel life in my entire body: my nails, my hair. Even my spleen was alive with pleasure. When I came, I silenced my groan and opened my mouth to allow full penetration by his tongue, which continued to caress me without ceasing. I was a wheel rolling out of its own center as I plunged into carnal oblivion. And we still had our pants on.

Chapter 14

The car's steel skeleton sizzled to black. We lay under the table until the fire consumed every spot of edible material; the white-with-blue-stripes cop-car paint, the plastic dash, the vinyl bench seats, the police radio, the plaid thermos, the overnight bag on the back seat.

The tires exploded in a mass of burning rubber. The frame collapsed, and the carcass eked out its final stench.

My sheriff and I lay on our bellies. I, propped up on my clutched fists beneath my chin, and he, touching my back with light fingers.

I pressed my torso hard against his side, like a four year-old mare shinnying on up to a stallion she'd known from fillyhood.

He slid his fingers from my back and shifted his pelvis away, the space between us expanding like a blister filling with blood. He held his breath, the blister growing between us.

"My back hurts and so do my shoulder blades," I said.

"Where does it hurt, Persephone? Maybe I need to take you to Dr. Barrett." He pressed on my back like an old farmer easing the rusty choke on an old Eight N Ford fifties tractor. "Does it hurt here?" He thumped my spine like a clumsy chiropractor. "What about that? Lower? Higher? How does that feel?"

I winced. "Try to be more sensitive. Do what you were doing before."

"No. I'm too old for you."

"*Au contraire, mon ami,*" I said quite seriously. "Haven't you figured out that it is I who is too old for you?"

"No. My job is to protect you, not figure you out."

"Says who? I can take care of myself. Obviously. My cousin Calliope, who is not a lesbian, makes me feel better by writing messages on my back with one foot of her stuffed teddy bear. You can't get any more innocent than that, Sheriff Pappas."

"I don't have a teddy bear."

"Then just use your index finger."

He traced words on my back with his fingertips, like Calliope and I did when we lay last summer on the Black Beach of Paxos, Circe's Beach, beneath the crenulated towers of the Matepas' Venetian castro.

N, he wrote.

"You are perfect," I whispered beneath the cacophony of collapsing tables and sirens.

O, said his fingertip.

"I have heard all women become their mothers," I said, realizing we were already in the say-anything phase of our relationship. Thanks to the deafening effect of the blast, he couldn't hear a word I uttered.

A ceiling beam crashed onto the counter. Pizza slices flew around the room like doughy shrapnel.

But I could hear the wings of butterflies fluttering around the morning glories on the fence across Main Street. The flowers creaked as they turned their purple faces to the sun.

I blinked twice and rubbed my eyes hard. The haze dissipated, revealing a fire truck shooting javelins of water like cold steel at the smoking, sooty metal remains of the car that slumped in front of Vendetto's. Like a burnt goat for Baal, the smell of souvlaki burst balloons of memory. My hearing, attenuated by my recent loss of visual acuity and by a trick of nature, rendered conversation unfair.

"Can you go back to what you were doing, please?" I said.

S. His finger dipped to the small of my back.

"Don't add a 'T' to that 'S,' please."

He reached for the Providence Journal that had flown out of my hands with the explosion.

The newspaper was splayed open to the obituary section like unfurled moth's wings impaled by stick pins. The pages were smeared with Boston Cream. He scanned the obits and turned the page.

Sunlight penetrated the spaces between the rubble and illuminated the picture of a man in a black-billed cap carrying someone in his coat. The subtitle read: *Limo driver saves girl from near death after fall from Ferris wheel.*

He lifted his eye patch and stared into my eyes. "Well." He paused. "I," he began, then stopped. "You." His breath congealed in his throat. "I guess you are…you just might be… someone." He coughed. "Maybe you are older than I thought. A lot older than I thought," he muttered to himself.

H. His finger dipped into the small of my back.

"Your good looks are a snare I'd like to be caught in," I said. It was easy to confess when your listener was deaf as a beetle.

O. My back bowed like a cat's toward his fingertip, which now rested on my left butt cheek. His hand slid under my untucked shirt and into the top of my now unzipped jeans.

"I would go with you anywhere. To an empty beach, a corn field, a pumpkin patch. Your house, a motel. Any motel. To a sleazy demolition site with ripped out toilets, junkies in the stairwell, pipes hanging out of the ceiling and plaster falling down on us. This heat is too much for all these clothes," I said, pulling my hair off my sticky neck and onto my left shoulder. "I want to be naked with you."

W. Oblivious to the unveiling of my deepest disclosure, he drifted back to my right shoulder, my shoulder blade bare except for one dingy bra strap exposed beneath my loosened and twisted clothing. "These are so pretty," he said.

O, he traced. Then L, followed by D.

I knew he wasn't talking about my underwear, grey and pilled from laundering too often with black socks. I had been waiting for my breasts to grow bigger before purchasing additional lingerie. I dreaded shopping for personal items because Medea would insist on sizing me properly. I knew I wouldn't measure up to her operatic standards.

R, he drew. Then, a U. He paused and drew a question mark, dotting it with a stiff finger.

How old R U?

I wiped the plaster dust from my shoulders and chest. There was room enough under the table for me to sit up cross-legged and reach over for a bag of Famous Amos chocolate chip cookies. I ducked and put one in his mouth. I ran a finger down his back and leg until I got to his shoe. Standard military brown dress lace-ups. I struggled to untie the Gordian knot, but the hard plastic-coated laces clasped like a Victorian maiden's knees. Fumbling, I pulled the end of the string and the shoe sprang open, releasing his brown sock-covered foot. I stripped the sock from his foot. Naked flesh gleamed in the light. I stroked it, massaged it, blew on it, tickled it, prepared it. 7 of 7, scraped my fingernail on his sole.

"*Christos eleison,*" he said.

I crunched a cookie, then offered chocolate stained lips. He pecked at them like a baby sparrow taking a worm from his mother's beak, then sighed and licked the chocolate from my lips. "Tastes good," he purred.

The silence circled around us in a winding gyre, like the sonar of a bat feeling out the contours of his cave.

"I'm thirty eight years old. I'm a sheriff. A member of your church and a friend of your family," said Pappas.

I ate another cookie, offering him one. "Take this and me too," I said. "I command you to kiss me, again. This time, differently, like I want to be kissed."

He pulled me toward him by my empty belt loops, his lips within the magnetic field of mine. His face pulled back. Then, like two scraps of iron giving up, it flew back defeated by wicked gravity. His breath tingled. The scuff of his jaw prickled—caterpillar soft. His mouth was honey in mine. The scent of baby oil from his neck lingered on my face. We tangled, roots of live oaks on a swampy river bank, exposed, entwined, like braids of hair, cavernous, but a haven for phosphorus and the green glow of foxfire, sparkling like city lights.

"I have never seen shoulder blades like these." He cupped them as if they were breasts, making them flush.

The seams of my bra dented my nipples. This was not a quality undergarment. A humiliating excuse for a brassiere. I wriggled my breasts loose, looked over at him, and slipped the patch back over his eye with one cramped hand. I pressed my lips to the underside of his jaw, loving the oaky smell, the slow, sure rhythm of his breathing and slow-beating heart. I rubbed my cheek against his wet lips. "Thank you."

Beneath the charred and smoking canvas awning of Vendetto's store, a pair of cardinals, like crows dipped in blood, circled above the broiling car, then settled on a Ginkgo tree. The birds shimmered in the glow against the scrim of fire beyond, blooming in scarlet. My eyes seemed to be healing. I held my lids open against the strain of an intense urge to blink.

A tricolor beagle trotted to the fire hydrant, smelled the patch of grass at its base, then sauntered over to the pansy patch and lifted a hind leg in quiet relief to the yellow and purple upturned faces. Incensed, the birds fluttered skyward as Auntie Georgie's limo pulled up.

"That's him," I said. "He's come to get us. Come on."

The magazine rack had tumbled over from the compression effect of the bomb. Piles of vagrant magazines—an avalanche of Glamour, Seventeen, Sports Illustrated, Yachting and Good Housekeeping—lay spent among the rubble of dish washing soaps and broken spray bottles of Lysol. I reached under a New Yorker and grabbed a Cohiba, stuffing it in my cleavage.

We climbed out of our hovel, the paper folded under Sheriff Pappas' elbow, tripping over land mines of debris as smoke-dazed flies circled our heads.

"Did you know that if you took all of the weight of every living being on the Earth, including swamp flies, cockroaches, human beings, algae, and rhinoceri, one quarter of that mass would be ants?"

He smiled. "No. Didn't know that, honey."

#   #   #

The man in the black-billed hat opened the door of my Auntie's limo and we walked past the combustibles and climbed into the back seat.

"That your car?" said the limo driver.

"Was," said Pappas.

"Can you take us to Father Stavros?" I said.

"Yes." The driver turned on the radio.

"What's this piece?" asked the sheriff.

"Flight of the Bumble Bee," I said. "Haven't you seen Fantasia? You know, Disney."

"Yeah. Really hated that movie. I hate all cartoons. I can't stand the idea of fat dancing elephants in tutus. They weren't funny at all. Just gross. And illogical. I took my son to it." Sheriff Pappas turned his head away. "With my wife."

He held a deep breath.

"I'm sorry about your family," I said.

His good eye filled with tears. The bottom of the patch moistened, tears cupping and cascading down his cheeks and streaking down the side of his nose from his imperfect eye. "What happened to my family is no excuse for what happened in there, Persephone."

"I told you I'm old enough. Responsible for my own decisions."

"And I'm responsible for mine. I know you're older than you seem. No doubt about that. But that doesn't exonerate me, either."

"Yes, it does." I leaned over and tapped at the chauffeur's window.

The man in the black-billed cap slid open the glass. I touched his shoulder, the hint of a spark passing between us.

Sheriff Pappas jumped, jerking his leg away from mine. "Wow. What was….?"

"Never mind," I said. "Just friction."

"Let me tell you about ants," said the chauffeur. He reached into his coat and pulled out a pink cardboard baker's box labeled 'Citizen Cake.' "Care for a truffle?" he offered, passing the small box back to me.

"Love them," I said.

"I do too," said the sheriff.

We sat on the lemon-waxed leather seat and ate dark chocolate truffles embossed with tulips while the chauffeur told us about ants.

"Ants have a collective mind. They are not individuated, as people like to think humans are."

106

"We all know about the collective unconscious," I said.

Sheriff Pappas groaned.

"The hive mind is non-local, and goes wherever the parts go," said the chauffeur.

I sat back in my seat and considered for a moment what he'd said.

He took exit 7 to Blackstone Boulevard, past a grove of birch, their bark studded with eyes like a conclave of Acadians walking with Socrates in the warmth of an August afternoon. Over a paint-peeling covered bridge that crossed the rock garden of a swollen stream, we passed the cemetery surrounding a chapel that had once belonged to the College of Salve Regina. The road widened then disappeared below a hillock clustered with black-eyed Susans.

"Are you suggesting that through the mind of an ant you could be everywhere at once?" I asked.

"I'm not suggesting anything."

"Well, it sounded like you were."

"Well, maybe I'm doing it unconsciously," he said with a trace of a laugh.

"Wouldn't it be cool to travel through the minds of all creatures?"

He snorted. "I'm just talking about ants."

"Hand me that box, please," said the sheriff with a groan. "I think I'll have some more tulips."

"Hold it. Isn't hive consciousness relatively analogous to collective unconscious in humans?" Waiting for his answer, I scratched a mosquito bite until it bled.

"I'm not connecting the dots," said the driver. "It's important you come to your own conclusions. I'm not feeding you what to think here."

"But you catch me when I fall."

He said nothing to that.

The needle on the dashboard slowed to thirty so a guy smoking a cigar driving a horse trailer could pass us.

The horses swayed their hind ends with each curve and bump in the road. They looked like the baroque dancing horses on the Napoleonic vase, gilded by a tulipine art nouveau border, in which my mother stored cedar chips in the coat room at the Tent. The guy with the cigar slammed on his brakes and the horses' rears tensed and braced. The man in the black-billed cap pulled our limo onto the shoulder.

"Shit, that was close," said Guy Pappas, chewing his chocolate and swallowing. He folded the newspaper.

I leaned forward to the chauffeur again. "How did you catch me, anyway?"

"With my coat."

I took in a frosty breath, remembering Yiayia Friday's pale fist clamping onto a chunk of my hair. The Ferris wheel going down as she pulled up. I remembered the terrified look in Calliope's dilated pupils, the open-mouthed rictus of shock before I turned, facedown, the ground racing towards me. I remembered the rush towards asphalt and golden circus tents, their striped banners flapping, the pounding of the salty, grease-scented air against my face, then the lightness of his catch in the heavy swaddling of a wool coat that had encased me within its downy lanolin folds like a chrysalis. "Just how is it possible that you could catch me with a coat?"

"How is it possible that you can lock a door by holding your breath?" He reached back and slid the glass window shut.

I had no idea why holding my breath enabled me to lock doors, keep them shut, or stop knobs from turning. Yiayia Friday had tutored me until I could slam the heaviest door into the tightest jamb. The physics of it, I didn't understand. I'd been doing it so long, I'd ceased to even wonder.

I sat back, my arms folded. I gritted my teeth. We passed white square farmhouses and drove deeper into the woods, where a hint of sky filled in the puzzle pieces between the pitch pines. I knew I should ask again about my fall from the Ferris wheel. I wanted to hypnotize him and make him tell me. Everything. Learning the mechanics of my powers was vital to my sanity. I had known this for a long time. I knew the man in the black-billed hat had stood watching back when Georgie had dragged me away from the clamoring car at the beach house, when I was little. I'd seen Christy disappear, and this chauffeur take his place at Yiayia's funeral.

Why was he protecting me? Why did I need protecting? I had to know the answers to these questions. Yet I didn't want to know. Not really. I was afraid. There were things I needed to grasp.

I wanted to open that window and get the answers. But then, I just couldn't do it. I wasn't ready to know, exactly. Not yet.

Maybe I would ask Father Stavros.

I remembered the trail of his wings, so like a bridal train, when that cute doctor was picking shards of the candelabra out of my face with tweezers. I remembered them spreading to soften my drop from the air, straight as rain into his coat. He wasn't an ordinary chauffeur. He wasn't a human bodyguard. I reached up, exhaled, and slid open the window again. "Okay, then," I said. "Tell me about the bees."

"Well, bees are mostly sterile workers. Except for the queens. The workers feed and protect the queen." He looked into the rear-view mirror, staring into my eyes.

"So I've heard. They have group consciousness," I said, smart-ass style.

"The drones will even sacrifice their lives for the group. They fly through fire and smoke to save the queen."

"So you're my drone? Who are you, exactly?"

"I'm just your driver. And we're talking about bees."

"Okay." I relaxed into the beeswax scent of the leather seat again. "This one fact is fatal to Darwin's theory. At least, when it comes to bees, the altruists, the most self-sacrificial are the most vital to the hive."

"Then how do their genes survive?" I said.

"Inbreeding," said the driver. We passed a cornfield where the wind tossed a handful of grackles into the sky and blew them apart into a shower of tiny blackbirds.

"Sisters are more related to each other than to their own offspring. They're supersisters."

"And the supersisters produce the drones?"

"Of course. Bees share seventy-five percent of their DNA with their sisters. From the selfish gene point of view, it's more logical to raise sisters than to spawn offspring. Each individual, each supersister, every drone invests entirely in helping the group, leading to a perfect superorganism."

We passed a weave of honeysuckle vines where a skulk of red foxes nursed their kits in a tangle of flowers. The red bands collaring their throats shone through the splotches of leaves like the red stripes on peppermint candy canes.

"The hive mind is an intelligent version of the superorganism, like bees. What each bee knows, so knows the hive," the chauffeur said, looking back for an instant.

"Well," I said. "I think you expect me to draw parallels to other things."

He shrugged. "That's entirely your choice."

"Maybe the two of us are connected telepathically. How else would you have known to talk about bees? Or maybe you communicated about the hive mind to me when I was in Vendetto's."

"No, absolutely not. That was about ants." His smile caught in the glass of the rear-view mirror, spreading from one side of his mouth to the other.

On the right side of the road stood a small stone tower. Above its iron door, a punched-out aperture was open to the weather.

"Looks like the houses of Areopolis. Stone towers, one room wide, with narrow stairs to a landing and four portholes for viewing. Large enough to fire at Turks or pour boiling oil onto the head of an enemy," said Sheriff Pappas. His father's family had come from Mani, the middle finger of the Peloponnesus. Areopolis is the capitol of that province, the only city in a landscape dry, hot, and rocky like Mars.

The road forked into three branches. Tires squealed as we made a hard right, heading back again southeast. The surface changed from dirt to pebbles that flew up from the wheels and rat-tat-tatted on the undercarriage of the limo. We rounded a steep curve and headed downward into a hidden plateau surrounded by colonial stone fences whose ends disappeared into the forest of evergreens that lined both sides of the road.

We rolled to a stop, then crept up a pea gravel grade to face the magenta sun. The huge luminous orb hung before us, webbed with capillaries, like the embryo of a chicken cracked out of its shell. The great bell of a stone chapel rang seven times, and monks in brown robes scurried from their labors in every direction to receive us.

"Here we are," said the chauffeur. "Now you can go in to meet your Magus."

110

Chapter 15

Four monks in full brown robes appeared before the front windshield, one trailing behind the other three. A pair of small white goats scuttled behind him.

The foremost monk had the burnished olive skin of a Bulgarian soldier, dark heavy brows shading his hazel eyes, a large straight nose, chiseled cheeks and jaw, and purplish lips. He looked about thirty five.

"Welcome to the Monastery of Saint John the Theologian." His heavy Bulgarian accent persevered over his rolling rs. I recognized the Bulgarian because Yiayia had spoken hellos and good byes, terms of anger and endearment, and snatches of Balkan languages from Bulgarian to Czech to Hungarian.

The pair of monks behind the Bulgarian was quick moving, solid as rock, and had pure Macedonian faces with yellowish, twin features and flashing brown eyes. Their heads had been recently shaved; a stubble of black hair shaded their scalps. All three of the foremost monks were unhooded and shaved. Ten feet behind them, the other stood in a darker russet, unfaded robe. He wore the hood up, his face lost in its folds like the Spirit of Christmas Yet to Come.

Pappas and I sat in the car, seeking comfort from the warm emanation of life force from one another, our violet auras caught like slinky toys stuck in a coil of wire, zaps of electricity passing between us.

The chauffeur got out and opened my door. Pappas broke from me and opened his own. I stepped out of the limo and looked up at the sky. It was empty as a plain blue and white tapestry. Clouds were angels' wings against the heavens. In the absence of blackbirds and crows, the calls of the Bobwhite quail echoed in the woods beneath a butcher bird's trill.

The man in the black-billed hat turned to me and whispered, "Before we leave, let me tell you about the butcher bird."

"I'm staying right here as long as you stay with me," I said. "But no longer."

"*Au contraire, mon amie*. We will leave you here for a while, then come back and get you when you call me."

"Have no fear," said the Bulgarian, tipping his head to me in a slight bow. "We will take good care of you."

"I'm not afraid," I lied.

"Father Stavros is waiting to see you. But first he bade us to show you the monastery so you will see how we live and understand the sanctity of our vows. You must know we are men of God. You must trust us as we trust you."

"I will do my best to conjure up some trust," I said, feeling distrustful.

"Over here we have a herd of goats," continued the Bulgarian. As if I hadn't noticed. A horned, yellowed billy urinated on the grass and licked it, chewed, and spat on his own fur. Then he nibbled the lips of his ewe and mounted her backing rear-end. He reminded me of Yiayia's truffle sniffing Boar of Everholt, so free with his urine.

"You see the goats dotting the pastures like horned lambs of God?"

"I didn't know the lambs of God were *keratas*," I said. "Horned ones."

"My Holy brothers tend them with care," he said, ignoring my smart-assed comment. "They bring them purified water and sprinkle their troughs with olive branches dripping with holy water. See that barn ahead? That's where we make the cheese."

The hexagonal red wooden two-story barn stood in a freshly-sickled field of alfalfa. Horses grazed the quiet pastures or looked to the woods at the calls of birds and what sounded like the firing of gunshots.

The Bulgarian opened the massive sliding door, the cracking paint of the weathered board giving away its age. A sour gust of aging milk assaulted our nostrils. Peppercorn, bleu, feta, kashkaval, balkani, blended with the distinct scent of goat.

Sheriff Pappas held his breath. I dared not hold mine. The chauffeur laughed at our struggle. The monks paid no notice to our olfactory struggles.

The Bulgarian had an elegant strain of whimsy and a deplorable taste in cheese. "Don't worry, you'll get used to it," he said, snickering.

Vats of heated goat milk in various stages of fermentation simmered and bubbled in the cavernous space behind him.

"These tremendous cauldrons are five gallon Volraith stainless steel pots for new cheeses. In the loft, we age them before the buyers and bidders come." The Bulgarian pointed at one of the specimens. "Look here. This is the most important part of cheese making. The liquid must be cooled to exactly one hundred and thirty degrees Fahrenheit. The cheese cloths must be tightly woven, so only the liquid whey drips through when the Neufchatel is hung. Otherwise you will never get a good soft cheese."

The Bulgarian opened his robe and pulled out a skein dubh from his leather girdle, then drew a slash in the cheese cloth. He plunged a French-manicured fingertip into the inoculated, rennetted thickened milk and left a crater. "Properly coagulated goat's milk breaks cleanly and clear whey fills the hole if the cheese is perfect."

The Bulgarian pulled out his finger, now coated with curd, then looked down, snarling at the sack of cheese cloth hanging like a dead pig. A monk handed him a gold embossed kerchief. He wiped his finger. "This batch, it's no good… Bartholomew, come quickly!"

The Ghost of Christmas Yet to Come, face still hooded from view, stepped between the two shaved monks, brushed aside the Bulgarian, and stood over the vat and spat at it. "I spit on the devil!" Bartholomew screamed at full volume. "I stomp on his filthy curd.

Curse thee spawn of Satan, curse thee, cheesecloth, thou treacherous demon from hell! Out, I say. I will tie thy entrails in knots and burn thy filthy bowels in a rendering pot of curses and decaying brains. I hate thee and spurn thee. I cast my urine upon thee from a fountain of Pan, and my excrement upon thee, and my sins upon thee that thou shall sink beneath a sea of flames beyond the forked gates of Hades. Hades…that's Disneyland for assholes. I curse your fall, Lucifer. I curse the cocks you sucked in Hell, you sodomizing miscreant, fucked up the ass by the Minotaur! And you adored every fucking God-damned second of it. How exalted thou were with a trident thrusting up thine ass! *Gamato*! God damn you! God damn you." Bartholomew made the sign of the cross over the rotten cheese. "In the name of the Father, the Son and the Holy Spirit. Amen."

"Thank you, Bartholomew," said the Bulgarian. He turned to me and Sheriff Pappas. We both stood agape, stunned by the spectacle. The man in the black-billed hat only laughed.

"Bartholomew curses at sin, basil gardens, and bad cheeses, among other things," said the Bulgarian mildly. "I apologize. But really, Bartholomew's curses are quite necessary to our business. Bartholomew never says or does anything else."

Musty warmth emanated from the sack of foul-smelling cheese. Then the cloth, as if soaked in oil, spontaneously ignited. The cursed carcass of cheese disappeared into flames like a sacrificial wicker man.

"Pay that no attention," said the Bulgarian.

"I've had enough, I think," said Sheriff Pappas. "Thanks for your hospitality."

"Yes, yes," said the Bulgarian. "It really is time for you two to go—and leave Persephone with me."

## Chapter 16

I waved to Sheriff Pappas and the chauffeur as they drove back down the pebbly road, past a scarecrow and a conclave of male goats pissing and butting heads. I sniffled after their car disappeared. Then noticed two stone towers I hadn't seen before poking out of the forest, one to the North, the other where the pebbly road broke into the western hill. In the northern tower stood a man at the high window portal. I saw the flash of a rifle barrel.

"I can always stop all of this with my breath," I muttered to myself.

"Let's visit the chapel," said the Bulgarian monk at my side. "I am Father Alexander." He put a hand to his chest.

"I'm Persephone," I said.

"We've been preparing for your visit to Father Stavros for generations."

"You have an interesting place here," I admitted.

"The rocks along this path to the chapel were excavated to build the foundations for all these buildings."

We followed them. They glittered with semi-precious stones: garnets, peridots, and lapis lazuli, tessellated and swaddled by igneous stone that connected the buildings in an arching path imbedded in clay.

The chapel garden of japonica and ancient purple and white lilac had a central feature: a fire pit, embers still smoldering from the night before.

The chapel door hung ajar and the reek of frankincense wafted through the opening. The exterior white-washed walls were stained to zebra stripes by the resin of outdoor pitch-pine fires. Two silent monks were stationed on both sides of the chapel entrance, straight as an emperor's palace guards.

"*Dobra doshal,*" said Father Alexander.

"What?" I said. "I don't understand a word of Bulgarian."

"That means 'welcome,'" he said, nodding and holding the door open for me like the gentleman he was.

"I curse the word that does not explain itself!" said Bartholomew, stepping into the granite floored chapel.

Freestanding icons surrounded the perimeter of the chapel in a horseshoe that extended to the altar. Thousands of tiny votive candles, each no larger than a shot glass, slow burning, without smoke, yielded only a hint of paraffin. The Chapel of Souls had seemed tiny from the outside by some illusion or trick of vision. But from the vestibule, the chapel looked as large as a Wal-Mart superstore. I counted the first rectangle of candles, one hundred tiny wick lights wide by fifty deep. Five thousand candles in one corner making up a miniscule city. There were thousands of these slow-burning rectangles, like divided fields from a bird's view. I watched one fire go out and felt a spark of warmth leave my index finger.

"Don't touch any of those," said Father Alexander.

"But I didn't touch anything."

"Don't even think of touching them," he said.

"Well, there must be a million candles in here," I said.

"At least," he said. "And others elsewhere."

"What about this candle right here," I said. "The one that's sputtering. Shouldn't we scrape some wax off the wick? It might go out."

"What do you know about that candle? What do you know about its wick?" he asked.

"Well, I—nothing."

"Curse the candle that will not go out!" said Bartholomew, spitting the words like a bad taste of cheese.

"What did you say?" I asked.

"I can't give you much promise she will survive," said Father Alexander.

"Who?" I said, alarmed.

"The candle, of course."

"Christ, Jesus!" said Bartholomew. "She might wake up, but if she does, she won't be the same as she was before." Bartholomew turned to the candle. "Curse thy cancer. May it be consumed by a demon and pass through its bowels. May it lie in a stinking pit of refuse and be consumed by a kettle of turkey vultures fresh risen from Satan's red and sulfurous cock."

"Don't worry, Persephone," said the soft voice of Father Alexander. "I think she might live."

"Who?"

"The candle, of course," he repeated, and smiled.

The walls of the chapel were windowless to better preserve the ancient icons of Saints and Apostles. Frescoes depicting the Sermon on the Mount, the Sermon on the Plane, and all thirty-three parables revealing the heart and soul of Jesus covered every inch of the plaster walls. The ceiling was domed. A great blue eye stared from its center.

"I wanted to bring you here so you would know the eye of God is on you and on all souls, and that those souls may someday be in your hand," said Father Alexander, his Bulgarian accent disappearing for this statement, as if he had practiced saying it phonetically in English.

"What? What do you mean by that?"

"It is not for me to tell you," he said.

"Frankly, you little bitch," said Bartholomew. "It's not for you to ask anyone what they mean by anything. Damn thy curiosity, and lack of patience. And by the way, you were late. Curse thy God-damned car bomb making you late. Curse the tumult in the street after the bank robbery. Impulsivity is the sign of an undisciplined mind! May the jaws of the Minotaur consume thy lack of self-control with a slow chew! May he rip the flesh and tear the sinew with his rusty canines. Life punishes those who come too late."

I paused then turned to find Bartholomew's shadowy face within the oversized cape.

"Got it," I said.

#   #   #

Outside, to the left and the rear of the Chapel of Lights, the ground flattened and gave way to concentric rings of tightly mowed grass and garlic plats forming a sacred labyrinth. Seven monks sat on granite benches evenly spaced around the outer ring. The mandala pattern was cut from rye grass and stubbed garlic stalks, inviting a fragrant walking meditation, like in Grace Cathedral. Two monks slapped bos together, jabbing, blocking, spinning. But each blow that landed on a shoulder or trunk or thigh produced a shout from both the striker and the struck. The warrior monks each held in his fist a round tapered stick, 1.2 inches at greatest diameter and six feet long. The thwacks of oak bo against bo resonated in the valley, but the whacks of bo on flesh were absorbed by the fighting bodies cloaked in brown. The monks studying the movements at the periphery scored the match by extended arms, four to three. Both warrior monks bowed, their bos erect at each man's right side.

"Does this interest you, Persephone?" said Father Alexander.

I sighed. "Not really. Seen it a thousand times in Chuck Norris movies."

He studied my face. "I once fought a guy who was as good as Chuck Norris. Didn't end well."

"I imagine not." But I wondered, for which one?

"But these monks are practicing marksmanship. The oak bo is a practice device, not the final weapon, which, of course, is the rifle."

"I understand," said Persephone. "The eye is trained by the speed of the bo and the immediate pain of missing a shot."

"The hand is trained by the bo exercises to be strong and steady on the rifle. The bo requires much more finger strength than a two-pound trigger. The swing of the bo trains the breath to exhale when striking."

"If you exhaled during a gunshot, wouldn't you move and ruin your aim?" I asked.

"The transference is very easy. My warriors practice a form of Chi Gung in which they must inhale deeply against hardened abdominals and a tightened rectum with chin tucked as in shooting. They find the optimum sight picture and breathe slowly, keeping the sight within the top and bottom of the breath. If the sight deviates, the shooter must adjust. Once he has found the optimum sight picture is true, he exhales half way, stops his breath and pulls the trigger."

In perfect step, the monks began walking the mandala, their faces cloaked and heads bowed.

"They consecrate the mandala after the match. Everything we do here is holy," said Father Alexander. "As in shooting, when you strike with a bow, you optimize your sight picture. Remember this, Persephone. Write it down. Don't you carry a journal around?"

"No. I keep it in my head."

"One day you'll see something small that you will need to make bigger, in order to strike it."

"Damn her reluctance to believe," growled Bartholomew. "May her doubt swim in the jism of hell's skanky frog ponds, like a many-tailed monkey."

"Oh thank you, Bartholomew," said Father Alexander, turning from us. I followed him down the gemstone path to the rectangular stone common house.

A pair of glistening feline eyes blinked in the deep shadowed woods behind a stone tower. A passel of possums lunged out of a hollow tree, squealing as they ran off across the gemstone path.

"This stone house serves three functions. On the second floor are the monks' cells. Each has a bed, a bureau, a small desk, a nightstand, and a small lamp. Downstairs in the north wing is our refectory. The south wing protects our library from thieving hands."

The great hall was lit by natural sunlight distorted by mirrored ceiling glass embedded with chicken wire that cast a web of shadow on the stone floor. A huge archway lead to the gloving room, where monks donned thin, unbleached cotton gloves before handling antiquarian manuscripts. Two monks nodded as we passed into the library proper, where five others sat at a long primitive table of polished aged oak, copying the contents of one folio into another, dipping ostrich quills into indigo inkwells.

"These are sacred texts being copied. Some are Apocryphal. Not a word, not a letter, not a comma can be changed. The word of God cannot be reproduced by a machine."

Shelves of books reached to the ceiling of the windowless pressured room. None of the monks glanced up as we passed.

"They won't look at you," whispered Father Alexander. "They are trained to hyper-focus on those parchments and they will work in silence until the bell rings and their transcribing is through for the day. A single blot of ink or a poorly formed letter, a misplaced comma, or a sneeze on the page, and the entire manuscript must be thrown into the fire pit. Let's not disturb them."

I twirled a lock of hair around my fingertip.

"And let's not tempt them."

Casa Blanca lilies on a tiger-maple sideboard cloaked the stale aroma of musty scrolls. Some parchment carried in its fibers traces of dry Middle Eastern earth from ancient tombs and the burn of plant pigments fuming from clotted ink. The huge flowers stood at attention in various bisque vases, like arrows in a quiver. The lightly blushed, gleaming alabaster blooms were like faces of the dead set out for a final viewing. I stood transfixed, inebriated by their perfume and the luscious still life as their internal fires continued to cool. They were dead, after all, but oh, so beautiful. I reached toward a beckoning petal to pet its smooth pelt. The eyes of the monks all lifted from their scrolls, peacock-feather quills poised over inkpots.

"Don't touch that. Don't show them," said Father Alexander. "Remember the candles. This is not a place for you to touch without permission." But he'd stopped my hand a moment too late. The petal, firm at first, went limp and brown, and drooped on its stalk. The monks put their faces back into their transcripts. The scratching of quills on parchment resumed with a noise like cats scratching carpet.

I breathed in and held it, then let it go. "I see," I said. "Will everything I touch die? Does Medea know this is my great gift? Has she been trying to stop me from living a life of pain? Is my great inheritance to be Rapaccini's daughter? Is this my job description for the next seven hundred years?"

120

He pressed a French-manicured index finger to his lips. "Those are all questions only Father Stavros can answer."

The heavy door seemed to close itself behind us despite the pressure in the room.

"Please prepare to meet Father Stavros, now. He is the greatest teacher of our century. A great Abba, desert father, and you will never again meet any human being of his gravitas."

The monk showed me into a large paneled room, with rough granite floors and one small square table centered under a skylight with a blue stained-glass eye of God gleaming from the window above.

Father Bartholomew walked three steps behind us.

"Where is Father Stavros?" I said, stopping at the high back of one of the two ebony chairs.

"God damn thy impetuous and insufferable nature!" screamed Father Bartholomew, pounding a fist on the tiny table, which jumped with each strike. Lily-white candles bounced in their shiny silver holders, fell on their sides and went out, leaving two wisps of grey smoke.

"Father Stavros will be with you in just a few moments, my dear Persephone," said Father Alexander, pulling out the opposite chair and gesturing for me to sit. "First he bids us to make you comfortable."

"Thank you," I said, sliding into a chair.

"Shut thy trap, thy quencher of light and murderer of flowers."

"They were already dead in the vase, you silly monk," I said.

"Hush now, Father Bartholomew," said Father Alexander, pouring me a golden grail full of the deepest, reddest wine I'd ever seen. Absent was the purple cast of Burgundies. It was even less blue than claret. I smelled it, expecting rust. Instead, the bowl of the goblet cradled the smooth, silky sweetness of grape and the ripeness of oak casts with overtones of at least seven fruits: cherry, pineapple, apricot, blackberry, current, rose hip, and peach. It was like a parlor game. I detected no volatile acidity. Medea had been sure to train my nose for wine during my Christmas vacation in the third grade, when we'd sat at the Newport Musical and tasted the wares of the wine merchant, from the finest Chateauneuf-du-Pape to a basic acidic Mateus. Medea wouldn't quit until I could smell and taste the difference between them all. Like the Pepsi challenge. Of course, wines with acidic smells and aftertastes were not always bad. Their flavors could be neutralized by rich meats and sauces.

But this wine was, in a word, "frightening." Why? I had no idea.

"I don't want to drink this," I said, setting it down on a nearby table.

"It doesn't seem good?" said Father Alexander, frowning.

"It does seem good, but it doesn't seem possible. I can't find any acidity whatsoever in its aroma. It seems—" I paused. "Unnatural."

Bartholomew inhaled a hard breath, grunting and shaking his finger at the chalice. "Thou too perfect wine. No acid! How dare thee display thy foul perfection at this holy table? I command thee to become potable thou rich, arrogant bastard of a wine." He inhaled three rapid, thorough, cleansing breaths. "I command thee, on pain of fermentation and infestation with germ-carrying fruit flies, become favorable to the nose and palate of this mistress of the dark and unseen that she might partake of thy wretched, though holy aging."

My nose deep in the bowl of the chalice, I could resist no more. The temptation of perfection was too great. So I let a dribble of the impeccable vintage slip between my lips. I held and studied it on my tongue.

"Before you swallow, we must say goodbye for now, and leave you to Father Stavros. Enjoy your wine." Father Alexander rose from his chair, pulled his hood over his head, and left the room.

The wine warmed my throat, then twisted through the alleys and tunnels of my innards with each heartbeat. I sensed the absence of the two mad monks, closed my eyes and drank the rest of the cup, surprised by its lingering sweetness. The chalice was heavy gold. At its bottom was an inlaid blue glass eye, at the union of stem and bowl. It was the blue eye of God, the charm against the *kakomati*. I felt safe in that room deep in the monastery, as if the room itself held some supernatural power to protect me.

Chapter 17

"Hello, Persephone. You like the wine?"

"It's more delicious than a pomegranate."

Father Stavros' gaze descended to a dented golden plate that sat on the small square table, its lacquer worn and pitted. A half-eaten pomegranate painted a Rorschach on a golden brocade napkin with frayed edges.

"Oh—did I eat that pomegranate?" I said, watching the flaming orange and ripe green leaves wave hello outside the small square window, its stone casing eroded, chipped and pocked.

"You were eating it," Stavros said, "when I came in."

I licked my lip and tasted a trace of juice—sweet with a twang. "What else was I doing?" I squeezed a dried rosy kernel between my fingers. It refused to pop, so I picked up another, and another. They were all dried out like mustard seeds.

Rain knocked on the lone window. Wind howled through the spaces in the now-crumbling walls of the refectory.

"You're right. The room is similar, but not a duplicate," said Father Stavros. His wizened face was a topographical map of

the Balkans, complete with valleys, mountains, crevices, and dry
creeks. His near-black eyes were deep oceans, the moon craters
of a distant planet. His high forehead, peaked by a crop of grey
hair, slid to the ridge of his brows, trimmed, but thick like the
silver blush of Blue Velvet in autumn. Waves of hair fell to his
shoulders. This was the monk on horseback who visited Yiayia's
beach house the day before she died swimming.

"What day is this?" I slid my chair back. It rocked unevenly
on the stone floor, as though one of its felt pads had come unglued.

"These things get by me. I'm an old man." He folded
his hands on the table, knotty as gnarled cedar, the Venetian
waterways of his veins soft and yielding under weathered skin. He
tapped the trimmed edges of his opaque nails on the table, their
horizontal ridges like rings on a tree.

"How old are you?" I asked. A tiny piece of stone fell from
one of the huge neo-Gothic arches with a clatter.

"Forty-four thousand seven hundred and twenty two," he
said, clearing his throat.

"What?"

"And not a day older." Father Stavros smiled, his teeth
shortened by time, but still ivory.

"One hundred twenty-two years one hundred sixty-four
days?" I said. I sat silent, stunned by my own calculation, unsure
of its accuracy, but sure, nevertheless.

"Correct," said Father Stavros. "Have another glass of wine."
He stood and poured wine into both our glasses.

"You're six four and three quarters," I said, amazed.

"Correct again," he said. His black cape slackened over his
brown tunic and leather girdle, a skein dubh tucked into a knife
pocket sewn into the worn leather. He was slight, but powerfully
built in the shoulders and forearms. His boots carried dust from
all over the world. The heavy three-bar cross hung from his neck
on a thin leather braid, sapphires gleaming through a haze of
sand like eyes through a dirty window. On top of the cross stared
an unblinking eye of God, the stone in its center as blue as the
Adriatic. The worn initials, INBI, Jesus of Nazareth Basiliou of
the Jews marked the top bar. The only representation of the body
of Christ was the string of jewels. The middle bar held the initials

of Christ: iota, sigma, chi, sigma. The bottom bar crooked to the right.

"Why does the footstool point to the right?" I said.

"Jesus was flanked on Cavalry by two criminals. The one on the right asked for forgiveness, so the bar points towards him and his ascension."

"Why would they provide a stand for a crucifixion?" I asked.

"To prolong the victim's suffering," said Father Stavros. "Otherwise, their wrists rip and they bleed to death in minutes." He spoke as though he'd seen it happen.

I stared at the bottom of the cross, where the skull of Adam faced upwards through the cross's row of sapphires, looking toward the eye of God.

Stavros lifted his glass and inhaled the fruity spirits, his prominent nose magnified within the bowl. He finished his deep breath and swallowed. "The body of Adam is buried underneath the site of the crucifixion of Jesus. Thus the Apostle Paul called Jesus the new Adam."

"How long have I been here?" I said, slugging back more wine.

"How long did it take God to create the world?" He rose from his chair and picked up a metal basket from the sideboard, placing it on the table between two unlit candles, their silver holders dented and patinaed. He unwrapped a steaming loaf of bread from within a fresh tea towel, its borders brocaded with golden tulips. "Take this. Eat." He ripped a morsel from the yeasty loaf and put it in my mouth, then crossed me three times, right over left. He reached into his leather girdle and removed a purple vial. He released the gold cap and the ancient odor of hyssop escaped, like camphor, but vaguely minty, filling the chamber. He held the vial between thumb and forefinger, and tipped the contents, wetting his thumb. He made the sign of the cross on my forehead with the oil.

"What do you expect me to do?" I said, the unction on my forehead hot and prickly as a new tattoo.

"You are provided with the choices your heredity and talents offer. You must balance destiny and free will just like every other soul."

"You didn't answer the question."

"I didn't give you the crystal ball reading you expected, no. The answer is your choice. You have to decide how your destiny will unfold. You could opt out and play a lesser role like your mother, Medea, and your great grandmother, Penelope. You could let reason dominate and be like your Auntie Georgie. Or you could find a greater purpose like your ancestors Hestia and Theodora."

"Never heard of them," I said.

"They delivered messages from God a long time ago. Now you have heard their messages."

"When? I don't remember."

"You will when you need to."

"But what about Yiayia Friday?"

He smiled. "She is still helping you."

"Helping me? She yanked me out of a Ferris wheel and flung me to the ground like a killer throws a victim into the sea."

"She dropped you into a new life, into the arms of an angel who was waiting for you, wings outstretched, ready to fly, his garment spread to soften your fall."

I looked up toward the sound of pounding rain and to the great eye, the skylight imbedded in the ceiling above our table.

"Yiayia Friday's face floated in those bottles of poisons at the kewpie doll kiosk at the carnival. There's nothing wholesome about her. She torments Medea with her ingrained malignancy and green tongue. She's a creature of spite and envy. How can I trust her ghost?"

"She's not a ghost. She's your spirit guide from an astral plane and chooses to stay close to save you from the trappings of materialism. You have built walls around yourself and she's loading the mangonel on top of her siege tower. Surmount the walls of your spiritual fortress. She is an agent of the Church and is still wiser than you. That's why you need her. When you close your eyes and meditate you must ask for help from those who know more, and you must be gracious and thank them for their help."

I sneered. "Right."

"You must accept your spirit guides who are appendages of God, and you must thank them every time they intervene and every day of your life. And you must meditate and ask for knowledge of God's will, and the powers to carry out his will."

I wrinkled my nose. "I don't think so."

"From the time of your birth the Church has bathed you in the light and adored you and fed you. It will endeavor evermore to keep you safe from harm."

"Who'd want to hurt me? And why did those scum bags kidnap my parents?"

"They were simpletons, ex-cons, recently released from a prison rehab program. Rocco and Guido were postage stamp lickers working their way back into society. Hired because their profiles showed they could be manipulated by Mafia politicians and still stay quiet. Heretics with…family connections paid them to kidnap your parents for questioning. Medea knows very little about the rise of the Heresy of the Athanatoi, a flagellant sub-cult of Arianism. She has resisted her spiritual inheritance. She bites her nails and hides from her fear behind glitter and bling. Your father is a very decent, reverent person. He has no interest, though, in neo-Montanists and their alchemical agendas."

"So my parents didn't cave when this mafia interrogated them?" I flushed and smiled. Who would have guessed how tough the folks could be?

"Your parents didn't give them any answers because they didn't have any. They wouldn't have answered even if they had. In the course of her life Medea took only one step onto the path you are traveling, then yanked her foot back. Your quest will go far deeper into the woods than your mother could even imagine."

"And what quest is that? To dream the impossible dream? To fight the unbeatable foe? "

"Listen. You could turn back now, and sign up for something else. You have free will. You don't have to stay on any road until the end."

"But what's my purpose?" I squirmed in my chair so that it creaked, threatening to collapse.

"You already know. Soon the scales will fall from your eyes and you will be like Paul."

"My sight is getting better all the time."

"Your sight will be far superior, beyond imagination, Persephone." Father Stavros extended a hand, stood up from the table and pointed to the east corner of the chamber. "What do you see there?"

"An eroding stone wall."

Stavros paused. "Look again."

I studied the wall, my nose nearly touching it. Its coldness and a trace of mildew whispered of smoke and sandalwood. The granite unveiled its cloth of crystalline clusters, mineral deposits running in rivulets with flashes of moss and rust from their copper and iron oxides that sometimes opened into tiny geodes and miniscule jewels.

"Kneel with me," said Father Stavros. I bowed my head. He opened his black cape, kissed his cross, and showed the ends of the holy stole that had been tucked into the neck of his tunic. He draped the amethyst silk with crosses of golden thread over my shoulders. "These are the hands of God."

He shut his eyes and squeezed until tears dripped to his wizened cheeks. Father Stavros caught tears from each eye with his two forefingers and rubbed the lashes of my own eager eyes. "Heavenly Father, physician of our souls and bodies, who has sent our Lord to heal every sickness, visit and heal us. Grant this, Oh Lord, God of Hosts, that the thickened scales of dormancy drop from the eyes of your servant, Persephone. Provide strength of body and spirit, and recovery of her vision. Grant this, oh Lord, and give her vision of the *theotees* that she might see things whole. Lord, you have taught us to pray for each other that we may be healed. We pray that you heal, guide and protect your servant Persephone and grant her the gift of complete and divine sight. For you are the source of healing and to you we give glory, in the name Father, Son and Holy Spirit. Amen."

And I said, "Grant that I may know your will and give me the powers to carry it out."

We crossed ourselves three times right over left and rose from the damp floor. Stone grew out of the wall until a finished table appeared, its edges beveled, its corners rounded, its surface smooth and polished. I stepped back to avoid the thwack of the emerging altar. An icon of the Holy Theotokos and Child in a gilded lily frame stood on its left side. On the right leaned an icon of Agios Ioannis the Theologian in a similar frame. Between the holy candelabra and the splintered ash crucifix sat a globe, with streams of sandalwood incense rising in curlicues towards the oculus in the ceiling above. I bent over and opened my eyes wide to examine the altar born out of the wall before me.

With my next blink the scales in my eyes loosened, seemed to float like soft contact lenses. I blinked again. My eyes watered and pushed them out. They landed on the stone altar with a soft clink. Then, as we watched, the thin white scales melted like ice on a hot sidewalk.

The beating of the rain on the great eye above us echoed throughout the chamber. The outer darkness descended through the skylight. Like a stratus cloud, gravid with storm, it covered first the entire ceiling, then sank like a drop of food coloring in a cup of water into the room.

As the velvety blanket of darkness descended and touched the table top, the two candles in their dented and burnished candlesticks lighted. When I turned toward him, Father Stavros was gone.

Chapter 18

Father Alexander had grown the shadow of a beard since my meeting with Father Stavros. He led, and I followed like a spaniel to the boxwood garden, lit by the flattening sun. A line of monks in brown robes, heads down, walked in slow rhythm over tightly mowed rye grass and stubbled garlic stalks cast brown by the inspissations of fall.

"We are blessed to have a new addition to our labyrinth," Father Alexander said in a rough Bulgarian that I was amazed I understood at once. "Just three days ago, after hurricane Demeter, a quartz crystal the size of an elephant tusk washed up in its center, carried by the high tides of the Atlantic."

"Missed a hurricane," I said. "Did I sleep through it?"

"No, Persephone. You were merely engrossed in lessons." He continued in Bulgarian. "We have measured the crystal's energy field. Her magnetism yanked the ring off Father Bartholomew's swollen finger. He bit his runaway tongue and for once kept his curses to himself."

Father Alexander paced, voice curling up to a high, excited pitch.

"The monks all dreamt alike on the night the crystal landed in our meditation circle," he told me. "The next day Father Bartholomew bent a silver spoon by focusing his mind like a laser and directing his intention through her." Father Alexander glanced down at his pectoral cross. "The spoon glowed red, then sputtered and drooped. The iron crucifix on my sternum levitated right off the leather thong when I got within twenty feet. My very fillings drew me toward her. We call this gift from the sea The Ancient One."

I saw neat piles of kindling, mowed lawns, yellow blossoms of squash asleep in their beds. But no debris, misplaced stone, or scattered twigs. Fall leaves slept in steep piles in the field. Everything but the season looked newer than when I'd arrived at the Monastery. The cathedral's abraded walls and arches seemed fresh-built and radiant, garlanded with pumpkin flowers and creeping blue asters. Between tall cedars, skunkweed florets and beads of purple nettles nestled in cups of leaves like ninja stars.

I sneezed.

"*Gesundheit*!" said Georgie's chauffeur. He was in his black-billed cap, walking up the circular pea gravel drive in front of the monastery.

"*Zbogom*," I said, surprised at my fluency. "*Blagodarya*," I blurted, giggling,covering my mouth with one hand.

"*Molya*," answered Father Alexander. "Goodbye, and thank you, too." He took my hand and pressed a tender kiss into its palm. "I'll tell Father Stavros you're already speaking lovely Bulgarian. You've learned many new things in your seven days with us."

"Seven… days?" I squinted over at the man in the black-billed cap. "I've been here a whole week?"

He nodded. "All of Father Stavros' sessions last seven days. Everyone is always stunned to learn this, afterwards."

Walking toward the car I felt the pull of the Ancient One on the iron in my blood, on the calcium in my bones. She anchored the holy labyrinth and the mystery of my audience with Father Stavros, itself labyrinthine. She whispered secret knowledge, new but still buried deep within my brain.

The chauffeur drove Auntie Georgie's limo past granite towers topped with the dark voids of gun portals, vast fields of green timothy spotted with white goats. Then down a winding dirt road through the same long orchard of pears, their white cotton-candy blooms had been replaced by flaming scarlet leaves.

I watched the chauffeur in the rear view mirror. "Where are we going?" I asked, as the Newport Bridge carried us off the island

"To your father, of course."

To my amazement I'd forgotten my worry about my parents a week ago, when I'd met Father Stavros. "How is he now?"

"Perfect." He stroked the white peacock feather pinned to his lapel.

"Did he study with Father Stavros, too?"

"Well, he's not. Unlike you, your father was gifted by God with a rational mind."

The realization the chauffeur could read my mind hit me like a steel anvil. My heart thumped. I couldn't hide anything. I blushed. How I wished Angelo were like me.

My father had once trained a wild raccoon to eat daintily out of his hand. The orphan varmint he named "Zorro" developed a fondness for jelly beans, so Angelo had taught him to jump and catch them in midair. Zorro's favorite flavor was grape. Mine was sour apple.

Last summer, Angelo had spied a robin's nest deep within the branches of a heritage purple lilac. We'd spied on the secret lives in that thatched home nestled among sprays of flowers. Behind the blooms, through the window, Medea's wall of faded icons hung. We parted lilac boughs, careful to avoid disturbing the baby birds. The saints gazed at us, guilt-ridden, from cracked plaster.

The one person I'd have chosen to grow wings and guide me out of this supernatural mess was Angelo.

I frowned. "I meant magical powers."

"Today's magic is tomorrow's science." He shrugged and removed his black-billed cap, raking back blond hair. "He doesn't practice our kind of magic. Thank God for the iron in the blood of your mother's line."

The leather upholstery squeaked under my thighs. My jeans no longer carried the acrid scent of pyrotechnic dust from the car bomb. I missed the oak-leaf aroma of my little tryst under the table with Sheriff Pappas. Like a human sachet, I perfumed the car with hyssop from my week spent with Stavros, the Magus-Priest, spiritual patriarch of the Matepas motherhead from Gaios. I reeked, yes—but with a good scent, like the anointed feet of Jesus.

Funny, I felt very clean, but recalled no kind of bath, ritual or otherwise.

"Sabean odors from the spicy shores of blessed Arabia," said the driver. "Smell's more sure than sound or sight to help you remember."

"Ha! Total amnesia." I straightened my back, imitating the posture of the monks. "So tell me. I won't interrupt. Pinky swear."

The chauffeur channel-surfed to the blasting pipes of a Bach organ concerto, then turned the volume way down. I strained to hear. He said, "The Ancient One sits on her throne of rye and onions, washed up by the swells of the Atlantic. She answers a ritualistic call to heaven long practiced by the monks at the Monastery of St. John the Theologian. Now that she is here, they only practice our holy traditions with greater joy."

"Pfft. It's just a crystal." I spotted a family of deer loping in a wheat field, and worried about hunters.

He rolled down the window, slowing to keep the deer in view. I stared in amazement as he bent the bough of a tree with his mind, then let it snap back. Birds rose in a fluttering frenzy. No breeze. No other explanation. "You're missing the point," he said. "I'm preparing you."

"To be a holy stable girl shoveling golden stones and scraping out stalls of the horses of the Gods?"

The driver told me about the crystal, the monastery, the hive-mind of bees. He gave lessons on the leagues of angels, biblical prophets and miracles, and using Livani to open heaven's ears. How the resin-soaked woodchips are rubbed on the skin of those who've fallen asleep. How Queen Arwa of Cypress lectured on Sufi astrology and mathematics from behind a curtain soaked in Livani, a woven portrait of Saint Sebastian pierced by arrows. Her students remembered everything they heard. Then he described the world of the crossroads, where spirits sometimes lingered.

I glanced into the rearview. A red streak of light strobed across my face, leaving the rims of my eyelids glowing. "Thanks for catching me, that night when Yiayia yanked me out of the Ferris wheel." I gazed out the window and crossed myself as we drove past a road-kill squirrel.

The chauffeur was silent. Organ pipes on the radio droned. Outside, fields and woods alternated until a river, cloaked in congealing mist, flowed into view. Next a giant chokecherry bush laden with crows.

"Stop," I said. "Please." Those black birds were always a sign of death. I spied lumps of fur like graying snow beneath the shrinking sun. I saw everything now with tremendous acuity, despite the falling dusk. Slamming the heavy door, I ran to the carcasses, the chauffeur following with long slow strides. A passel of possums lay beneath the bush, jaws grim in a death rictus. Teeth protruding from half-open mouths, gums pale and rubbery as Pink Pearl erasers.

Crows rose from the bush like a handful of blackened pennies thrown up into the sky. They coalesced, then separated, disappearing behind live oaks whose limbs mimicked streaks of lightning in the late afternoon sky.

The chauffeur knelt on the moist brown grass.

"Got any *livani* handy?" I stroked the back of the smallest possum with a birch twig. "I don't suppose you can bring them back to life?"

"Wake," whispered the chauffeur. "It's possum day."

The mama twitched, belly expanding and contracting like a balloon, grey fur bristling, tail slapping the ground. Her black marble eyes glared as we backed away. She sniffed and her babies twitched, then clamored into the briar.

We walked back to the car. "Are you an angel of life, or death, or a guardian angel?"

"I'm here to help. I am not your guardian angel."

"Help me with what?"

"Your lessons," he said. "Right now I'm teaching you to use clairvoyance. To fast and meditate. You're a little behind on your studies."

"I don't care about studies. I care about possums waking from the dead."

"You woke them with the *livani*." He sniffed my neck. "The monks pass the steaming urn amongst guests seated on their stone benches as a gesture of hospitality. In the east, it's called *bakhoor*, and makes the air swirl with sweetness. Camels carry the blessed incense to the shores of the Black Sea where it's loaded onto dhows. Now it's found its way to you." He inhaled deeply and threw his head back in a kind of ecstasy. "It's embedded in your clothes."

"Were you ever human?" I looked into his topaz eyes. My own were still tearing. They felt impregnated with grains of sand. A low hum shimmered in the air, as on the day I'd ended up under the table with Guy Pappas, his huge warm hands wielding my skin. I wondered if angels could sleep with humans, if they even had the right parts. Yet I couldn't imagine being this angel's lover. The current flowing between us was beyond lust. More convincing than my new, strong vision despite my being blinded by the eclipse, retinas burnt.

Whatever he really wanted from me, I was sure he could get it. I sensed surges beyond my control, a straight-wire to my personal power grid. Regardless of my will, I felt he could pull force up from my thighs, through my torso, permeate my heart, then shoot it like lightning bolts from my fingertips. He must have plenty more to teach me.

I yawned. "Well, all this talk sure creates a pious atmosphere." We reached the car, but I was just getting rolling. "Dad says I'm a quipster. Does it make you want to strangle me? That's what Mom says."

"No," he said. "It's merely distracting, which, of course is your intention."

"Know what a lamster is? I just made it up. Someone who likes to make geographic decisions. You know… like when people go on the lam?"

The chauffeur slipped on dark grey, metal-framed shades. Their lenses reflected my own face in the rear-view mirror.

"Could you turn that up?" I pointed to the radio. "Love the organ. The king of instruments. Spooky, even how it works."

"Persephone! *Skasmos*. Shut up."

I imagined chasing him with thumbscrews and a rack. But I barricaded the thought, keeping it from escaping my mind. "Why should I care about *livani*. It's just incense."

He lifted the shades and stared into my eyes. "Meditate more and you'll be able to call upon the Archangels."

A flink of cows grazed in a field. Grasses and red clover buds bent in the wind. I folded my arms and squeezed my sides with my hands, grabbing ribs. "Why should I believe that?"

"I cannot tell a lie," he said.

My stomach gurgled. I twirled hair around one finger. Silt clogged a rivulet meandering through a field of low grasses. Cattle drank from the puddle of overflow. I might be on a smooth, slow-moving train, though our limousine rocketed over state roads and onto I-95 like a missile.

The organ concerto was replaced by a newscaster.

Shawn Fitzgerald, spokesman for the Boston's 'royal family,' has announced that both O'Malley senators have received near-perfect kidneys from an anonymous donor. The brothers are doing well, and the curse on the O'Malley family appears to have lifted. After the two senators were shot back in March, and the unfortunate lobotomy of one O'Malley sister, it had been conjectured the political dynasty had been cursed. Most theories involved "A Broch," a potent Jewish curse due to the Nazi leanings of the family patriarch, Andrew O'Malley. However, the youngest sister, Carol, says their long-term ill luck had actually been brought on by sister Kathleen, who was mentally challenged, and had once kicked over a fairy ring. A band of homeless wee people had then pronounced a curse on all future generations…. Breaking news: the President has just received a successful corneal transplant after an unfortunate accident with a telescope during the recent eclipse, while visiting the Mexican president.

The chauffeur clicked off the radio.

"Hey!" I protested. "That was interesting. Tim would've made a good president. Where do you think they got those kidneys?"

"Listen to what I'm saying."

I knew angels didn't lecture just anybody, but I felt imperious. My inbred appetite for opposing authority called to me like fresh-baked brownies. "I need to go tee-tee. Can you stop at that field over there?"

I was a pro at peeing outside, thanks to Medea and her bathroom germ phobia. I knew where to go and how not to get a rash or a bug bite. I chose a large walnut trunk to hide behind, then watered the crabgrass. Pointy grey caps poked up through the blades, forming a fairy circle. An undulating path of fungi lead to a small, dark wood. I followed the mushrooms, laid out like nuggets of moldy bread. Glimmers of foxfire haunted the recesses of the woods. The path stopped at a hollowed-out tree. Squirrels scurried, their scampering echoing within the oak chimney. I knocked: Nothing but echoes. I reached into the largest hole and my fingers brushed cold metal, straight edges amidst soft woody pith. I gripped the hard object and drew it out.

A tiny box, the size of a pack of cigarettes. Tin, rust-spotted with age. I pushed on the lid with both thumbs. It didn't budge, so I slipped it in the pocket of my jeans.

I followed the fairy trail back to the car, careful not to make Kathleen's fatal mistake and squash any mushrooms. I believed the O'Malleys. They were all smart, except for the poor sister with the lobotomy. I didn't want to upset the little people and bring their wrath down upon my family, too.

"What did you pick up?" said the chauffeur, frowning.

"I'm keeping this to myself."

"Why keep it at all?"

"I just feel I should, that's all." I shrugged. "You keep a lot inside. I've decided to take after you, now."

"Well. Why not make an offering of it? We can light the *livani* and call your guardian angel. Maybe the box has something inside that will tell you about yourself."

I fingered the cool rectangle, pushing it deeper into my right front pocket. Somehow, to open the box in front of him would be like taking off my clothes. I wanted to get somewhere private and see for myself what was inside. But not for a while. Maybe not for a long while.

"Seekers of spirit guides make offerings for intercession to human ancestors who've expanded into new realms of existence," said the chauffeur.

"Everyone expands into a new realm when they die, don't they? My thigh felt cool, as if the box contained some kind of chemical ice-pack, just activated. Tell me everything."

He laughed. "Petulant one, they don't tell *me* everything."

"Just read their thoughts then."

"*Verboten.*"

The muscles between my eyebrows ached. "Who are they?"

"Perhaps Stavros told you." He picked a possum hair off his coat, not looking at me.

"Who knows what Stavros taught me," I said, secretly tapping the tin box. "Except now I speak Bulgarian."

"Stavros doesn't confide your destiny to others," said the chauffeur.

"Who am I?"

"In order to discover who you are, first learn who everyone else is. You're what's left."

"Does my father know I went to see Stavros? Does he know about the car bomb?"

"Stavros, no. The car bomb, yes. It was on the news. They were after you, not Guy Pappas."

"Does Dad know I saw the black mare of the apocalypse with the starred forehead? That I fell off Agrippa the Ingrate, went to Mexico, saw an eclipse, went blind, and now have the senses of a wolf-bitch? No, something supernatural, way beyond animal senses."

The chauffeur shook his head. "No one else knows. My advice is keep it to yourself. Except, you can tell Christy and Georgie."

"And you?"

He smiled. "Anything."

"Why were my parents robbed and stuffed in the trunk of Dad's T-Bird?" I asked. "Why'd they shoot him in the head and leave him to bleed to death all over Medea?"

"The kidnappers tried to question your parents your powers, Persephone. You were too well-guarded to snatch."

"Medea was right, then." I fingered my cross, sliding it back and forth on its chain. "Because of me they were kidnapped. At least we know whose fault it is." I sighed. "Mine. As usual."

"Relax, perturbed girl!" said the chauffeur. "The responsibility lies in the hands and souls of the men who flogged your parents. And those who paid them."

"These kidnappers. Father Stavros said they were, like, Mafia."

"They dig for treasure upon the earth, where mold and rust doth corrupt," said the chauffeur. "They have sown the wind, and so they shall reap the whirlwind. He that digs a pit will fall into it."

A draft encircled me. I closed the AC vents tight, and pressed all window controls. Still it blew. I took the breeze in the enclosed vehicle as a sign. "But who were they, exactly?"

"Goons hired by the Athanatoi."

"Oh, well that explains it." I gave a sea lion snort. "And who are they?"

"A heretical group from the time of Arius. *Klysty* flagellants. They perpetuate the primary Arian heresy—that Jesus was not begotten before all time, but made. That death is an enemy, hovering like a goddess in the night. They believe that without angels of death, life on earth would be eternal. That's why it concerns you, Persephone, born of Medea, emerging as a shadow from the underworld."

The chauffeur turned his sparkling face back towards me, one eyebrow raised. "You ate the pomegranate, didn't you?"

"With Father Stavros? Well, yeah, a few seeds." I tapped my knees as if they were bongo drums, bored yet uneasy, wanting the talking to be over, but also wanting to know. My destiny he was talking about, after all. "So?"

"Those who transform from human to angel are protected. The Athanatoi will be stopped. We always stop them. They re-form out of dust, but to dust they return. They crumble."

"Huh. How about that."

The limo pulled into the parking lot of Providence General Hospital, then around the back into the garage, a huge rabbit warren held up by steel beams like the shoulders of Atlas, never shrugging.

I heard dust settling on windshields and bare concrete.

The chauffeur opened my door.

"You're coming too, right?" I squinted against the light of his glistening skin. Outside a moon bow slowly formed over Federal Hill.

"I've been with you ever since you were born. Soon you'll be like me, and need no protection."

"As if! I'll never be an angel." I laughed, fluffing my hair.

"That snort of yours is unbecoming of an angel. Or anyone." He raised an eyebrow. "Try to be more demure. It goes better with a chiffon gown and diaphanous wings."

In front of the hospital a massive stone fountain spewed chlorinated water. I threw a penny into the pool of spare change, wishing for lots more time. For many more human experiences like the one with Guy Pappas.

The chauffeur coughed behind me. "You're youth will be filled with tough lessons at earth school."

On the other side of the fountain stood a man who'd clearly worn the same gym socks three days in a row. I felt a great pull towards him, like gravity. His lips weren't moving, yet I could hear his pleading. "What will I do with the children? Please, keep Rose Marie alive long enough to see Paris." Swollen tears rolled down his cheeks. "Jesus, just do this and I swear, I won't sleep with Kitty. And I swear no more greyhound's. And goodbye, Johnny Walker. No cheating. At anything." I felt like I was falling in slow motion, not down, but toward a person I'd never seen before.

"Stop!" The chauffeur scooped me into his arms and blew golden dust in my face. His breath was sharp as smelling salts. I folded into his embrace like a tea bag dropped into a cup and looked into his pupils, black-hole black. "You aren't ready to enter anyone but yourself! Be careful!"

He stood me up and straightened my shirt, then took my hand. We walked toward the great glass doors of the hospital.Grass crushed under foot with the sound of crackling paper. The permethrin smell of mums permeated the beds of dark earth flanking the hospital's entrance.

"Dear girl, you must have a full life, but also a taste of the process of dying. You must feel the horrid grind of human existence. They fear death—a thing to them that seems to stain the radiance of God. You will help people in the gleam of time between two worlds." His hand radiated warmth that instantly evaporated the sweat from my clammy palm. When he let go I felt the heat fly in a circuit through my body, down to my toes.

"Everybody wants to keep their lives, regardless of the tragedy in them," I said, counting the pennies under water in the fountain behind us. The slow heartbeat thumping in my ears was his, not mine.

"Who are you, really?"

"Your guide." The sparkling dust around his face expanded as he smiled.

"Don't angels have names?" Could everyone see his aura, or was it just me, part of my new fund of knowledge?

"Call me 'Azrafel."

I bent over to tie a dragging shoelace. Sticky gum glued my heel stuck to the concrete walkway. A spearmint miasma wafted upwards as I scraped off the nasty wad with a greasy French fry box.

"Ha! Some angel, me. I'm organoleptic and need to sleep a lot."

I threw the filthy box into a fluted metal receptacle that reeked of soiled diapers. He grasped my shoulders and turned me around.

"Look closer at that fountain."

"With your new vision you can see every detail, even from here."

I studied the marble figure of a titan, sculpted planes of gnarled muscle and granite legs. Kronos held a naked child, winged like Cupid. At first, I thought he was kissing it. Then, to my horror I realized he was devouring it, hair and wings first. In the other arm he gripped more wide-eyed children, stone faces desperate in their struggle for freedom.

"Kronos ate his kids to keep them from stealing his throne," I told the angel, as if this would be news to him.

"As the Athanatoi want to devour all human-born angels of death," said Azrafel. "Now come."

Chapter 19

A gum-smacking redhead with deep cleavage leaned over the information desk just inside the main entrance of Providence General Hospital. Azrafel seemed taken by the view. She winked at him, and rattled off the floor where my father was staying. "Bed seven, neurosurgical unit, honey."

Azrafel had told me Dad had gotten a cadaver graft to the pocket-pistol wound which had grazed his occipital bone. Most patients in the ward had brain hemorrhages, tumors, horrible disfigurements. But Angelo looked great. He was just then strolling to the Jacuzzi, a cappuccino in one hand, The Wall Street Journal tucked under an elbow. I ran to kiss his clean-shaven face. A small bandage was taped to the back of his head. Fresh sutures peeked from under the dressing like spider legs.

Behind his right ear I spotted a new tattoo—a yew-green Mobius like the bilobed vine snippet Medea had once smuggled from France in her satin pumps, under an arch support. She'd hidden the crimson shoes in a secret luggage compartment and gifted it to me as a special souvenir from the Riviera. She'd called the plant "Goat's Foot" because each set of leaves resembled a cloven hoof. She'd planted the clippings in a flower box on our tool shed. Long runners soon covered the shed with anemic pink trumpet flowers and thick cascades of tiny leaves.

I stole another glance at my father's tattoo. Did he know it was there? It could've been mistaken for a bug or a mole, invisible from the front. From the side, nearly hidden beneath his hairline behind that ear. I wondered if Medea had noticed it yet. It swelled from a pink base of clean skin, a gift from his former captors.

"Anyone for cappuccino?" he asked. "This place is great. A Japanese nurse massages my feet with Kama Sutra oil and brings me hand-rolled sushi from home. She sneaks it past the charge nurse in a cooler in her duffle. Medea hasn't yelled in a week. Not at me at least. I get to read all day and drink coffee and eat ginger pecan scones. Whenever I get a touch of headache, that same nice nurse, Sulo, brings me morphine. Helluva place, I tell ya."

On the way to Dad's room, we passed the nurses' station and I waved at the beautiful smiling nurses, turned out like thoroughbreds at a brood mare inspection. I smiled back, lips glazed with Saucy Sangria that now tasted like wax. The team of nurses wore slim white dresses and little hats like starched origami swans. My dad winked at a blonde pixie of a nurse carrying a clipboard. She stared straight into his eyes, bit the corner of her bottom lip, looked down, away, then gazed directly at him again.

My father was the pride of the unit. He could walk, talk, brush his own teeth, and banter about midbrain bleeds, having studied medicine in Athens before he'd fled Greece with emeralds in his boot heels and gold powder in his pomade. He'd wriggled out of his fascist "obligations" like a shot during the Nazi occupation, drilling some well-placed holes in airplane gas tanks in the process.

"My cranial nerves are all working." He laughed. "I'm a lucky man. Not your typical neurosurgical patient."

Guy Pappas sat on a stool, his back to the window of my dad's room that overlooked the Providence River. His chin rested on a fist big as a cow heart. His brow furrowed. He reminded me of a photo of Josef Stalin. Except for the eye patch; under its convexity, I could see his green eye moving. He was leaning over the Go board that occupied Dad's overbed table. Guy placed the black stone on a space on the wooden grid.

Good evening, Sheriff Pappas," I said in my softest whisper, looking as innocent as possible, affecting an alluring lip-pooch. I fastened the top button of my shirt, then played with the button in its hole. If I was truly magical, couldn't I, too, conjure up some cleavage? These older men seemed to really notice breasts. And lips. Even the angel had regarded that well-endowed receptionist with interest, if not astonishment.

"Hi Persephone." Guy's eyes were smiling. "Your father looks ready to go home."

Dad nodded. "I could've gone yesterday. But they wanted another brain scan and EEG, just a routine check. I don't mind. I like it here."

Nurse Sulo entered, compact and efficient, blackwood hair tumbling down her back in curling-iron waves, watermelon lips coated in perfect shine. White rubber heels squeaked as she trotted across the polished tiles to attend to her reclining patient, who was sunning himself in bars of light passing through the horizontal blinds.

Medea's antithesis, Sulo smiled without a sneer, chuckled without ridicule. Her skin carried jasmine perfume. Astringent chemical floral potpourri and mothballs were Medea's signature scent.

"Couldn't something else go wrong?" I said to Sulo. My father was happy here, after all.

"This must be your beautiful daughter," she said, pouring ginger ale into a cup of ice. "What an angel. She has your eyes."

Sulo, lids darkened with Isis-eyeliner, turned to me. "Dr. Bett has already spoken to your mother. The tests are just a precaution."

She tipped her delicate chin towards Dad. "Need anything else, Mr. Angelo?" Bat, bat, bat went her eyelashes. Angelo shook his head and winked at his own personal geisha.

"Dad. What happened? How could you be shot and still be okay? Are you really? Tell me everything."

"A guy named Rocco held a 25 caliber Beretta to the back of my head, execution style and pulled the trigger, mumbling in some Neapolitan dialect. The bullet got stuck in very hard bone, about

144

an inch thick…. A contact wound. The guy must've slipped. Poor concentration, typical lame-ass criminal. Then I woke up here. I don't remember anything else."

He sounded so analytical. And casual. "And that's it?" I said, wide-eyed.

"As I was just telling Guy, here," He sipped coffee foam head off his brew. "That's all. I don't even remember my sleeping arrangements in the trunk with Medea. Probably a blessing."

"Yeah, I'm sure that was pretty." I pushed visions of Mom's ample thighs straddling Dad's neck out of my head. "Can I see the wound?" I peeked under the loose, dry dressing. What I was really studying was the tattoo of the Mobius. About the size of a lima bean, just behind the right ear.

"Look all you want, Persy." He tilted his head under the light. "The bone and skin come from a transplant donor, trimmed and chiseled to fit perfectly. The donor skin is like a bandage as new skin grows under it."

"You mean," I said, stunned by the now-personal miracle of organ transplantation, "that bone is really going to become part of you? Wow." The cadaver tissue fix was nice, but who put that Mobius there? Not a doctor. Had he been unconscious when they injected his dermis with ink? Was this mark always left by the Athanatoi on their victims? Did he even know it was there?

Dad rubbed the inflamed spot of skin bearing the tattoo. "Those thugs really wanted to know your whereabouts, my dear. They also wanted some secret Medea possesses, but couldn't torture out of her. She's loyal and tough as gristle."

The ink green Mobius was so fresh; the surrounding skin so pink and swollen. I struggled not to stare.

"Matepas secrets always were impossible to extract from your mother," Dad continued, fingers reaching again toward his graft, then stopping. "Medea never talks. Chinese water torture, water-boarding, iron maiden. Forget about it."

Sheriff Pappas' eyebrows rose.

"Nothing could ever break her," my father continued. "You inherited something from her. A strength I don't even come close to. Medea doesn't use psychic skills much, except at Belomancy. She still loves archery. Likes to use food, too. Like messages baked in dough, or interpreting the budding behavior of onion plants. But after that one weekend when she blew it in Atlantic City, she won't even read coffee grounds anymore." He shrugged. "Too bad."

The tiny box in my pocket warmed, heating a rectangular patch of my thigh, making it tingle. "What else, Dad?"

"Oh, yeah." He set his coffee down and looked over at the chauffeur. "Rocco wanted to know why Georgie's chauffeur is always either with you, or shows up just when you're about to get killed. They wanted to know if and when he ever leaves. And where he lives."

"Hmmm. Tough questions," I said.

The chauffeur was studying the Go board in silence, as if the pattern of stones held the answers.

"That's all I got for you," said Dad. "They spoke a dialect I'm unfamiliar with." His forehead strained to concentrate. "But if Mr.,uh—"

"You can call me Azrafel," said the angel, skin yellowish and aglow, like a vampire from a campy teen-sex movie. But he was not undead, nor a creature of the melodramatic dark. Just an angel with an audible heartbeat, who breathed like a human being. Blood whooshed through his sacred body, alive to my ears as a heliotrope garden caught in the whisper of blossoming. A solid spirit who'd leaned over the gold bar of Heaven. He, like me, was on loan.

Azrafel's eyes locked on mine. Be not forgetful of strangers: for thereby some have entertained angels unawares. His voice whispered in my auditory cortex. My ears buzzed as if with the secret humming of a bee.

So tell me Azrafel, how many angels can dance on the point of a very fine needle without jostling one another? I sent back. This was indeed the fun part, at least so far.

Two, he responded. "I'll take over your stones," he said to Dad.

"Only if I get credit for the win," said my father. "White is all over the board and very well-defended."

Had that angel over there ever had sex with a human? I couldn't help but puzzle about this. He seemed so alive, a flesh and blood creature. But weren't angels supposed to be androgynous? Now my hot sheriff, his ass tightly cupped by those faded 501s and

146

his triangular chest wrapped in a hand-knitted cardigan—he was definitely alive. I wanted to wrap him, and myself, in a hospital blanket. I pulled on one eyebrow. I cleared my throat loudly, hoping to dispel the image.

What if Azrafel could hear my thoughts? What if he knew everything I was thinking without me transmitting deliberately? Poor me, just beginning to turn on to sex. Now what will happen? Can one date in a chiffon dress and diaphanous wings? Would I have to die? Worse, would I have to die a virgin? No! I was way too imperfect, way too impulsive. Way too ready to drop everything and sneak into a bar, chug a beer, find a fisherman or a submarine builder to slow dance with and tongue kiss. Go home to a shack by the sea. I was no angel. Nope. Not me. Not really. Not yet, anyway.

"Let's take a walk," my father said, breaking into my guilty reverie.

Chapter 20

My dad and I took the elevator to the top floor to see the garden. The box, still deep in my pocket, heaved and vibrated. In the shadows of the dimly lit elevator, a ghost of a child stood in front of me, eyes gleaming, hair streaming as if wind were blowing through the dead space. She pointed up into the dark ceiling tiles of the elevator. The mouth of the ghost child opened in horror. I sensed a vague figure hovering up there as I stared overhead. It was crouched in one corner of the shaft, riding it up. In a twinkle, the ghost child shrank and flew away like a butterfly. An ectoplasmic trail glimmered away as the doors opened to the top floor.

We stepped out into a room with three floor-to-ceiling windows. New Age spa music hung in the air. We looked down the bluff upon roofs dotting fingers of land poking out from Roger Williams Park. The atrium overlooked the Providence River, sprinkled with small glistening boats.

In a quiet neighborhood surrounded by native conifers, the textured garden of soft ferns begged to be caressed, tempting me to lie down and take a nap in the soft palms of its prehistoric hands.

A plaque, above an indoor fountain of Pan playing hornpipes that squirted water, read:

In 1977 the Elizabeth Blackstone Botanical Garden Trust was established to preserve and showcase the remarkable garden of Betty Blackstone. Known for its exceptional collection of rare and unusual trees and shrubs, in addition to an expansive collection of woodland herbaceous perennials and seventy-seven species of ferns, the garden continues to reflect the horticultural spirit of Mrs. Blackstone.

We sat on a stone bench in front of the fountain, little drops of rain bouncing off Pan's haunches misting into the air.

Dad reached for my hand. "Remember the mulberry trees?"

A pair of red mulberry trees behind the Newport Musical Theatre had always housed mockingbirds where cow paddocks leaned into the high grasses. Under those mature trees, twenty-five feet high, we would sit in the shade of the domed crown and coax squirrels and geese to come visit by offering walnuts, Ritz crackers, sesame crisps, stale rolls from the restaurant's bread box, and of course, mulberries.

"We met Merrill there," said my father, inching closer to me on the stone bench. "Remember how he got so tame he would scratch on the kitchen screen door?"

"He loved pecan pie. He ate some out of my hand, and I had that little cut on my finger. So Medea tried to convince Dr. Barrett to order Rabies shots," I said, laughing.

"You're drooling," screeched Dad, mimicking Medea's practiced contralto. "Now you've done it. You two and that squirrel! You've gone and gotten yourself a case of the rabies!"

I giggled and hugged him, in a teen-age girl way that ended too quickly and involved only above-the-waist contact.

"I liked it when Merrill would climb up the steps, jump up on the screen door and make it flap in its frame," I said, sitting cross-legged on the bench, facing my father. "Merrill's way of knocking. He looked like a superhero squirrel, stuck like Spiderman, his claws gripping the screen."

Dad cleared his throat. "I want to tell you something." He always said that first when he'd been resisting telling me something.

"What, Dad?"

"You're an academic star."

"So what?" I said. "I'm not motivated by grades. I want to know more, make connections. Like why I'm here. So tell me. Why do I have this spider sense?"

"It's more than spider sense," said Angelo. The dew from Pan steamed his skin, reflecting light from the ferns. "I've seen you apply your brain to thorny problems. You paid for an all-day spay-and-neuter clinic when you were seven years old by organizing your little friends into making and selling pet-paw prints at a street art fair."

He tucked my loose hair behind both ears, watery eyes fixed on mine. "You're involved because the world matters and you matter in the world. And I want you to be safe."

I blinked and stared down at the cobblestones under the bench. He reached over and pulled off a bud of sage, rubbed it between his fingers and took a whiff. He was right. These plants were begging to be touched and sniffed. If I were a dog I would've rolled in them deliriously.

"Do you remember when Calliope stole one of Medea's golden tablecloths?" My thigh was burning. I lifted the box from one pocket and stowed it in the other. "We spread it out under the mulberries and Calliope climbed up and shook the branches. We caught all those mulberries and dried them in the sun."

He laughed. "You and Calliope ate so many, your teeth were purple."

"And Medea said we looked like a couple of Transylvanian blood suckers."

"Yeah. That was cute."

A butterfly lighted on Dad's hand, fanning its large yellow and purple wings like folding and unfolding paper in the wind. Soon the room was thick with them—giant Papillions with powdery wings and strange insect bodies, ugly as roaches, but wings as beautiful as lilies.

"Do you think when we die our souls ascend to heaven as butterflies?" I said.

"Sometimes," he said. "It depends."

A butterfly with wings that ended in teardrops landed on the lip of a moss-covered urn. It let me reach out and touch it. I turned to my father and held his soft cheeks in my hands, then brushed the roughness of his sandy jaw.

"The ancient Greeks called butterflies 'Psyche', which means 'soul.'" He turned to me and laughed. "But some of the misfits of history said night witches turned into winged creatures and stole butter."

"Seems like a lot of trouble," I said, "for those witches." Inside the left front pocket of my jeans the box rotated as if magnetized suddenly. I turned left on the stool and the box lined up with my thigh, as if it were a compass aligning itself with a great navel meteorite.

"Dad," I said. "You are the best man in my life. I love you. But I need to go."

He grabbed me by my thigh, then jerked his hand back suddenly as if it'd been burned.

"Oh, that's just static," I said. "Such dry, cold air."

He frowned. "I want you safe. It's time for you to go away to college. Christy will be nearby. He'll help you whenever you need him."

I'd known this was coming. I needed to let go of the little soul inside me that yearned for the domestic bliss of television sit-coms.

"I'll miss those mulberry trees," I said. "Their leaves were like yellow mittens in the fall."

"They're the last to bud in the spring," said Dad, patting my cheek. "You'll be eating them all summer."

"What about Calliope?" My thigh burned. I wanted to take the stairs to return to his room.

"I don't know," he said.

Tears scorched my cheeks. I pressed my face into his shoulder to stifle my weeping.

"Work to break out of that cocoon and fly, my beautiful, rainbow butterfly," he said. He says such corny things.

He patted my back under the canopy of giant, dripping cinnamon ferns. I would carry his hug with me forever. I would keep it. I would.

I felt as shipwrecked as those sailors whose boats got tossed in whistling sleet and snow while they slept, only to awaken to the hollering of a drunken captain staggering down the stairs, crying "Wake up! We're lost!"

Chapter 21

"I promised Medea I'd take you to see Dr. Barrett," said the Sheriff, the Go disc hovering over one square on the board. He plopped the white disc down with a thump. He'd dropped a few inches off his waist in the last few weeks. His hair had grown and soft curls turned up at his neck's nape. He looked delicious; playing Go with an angel.

"My eyes are fine," I said, looking across room seven at the glittering angel in broad daylight. Can normal people see all that shimmering, too? Don't they wonder what makes him glow?

"A promise is a promise," he said, putting on his bomber jacket. The tan of his coat reminded me of a butterscotch sundae, or a snifter of cognac, either of which I would like to share with him. Maybe I could entice him into taking me to an ice cream fountain. Or better yet, a dark bar. I knew I looked best in light broken up by shadows. Older, too.

"You busted your zipper," I said. I knew this not because I saw it, but by anomalous cognition.

"No I didn't," he said, zipping his jacket.

"Try the pocket," I said.

"What're you talking about, Persephone?" said Pappas, fighting with his zipper.

We Matepases excelled at anomalous cognition. "I told you I could see just fine."

"A promise is a promise," he said again.

"Go ahead, Sheriff Pappas," said my father. "I see you've lured the tiger out of the mountain, and I have a high-level Go player to deal with here. So go on. Let me finish."

My father turned to Azrafel. "You have time. No?" My father's soft parsley-snip eyes reminded me of willow groves in the breeze, when he was happy. I wanted to fall into them and onto a swing suspended from willow branches by a stream, grasses bowing their heads to the wind.

"Yes," he said.

I kissed him and tossed Azrafel a thought.

Let him win.

Okay.

But don't let it be easy.

#   #   #

Dr. Barrett's office was a stand-alone, one-story building near the medical supply store where equipment for the handicapped and infirm waited to be purchased: reachers, canes, wheelchairs, surgical corsets, bunion care items. Next door was the pharmacy and down a row of gusty trees made naked by the wind, about a half a mile, stood the hospital.

Sheriff Pappas and I walked beneath the high branches, through dead leaves gold as lightning, some dry and dead. But my autumn favorite was hectic red.

The door to his office had been covered with boat paint, a slick and shiny U.S. blue.

Sheriff Pappas pushed the door open and held it for me. We stepped inside and it closed with an accidental slam. The unmanned table in the waiting room carried three phones, all jammed together in one corner, each with several clear, reddish, important-looking buttons. The phones watched over a prescription pad and the yellow pages. A powerful smell of ether rushed ahead of Dr. Barrett before he greeted us. His secretary, salt and pepper hair, formal and trim in a grey suit and oxford pumps, invaded the privacy of the ether and squeezed by him, arching her back to avoid chest contact to get to her desk.

I followed Dr. Barrett back to the wood-paneled hallway where he made me stand behind a black line. He put a plastic spoon over one eye at a time while I reported the letters on the eye chart. He flipped the pages of the chart and moved me further down the hall with each try until my back had reached the warm wall.

"Your vision is superb. In fact it measures twenty over five by my chart, but you read the letters with such ease, I'd wager it's even better than that," said the doctor, pulling the ophthalmoscope off its bracket on the wall.

He closed the door to darken the room and shined a tiny crimson light into my squinting eyes.

"Hmmmm…." said Dr. Barrett. "Huh." He paused. "Hmmm."

"What is it?"

"But you shouldn't see that well, if at all." He replaced the scope.

"Why?"

"Your retinas are swollen. Some parts burned, especially near the areas where the cones are concentrated. The part that sees colors." He scratched his chin. "Wait a minute. I need to get something."

I sat on the white-papered exam table and studied the Norman Rockwell prints in poster shop frames that hung from the exam room walls. Ether saturated the recycled air.

Dr. Barrett returned carrying a thick fan of swatches like decorators use and a book with red shapes in a sea of green dots. He showed me the book of dots first. I was tasked with identifying the red shapes inside the green backgrounds.

"The number twelve, the number seven, a circle, a square, and a triangle."

"Well you got that all right," he said, chewing his lower lip. "Let's try the swatches. I want you to describe the colors as accurately as you can. You have macular swelling. Yet you see everything. It's odd, to say the least."

154

He opened to a leaf of purples and covered the designerly names of the colors with his palm and fingers. "What's this one?"

"Misty rose," I said.

"Right." He removed a finger from the typed name. "And this one?"

"Countryside pink."

"Exactly," he said, forehead lined with worry. "And this?"

"Cranberry ice."

"How are you doing this, young lady? No artist could distinguish these colors one from the other without putting them side by side, much less rattle off their marginally significant names." He touched the breast pocket of his blue pin-striped suit, feeling for his cigarette case. "Let's try the greens." He flipped through hundreds of color chips to find obscure greens. "What about this one?" he said, extra careful to hide the printed names on the lower right-hand corner of each little rectangle of color, with a thumb.

"Parsley Snips," I said, giggling.

"And this one?"

"Winchester sage." I smiled wider.

"Okay, then." He held his breath. "Let's try this group."

"Little Angel Yellow. That's me!" I snorted.

"That's impossible," he said. "Not only is your level of sight impossible, your memory is apparently eidetic. You must've seen this paint fan before. I don't know what to do about this. I just don't know. I…." His voice trailed off. "From my physical examination of your eye grounds, you should be legally blind, hardly able to see anything. Shouldn't even be able to tell red and green apart."

"Try another one," I suggested. "Maybe I won't get it right."

He flipped to a new chip.

"That would be Sunny Side Up."

"And this one?"

"Dune White."

"This is impossible," he sighed. "Lie down please."

He covered my eyes with a blue cotton surgical cloth. "Now try. No cheating."

"White Goose Down, Olympic Mountain Snow, Alaska Skies, Ice Formations, Soft Chamois, Cloud White, Eggshell."

He shuffled through the color sections, breathing shallow and fast. His stomach gurgled.

"Okay. Try now."

"Revere Pewter, Puritan Grey, Kennebunkport Olive, Queen Anne Pink Beige, Iris Bliss."

"And this one?"

"Under the Big Top. It's a kind of windy sky blue."

"How can you do this? Impossible. I'm sending you to a retinal specialist. I'll call now."

I removed the cloth and sat up.

"I can't go to any specialist. Please, Dr. Barrett. Please tell Sheriff Pappas out there my vision is intact and let me go now. I need to see my mother."

"But there's nothing like this reported in the literature. Nothing. I need to write up an article."

"With my blessing, Dr. Barrett," I said. "Please do. But—"

"No," he said. "You can't go. I need to get your retinas mapped. And you need a PET scan. And an EEG."

He took out a cross pen, a prescription pad and dropped them. He bent over to pick them up. Paper clips, a reflex hammer, and a penlight fell out of his pockets to the linoleum. Thuds and tinkles, out of tune and harsh, mingled with the ether mist that hovered around him like Pigpen's cloud of dust.

"I can't let you go," he said, gathering up the spill, walking toward the wall phone. He was loud and frantic now, heart thudding hard against his ribs, racing with extra beats, blood rushing and torrential, almost deafening.

"I've got to get out of here," I said, hands clamping my ears against the percussion of his nerve-racked circulation.

He blocked the door with his body.

"I can't let you go, Persephone," he said. "Don't you realize you're a medical miracle?"

"Step aside, please, Dr. Barrett."

"I cannot," he said, forcing his voice down. "I owe it to my colleagues. How did you burn your eyes?"

"Looking at the eclipse," I said. "Please let me go."

"What eclipse?" He rubbed his neck and scowled.

"When I went to Mexico."

"When?" He sniffed.

"For vacation. A few weeks ago," I said, working on opening the storm window.

"Impossible, Persephone." Dr. Barrett loosened his tie. "What if I tell Sheriff Pappas? I've cared for you since you were a baby. Through all the cases of strep throat and your mother's frantic worries. It's for your own good. Get away from that window. My colleagues…"

"If you don't let me go right now I'll scream. Then I'll have to tell Sheriff Pappas about the three rolled joints in your cigarette case," I said. "Think of your colleagues. I'm sorry, but I have to go."

"My cigarette case?" he said. "But—How could you know that?"

"I can smell them," I said. "So please, let me leave."

He opened his mouth as if to say something else, but no words came.

"Dr. Barrett," I said. "I appreciate everything you've ever done for me. You're a great doctor. Now please, let me out of here. I have someplace I need to go with Sheriff Pappas. Just tell him I can see great. Just tell him."

I walked right into the middle of his ether cloud and looked hard into his face. "Just tell him."

He stepped away, looking flustered. He followed me down the hall to find Sheriff Pappas sipping coffee and eating a shortbread tart with cherry filling.

I looked at the prim secretary who smiled her Cherries-in-the-Snow smile, and shrugged.

"Would you like one?" she asked.

"No, thank you. My mother says sweets and a foul temper cause pimples." I looked at the name plate on her desk. "Bye Mrs. Duer. Sheriff Pappas and I need to be somewhere now."

"Do I need to talk to Dr. Barrett?" asked the sheriff, as we yanked open the door that still seemed sucked closed by some strong vacuum force.

"No," I said, descending the stairs. "You can talk to me about it over a butterscotch sundae. Or better yet, a warm cognac."

Chapter 22

Sheriff Pappas swirled the dregs of his third cup of espresso, lifted it to his nose, and put it down with a clatter that echoed from the bottom of the stairwell above our heads.

"What's wrong?" I said, peering into the cup. "Got a bug in there?"

We sat in a corner at a metal bistro table hidden in the shadow of the stairs, across a dimly-lit alcove, a spot usually reserved for Mayor Cianci. The hostess at Capriccio let us have the table because Buddy Cianci was in jail. The mayor of Providence had kidnapped his wife's lover and tortured him with burning fireplace embers in an abandoned warehouse on Federal Hill. He was now running his campaign from a prison cell equipped with a phone, computer, and fax machine.

I reached over a basket of peppered bread sticks and picked up the demitasse. I examined its contents and poured a few drops of remaining coffee into my drained water glass. I turned the cup upside down and pushed the saucer towards Sheriff Pappas.

"Rotate it three times to the right for the future."

He took off his patch within the bower beneath the stairs. In the quiet light he showed me his eye, hazel grey like a seagull's wings, a wedge of iris missing at seven o'clock. "I want to tell you about the past, about my eye."

"Okay. Tell me."

"It happened the night my wife and boy were killed," he said, voice so low and hushed I could barely hear him over the chatter of the restaurant's other patrons.

At the table next to us, by the window, a man lit a cigarette. Guy Pappas coughed. After two puffs the man crushed the cigarette in an ashtray. The sheriff twirled a Calla lily tipped in its narrow vase. A candle the color of tupelo honey cast fingers of light on the pair of coffee cups stained with grinds that touched each other in the middle of our small table.

My soul fell upward into the wedged hollow of his injury like a gull on a thermal updraft. The left pupil of the damaged greenish eye was slow to constrict in the candlelight. Unlike the uniform grey of his good eye, it projected a fairy aspect that drew me closer than Medea would've deemed…necessary.

You don't need to do that, she said in my mind.

In the shadow of the masked sun looming through the bay window, Sheriff Pappas said, "the car slid on black ice. The right rear tire hit the curb. We had a blowout. My wife stood in the sleet with the car manual while my son and I changed the tire. He was an Asperger savant, one of the lucky ten percent with a notable gift."

Pappas sneezed into his sleeve.

"We argued about rotating tires. He was also a math whiz."

His voice grew shaky. "He insisted the tires needed rotating at ten p.m.… in a freezing rain storm! On Highway 95. We took the wheel off. I said there was no way we were rotating tires in the dark. He slugged me in my eye with the tire iron. Then my wife insisted on driving."

Pappas fingered his cuticles. A girl in a plaid skirt, navy coat, and club tie slurped spaghetti that hung from her chin, beardlike.

"Stop it!" said her mother. "Mind your manners!"

Guy exhaled, raised his eyebrows and waited for the commotion to die out.

"But, still, I drove," he said. "I'd made it up to about twenty-five miles per. Then a four-wheeler skidded around a blind corner. He struck us on the passenger side."

He held the back of one hand against his forehead like an aegis against the restaurant noise. He ducked his head lower.

"My wife's face smashed through the windshield."

He sniffed as if offended by the spice of meatballs that rode by on a waiter's tray.

"She bled to death on the dashboard, before the paramedics came."

His voice fell to a whisper in spite of the shuffling of feet, the battlefield clanging of forks and knives.

"My son hadn't buckled his seat belt. He burst through the window out onto the dirty snow."

Sheriff Pappas' words slowed. His face blanched. "He died sputtering blood in my arms, the hole between his ribs gurgling. He was ten years old."

"I'm so sorry." I didn't know what to say, struggling to hold back from him. I gulped some espresso. "There's life after death," I gasped. "I know there is."

"How do you know?" he said. "You're fifteen years old. Did your Father Stavros tell you that?"

He stifled a cough with a curled fist.

"He didn't need to," I said. "I've seen spirits, human and animal."

"Have you seen the spirit of my son?"

"Not yet," I said.

"Do you think you will see his spirit?"

"I don't know," I said. "I hope so."

"Okay," he mumbled. "I guess you might."

"Rotate the cup three times clockwise for the future," I said, in my softest voice. "Then turn it over."

I looked into the dregs. My chest grew tight. The mud-brown smudge seemed like death.

"What is it?" he said. "What do you see?"

A great sadness grew within me as amorphous as the music of Debussy's The Afternoon of the Faun, which was drifting through the restaurant. He waited for my answer. While he waited, I grew weaker, sweating, my heart sinking, sullen. For a long moment I lost track of where I was; busboys folding and unfolding napkins, patrons going in and out the front door, people waving from outside as they passed in front of the big bay window. The cold air from the stairs descended step by step. An Icelandic foggy vapor settled over the table. I breathed it in. The hairs on my arms stood up like needles. My palms went blue.

"Come on. Tell me now. What d' ya see?"

"In the cup?"

"Yes."

I pressed my lips together and swallowed.

"All I see is a…a box turtle," I stated.

The candle hissed.

I desperately wanted to change the subject. I wanted to grab him by his hair and kiss him with a deep questioning tongue, but the chill that had blanketed me and my sense of loss remained. I was paralyzed.

Guy's hair rose in a thick mass of tangles, still windswept by the ride to the restaurant. He had insisted I wear his helmet. He'd snapped closed the chinstrap himself and checked it with a tug. I had always loved to talk to Guy Pappas when he couldn't hear me, especially on his bike. On the way to Capriccio, in the middle of a wide-mouthed proclamation of eternal love, I'd swallowed a fly. But that seemed so distant now, so hollow.

"Excuse me," I said, rising.

I ran to the bathroom and flipped my head down and up, fluffing it to match his mane. I licked my finger and scrubbed the mascara tears from my cheeks. I added a few drops of water to my forelock to keep the hair out of my eyes and licked my lips. Out of habit, I practiced a flared nostril three-quarter profile and let my lips unlatch, showing my upper teeth like the girls in underwear catalogues do. I sighed. What was so sexy about that opened-lipped, dazed look anyway? I stared at myself. Intriguing enough. But, really, I only looked ready to vomit.

#   #   #

The waiter wore a penguin suit with no coat or tie. A gold lucky chili pepper hung on a thick twisted chain, trapped in chest hair that I assumed extended clear over his back.

"Would ja like anythin' from the ba'?" the waiter asked, in a mist of Aramis and cigarettes.

I straightened, and in my deepest voice, said, "A warm cognac, please."

"And what can I get you, sir?" he said to my sheriff.

Pappas studied the waiter's shoes.

"Cognac?" He turned to me, shaking his head.

The waiter turned on one heel of his patent leather loafers and squeaked over to the bar.

Pappas bent forward, close into the candle-light, until the flame shone in his pupils.

"What're you doing, Persephone?" he said. "I am a sheriff. You're underage. I can't let anyone serve you liquor."

"Relax, Guy Pappas."

A chunk of bangs fell forward, tickling my nose. "We won't get caught. My chronological age is totally irrelevant. If I seemed young, I'd get carded."

"You can have just one," he said, sighing.

"And by the way, I happen to have a fake ID in my wallet."

"Let me see."

"Never," I said.

He tucked a strand of hair behind my ear, but it bounced out like a spring. He pressed toward me against the table, examining my scalp like a numismatist studying an Indian head penny.

"See?" he said. "You've got one."

"Got what?"

"A white hair," he said, separating it from its tress.

Straining, I crossed my eyes at the curved silver strand.

"See?" I said. "You don't have any of those. Obviously, you're just a kid."

"Thank you," said Pappas to the bowing waiter, who made a ritual of placing our glasses before us, waving them in the air like a conductor.

The sheriff swirled his cognac, put his nose in the snifter, then leaned back in his chair, eyes closed. I dropped my spoon.

He stroked the edge of the cherry table not covered by the white cloth, then shifted his weight in a wine-colored, leather-upholstered chair studded by big brass tacks. His eyes glazed over as if he were recalling some sweet memory of his childhood.

"Lucky Luciano and Ray Patriarca used to have business meetings right here in Capriccio," he said. "Luciano controlled the Port of New York."

He paused, rubbing the rim of his glass.

"Ray Patriarca, Sr. controlled the Port of Providence. Capriccio was the epicenter of hooch during Prohibition. Luciano kept Ray supplied. And Ray kept all of Providence supplied. And guess where his headquarters were?"

"Where we're sitting?" I said, droll, monotone.

Guy Pappas bit into a crisp breadstick.

"Bingo." He chuckled. "You're about ten times smarter than I gave you credit for. You're sitting in his chair. This was his favorite table."

The bell of a Good Humor truck rang in the alley beside the restaurant, rattling the pendant lamp that swung in the bay window. Across the alley, through glass streaked with car exhaust, a dark man dressed like an undertaker appeared between the double doors of the printing office. He adjusted his wire-rimmed sunglasses and climbed in the backseat of an idling limo. When it drove off, a black Labrador on the sidewalk seemed to materialize in the man's place. The dog was stout, even for a lab, with big ears, muscular hunched shoulders, bowed hind legs, and narrow hips.

A crow in a ginkgo tree looked down on the dog and chattered. Not thinking, I held my breath, my blood running cold. A Capriccio customer struggled with the front door until I realized it. Then I exhaled and let him in.

The dog lowered his head and coughed, his tail clamped tight. He struggled to breathe. His sides heaved six or seven times, mouth open, neck extended as he planted his forelegs wide apart.

"The dog," I said, pointing. "Look."

Sheriff Pappas turned towards the window. The Labrador resumed coughing, pink tongue protruding from his mouth. Pappas stood, threw his white napkin onto the table, and hurried to the door. I slipped my clogs back on but dropped one, almost tripping as I ran to catch up. From the alley, I watched the dog's chest wall collapse and spring outward in a strained stertorous rhythm.

"Quick," said Pappas. "Maybe he swallowed a ball."

The dog coughed and breathed a deep-sleep snoring breath. He gasped and rattled.

"Here boy," I said, kneeling on the pavement.

The dog halted, hung his head, and coughed. I crept toward him. The box in my pocket hummed.

"Persephone," said Sheriff Pappas. "You hug him, and I'll check his mouth."

The dog cowered from Pappas and took a few staggering steps toward me.

My pocket grew warmer.

The dog wore a simple braided leather collar. Tags and a three-bar cross hung from its ring.

"Stavros," I muttered. "Or sent by Stavros."

Pappas frowned at me. "What did you say?"

"Never mind," I said.

The dog staggered into my arms and I enfolded him like jasmine vines surrounding an old stump. His lower eyelids drooped, the pink rims wet, brown eyes dilated.

"Please be okay," I said.

The box in my right pocket radiated painful heat.

"Don't worry," said Pappas.

His many keys rattled from his key chain. He reached toward the lab. The dog retreated into my lap.

"It's okay," I purred.

The dog's muscles relaxed. I embraced him as Pappas tried to open his mouth. The dog growled.

"I'll do it," I said. "I know this dog."

"You what?"

"I know him," I insisted.

Enveloping him in my lap, I applied slight pressure to his jaw with thumb and forefinger. He opened his jowls. Sheriff Pappas knelt beside me and shined a flashlight into the dog's mouth, pulling his tongue to one side like a great pink worm.

"I see something," he said. "But I can't reach it."

He pulled up a leg of his jeans and slipped off a shoe. I stood and leaned over the dog, finding a spot below his ribs. I lifted his rump into the air and shook him.

"That's good," said Pappas, removing his boot and then his sock. His great toe had a curly tuft of hair like a hobbit.

I delivered six or seven thrusts like I'd practiced on the drowned dummy Annie in my lifeguard class. The dog coughed, managed two or three normal breaths, then convulsed.

"Hold him," the sheriff said.

I clung like twine, ignoring the buzz of heat warming my pocket, scorching my thigh.

"Careful," said Pappas.

He reached into the dog's mouth; hand gloved by the sock, and pulled the tongue away with the other hand. The dog pushed against me, recoiling. Guy Pappas drew back his hand, holding something soft and doughy, with streaks of red.

"Got it!" he said.

He pitched two tomatoey lumps linked by mucous onto the cracked sidewalk.

The dog stopped gagging and wagged his tail. I sat with him on the ground and scratched his side at the perfect place to cause one hind leg to beat up and down like a piston.

"Pizza bones," said Sheriff Pappas, pulling off his makeshift glove. He laughed as he held the slimy sock up, dangling it by two fingers over a trash can.

"What's a pizza bone?" I said.

"The crust."

"Oh, I never heard that," I said. "But that's not pizza. Maybe apple sections?"

"Doesn't feel like apple sections," he said. "Feels like dough."

I rubbed the dog's ear. He lay down and fell asleep, exhausted.

"You saved him," I said.

"We did," said Sheriff Pappas, beaming. "Where did you learn that Heimlich?"

"Well, life guard class," I said. "But I've seen it in real life. I'm deathly afraid of watching dogs eat ever since I was dog-sitting at our next-door neighbor's and the little white thing almost choked to death on some gristle off a prime rib. The bone was as big as she was. I called my dad. He ran over and Heimliched her four or five

times. It didn't work, so he carried the dog across the yard to the car.
I got in back and he threw the dog on my lap."

"But it didn't work," he said.

"I still memorized what he did," I said. "It could've worked."

"True. Then what happened?" he said, putting on his shoe
again.

"By the time we got to the hospital, the dog was having
seizures in my lap."

"That's a terrible story," he said. "What kind of dog?"

"A Bichon Frisé," I said. "The little white fluffy kind."

"And?"

"The vet had to do emergency surgery, put a tube in her throat."

"Ew," he said.

"But she lived," I said, laughing.

Pappas patted the Labrador's head, then my head. He reached
up and twisted a branch off the ginkgo in front of the door of the
printing office.

A crow cawed.

"What is it?" I wanted to rub the furrow that had formed
between his brows.

Pappas poked at the starchy pile of mush with the stick, as the
dog slept, sunning himself.

"I don't know about this." He looked concerned.

"What is it?" I reached for his free hand, bending over the
coughed-up food.

"I'm trying to get under this mess and flip it over."

"Whatever it is, it's gross," I said. "I'm phobic about watching
dogs eat." I squeezed his hand. "Is that normal?"

"Persephone," he said. "You're funny."

"Maybe it's a sausage."

His eyes squinted down to slits.

"Maybe. Or two." He pushed the cylindrical objects, rolling
their edges with his stick.

The gooey glob collected tiny bits of chewed-up concrete and
dirt. Dust from the sidewalk stuck to red smatterings of sauce. He
cracked another stick from the ginkgo, driving away the crow who
still called darkly, flapping above the building tops.

166

Pappas worked the ginkgo branches like chopsticks, one in each hand, poking at the sticky mass from opposite directions. Finally he flipped it.

Acid filled my mouth. Prickly heat flooded my face as I buried it in his chest, sobbing.

"Go sit down, Persephone," he said. "Over there, on the sidewalk."

But I peeled myself off him and squatted down next to the sheriff as he removed the tweezers from his pocket knife and an evidence bag from his bomber jacket. In stony silence he dropped the pair of bloody fingers into the plastic baggie and zipped it shut.

Chapter 23

"Don't worry about the dog," I said, struggling to ignore the heat radiating from my pocket. The box squirmed like a snake egg trying to hatch.

The dog's sweeping tail lifted and waved. His ears pricked forward. A high, sharp whistle sounded, almost out of human range. The dog ran up the alley, looked right, then left, crossed into Roger Williams Park and disappeared behind a ridge of cedars.

Sheriff Pappas wrapped the baggie containing the fingers in a rag. He stowed the bundle in an evidence container that hung from the side of his bike.

"Where're you going, Persephone?" he said.

"I'm just following the signal." I was half-way up the printing office steps by then.

"What signal?" he said, unzipping his jacket. "Did you hear that whistle?"

I rolled my silver cross back and forth on its chain. "That's not the one I mean."

I tried the black iron knob on the great green door of the old brick building, but it was locked. Then I had an idea. For the first time, I held my breath and a door opened.

"It works the other way, too?" I muttered, assaulted by a waft of inky air. "I had no idea."

"What're you talking about?" Pappas said, following me into the printing office. I turned the brass lock behind us.

The room was paneled in pickled oak, and filled with sheet-fed offset Heidelberg printing presses, die-cutters, letter presses, and manual business forms machines. Library tables were topped with stacks of paper, menus from restaurants, and wedding invitations embossed with fancy metallic letters on heavy parchment. Light slid between slats of Venetian blinds illuminating everything in dark, pale ribbons.

"This is trespassing, Persephone." Pappas inhaled sharply, his injured eye re-patched, the good one rolling up toward the ceiling.

"It's only a shortcut," I said. "Come on."

"You're coming with me." Both hands rested on his gun belt. "We can't just break into an office. That's a felony."

"I thought a cop could enter a building if a crime was being committed."

"There's nothing going on here." He reached for my arm to escort me out.

I pulled away and hurried toward the basement. With every step, the box grew hotter. I pulled it out of my pocket, singed my fingertips, and dropped it.

"Stop playing around," he called behind me. "We're leaving."

He picked up the box, gasped, then fumbled it like a freshly-roasted chestnut. "Shit," he hissed, eyes widening in the dusty light. "Damn thing's hot as hell."

It slid out of his hands and hit the floor with a thump. "What's in there?"

"I don't know," I admitted. "I found it in a tree stump a while back, and can't open it. But it led me here."

"Well, we're getting out of here." He reached for my arm again.

Again I stepped away, behind a fire-proof office safe the size of a refrigerator.

A cockroach scrambled across a dessert menu for Gaspare's Restaurant. I picked up a ledger and smashed the bug, smearing greasy brown and white schmutz over the description of the Kahlua tiramisu.

"We're breaking and entering," he rapped out, the words like bullets on steel. He made a sound somewhere between a laugh and a huff. "Now I'm contributing to the delinquency of a minor."

Pappas turned back to the front door, grasped the stiff brown latch and twisted. I took in a deep breath. The lock jammed.

"Damn, it," he said. "I know you're doing this. Let the knob go. I'd like to keep my job."

"No one knows we're here," I pointed out.

"How do you know?" he said. "You're just guessing. And you're fifteen years old."

I picked up the box, which had cooled. It lay dormant in my hand like a seed waiting out winter. On impulse, I turned toward the back of the office.

"Look, the box was cold. Now it's warm again," I told him. "You see?"

"Respect your elders. Let the door open. Your imagination is way out of control."

"No it's not, Guy." I held the box out in front of me as I wove between chairs and printing equipment. "Hmmmmm. Warm… warmer…colder… cold…warm, warmer…warmer….warmer…. hot!" I stopped in front of a five-foot wooden door obscured by the shadows in the back of the shop.

"Give me that box!" The sheriff rushed toward me, roaring like Ahab calling for the death of a whale.

I offered him the box. He snatched it up, then fumbled again, tossing it between his hands, cursing at the sizzle of heated metal. He tried to open it with his thumbs, but the lid wouldn't budge.

"Damn this thing." He took out a handkerchief and his pocket knife.

"Fuck!" He fiddled with the lid, using the kerchief like a potholder, prying at the edge with his penknife. But the jaws of the box wouldn't give way. "What a damned stubborn clam."

"It's not a shellfish, it's a compass," I said. "It's trying to lead us somewhere."

"It's just a damned fucking box," he said. But his forehead was sweating.

"It wants us to go through this door." I pointed at the dwarfish pair of book-matched wooden panels stained dark walnut.

"What do you mean, it wants us to do something?" He rubbed dust from his eye. "It doesn't want shit! How can it be a compass? It's just a damn fucking metal match-box."

"It wants to show us something inside here."

"The box isn't a person," he said, slapping it back into my hand. "God is not inside the machine."

"We need to find out what's behind this door."

"I know what's behind it. The whole neighborhood is filled with basements connected by tunnels. Patriarca used to store liquor right under us to escape the law during Prohibition. The largest illegal stash of absinthe in the world was found only three years ago, buried behind the locked doors of these spaces. The basements were speakeasies, the tunnels storage vaults. There's nothing down there now except empty corridors between stores. Most of the rooms below are sealed off. Just forget it, Persephone. You're letting your imagination run wild."

Pappas ranted on. I opened the door of the basement expecting to see the ghost of Luciano and Ray, Senior, or musty cases of moonshine and old ammunition. And prostitutes in flapper dresses. "You wanted to go," I said. "Well let's go, then. This is as good a way out of here as any."

"No, it's not." He looked stern, parental, arms crossed. "The front door is the best way out."

"But someone might see…." I swallowed. "See us together. And besides, the box wants us to go this way." I started down the stairs in total darkness.

"Jesus Christ."

I glanced back to see Pappas pulling a mini-Maglite out of his bomber jacket, aiming so its narrow beam pointed at my mouth.

"Let's make a deal, then. If we go down these stairs," he said, "and don't find anything—which we won't—do you agree to leave with me out the front door?"

"Of course." I tossed my hair over one shoulder. "I don't actually like basements. This one smells like stale cat pee."

"Fine then," he said, jaw set. He shone the light down the narrow, worn steps. "Let me go first."

"Sure," I said. "And I'll carry the compass."

"It's not a compass. It's a box."

"Whatever you say." I smiled. "It wants us to go through the basement, over towards that wall."

I felt his breath warm on my neck as he passed me on the stair. He was sucking on an after-dinner mint.

"Nothing down here," he muttered from the bottom step, swinging the light in an arc toward all four brick walls. They glistened with water that leaked through cracks in the mortar.

The concrete floor slanted toward a central drain that emitted a reek like old gym shoes. A shower head with a rusted chain pull attached to one wall. In the corner, on the far left, between a water heater and a thirty-gallon sink of soapstone, hung a grey-painted metal door with a barred window at head height. The walls were streaked with black mold and eroded by drops of water that slid from the slanted edges of the ceiling. Torn asbestos insulation draped over us like horror-movie cobwebs. Water trickled from the ceiling, echoing through the cavernous stillness like the inside of a seashell. As I moved toward the barred door, the box activated.

To keep my fingers from burning I slipped the compass back into my pocket.

"The box wants us to go through that door," I said, pointing.

"That doesn't go anywhere," Pappas objected. "These catacombs are filled with sealed-off ends. Bricked in decades ago."

"Nevertheless," I said.

The padlock of the steel door opened to a slight touch of my finger. Beyond the doorway, the corridor switched back to the left like a mountain trail.

"Stop," he said, flashlight on his shoulder. "Let me go first. Someone's been down here—I mean, recently." He sighed and adjusted his eye patch. "See? The padlock's broken." Puncturing near-total darkness, he cast a flood of light between the bars.

"What's over there?" I asked.

"Water. Rat droppings. The corridor's winding," he said.

"Oh, Jesus Christ, there's another door. Hanging open."

My lungs constricted as dank air reached them. "The compass says go."

"Well, I say stop. You don't just blast through a place like this. It's unsafe. The ceiling could cave in."

"I trust the compass. I can almost feel Yiayia's hand upon me. My yiayia would be disappointed if we didn't go in."

"She isn't here," he said.

I looked straight into his eye. "Yiayia's always here." I inhaled mildew deep into my lungs, then coughed.

He sighed a long dreary sigh, the woeful kind that goes with a scowl and gets stuck in your throat, then trails off like the moaning of pigeons.

"You sound like Medea. She groans like that whenever she knows I'm right."

"Let me tell you something, young lady." But then he didn't. He just chewed his upper lip, as if he had forgotten what he was about to say. He pressed his palms to his eyes, inhaling the moist decay of broken underground rooms devoid of fresh air, of soil seeping through the cracked foundation. His voice dropped an octave. "Okay. We're going into that room, and we're going through that door. We'll obey that compass of yours. It's ridiculous, I know. But I can see stepping through is the only thing that's going to satisfy your morbid curiosity and show you how silly this is."

"Fine," I said. "You wouldn't do it if you didn't think I might be right."

"Okay." He motioned me over. "Hurry up, then. Stay right behind me."

The sheriff opened the dusty door and we slipped into a looping brick passageway. The dripping of water and the scratching of rodents resounded through the halls like bats scurrying across a rocky wall of a dark cave. A gradual rumbling sifted down from the ceiling, low and distant at first, then gathering force and volume.

My pocket swelled with heat.

"A car," muttered Pappas. "We must be under an alley." He pressed me up against a decaying wall and looked up at the warped plaster ceiling. The noise overhead faded, passing into the distance.

"What is that?" he asked. "Do you hear that low buzz?"

I shrugged. "You mean the box?"

"No. Something else at the end of the hall. Behind that steel door."

"You think someone's in there?"

"No." He hesitated. "A water pump, maybe. Used to be a butcher shop, across the street from the printer's. We must've doubled back to it." He scratched his forehead. "The hum must be a compressor."

"Sounds pretty loud," I pointed out.

"It's magnified by all the space down here," he said. "There was a huge meat locker in the basement of the butcher shop. Kosher. They slit the throats of live animals and let the blood drain out. Then made sausages out of the scraps they swept up."

I shuddered. "Sounds gross. My associations with meat lockers aren't the best."

"That compass of yours must really be hot now," he said.

"Yeah, it is." The box in my pocket was burning my leg through the denim of my jeans. "We're here now," I said. "Whatever we're supposed to find is here."

We stopped ten feet from the meat locker, shoulders touching. Squeaking tires rolled across the road overhead. The strain on the stone and plaster from the weight of the vehicles passing overhead and the steady hum of the compressor filled the dead space with magnified groans as if the sighs of the sleeping dead were caught heaving all at once. Dust sifted down on us from the cracked ceiling.

On the dented steel door of the locker was a perfect print of a human ear, where someone must've leaned or fallen.

Its job done, the box began to cool.

"There are human bodies behind that door," I said, committed to the sudden conviction. "I know it."

Pappas frowned as if he didn't believe it. "I'll open the locker. You stay back." He rummaged through the inside pockets of his bomber jacket for gloves and a 35 mm mini-automatic camera.

"I'm the one who got us here," I said. "I'm the one who opens the door."

"Oh, no you don't. I'm the cop. I'll do it. You stay back, and— here, hold this." Pappas handed me his mini-Maglite like a surgeon handing off a bloody scalpel to a nurse.

"Look." I pointed the beam at the tracks on the floor. In the circle of focused light, bloody paw prints met the muddy outlines of shoes. I traced the perimeter of the door with the beam. "It's not closed."

"What?"

"When is a door not a door?"

He shook his head. "Huh?"

"When it's ajar." I snickered once, then stopped myself. I stepped around the trail of prints on the floor and illuminated the three-inch-wide gap between the door and its jamb. Just inside stood a stack of newspapers bundled and bound with twine.

"Massachusetts senator receives new kidney," blared a headline on the top sheet of page one.

"Stop," he said. "Don't touch anything. This is a crime scene. It's all evidence. Don't screw it up."

He'd spoken too late. I was already on my way across the threshold. I tapped the edge of the frame with the flashlight, then opened the door wide and swung the beam across the vault of the room. The cement walls were pitted, streaked with bleach stains and greasy smears. Bare meat hooks hung in rows from a steel cable the full length of the room. Built-in shelves were cluttered with dozens of flattened cartons, bolts of string, and serrated blades of various sizes. The floor was littered with empty soda and beer bottles, scraps of old newspaper, flaky and curled with age. The light beam cascaded across two steel tables in the center of the room. I inhaled a sharp blow of frigid air and a sulfurous aroma of slightly rotten beef and hot metal, as if someone had been welding.

On each of the tables lay a corpse clad in a white hospital gown.

"Jesus Christ." Pappas gripped my shoulders, thrusting himself forward and pushing me behind him.

I leaned around for a better view. The dead men were posed on slabs like recently deceased twins. I shined the beam on the face of the larger corpse. An endotracheal tube rose from the man's mouth, like a spigot. His broken nose listed away from the swollen orbit of one raccoon eye. A trickle of blood had dried in a black puddle within the cup of his ear. His eyelids were sunken, as if the globes had caved in, dried up, or perhaps had been removed. A sheet shrouded the body, and both arms rested above his chest, as if he'd been tucked in for sleep. An I.V. with short tubing curled back, taped to the man's knuckles. It'd been inserted in a hand with two fingers missing.

Pappas lifted the wrist and studied the stubs.

"No bleeding," he said. "The finger amputations were post-mortem." His set his jaw. "I guess we knew that already. Didn't we?"

"Yeah." I nodded and swallowed. "We knew."

"I've seen that tattoo before." The flash from his camera lit the room for an instant like heat lightning.

"It's a Mobius," I said. "They're not just a couple of goons. They're Athanatoi thugs. See? Both have the same tattoo."

"They're what?" Pappas was measuring the Mobius on the pale fleshy part of the second man's forearm with a tiny ruler he'd pulled from God knows where. He was apparently well-prepared for impromptu crime scenes.

"A sort of cult. Stavros told me. Assassins, killers."

"Well, they're dead now," he said. "Why did Stavros tell you about these men? What've they got to do with you?"

"They staked out the Newport Musical. Calliope and I were hiding and heard them talking. They did the burglary you investigated at 140 Red Chimney. They robbed my parents at the bank, then threw them in the trunk to suffocate. They shot my dad in the head! That's what they have to do with me."

Water dribbled from the ceiling and plinked onto the floor as if we had stumbled into Tom Sawyer's cave. The sheriff stood without speaking, not moving, barely breathing. A shower of drops hit the floor. At last Pappas took in a slow breath and put his hands to his forehead, wiping away the sweat. He pressed the heels of his palms against his closed eyes.

"What're you thinking?" I asked.

He leaned over the first corpse and studied the tube. His gloved hands descended to the lip of the sheet, hesitated, then pulled the white cloth down. It rustled as he rolled cool damp cotton to the man's knees.

The sheriff whistled through the small space between his front teeth. He untied the strings of the hospital gown and opened it.

The sheet swept to the floor like the wing of an angel.

Cuts angling down from the man's shoulders met at his sternum, and a single midline incision extended to his navel. The V-shaped chest opening had been stapled closed, the midline abdominal incision

176

sewn back together with a long, coarse, running catgut suture. Symmetrical gashes on either flank below the ribs were stapled closed.

Pappas scrutinized the incisions, squinting. Then his gaze went distant while his analytical mind formulated answers. "These incisions look post-mortem. Or at least perimortem. See? There's very little blood or bruising."

"I see." I chewed my lip and tasted blood.

The belly of the corpse was concave, almost hollow, despite its overall corpulence inciting my question, "What's been removed?"

Guy lifted the sheet, exposing the second corpse, and opened the man's gown. The body had been dissected just like his partner, eyes and belly deflated. He slept with his arms crossed. Both cadavers wore hospital ID's on their wrists, yellow tags on their toes. The sheriff copied the names on the tags into a small notebook.

"I sleep like that, too," I said. "Flat on my back, with my arms crossed, as if I'm dead."

Pappas closed his eyes in silence, chewing one cheek, his breathing slow. I waited for an answer, careful not to interrupt his train of thought.

"These men were after you." He shook his head. "Now they've been dissected like lab frogs." His forehead wrinkled. "They have organs missing, for Christ's sake!" He pulled out his phone, then snapped it back onto his gun belt. "They must have friends. These Athanatoi, who'd they work for? How big an organization?" He frowned. "And how powerful?"

My ankles turned in my clogs, almost giving way. I pulled sweaty hair off my forehead and knotted the frizzy mess into a loose bun. My shoulders slumped, my chest caved, breathing exhausted. Fear struck me like never before—like a sickening pang deep in my gut—like a dagger in my mind.

"And now you've found the bodies of the kidnappers," he said, "by a means you can't explain. A metal box. Of course, they'll blame you."

He turned me toward him, lifted my face, and cupped my cheeks in his hands.

"We've got to get out you out of Rhode Island, Persephone," he whispered. "Now."

                    #   #   #

Guy held my hand and we left the printing shop the way we came in, just as I'd promised. My hand was warm and small in his, completely enveloped by his palm, like a baby chick. He squeezed my hand every time we took a turn through the underground maze. "You're okay, baby. I'll make a quick call. Then we're getting out of here.

Guy's bike was parked in the shade of Capriccio's façade. We crossed the street, the moon upside down in the sky, as if it were dumping something on the Earth, like cream, or luck. Up the hill at the terraced entrance of Roger Williams Park, the sun escaped from behind tree branches that locked their limbs together and wound around the wrought iron gate to form a great trellis. Guy made calls while I stared at the interlocking branches, looking to find where one tree ended and the other began, and finding no sign of separation.

I walked over to Guy and buried my nose in the place where his shoulders and neck came together. He cocooned his arms around me and kissed the top of my head like my dad used to do.

I turned to face him, his breath cool like eucalyptus leaves. We breathed into each other's mouths for a minute. It lasted a long, long time, but not long enough.

"This is why life passes so slowly for kids, and why it flies by for older people," I said.

"Why?" He squeezed my hand. I felt my own pulse in my fingers, faint and rapid as a baby bird's.

"Because children notice every tiny thing that happens. Every shade of color, every sound. Adults learn to skip over things. They summarize."

"I love you," he said. He looked away, then turned back. He took off his jacket, arranged it over my shoulders and arms, and zipped it up. He found my hands through the too large cuffs and pulled them through.

"I want you to take me to bed."

"I think that would be the right thing to do." He seemed earnest, as if he had really stretched his mind around the morality of having sex with me, all things considered.

I kissed him again. His spirit was in his breath. I was breathing him in, as much of him as I could. I pressed my nose against his chin. It was rougher than it had been under the table at Vendetto's when his car had exploded. The bomb had been meant for me. I inhaled deeply, hoping to suck in cells, tiny pieces of him, little bits of invisible DNA, perspiration and oil his glands had made. I could still smell the coriander from traces of Metaxa on his breath. He kissed my eyelids, nose, ears. I brushed my lips across his neck, his chin, his cheeks, behind his ear. I rambled across his skin, savoring the winding boundary from rough to smooth from dry to moist, from salt to oak leaves.

"As far as I'm concerned there's no better way to explore the road than from the back of a bike." Guy Pappas fired up his engine and handed me a helmet. "Hop on!"

His smile slashed me and burned. For the first time ever I saw he had one dimple. It was deep and cute.

#   #   #

Since preschool, my favorite mode of locomotion had been by horse. The second, by bicycle. When I was nine I discovered motorcycles. I had become adept at riding Calliope's Honda 350, passed down to her from her big brother, Christy.

We would take turns riding bitch behind him on his orange hog. One of us would get to ride the girl bike, ponied alongside by Christy.

"If you want to get good on the road, you've got to get good on the dirt," he would say.

At one point, I can honestly say I felt one with the dirt, flying over the air, birdlike, never thinking about my wings.

That all changed when I took drivers' ed. I was preoccupied with manual transmissions, and what that funny H-shaped pattern the gear shift made actually did inside the transmission. What was happening when it made that horrible grinding sound?

In my absent-minded state, I'd squeezed the hand brake of the Honda, thinking it was the clutch, and went over the front of the bike head over heels. I ate dirt and broke my thumb.

"You should have crossed yourself at the Fairy Bridge," Calliope had said, attributing the first of my series of motorcycle mishaps to the displeasure of local wood nymphs at my failure to show them appropriate respect.

\#   \#   \#

Guy and I meandered through the streets of Providence, up and over the knoll and passed the twining trees locked in an embrace that was part bondage.

Riding bitch was humiliating for a seasoned advanced novice like me. I was definitely not a tadpole or a guppy, more a flying fish, though not yet up to dolphin or shark. But the natural, instinctive connection to the road I once felt was gone. I think it'd left the last time I'd eaten asphalt.

"Hug me harder," he yelled over the engine.

I pressed up against him and gripped him with my knees and arms. When we got to the highway the world flowed into a great big blur streaking by on all sides.

We banked through turns without effort, the wind pounding us. There we were, whipping along, feeling free, with this giant vibrating machine between our legs. I still felt embarrassed about being driven. But okay, I'll admit it, the BMW K100 with its new technology, the counterbalance shaft, made our little girlie Honda look like a tricycle. This thing was hot. I got the giant vibrator reference. Guy's bike was a testosterone torpedo.

But the best thing about being behind Guy Pappas on his bike at top speed was I got to confess everything to the wind, to the air that was teeming with spirits.

"I love you, Guy!"

I knew Guy couldn't hear me, but the spirits could.

"I think about you every night! You will be mine—as God is my witness!" I proclaimed, a la Scarlet O'Hara, a fist quickly raised to the streaming air.

He balled up my hands and pressed them against his belly.

"Hello out there!" I said to the spirits. "I know you can hear me."

Then I swallowed a fly, a big one that got stuck halfway down my throat. Its wings tickled my windpipe. I pressed my face into Guy's shirt and stifled a cough. I pocketed sputum until I stored

180

enough for one giant gulp. At last I got the insect down.

We arced around the old water tower and rounded deep curves as we made our way to South County and took the North Kingston exit. We bounced over trestle bridges and passed by old farms and cemeteries as we approached Eastwick.

"You all right back there?" He laughed over his shoulder.

"Good," I said, leaning into him.

The whirling slowed. On the main road into town, the first sign read:

Eastwick, established 1637. The next sign said: Wickford House, and the third said: Smith's Castle, the site of the first and only drawing and quartering for treason on American soil.

Old oaks stretched out their arms toward each other across the lawns of the historic neighborhood. The road ended in dirt and the distant sound of laughter floated up from Eastwick Beach. We stopped there, idling. The sounds and smells of the sea came bouncing through the air like beach balls.

"We take a right here," said Guy. He turned his head to snatch a look at me with his good eye. "I'll get you home in twenty minutes."

"That dimple." I was delighted. I fingered it like cookie dough. "I'd never seen it until today." Then I pressed my cheek to his neck, feeling his pulse against my chin.

He took off his sunglasses and blew on them. Then he polished them on his shirt.

"Look!" I said. "A box turtle."

I climbed off the bike and turned to the turtle, marking its location. The turtle was about seven inches long loitering in the street. I took off my helmet and flipped my hair.

"I want you to keep that coat," said Guy. "It looks good on you."

"No. I can't."

"I have another one. He opened his arms for me to climb in and wrapped them around me like vines. "It's a present."

My cheeks tingled as blood rose up my neck. "I'm getting that turtle and then I'm coming back for you."

I dashed about twenty yards to the turtle, picked it up, and stroked its domed shell.

"It's not hurt," I called back to Guy, who was balancing the purring bike between his legs. The turtle's head retracted, then its legs disappeared.

"Death," said the turtle.

I looked into the trees for birds, for leaves rubbing, for breezes interrupted by strange slinging branches and the rushing of water. I looked to the beach. Perhaps I'd misunderstood someone's conversation across the grassy field. Or maybe the voice had sifted through the undergrowth and distorted the word.

"Death." I heard the word again. The closed-hinged shell was marked by orange stellate rays spreading across mahogany rings.

I carried it, arms outstretched in front of me, to the marshy side of Old Route 2—on the same side of the street as the beach. The air was filled with brine and the sulfur of primordial swamp. The aroma of a local coffee roaster penetrated the thickened air. It was low tide in a nearby marsh, the crunchy-shelled mud like dregs in the bottom of an espresso cup. I smiled and waved at Guy. A murder of crows blew in the wind overhead. The hairs on my arms were spines spiking the lining of my coat. The green-black plumes of pitch pine lining the street stepped toward me and the lid of the sky descended in a smoky cold carpet of clouds. Damp clothes on a line billowed and waved excited arms in the late afternoon coolness under a sullen and sinking sun. I slid over the bank to put the turtle back in the marsh grass. Then, I noticed the smell of pyrotechnic dust on the breeze, like gunpowder, like the stench of the car bomb's explosion at Vendetto's. I heard the metronomic click…the click of a timer. I saw a key… the key was in a lock that turned an engine off… a secondary trigger engaged.

And I was too late to stop it.

"Get out of there, Guy!" I roared.

He straddled the idling bike, sleeves rolled up, hair blown back like a tangle of lion's mane.

I'd crawled up the slope toward the street on my elbows, struggling not to slide down its muddy slant. "Don't turn the bike off!" I screamed, hysterical, ferocious, filled with panic. "Get off, but leave it running!" I was huffing and blowing like a steam engine.

The identical black car that had picked up the man dressed as an undertaker at the printing office turned the corner into Eastwick. Just in time for the explosion. I'd seen the same man before, right after the incident with the choking dog. And I recalled the car.

Athanatoi henchman, I thought.

A core of sorrow blasted up my neck and sent flashes across my cheeks. The burst threw me to the foot of the marsh. I climbed back up the bank, slipping, my soul bleeding. The BMW had erupted into flames and shrapnel. Jagged metal whizzed by my head. The man I'd clung to moments before was now fragmented into bits of burning flesh and rags of cloth.

The blast vaporized Guy's body. He was strewn all over Main Street in Eastwick. Obliterated. Bits of bones and teeth.

"No! Guy! No!" I ran to the sizzling carcass of the bike, an amorphous mass of flames, convection currents pushing me away. I cried for Guy and for my Yiayia. I cried for Guy's dead wife and son. I lay down on the grass and cried like a woman. I cried for all the suffering and loss and misunderstanding in the world. For fascism and murder. I cried for the suffering of spirits and lost souls. I writhed and moaned and screamed. I cried for my one day ruled by love, and my night to come ruled by horror. I cried so hard I snuggled into someone's damp lawn then fell asleep, leaving the imprint of a grass angel laced with ashes that must've been pieces of Guy.

Chapter 24

Following an Explosives, Ordinance, and Demolition (EOD) assignment dismantling submerged warheads off the Ivory Coast as a Navy Seal, my *kumbaro,* godfather, Cousin Christy, had become a mercenary in Cairo. But from the time of his hasty meetings with agents of a Saudi Prince in Orlando, Florida, to his expulsion from several African countries, he was rumored to be a spy. He'd sailed to Madagascar and joined a team of private-duty live combat system specialists who had chased the Madagascarian dictator into exile at the point of a tank, and had intercepted armed gangs carrying endangered rosewood timbers bound for North Korea. He had disappeared into a rainforest ravaged by illegal loggers during the aftermath of the coup, and resurfaced at a Chan temple Monastery on the north side of the western peak of Mount Song.

Between jobs he would come home and lavish me with gifts.

"I see an angel and I think it's you," he'd said on my fifteenth birthday, presenting me with a sweeping headdress, a crimson explosion of chicken feathers, wrapped in tissue paper.

"It's beautiful." I'd opened and closed it like a flower. "I'll hang it up in my room over the poster of Captain Picard. Where'd you get it?"

"A merchant in the Cameroon highlands wanted my cigarette lighter and binoculars."

Then he and some guy from work had excused themselves and gone out to the garage to clear out travel trunks. The man, dressed totally in denim, pulled back on the slide lock of a new Taurus Centurion nine-millimeter pistol. The shot had flown out the window of the garage, ricocheted off a water tank and landed in the plaster wall six inches above the top curl of Medea's wig.

"Are you crazy?" Medea had shouted at the man in denim, wagging her finger. "When you clean a gun, make sure it's unloaded. And never point it at anything you aren't willing to destroy. Damn Tavros, piece of shit."

The man let the screen door slam behind him on his way out.

"Incompetent dork," she'd mumbled under her breath. "Shit for brains.... Government asshole."

Christy would disappear for weeks, sometimes months at a time, but as my godfather, he never missed a religious holiday or my birthday.

Back home in Newport, he'd laughed at my vegetarian ways and my probing interrogations during Christmas and *Pascha*. His chief concerns were giving me kisses and keeping the gas pedal of his blood-orange Corvette floored.

"Sluggish bitch of a car," he always complained. "I shouldn't have trashed the Foxy Lady."

"But I love the Old Spice!" Medea had squealed, holding onto her wig. Christy sat a full forearm's distance behind the wheel and hugged the corners of the black-topped back-road edged with pines all the way to the Country Inn. I'd lain sideways on the bench backseat counting barns, wind slapping my cheeks pink.

Back in Cairo, Christy had served as royal family bodyguard with forty other American mercenaries, where he'd personally supervised the playtime of the prince's twelve year-old, obese diabetic son, Mukhtar. He'd tried to persuade the boy, without touching him, that he should desist from beating to death smaller children he taunted on the streets of Cairo.

"Please, Mukhtar. Stop beating him. Allah would not have you kill the innocent. If you kill the innocent, you kill all men. If you spare the innocent, you spare all men and will one day awake in paradise."

Sometimes Mukhtar would look up and listen. Other days he would not. Then all the palace bodyguards with their heavy gun belts and uzis, and the Prince's fork-tongued wife, would rush to face off with the poorly-armed Cairo police under the portico of the former hotel's lobby.

The prince's foreign wife, Reina, wore poison rings and carried an Austrian dagger in the cleft of her bosom. The blade was stamped with the Bulgarian frog, Zbrojovka Praga. Its Yin and Yang maker's mark shone on the hilt.

"Kill the infidels," she would say. "And Allah will have a place for you in heaven."

"She was the most evil and ugly woman on earth." Christy would whisper and laugh about it, even at weddings and funerals. "She once tore out a woman's heart and drank her blood. Reina would not let me go because I knew from Mukhtar that her frequent mutilations and schemed murders in Arabia had caused her family's expulsion from Beirut. How I escaped her is classified. Others weren't so lucky."

Christy was a gorgeous blond Greek with an olive complexion; his mellow, chiseled beauty threw off rays like a star. His eyes, so lacking in pigment they glowed azure blue like a goblin's. He hid beneath Serengeti sunglasses, category 15, black.

I never imagined him naked, as I did other men, like Guy. But when I'd lost Guy, my cup of misery had been drained to the dregs.

When I thought of Christy's bronzed hands fiddling with an Orthodox blue bar cross that hung from his neck, I sculpted in my mind his suggested, bulging chest. I loved the nape of his neck, his scent of leather and ocean water. In daydreams, I pictured his gloved hands locked onto the perforated wheel-skin of one of his small fleet of blood-orange sports cars. We both loved to race, top down, over the tortuous roads of the sea cliffs of Newport. Once Medea had lost a wig and a silk scarf to the wind on a twisting road to the Newport Musical while my cousin drag-raced a local Jai Alai player in a souped-up Dodge Charger.

Christy had a side job as the first importer of disposable diapers in the Middle East. He'd made a small fortune and purchased currencies from the four corners of the world which he stashed in a safe deposit box on the Isle of Wight.

Christy and Guy Pappas had advised Auntie Georgie to spirit me away from Rhode Island as a precaution. So Azrafel, the angel with the black-billed hat, drove us in a midsize blue rental sedan in the middle of the night to Logan Airport. We fled by commercial plane to San Francisco. From there, we traveled by beat-up Chevy station wagon to Christy's vacation home in Half Moon Bay, California, a modern Frank Lloyd Wright-influenced structure that hung, espaliered, from a craggy bluff over the great, wide-awake eye of the looming Pacific.

#   #   #

My relationship with Guy had a tangible core. And alive or dead, the bond was irrevocable. I tried to summon his spirit, but couldn't. Not yet. I knew there must be a reason. I was in mourning.

"Christy won't be home when we arrive," Auntie Georgie told me, munching peanuts and sucking down Bloody Mary mix, as we flew above the cornfield discs of Nebraska. "But he'll be back by tomorrow."

"That will give me time to freshen up." My nervous finger fiddled with the cuff at my wrist caught on my Mickey Mouse watch.

"No worries, though," Georgie said, "He'll have some tough guys at the airport there to pick us up. They'll be armed. Don't let his absence bother you."

I shut my eyes, imagining coasting in thermal sea winds and brawling storms.

"Okay," I said. "I'll try to stay calm."

"Just don't draw any extra attention to yourself." said Georgie. Georgie tugged to cover my thighs with the hand-sewn hem of my dress, then patted my knee. "What's the use? You'd be lovely in a sack." She smiled and pushed her sunglasses back up her nose.

#   #   #

At San Jose terminal, giggling nuns scurried past us, chatting of Holy Land pilgrimages. Their lives gliding by on winged feet, cushioned by miracles of healing springs and visions of the Holy Mother gifting sheaths of red roses to the humble. Schoolboys tossed each other's caps as two policemen scarfed down soggy BLT's and steaming coffee in a lobby cafeteria. Loudspeakers blared homage to San Francisco, Dallas, and New York above the rumble of arriving and departing planes. Two goons smelling of Musk for Men approached us, wearing Italian shoes and firmly set fedoras. But they strolled on by with hardly a glance, while displaying hand-written signs to find their customer in the crowd.

"Have you heard the news?" said a pimply-faced blond Mormon boy, who offered us a pamphlet highlighting the teachings of Brigham Young, and then followed behind us.

"Heaven is in your hands," he yapped and pleaded.

No older than I, he carried a Book of Mormon and wore a fresh white shirt with suspenders and neatly pressed khakis. I knew he must be wearing a magical mystery Mormon undergarment beneath his clothes, and I mused about how it must be to take a shower without having to get naked. Intrigued, I wondered how I could get a pair myself—not out of disrespect but out of utter fascination. The undergarment was a symbol of purity, and supposed to protect the wearer from "the world." Did girls wear them under or over their bras and panties? The blonde boy walked a step behind us, the patter of his feet soft and springy like a cat's. Neither Auntie Georgie nor I looked back.

"Whatever happens next, don't say anything," Georgie whispered. Behind her dark sunglasses, the flat solemn mask and unpainted lips were out of character and disquieting. "Mormon women don't talk much or hug in public, so neither will we."

"But why…?"

"Don't ask." She straightened her cotton kerchief. "Just be cool."

After a few more steps, a second Mormon boy, a few years older than the first, slipped to Auntie Georgie's side and fell in step, saying nothing, a black prayer book tucked under his elbow.

"Straight ahead," the older one whispered. "We're going to exit through that revolving door directly in front of us. Someone else will pick up your luggage."

"Caleb, Jeb, Sara," said a heavily-whiskered older man with an Abe Lincoln beard. He wore a crisp white shirt and suspenders. Approaching confidently as if he knew us, he stopped all four of us for a moment.

"I'm mightily glad to see you home safely," he said, nodding.

He kissed the air in the direction of Auntie Georgie and me, and turned and led us all to the exit. In an instant, we were a reunited Mormon family headed for the parking lot to our wood-paneled station wagon. And finally I understood why Auntie Georgie was wearing an uncharacteristically modest brown wash dress. And why she'd insisted I wear a pale blue gingham homespun frock for the flight west.

She slid across the vinyl front seat to sit between the muttering Mormon elder and his suddenly-materialized doughy wife, who was also carrying a prayer book. I was wedged in between the two Mormon boys. No one smiled, which was just as well. I'd forgotten how.

"We'll go carefully now," said the elder. "But there's no one following."

"Not yet," said Auntie Georgie.

Soon we had left the San Jose Airport behind. Within two hours, we were weaving through a maze of narrow Monterrey streets. The boys who flanked me gripped their books on their laps as if they were holding hollow leather cases containing revolvers. We glimpsed an edge of blue water, and then the curve of Monterrey Bay that disappeared behind squat stucco cottages.

"Careful now," said the whiskered Mormon at the wheel.

The station wagon debouched from the neighborhood and glided into the swerve of highway that raced the last few miles to Half Moon Bay. The Mormon boys and matron opened their books, the pages flipping like a flutter of butterflies. I saw that I'd been right: the Bibles were indeed cutout to fit the handguns I'd imagined before.

"Okay," said the elder. "Clear."

The blond boys and Mormon woman slumped and grinned. We drove the streets of downtown Half Moon Bay between its rows of small tourist shops and quaint restaurants, the car rattling, then accelerating from the business district to an ocean-side drive between rocky hills rising like the sun, sprouting clinging mansions like morning glories on a vine.

Beyond the foaming swirls and white-capped breakers of the Pacific Ocean hurling against a rocky shore, seals were gathering in rookeries on guano-surfaced islands of granite. In three more minutes the wood-paneled station wagon turned right. We headed up a winding road that dipped and rose again and at long last reached a driveway half-hidden by massive tree-trunks and tangles of foliage.

The car halted with a jolt amid burning brake fumes. We all disembarked. The Mormons lined up in descending order of height at the truck and gestured toward Christy's house.

"We'll stay right here until you're locked inside," said the Elder. "Then we'll wait in the garden cottage. It has an intercom."

"I know the drill," cut in Auntie Georgie, winking, her glasses parked on the top of her head. We climbed the pavilion's flagstone steps up the switchback.

Christy wasn't home, as we'd expected, so we found the hollow mock-rock hiding the keys within it. Next, we turned off the security cameras and alarms set within phony gopher traps and let ourselves in.

"That key was a fake," Auntie Georgie said, "The door recognized my retinas, and it's already trained to recognize yours."

The expansive house jutted over a rocky bluff in the guise of a white swan stretching it wings. That evening it seemed prepared to leap into the salty streams of air rushing over the Pacific, perhaps to circle the nearby stone tower built by the bloodied hands of the poet Robinson Jeffers, and then dive for a voyage over the gleaming golden arc of sand that verged on Monterrey Bay.

"You're associating Jeffers' verse-play Medea with your mother." Aunt Georgie sat, chuckling over her morning fondue of grapefruit wedges dipped in Port. "But, so far, your mother hasn't killed any children. Not even her own."

"I argue not, Jason," I said. I felt humorless. I missed Guy.

Auntie Georgie's pleasure in my stupid precocity as a fifteen year-old pubescent playing with myth in the darkness of her omnipresent shades filtered into her voice. I was easing from my first life as frightened innocent into my next as golden child.

The next afternoon, my new tutor, Father Montagnus, hired by Auntie Georgie, released me from my study of biblical psalms relating to fear of the dark and the death of loved ones. "When the night falls the darkness is so deep it causes everyone to shiver."

My aunt departed for her announced tour of Half Moon Bay's boutiques and flower shops, while I plunged into the mysteries of Cousin Christy's wise and wondrous house.

Because of their acquaintance with the sea, the house's acres of glass windows filled the rooms with endless sky and water. Two enormous foyers, one in the back opening onto the cliffs, and one beyond the facade opening onto the balcony draped with magenta bougainvillea, awaited the arrival of guests with all the delicious sanctity of quiet church vestibules.

On the east wall of the front hall, Father Montagnus had hung an icon of the patron saint of Agia Katarina Monastery of the Holy Myrrh-bearers, where he was a heirodeacon who instructed seminarians in the art of scenting and unction of the putrefying flesh of the recently departed.

Above Agia Katarina hovered the gold leaf icon of the Byzantine "tender mercy" Christos Kai Maria. The faces of the *eikona* shone flat and ancient, lined with worry and wisdom.

To the left of the patron saint of the local monastery at the second quarter of the cross rode Agios Giorgos on his great golden horse. Agia Paraskevi and Agios Kostas stood at the third and fourth quarters.

Below the wall of icons was a long lacewood table draped by a blanched eyelet cloth tuelled by Yiayia Friday when she was aboard the immigration ship that had carried her from her life as the Countess of Gaios to the cold, ashen barracks of Ellis Island, where she'd been examined by heavy-handed physicians.

Burnt-out wicks floated in oil in three glass cups resting in iron stands with filigree of lily. Daguerreotypes of my great-grandmother Penelope and my great-grandfather Capitan Matepas, a freedom fighter who'd been impaled by the Turks in 1876, three weeks before Yiayia was born, glowed in light reflected from the buttery walls.

Penelope's eyes were flat black, her lips a tight line, as if she'd already had prescience of the nearness of her husband's death and Yiayia's birth. Penelope sat in an armchair, her empire-cut dress, retro for the period, hid her figure. Capitan Matepas stood behind her in disguise as a Greek Orthodox priest. But knives were strapped to both thighs and up both sleeves.

A slight, swift breeze rippled the glow of the portrait. Cousin Christy's reflection wavered in the convex glass protecting the photograph. His torso zigzagged as though he were standing in a funhouse mirror. He was crooked, his chest too broad, head too small. I laughed at him as he grinned in the doorway behind me—the first smile I'd been able to crack since the incineration of Guy.

"So you think I'm funny?"

"Yes," I said. "You're the funniest man alive."

I meant it, but knew he wasn't funny to everyone. Certainly not to the henchmen of Syrian madmen whom he kidnapped and strung up with wires—until they broke into tears and blabbed their state secrets. But, still, despite his tales of violence, I knew he was righteous, like the vengeful angel Michael who had expelled the first humans from the Garden of Eden. Christy sent a thrill up my spine that was part attraction, part fear. Whenever I saw him, I felt an overwhelming sense of safety and ineffable joy.

I ran to him and threw myself into his outstretched arms. He was short and heavily muscled, with the face of a hero in a pre-Raphaelite painting. I kissed his cheek, missing his lips by an inch. It was like kissing a mirror.

"You're not the fourth in line, as you think," said Christy. "You're actually the seventh."

So he had been watching me study the daguerreotypes of my ancestors. "I didn't know that."

"Before Medea, Yiayia, and Penelope, there were Theodora and Hestia."

"That many?" I said.

"And many men and women before Hestia, all the way back to Circe."

"Oh, well. Circe wasn't real," I said, shaking my head.

"She was," said Christy. "But it wasn't until Seraphim, the Father of Hestia, that our line became confirmed to produce a different kind of angel."

He admired the light reflecting on the shallow ridges of his shiny fingernails. He cleared his throat and looked up again, straight at me. "An Angel of Death is a rare creature."

"Ha!" I sneered. "It sure is."

"Hestia was the most advanced in our line. During her life on Earth, the focus of the inheritance shifted beyond healers and alchemists to theosis."

"What inheritance?" I said, examining a chip in the gilded gold fame that surrounded the icon of Saint George. "You mean heirloom jewelry and sets of bone china?"

"Stavros knows," said Christy.

"Where are the pictures of the others, then?" I said.

"There are no more pictures of Penelope, or even of your Auntie Georgie without her sunglasses. Or even of me," said Christy. "They've all been burned."

"What? But what about all the pictures of Yiayia, Calliope, and me? They're important to me."

"We're destroying them now," said Christy.

"Isn't that bad luck?" I said, fingering the blue glass eye on my charm bracelet.

"Not in this case," said Christy. "We're trying to preserve our luck. To be wise is to be lucky."

It didn't matter to me what he said. I wanted my pictures back. But still, I loved and trusted him. How could I not? I turned toward him and hugged him again. He lifted me high, tossed me down and rained kisses on my face. His rough cheeks made my chin tingle.

"Get your shoes on," he said, squeezing my cheek hard like an Italian *nona*.

"Why should I?" I teased. "I like going barefoot."

"Because you've been cooped up here long enough," he said. "And just because I said so. I am mightier than thou, for now."

Chapter 25

Christy leaned back in a chair at our small table under a pair of gold-rush wagon wheels at The Boar's Snout Cafe. My cousin laughed and pulled out a dried-out loosely rolled cigar, a Cohiba Especiale. He posed as if he'd plopped out of the set of "The Good, the Bad, and the Ugly" in modern sunglasses, incongruously playing the Man with No Name—the tall gunman Eli Wallach had unwisely insisted on calling "Blondie." I love classic movies.

He took a few puffs, watching me through blown ovals of smoke.

"Centuries ago," he said, tapping an ash into a stone tray, "a heresy arose among some confused and vehement Magi of a Greek Orthodox sect."

"Can't we just chat?" I sighed, crunching a pickle.

"No, we've chatted long enough about Calliope and your horses. I already know all I need to know about the Ferris wheel incident and your trip to Mexico."

"My imagined trip."

"Your imagined trip was real," he said. "And Yiayia pulled you

194

out of the Ferris wheel. And Sheriff Pappas was your lover. Almost. You're a shark, Persephone. You can smell blood in the water when no one else can. If you doubt that for a minute, you'll likely go mad." He puffed out his cheeks like a blowfish, then blew a long stream of "O"s like the segments of an earthworm creeping through dirt.

I sat stunned, not blinking, in my chair at Boar's Snout Cafe Restaurant, where the steady chatter of customers in jeans and golfing outfits melted into a hum. Then, relief flooded over me like spume over high rapids.

"You must be strong enough to avert the misfortune already rooted in your life. Death brushes up against you every day." Christy leaned across the table, rolling the cigar between his thumb and two fingers. "Listen to what I'm about to tell you. If you need a few minutes to walk around outside, I'll walk with you. If you don't, I'll continue."

"Okay," I said, lying about needing the few minutes.

"Don't lie to me," he said. "Let's go for a walk."

"Okay." I felt my jaw clench as I went over the memory of Guy Pappas' death, finally interrupted by belted laughter from four waifish women dressed in tennis skirts and drinking pink cocktails topped with little paper umbrellas at the table next to us.

After Christy asked the waiter to leave our plates there, we walked once around the block without saying a word, munching Altoids.

"Are you ready now?"

"Yeah. I'm ready."

Once back at our table under the wagon wheels, Christy stabbed a forkful of asparagus. Then he set it back on the edge of his plate.

"These misguided magi," he said, "because of their compassion for sons and daughters of heathens and excommunicated men, wept bloody tears. They rejected God's gift to humanity. The gift of Grace. They hoped to find an alternative route to immortality for all. The traditional one of death and resurrection being fine, theoretically, for the blessed and fortunate, but not so convenient for the sinful and worldly."

Christy's voice lowered to a whisper. He leaned forward a few inches. "They were called 'the Athanatoi,' as you know. They considered themselves sprung from the literal head of God. And known by the sign of the golden bull of the apocalypse that bellows thunder, and the black horse adorned with stars, and the Mobius that has no beginning and no end."

"Jesus Christ."

He frowned, as if I'd belched or blown my nose in the tablecloth. "Don't use the Lord's name like that."

"Okay."

"And don't mention that horse again."

"Alright. But—"

"But what?"

"You brought up the horse. I also know the golden bull that bellows thunder," I said. "Personally." I poked the crust of a parsnip tart with my fork. "It chased Calliope and me under a fence at Medea's place in Newport."

"Of course it did." Christy poured two glasses of champagne. "Be wary of that bull, and of the black horse adorned with stars." He showed me the Perrier-Jouet label with its swirl of dainty lilies before replacing the bottle in its sweating ice bucket.

I swallowed the laughter in my throat. It ran as a chill halfway down my spine and bottomed out in my stomach as nausea. I pushed away the glass of champagne; Christy had omitted my age to have it put before me. I didn't need my fake ID.

Now he kept on, not bothering to react to my chill, my sickly look.

"The Athanatoi operated as a secret society. They began an exploration in diverse directions to ensure immortality for all, exploring all possible correctives for death: medicine, physics, chemistry, alchemy, sympathetic magic, etc. Among the cult's activities were attempts to kill God's angels of death, and efforts to prevent nascent angels from developing to maturity."

"Are angels material?" I interrupted.

Christy put his champagne glass down on the table, making indentations of overlapping circles by twisting its base into the tablecloth.

"It's not my business to guess," he said. "It's my business to know. The Athanatoi are real and breathing. I am an agent of the Greek Orthodox Church, regardless of what is perceived about me. The Church has always been a fierce enemy of the Athanatoi."

196

I didn't want to hear any more. I had hoped to be closer to my cousin, but instead felt driven away. I loved the splendor of Half Moon Bay, its rocky beaches and quaint artsy boutiques, its endless truckloads of rain-blessed flowers. But I didn't like Eastwood's cafe with its oxen skulls and cowboy motif. Not anymore.

"You do know I've killed people, don't you?" Christy's long white fingers fidgeted with his necklace, a miniature icon of Agios Georgios on his horse driving the broadsword into the neck of the dragon. "But only when I had to."

"Of course I know," I said without thinking.

Everyone in my family knew Christy had killed people. He had been a SEAL, in underwater demolition in the navy, and had the medals to prove it. And then there'd been his much-discussed career as a mercenary, which was not as hush-hush as it might've been in other families. Instead, it had been a source of pride. Then, of course, there was his cloak-and-dagger rep as a spy, which, in me, had left not so much distaste as a golden, romantic glow. So far.

"Actually, I know you know," Christy said, with a smile. "And still you trust me and love me, as I trust and love you."

"Maybe even more," I said at last, looking down at my half-eaten parsnip tart, heart beating away at my ribs with feathers of pure excitement.

"Then while you're here you'll put yourself in my hands and do exactly what I tell you, regardless of what it is. And you'll try your best to learn from me whatever you can."

The waiter came again and half-filled my glass with champagne. Christy put a finger over the top of his own glass.

"It's too good to waste," I said.

"Then you can drink the rest of it. I have to stay sober."

I sipped, savoring the explosion of tiny bubbles and how they ignited the roof of my mouth.

"Does this have anything to do with Guy?" I said.

"Of course it does," Christy said.

"The kidnapping and bombing?"

"Yes."

"I see" I rubbed a cramp out of the base of my neck. "You're offering to be my guardian angel."

"I'm not offering anything," Christy said. "I'm informing you as to the nature of our relationship. I am fulfilling the dharma."

I was frozen by his cold change of tone, a hard darkness in his eyes I had never seen before. His pupils dilated. I turned my eyes away by reflex and felt my breath catch when I discovered, on a far wall of the restaurant, a portrait of Eastwood as Dirty Harry, complete with magnum.

"Please understand me at once," Christy continued, his words becoming staccato as he lowered his voice. "You have to accept my protection as an absolute."

"I do," I protested, "I'm accepting it now."

"You are under the absolute orders of your family and church— and me personally—to accept my protection and instruction in all the things I must impart." Christy said.

"I know that," I said, stacking the bread plates, brushing crumbs from the table, willing my hands not to tremble.

"Don't do that," said Christy. "The busboy needs a job. Besides, it's gauche."

"Okay, Mr. Manners." I leaned toward him. "I accept everything. Auntie Georgie told me on the plane already, and I've already accept it provisionally."

He cleared his throat. "Provisionally? You're still only fifteen." Christy emptied the bottle into his glass. "No matter what you think."

"I'm old enough to accept what I want."

"Okay," he said. "But I repeat, you have no choice in any of this. All I am really requesting is that you trust and love me as before, even though the discipline I must subject you to might cause a weaker person to abhor me. Now, tell me at once, without hesitation. Do you promise to comply?"

"I promise," I said, raising my glass, as if to toast a new contract, or a marriage.

"Do you promise to continue trusting and loving me throughout all this? If you do not, I will take you to some quiet place and thrash you until you do. Now what about it? Do you promise to comply with my two requests, or do I take you out of this place and beat you with a switch at once?"

The words, "Fuck you and the griffin you flew over on," rose to my serpent tongue. But I stopped before they escaped my mouth. I

198

tipped my glass against my cousin's. Our flutes clinked in acceptance.

Christy was crying, tears streaking his lovely cheeks. Soon, I was crying too. So the customers at Eastwood's Boar's Snout Cafe Restaurant were treated to the sight of two related people, one much like Adonis, the other feeling more like the Witch of the West, sobbing over their asparagus salads, parsnip tarts, and champagne.

"I comply," I finally coughed out, as if I were a Chinese bride auctioned off to an overweight Wild West miner.

Christy dried his eyes with a cloth napkin embroidered with six-guns. "If you're uncomfortable here, we can go."

"Like where?" I said. "The Northwest Territories? I'll stay, thanks."

"No, we'll go now," said Christy. "There's something I want to show you."

Chapter 26

The wind tore through my streaming hair as Christy twisted the Evinrude's throttle. The dinghy shot over the infant waves of Monterrey Bay, the draft slapping my black ringlets into damp Medusa locks. I watched from the bow as the sharp hull cut across the water, slicing the bay into two perfect halves. Salt spray soaked my storm-grey, burn-out velvet dress, driving away the sun's warmth. My teeth clenched against the stomach-lifting sensation of flying without wings.

"What does my little shark smell?" shouted Christy over the wind, flashing a grin at me. His entire body vibrated with the pulse of the motor.

The strain of the dingy at top speed shook us both. Water sprayed our faces and tumbled down like beads of sweat.

The seismic vibrations reminded me of my next door neighbor back in Newport, whose yippy dog once had a grand mal seizure and peed in my lap on the way to the veterinarian. His owner, Mrs. Guppy, had one of those belts she put around her waist that all but shook her fillings loose while she watched the soaps on CBS in the afternoons. The Bold and the Beautiful, The Guiding Light, All My Children, One Life to Live, and The Young and the Restless. She sweated and undulated through two and a half hours of soap-opera passion. Mrs. Guppy jiggled in her plastic suit like the waves that were bouncing our dinghy up and down. I'd been her dog sitter at the time. I used to dress her twin Bichon Frisés, Lovecraft and Poe, in sweaters, clip-on bow ties and snappy retractable leashes. Poe was the one with seizures who'd swallowed a ham bone and needed a trach. I also babysat a pair of dachshunds, Girlie Girl Eye and SBD, short for Short Bus Dachshund, who was mentally challenged because his skull had been cracked by an Amtrak train bound for the Big Apple one New Year's Eve.

Not wanting to overdo it, we'd go for our casual walk-jog a quarter mile to Joie de Vivre Farms where Agrippa the Ingrate was then stabled. I'd ride while the dogs played with chew toys and chomped hoof trimmings in an empty stall. Then we'd all walk-jog back home and I would drop off the two dachshunds at my neighbors, the special-ed teachers, and find Mrs. Guppy still in her plastic suit, still flouncing on the vibrating machine.

The Evinrude coughed and sputtered as if it had inhaled water down the wrong pipe, or swallowed something nasty—like fingers or a ham bone. The clamor yanked me straight out of my dream world.

"Something wrong with the engine?" I asked, my open hands scraping water off my arms like sweat from a horse.

"Nope," said Christy, who gave the motor so much gas at once we bounced off the swells and hopped across the channel like a flat skipping-stone.

"What are you thinking?" Christy yelled over the roar of the outboard.

"The smell of death. It always smells like rust."

"I smell it too."

I looked at my bare feet, stained with algae, my Heli-Yum toenail polish glittering in the reflecting sunlight.

"Your cheeks look like Jell-O," I hollered, laughing, to my cousin, whose face shook as though his arms were attached to a jackhammer. He bit his determined lip. His blood was up. I could tell.

Christy shrugged and his lips twisted over to one side of his face in an ironic smile. "One way to avoid death is to not feel too much aversion to it," he said, lifting an eyebrow.

The bow cut through rhythmic arcs of water rushing underneath. I lifted my bare foot from the middle of a coil of anchor rope looped on itself like a snake. A twinge of worry at my carelessness startled me. I braced both feet on a green boat rib, giving my thrill-seeking toes something to do. Droplets of water coalesced on boat paint like liquid mercury. A sour taste lingered on my tongue over the salt.

"Blood in the water," I shouted, without looking back.

My fingers paled to indigo with cold. I gripped the dinghy's gunwale as the bow climbed over the swells and crested over the water before wavelets could break, feeling as though I'd slipped into a warm bathtub only to find myself slapped around by a tidal sea of tears.

"Something's wrong. Where are we going?"

Up ahead, a moored Benetti Yacht swayed with the quiet motion of a pendulum. Gulls dove for fishes.

"And the profit and the loss," I whispered, my head lowered.

"There," pointed Christy, his voice almost drowned in the rattle of the dinghy's motor.

The cruiser lazed, its command bridge rakish, its wrap-around windows tinted and canted like the sunglasses of a woman tanning on a beach. Christy throttled maximum revs from the Evinrude until we were running at top speed, then eased up when we were close enough to drift alongside the Benetti.

"I don't want to go aboard." I coughed, my throat dry as if I'd swallowed a pickle. "Let's stick to the Dyer Dink."

"The owner asked us to come see him," Christy said, tying up to the yacht's stern and nodding for me to climb aboard the swim platform. "Just hold onto the guard rail."

The height wasn't the problem, nor did I have trouble with the motion of the boat.

Although the hull of the yacht shielded us from the waves, the splash of bay water against my feet sent cold teeth of froth nipping at my bare heels. My legs itched as the air dried briny residue on my skin, but I dutifully climbed the ladder. Then, feeling groggy on a wide sidedeck, I brushed seaweed ribbons of hair from my eyes.

Christy pulled a key from a sagging cargo shorts pocket and inserted it into the salon door.

"There's a fully-stocked bar in the salon. I think we're obliged."

"You said the owner wanted to see us." I turned to him with a sudden quarter twist of my neck. "Why?"

"He'll be here soon." Christy peeled a fleck of dried seaweed off one knee and flicked it over the side into the water.

He turned the key in it. I considered holding my breath to jam the lock, but didn't. The door swung open. He stepped in and down the stairs.

"I hope this doesn't turn you green with envy," he said, offering a hand to help me across the marble foyer, slippery under my wet soles.

I ignored his hand. "How much does this behemoth weigh?"

"Oh, she's about one hundred tons."

"I can feel her engines running. But she's so quiet. Can you show me?"

He squinted, his face askew, "Okay. Let's go see the guts."

The quiet interior of the engine room belied the fact that she had over two thousand horse power and three generators. My heavy eyelids drooped with the soporific purr. The room hummed a consistent smooth sound of distant murmuring air like a giant white-noise machine.

Christy displayed the engine room of the cruiser like Martha Stewart demonstrating extra sharp knives slicing through hard boiled Easter eggs. Better than Ginsu knives…sharp, almost too sharp, Medea liked to say, all decked out in her French maid costume and patent leather pumps.

She'd put on the annual Holy week show for Christy, who never missed a religious holiday. She'd hold one big knife with a super-sharp edge up to the light and twitch her wrist. Fiery glints reflected off the blade, blinding us. She seldom cooked because my dad was a great chef. But for a special treat every year she made a show of decapitating cabbages from their trunks to prepare Palm Sunday's Lenten cabbage rolls, *yemistes* stuffed with rice and chopped parsley, anise, and pine nuts. She rolled each one by hand

and lined them up in a baking dish like corpses in a graveyard. After dressing them with bread crumbs she would dribble olive oil that had been blessed by the Archbishop over their little bodies, muttering Paschal Matins, and then slide the pan into the oven.

"Get your knives professionally sharpened and you will always have an edge in the kitchen," Medea would say, cutting her raw potatoes into paper-thin slices.

Christy jolted me back to the engine room with a nudge of his elbow, then tickled the back of my neck. "I'll meet you in the salon."

He smiled at my murkiness and pointed the way to a restroom, where I patted my damp briny hair and legs with a towel. I wasn't normally a snooper, by nature respecting the privacy of others. But as I straightened and saw myself in the full-length mirrored door, I had the urge to open it. My fingers grazed the edge and it popped open. Rows of leather strips were looped over a dowel. Some were attached to wooden handles, and some had metal buttons on the end of the lashes. Oil-treated latigo was caked with dried blood. Cardinal-red rags filled a wicker resin box of rattan vine.

I closed the door on some twisted person's idea of holy relics and wandered the boat until I found Christy leaning behind a teak bar sniffing his glass of Metaxa. He was easy to locate by the rich aromas of mochatto, pepper, nutmeg and oak. He sipped the plush caramel liquid, his eyes closed as if seized by some private memory.

"Umm," I said, still standing in the doorway, eyes cutting over to a strange, spicy-but-sweet flower arrangement sitting on the edge of the bar in a vase the size of a wine barrel. Undertones of overripe banana drifted from the thick grey-green oval leaves. I looked back into Christy's eyes, their gentle curves rimmed with water.

"Whatcha thinkin'?" he asked. This may have been a rhetorical question, because, like Azrafel, Christy was an angel. Couldn't he hear my thoughts?

"Religion," I shrugged. "Home, I guess."

"Well, this isn't home but just take a look around. What's not to like?" His voice sunk to almost a whisper. His eyebrows arched and fell. "The Italians have been building yachts for generations, and you can see the results, inside and out."

"I'm sure you're aware your yachtsman is a flagellant," I said. "I found his leather scourges and bloody robes in the bathroom. I'm not fond of self-mutilation as a path to God. ”

"Yes, he belongs to a group who use extreme mortification of the flesh to produce altered states of consciousness. Self-flagellation as devout worship. They also practice self-crucifixion."

"Well ho-hum," I said, shaking my head. "Just another pain-filled day in Purgatory."

"I agree," said Christy, swirling his drink. "But as you know, great pain releases endorphins." He pursed his lips and swallowed. "It also attracts fetishists who are already pain addicts."

"Nice," I said. Nothing he taught me had surprised me, yet.

"Pope John Paul II has beat himself with a whip and slept naked on the floor to bring him closer to God. That's confidential, by the way."

"I won't tell a soul," I said, walking over to the bar, feet still moist and sticky on the marble tiles.

"I, too, prefer more soothing forms of devotion," he whispered, eyes gentling, unstirred, his patience sovereign.

I could have exploded in a volcanic stream, like Medea would, at the weirdness of my bathroom-closet discovery. Instead, I decided to be cheerful, despite the aftertaste of pickles that had somehow found its way inside my mouth.

Happiness is a choice, my mother had drilled into my head.

"I've always liked the dusky blue-green fruit of the moth plant." I said, walking over to the sofa and running my fingers over its oceanic turquoise velvet.

"Brandy?" Christy displayed the black label with seven gold stars and bid me sit as he slid over to the glass rack behind the bar.

"No, thank you. More Champagne!" I ordered, in my finest Norma-Desmond-from-Sunset-Boulevard voice. I pulled my cheeks up toward my ears, mocking a bad facelift. "Got any tape?"

I examined the blue-black suede of my poor drowned Italian shoes I'd been dragging around with me by two fingers, and set them on the drain rack behind the bar. One rolled into the sink with a splat. On the skin of my dead shoes, water had drawn wavy lines of salt like a very, very bad Jackson Pollock, or a network of veins, or a tiny spider web warped by wind. Ruined. I wafted a sigh, then sat on a sculpted swivel chair. Its leather finish swirled like claret sauce on ice cream. I stretched out my legs.

"Isn't she amazing?" said Christy, handing me a cool glass filled with brandy that warmed me.

"Who?" I said.

"The boat."

The batting of his eyes thumped like rabbits' feet. Pushed by his diaphragm, his exhalations began low in his belly. His breath was elemental, like the first blaze of a fire or the first gust of a storm on a salt sea. His heart and all the tubes connecting to it pulsed a bass drum song that reverberated with the buoyancy of cork.

I slowed my breathing and tried to dampen my senses, but failed. "What happened to the good champagne? I like the kind with the lilies painted on the bottle."

"Don't act so spoiled," said Christy, lifting his chin. The boat tipped to and fro in the tide. "You'll love the brandy. Seven star Metaxa VSOP." He twisted the clasp of his gold chain back to the nape of his neck. His Agios Giorgio medal cast reflections on the polished wood.

I lifted the glass and drank all of it.

#   #   #

I glanced toward the center of the warm wood bar. A giant porcelain vase of glazed ecru exploded with big-thorned white roses and branches of glowing pink blossoms, heavy with oval petals and dark waxy leaves. The beeswax-infused countertop leaked a secondary scent of cedar that nearly overwhelmed the faint smell of gasoline clinging to the yacht's interior, and even the pungent spice of the centerpiece of whorling leaves and closed buds.

Beneath the duvet of smells lingered an old telltale aroma of garlic and yoghurt, so I knew the owner of the boat had to be Greek. Christy went into the long open galley and brought back a white tea towel with an embroidered black Mobius in one corner.

I sniffed. Hints of onion, paprika, and poppy seed leached from its Egyptian cotton fibers.

"Greeks own this boat. And they have a Hungarian cook. Don't they?"

"Never met the cook." He wiped a dribble of brandy from the honey-soaked countertop with the tea towel.

My eyes lifted from the Mobius to the cresting water. Next to a window hung a lithograph of a wood-block print I knew from a visit to the Metropolitan Museum of Art to view the works of Escher with Medea for my fifteenth birthday celebration. I had called the block print "Shred Heads."

Algemene kultur, my dear, answered Medea in my head. You silly girl. It's called the Bonds of Love, not Shred Heads.

Waves beneath the boat bellowed within my ears.

"This boat's too big. I feel lost."

Christy leaned forward, eyes blazing. "This cruiser has five heads, four staterooms, a master bedroom fitted with a whirlpool bathtub, a separate bedroom for their pair of poodles who sleep on bunk beds, and quarters for eight crew."

I shrugged. "Okay," I said. So fucking what? I thought, chewing my lip.

I picked up a coffee-table book about the O'Malleys off an ottoman topped by a leather cushion. When I pushed on the cushion, it slid a few inches. The table beneath was a separate piece, oblong, about four feet wide, its burnt finish bordered with carved olive branches. This wood, too, smelled of honey. I stroked it with my fingertips: smooth and greasy. I trailed one finger along its edge like a puff of smoke drifting around corners. I knelt down and tasted it with parted lips.

"Stop it, Persephone," Christy warned. "Turn your senses down." He slapped the table, and I jumped. "We have business."

I continued to sniff the edge of the ottoman. When I lifted the lid, out poured the odors of winter beaches, coppery rust, and cold whispers in the night.

"It's an antique child's coffin from Cameroon made into a coffee table."

"That explains the rust," Relieved, I closed the lid and leaned back into the firm embrace of my chair.

"About this boat. The owner is a family man," Christy went on.

I inhibited an almost overwhelming reflex to roll my eyes by staring straight through Christy's.

"He's a decent guy, with two kids and a loving wife. Teaches Sunday school. An entrepreneur with a bee farm. Some people probably think he has everything. But the truth is far from it. Now you tell me, Persephone, for whom does he work?"

I smiled. "Himself?"

"Very funny."

"The phone company?"

"You know the answer."

But I refused to play. I covered a yawn with my salty palm, tired of the mysterious riddles, the Sherlock Holmes and Dr. Watson routine. Next it would be Colonel Mustard in the billiard room with the dagger. This was like a bad Scooby-Do episode. Oh! No! Shaggy! Shaggy! I dropped my glasses! The wolfman is really a banker!

"Let me finish my brandy," I said. "And why are you speaking to me in those weirdly perfect Victorian sentences? Been spending time with Jane Austin? Or those awful Bronte sisters?"

Christy sat and silently watched. I polished off the brandy, sip by sip, my shark brain twitching. I inhaled the crescendo of blood and death that hovered in the air—it was on the cushion covering the casket. It slid off the walls. Emanated from the galley, from port and aft, from deck and sole, starboard steps, the swim platform, the shower. Even within the goose down of the velvet cushions. And something else. Something rancid, something poisonous was coming from those flowers.

"It smelled strongest on deck," I said at last. "Rust, the whisper of blood. Its fingers reaching out for me."

The sun's rays illuminated dust in bands of light. I kneeled with my hands on the casket for a moment, then rose and walked through the bespangled beam. The agitated particles felt like tiny warm drops of rain. I opened the salon door and headed for the deck, my skin prickling with airborne static.

Chapter 27

The sun was low in the sky and the tiny currents of water glistened with waves of reflected light. How could I have forgotten about the little magic box I'd stuffed into my bra? Now it was loud with heat, beating a Cajun rhythm against my breastbone.

Christy exited the salon door to the side deck. He stood beside me and shrugged, palms turned upward. "So where's this blood? On the bridge? The stern? The bow? Maybe down below, or in the bilge. Go ahead and follow it. You're on the right track."

Two fins of a ray carved concentric circles in the water in perfect parallel swirls.

The bay seemed to exhale, as if exhausted, and the fragrant air lashed at me in waves. The box was pulsing pizzicato.

"It must be coming from the water." My heart was racing faster than my mind could keep up—not a good sign. I stepped on a shell fragment just sharp enough to make me look down and notice the strand of dried seaweed stuck to my foot. "When I climbed aboard. I dismissed it. But I shouldn't have. Thought I was overreacting."

"Okay," he said, bending over the ladder's rail. "I don't see any blood down there." His black moonstone pupils undulated glints of light from the lapping water's surface. Christy cranked the windlass and the line withdrew from the water and exposed the sharpened shank of the oversized grappling anchor. I shuddered. The wavering silhouette of a body rose out of the inky blackness as if speared by the pointed end of one shank. It dangled, like a lettuce leaf, umbrella-sized, impaled by the tines of a fork.

Christy's forehead knurled with concern. "Don't be frightened by this." With a gentle finger he wiped a tear from my eye, which had grown there as an irritant, like a translucent pearl. "Nothing brutal was done," he assured me. "This display is designed merely to horrify the Athanatoi. It's grand theater, my dear. I fed Mr. Economou honey made by bees that had ingested oleander nectar. Then I floated some of those oleander flowers you so admired on the bar in rosewater—his preferred beverage."

"What?" I cried, throwing my head back, clamping my palms over my eyes. Late afternoon rays squirmed between my fingers and burned into my brain.

Christy cleared his throat. By the time I lowered my hands, his cheeks had relaxed into a mask of smooth Elgin, silent and placid. He was an Athenian marble of a Lapith, the human brother of a Centaur.

The sodden body rocked with the current. Economou's arms floated up, a faded Mobius tattooed on each deltoid, then sank again. His limbs were bloated from submersion. Crabs gathered around his fingertips, feasting. I imagined them clinging to his underside, beating their antennae, scraping at his flesh, filtering wafting particles that once were called Mr. Economou. I remembered my dad's recently published cookbook of Forty-three Fantastic Crab Recipes. He'd tried out each recipe as a special at the Country Inn and Newport Musical: crab-stuffed crepes, golden crab puffs, crab and avocado cocktail, sole stuffed with crabmeat. The nauseating waves in my stomach surged in jumps and fits. I gripped the edge of the boat, then sank to my knees.

"The man didn't suffer," Christy explained. " He passed into the next life in a bucolic delirium, similar to digitalis poisoning. Once he was dead, I prayed for both our souls, then closed his eyes with my fingers. I blessed him with the Song of the Parting of the Soul from the Body. Earthly death is a gateway to life eternal, you know. Mr.

Economou was prepared, whether he knew it or not. To be fair, he'd thought he was doing the right thing by joining the Athanatoi."

"But they're killers," I said, sniffling.

"Yes. But they believe they are saving man from death." His eyes were taking on the gradual cast of the setting sun. "By killing God's future messengers."

"Wouldn't it have been simpler to just let his body float away for the sharks?" My stomach turned over, its contents rising with the tide. "I don't understand how he was …pierced like that."

"I skewered his abdomen with the sharpened anchor shaft, attached the anchor line, then cranked the windlass down."

I nodded, witless for the moment, neither formulating any clear thoughts, nor wanting to.

"Look there, now," said Christy. "The drama presents itself almost whole."

I looked again, surprised by my own ability to still follow his directions as the body resurfaced. Five bills of the anchor flukes clutched Economou's back like a giant steel hand. He wore a buttercup-yellow shirt with a print of red crawfish scuttling across it. The stingray cruised by again, a phantom demon in search of its mate.

"I drove the shank through his chest, there," Christy explained, pointing. "Then set the flukes upward. That's a grappling anchor. I inverted the flukes and drove them through so they'd protrude from his back. I'm telling you, Persephone, I had to do this to help ward off the Athanatoi."

Christy sighed. "So, here's my big fish, caught by multiple hooks. The body will not be found before the Coast Guard starts poking around."

"What about sharks?" I said, tears slipping into my voice, clogging the words. "The Coast Guard may never find him, if the sharks do first."

He shook his head, smiling, as if this whole scene was some great benediction. "My blessings will save his body from the sharks. His soul is in a better place. He's no longer faced with the cruel imperative to kill that each Athanatoi operative must accept."

"What're you talking about? You killed him. Now you'll get caught," I swallowed back a sob at the thought of Christy in a cage.

"I'm not susceptible to getting caught."

Christy crossed himself three times right over left and kissed his icon. He cranked the windlass down and the horror of Mr. Economou's mutilated body disappeared into the sea again. I recovered the ability to think and cry, all at once.

"Why did you do it?" I sobbed, patting my damp cheeks with the hem of my dress.

"You know why. It's my job."

"Your job!" I cried. "What sort of job—"

"For the Archangel Azrafel," Christy went on, as if annoyed I hadn't already figured everything out. "And of course, for God."

"This is for God? My God? My God is the God of peace," I shouted, then dissolved in tears.

"Yes, I did this for your God, the God of Peace. For all Eternity," Christy said, turning to smile and wave to a husband, wife and two little children passing by in a Bayliner three-hundred yards away.

"Why would Azrafel want you to kill Mr. Economou? Why would he want you to kill anyone?" I swallowed my nausea back hard and willed it to stay put. I thought of Guy, tears strangling my words.

"You know why, in general."

"Well, I mean in particular," I said. My lips were numb as I spoke.

"Azrafel is completely connected to God," said Christy, as if that explained it all.

"There is a commandment against… you know, this big rule…."

"Mr. Economou's earthly death has been sanctioned." He fingered the blue three-bar cross that dangled below the Agios Georgios medal from a silver chain at his neck. "You're resisting what you know already. Stavros taught you many things. Access something useful, not just quips in Lebanese. You know everything about the sanction."

"The sanction?"

"Stop repeating everything I say like an Amazon parrot," said Christy. "Some deaths have very much to do with our family. Maybe this is one of them. I suspect it is, but to me it's justified, whatever the particular reason, and you must assume the same."

"But I don't assume it." My eyelid twitched. "No. I do not."

"Who have you known well that hasn't worked for our family?"

"Pappas," I blurted.

He frowned. "Bad choice."

"I know he didn't work for our family because..." I bit my tongue.

"Because he was around when you needed him?"

My tears gathered and hardened. Christy wiped them away, his voice growing soft and mellow, almost angelic again, the familiar tones of the older cousin I knew. The same voice which had sung me to sleep when I was a child. Oh, how I abhorred him now. But how I loved him. Still deeply, deeply, loved him. No matter how much I hated him for the horrors he'd done. And all with that damned odor of sanctity.

Then it hit me. "Auntie Georgie doesn't work for the family!"

"Your aunt brought us both up in the church and protected our earthly lives," Christy said. "She protected us so we could later do our sacred work."

"My Auntie Georgie never had anything to do with this," I cried.

He opened his arms, palms up, his skin golden. He appeared lighter, almost hovering on deck. "I am your Guardian Angel. It is God's plan that I protect you."

"By killing? Have you ever heard of the Ten Commandments? The ones in stone?"

"First of all, young Persephone, the Law is made for humans. I am beyond human. Second, life is eternal."

"You were born to a human," I said, feeling victorious. Now I had him.

"Was I?" He pushed back the hair from over his forehead, combing it through her fingers. "I was commanded by Azrafel, the Memetim, to feed Mr. Economou the oleander honey. I am not the one to decide when to bring a man's soul to God. The time of a death is never my decision. I protect his soul in life, then help prepare it for death."

"But what about your secret adventures for the government? And skulking around the Middle East, your mercenary trips to Syria? What about your spy antics during Desert Storm?"

"I served my country and my God. I have never yet had a problem serving both. If ever I did have a conflict, I'd choose God. Of course."

I sat down on the deck and wept. He sat beside me and put his arms around me, rocking me as Auntie Georgie would do.

I panted until I found my voice again. "But isn't death the enemy? The ultimate enemy? The final enemy?"

"No, Persephone." He wiped my face with one hand. "Death is just a beginning." His hands smelled like Ivory soap. I was beginning to see that my wishes had nothing to do with what I had to accept as truth. My mind spiraled toward death. I pulled myself up on the railing, hung my head, and cried to the sun that fell over the bay like the fall of a thousand leaves,

Why Guy Pappas?

Oh, the fingers in the throat of the dog...

Oh, the open body cavities, the liver, the kidneys, the eyeball...

To be part of the end of life is...is the worst possible end...to end a life would make me sick...to feel and hear the pump stop.... And then what? I don't want another lecture about the expulsion from the garden...No one deserves to die...it must hurt....I can't close my fingers on the wick of another person's life....Why would God choose me? Why not someone willing? There are plenty who are willing....For god's sake, I'm a vegetarian....Don't make me part of the end I want to be part of the opening act....I am not a killer....I can't stand death....I still don't understand why we need to die, I don't understand how death is a cosmic experience.

Oh God help me.

"Listen carefully, Persephone," Christy whispered. His voice seemed to come from all around me. "Azrafel is a great angel with four pairs of wings as soft as air, each filled with compassionate eyes. Azrafel draws his sword, to which clings a drop of gall. When a person is about to die, he simply opens his mouth and Azrafel drops the gall onto his tongue. I guarded Economou's death angel when she closed her hand on the light of his earthly life. Then

Azrafel took up his soul in a gentle embrace. And you will be the next death angel. It's as simple as that."

Suffering showered upon me with a roar of heavenly gulls and the speed of an electric eel slithering in pursuit of some helpless crustacean.

No way, I said to myself, knowing Christy could hear me—if he wanted to.

Chapter 28

A thin, bloody line remained on the horizon as we climbed out of the dinghy and dragged our salty bodies back to the blood-orange corvette, its leather seats hot and sticky from baking in the sun. We drove up the eucalyptus-lined hill in deafening silence, back to Christy's house.

"Open," he said, and the massive front door swung wide.

While waiting there for us in sunglasses and form-fitting cocktail dress—black with knots of silk violets—Auntie Georgie had laid out the equivalent of a Scottish high tea on the reflective oak trestle table. I could see her through a clear panel of the dining room's stained glass door. She sat lost in thought, staring through the bay window at a hillside of climbing nasturtiums.

"Ah," Georgie said when we entered. "My timing was perfect."

I pressed my face into her violet-splattered bosom. I'd never doubted Christy's words. Yet somewhere in my brain there must've been a block. Now, my chest heaved and I almost collapsed before they could get me into a chair at the table.

After Christy had carried me into the boat's salon, I'd cried for about twenty minutes. This time I held it to ten.

If the idea was to get my mind off the events of the afternoon, Auntie Georgie had done very well. I was devastated, yes, but also famished. A pot of green tea was accompanied by cold milk, Demerara sugar cubes, and thin lemon slices. Beside the tea service was a tray of cucumber-mint finger sandwiches, my favorite of all of Auntie Georgie's borrowings from the Scottish and British isles. In the middle of the table sat the traditional tower of platforms: raisin scones and Eccles cakes at the bottom, Madeleines next, then an assortment of petits fours and Russian tea cakes, topped by an array of miniature chocolate truffles, candied violets, and pastel Jordan almonds.

"We'll wait for you to eat something," said Auntie Georgie. She sat down at the head of the table. "Then we'll talk".

Christy pulled up a scroll-back chair and sat across from me, his eyes on mine as I sniffed back tears and tried a bite of cucumber sandwich.

"Hungry, cousin?" I said, offering to serve him. "Scone?"

"You're almost ready now," said Auntie Georgie. "The tears you've shed over what you've seen today are close to their end."

"But I—I think I'm dangerous." I collected more tears with the tip of a linen napkin. "People around me aren't safe."

"No, it's true—but it's the Athanatoi who are dangerous." She dragged a silver Edwardian crumb-scraper with a molded lily handle across the tablecloth. "Soon everything will be fine. You are a lovely soul, my dear. You've been well prepared."

She poured a small crystal glass of vintage Port and set it in front of me. Sunlight streaming through the window refracted off her darkening glasses. Shredded mint from the tea sandwich rolled bitter on my tongue and I sipped the fortified wine to wash it away. I felt a whole bucket of tears settle into the back of my throat. I swallowed. I'd long feared my fate. My sins would return to visit me. Now it seemed the cost was more than I wanted to bear.

"Father Stavros knows?" I whispered, my voice hoarse.

"Of course." Her voice was low, melodic. Georgie made a large circular gesture with her smoking hand, leaving an arabesque contrail in the form of her signature.

My head cleared quickly, as if on cue. The dizziness of the

moment before dissipated, leaving only a dry throat. I succumbed to another bite of the bitter sandwich, another sip of wine.

Auntie Georgie's dress of black silk and violets seemed as formal on her perfect shape as business slacks and jacket would appear on anyone else. She sat with palms flat on the table, like a corporate head finalizing a routine negotiation—all the papers signed, the secretary, Christy, ready to bundle up and whisk them away to a security vault.

"Father Stavros has sharpened you like an axe broad enough to cut down a forest of trees," Georgie said. "Just as he honed many of us before you: Penelope, Yiayia, even Medea. And of course, Christy and me."

"Well, that makes me want to run." I looked around for a way out.

"You don't really want to get away," Christy said as he buttered a scone, his pinky finger pointing up in princely fashion. "You're like a fish on a line swimming toward a boat."

The violets of Georgie's dress lifted themselves off the fabric, nodding their lavender heads on tiny green stems before my eyes.

"Father Stavros has readied you to do extraordinary things," she said.

"To oppose the Athanatoi?" I reached over and stroked one of the velvety, frail violets, now floating above the walnut table, their glassy silhouettes mirrored in the thick layer of beeswax polish.

"Yes," said Georgie. "Their society has grown into a world force that infiltrates governments and finances banks, think tanks and universities, even as it produces murderers. It kills nascent death angels, primarily in their youth, before their powers can protect them. The object being to bring about a universal eternity, a human race that will never die. The Orthodox Church has always been a fierce enemy of this heresy. For almost a hundred years, Father Stavros has been the church's guardian."

"Ha! That's hard to believe." To keep from rolling my eyes, I gathered Georgie's violets, one by one. I tied the bouquet together with the stem of one of the violets. "And what if it's all bullshit?"

As the words popped out of my mouth, unbidden, I felt a tempest of mortal fear spinning within. As if my own Cousin Christy and Auntie Georgie were Gorgons who would swallow me whole.

218

But when I looked up, both were smiling at me, lips twitching, as if about to laugh.

"We know you believe us," said Christy. "It's amusing to see that you simply don't know it yet. It's just the way Father Stavros does things."

"Sharpening the axe…." I sniffed my tiny bouquet of freshly picked flowers. "Hmm."

"Here's a bud vase," Georgie offered, pouring a few drops of water from the pitcher on the table.

"Mom." Christy smiled. "I like that dress better without the violets. It's more elegant that way."

Auntie Georgie nodded. "Perhaps, my love." She moved the bouquet of violets next to the pastry tower, then cleared her throat and bit into a small biscuit. "The heretical leaders of the Athanatoi have created what they call a divine presence." Powdered sugar dusted her lips, and she patted it away. "This so-called divine presence may seem like a hunter or a search party without a body, but it's an entity, nonetheless. This spiritual force can be perceived or felt as darkness, wind, the damp, a smell of sulfur, mildew, or poison. It's heralded by the appearance of large black crows. Have you seen them?"

"I have seen them blood red," I murmured.

"Then tell yourself what you already know."

So many confirming images jumped into my head. I took another sip of port to shut them out, and failed. I had no retort, no new objections to offer.

"The force can be lethal to a new death angel, but doesn't have to be. The nascent angel can use faith and skills and mentors to survive the efforts of the Athanatoi to derail her. Or she can be diverted from her development. The Athanatoi stopped Penelope in a field, where she buried a placenta. They stopped Yiayia Friday in a convent, converting her into a mere harbinger of angels to come. In the convent, her fate might've been much worse than insanity if her guarding Magi, Father Stavros, had not pulled her from the grip of the force."

I frowned. "Yiayia Friday was a little different, sure. But, insane?"

"Of course she was," said Auntie Georgie. "But still, she helps. Just as I do. As did Sheriff Pappas, who helped without quite knowing it."

"Auntie Georgie." I swallowed back new tears. "Please don't mention Guy Pappas." Heat rose into my face, scalding my cheeks. "And so—what's your role?"

"I'm the sensible one," she said firmly. She smiled a little, and winked, hinting that no one else was—present company included.

"Ah. Hmm. So we all have some little role?" I sneered. "Christy? Medea? The man who drives your car?" I snorted. "Oh, yeah! That's right, I forgot. He's no ordinary limo driver. He's Azrafel, the Seraphim. Well, sorry, but it all sounds nuts."

"Yes," said Auntie Georgie. Again the broad, languid gesture with her smoking hand. "It does. But it's true nonetheless. Everyone in our family, even our associates, like Father Stavros. Even the monks you know, and the Mormons at the airport."

"Right. Gotcha." I rolled my eyes. "So what's Medea's purpose?"

"To try to stop you from becoming a death angel of the Lord, of course," said Georgie. Then she bit her lip and looked at Christy. He paid attention only to the scone he was nibbling.

I clenched my hands into fists in my lap. "My mother hates me."

Georgie's eyes grew wide. She leaned forward and grasped my chin in one soft hand, looking into both pupils at once. "Medea loves you. No one asked her to divert you from our business. She does it because she loves you…the same reason she bought you that piano. I've told you before. Each night she cries because you continue to disobey her. She wants you to enjoy a simpler life. To have some fun. She worries that you will soon be lost."

"And so I'm supposed to become a death angel. What does that mean, exactly?"

The room grew so quiet I could hear Christy swallow his mouthful of pastry, in anticipation of Auntie Georgie turning the conversation over to him. He finished and put his hands flat down on the table, just as she had done.

"You're going to live a long and healthy life as long as I have anything to say about it. However, neither your Auntie nor I know what your path is, exactly. Only that you've been chosen as a potential death angel. And that the Athanatoi will destroy you if it can because their suspicions have been aroused."

"By…the photographs?"

"Those have been destroyed. No negatives, no microfilm. But someone obviously saw them first. There are other things, though. You've survived at least five near-death experiences." Christy drummed his broad manicured nails on the table. "But, as of yet, you're merely one of hundreds of suspects across the globe. Who knows? You must understand this very well. There are many unknowns and few certainties—one of which is extremely important."

"Which is?"

"Ultimately only you know where you are going."

"Me?" I said, a chill of sheer cowardice streaking down my spine. "How the heck would I know?"

He looked at me as if it were clear. "Because you have the will to choose."

#　　#　　#

That evening Christy built a fire in the great room at the main crossroads of the cruciform house. Its buttery walls were topped by oversized egg and dart molding. In the fireplace, long-roped iron snakes rode the flat curves of French andirons caught in the act of coiling. Outside, rain splashed the windows. This great room had always been Christy's favorite. He loved the icons from Russia he'd smuggled out of a communist bomb shelter that hung above a thick white mantle of stone beneath a recessed white ceiling crossed by dark, stained beams.

An enormous fully-equipped bar gleamed in the shadows to my left. To the right of the long, moss-green velvet sofa, where I sat alone, five mahogany Victorian bookcases stood elegantly crammed together. Behind their glass doors arcane leather-bound books from dank, dark rare-book stores propped against each other. Christy and Georgie perched in two matching armless leather chairs set halfway between the fireplace's gaping mouth and the sofa.

I stretched my legs out on a coffee table as large as a chapel door. "What did Father Stavros teach me while I was stoned?"

Auntie Georgie chewed the inside of her cheek and looked at me blankly.

"I mean," I said, "when my mind was stretched."

She arched one perfectly-shaped eyebrow, but remained silent.

"I've already discovered a few languages I didn't know before."
I sat on my hands and leaned forward. "You know, like Bulgarian."
I felt the coolness flush out of my cheeks, as the fire warmed me.
"Somehow I've picked up a trick for multiplying large numbers in
my head." I reached for a Queen olive and sucked out the pimento. I
considered putting the hollow green shell back, but changed my mind.

Auntie Georgie smiled, her sunglasses so transparent in the faint
and flickering light that I could almost make out the color of her brown
eyes. "What's the trick, then?"

"Imagine a calculator," I said. "Simple, really."

"What else did Father Stavros teach you?" She took off her
glasses and cleaned them with a hankie. "Yiayia Friday liked to brag
about how she could beat the house at Vegas. She was very fond of
card tricks and Black Jack. But we don't really know what Father
Stavros taught her, only what she discovered."

"You probably won't know what you know until you use it,"
said Christy. "I didn't know my own skills until I used them. Then the
memory of learning came back in a rush. Things came in waves, when
I needed to know."

"That's true of me as well," said Auntie Georgie. "Father Stavros
is very thorough. Yet subtle." Her eyes glowed honey-brown. "Yiayia
Friday learned languages as they were spoken to her and then spoke
them back…like a child learns."

She put her glasses back on and reached for an olive, then
contemplated the pimento. She sucked it out, like me. A family trait,
I guess. "He sharpens you, like a woodsman sharpens an axe," she
went on. "Things you've heard once and forgotten will meet and
make connections. Father Stavros must have something to work with,
probably in our genes."

"You have access to all the knowledge acquired by your
ancestors," chimed in Christy.

"Maybe she does and maybe she doesn't," said Auntie Georgie
turning to my cousin. "It's not yet confirmed."

"I think she does." He pressed his lips together. "Seven
generations of women in our family have opposed the Athanatoi, after
all."

"So we believe," said my aunt.

"Let me refresh you as to your progenitors, Persephone, in chronological order," he said. "First was Theodora, then Hestia. After Hestia, there was Penelope, Yiayia Friday, Medea, and Georgie. Each found their place, but none of them reached the highest level."

"It seemed each of us fell short in some way." Auntie Georgie shrugged. "But maybe it wasn't failure at all. Maybe we all did exactly what we were supposed to do in preparation for you."

This sounded ominous. "How do mean you 'fell short'?"

"Theodora delved into witchcraft, but wouldn't burn or drown, so they hung her. Penelope gave way to grief. Yiayia Friday was too loose a cannon. Medea, too in love with a trivial life to leave it."

I smirked. "You mean she's shallow?"

Georgie frowned at the slight to her sister. "Okay. In some ways, shallow. But still a good person."

"And Hestia?"

"Father Stavros forbade me to tell you about her."

Auntie Georgie was trying to entice me with a secret, I think. She and Christy whispered between themselves. I didn't listen. Of course, I could have. But since they seemed to be tempting me to eavesdrop, I didn't. I did hear a few snippets like "prohibition," and "how important Hestia's history is to Persephone." I turned toward the fireplace and tuned in to the pops and crackles.

The fire spat with steam from damp pine-needle kindling. The enflamed wood was ocher. Blazing bands of fire curved backward deeper into the fireplace, encircling the large central log. My gaze softened to see the figures that appeared between fingers of flame. I studied the shovel, whiskbroom, and poker of Christy's antique brass fire tools. The light leapt between hammered indentations and serpentine coils. Hestia, Hestia, Hestia, the serpents seemed to hiss through gleaming fangs.

I looked at the reflection of the fire in Auntie Georgie's glasses again. "And why aren't you a death angel, Auntie?"

"You know why." She laughed. "I'm far too rational."

"You're right," I said. "I did know that."

"Thank you."

"If you can't talk about Hestia," I said, "tell me about Yiayia. I can still feel her hand yanking my hair."

"Why don't you tell us about Yiayia," said Christy, turning toward the window as if receiving a message from the rain. "You probably know more about her than either of us. Tell us what you see in the fire."

I let a minute or two pass without speaking. Heat grew within my chest as the port spread its drowsy influence throughout my limbs. Yiayia's face materialized out of the blue flickering flames. I remembered the carnival, when she had appeared within the head of a kewpie doll, then in a bottle of poison.

"Okay," I said. "I think she was taken to some monastery or nunnery in Europe to see Father Stavros, but something went wrong… I'm not sure what. Something was corrupt about that place. Maybe it was occupied by the Athanatoi. The sky encircling the belfry wasn't blue and white with clouds. Instead, crows crossed the sky like stones tossed by a catapult."

"That's right," said Christy. "Go on. What else do you see?"

"I don't see anything," I said, blinking. "I'm simply thinking about what might have happened to her. Visualizing it." I felt like The Amazing Kreskin, scamming the yahoos. My intuitions seemed so far-fetched. "Yiayia had a mean streak. She must've been a victim of cruelty." Then I started feeling like a would-be medium, entranced by my own dreaming. "I am guessing someone was cruel to her at the monastery. I've read too many Gothic novels to think otherwise, and know from family talk that she was changed after her visit to Father Stavros. Or rather, by the Athanatoi, who'd lied their way into the monastery."

"I'm glad you know they were involved," Christy said. He looked away again, into the fire steaming with damp pine, nodding.

By peripheral vision, or some other mechanism of my mind, I could see the blazes in Christy's eyes, and feel the heat of the fire itself in his body…in his legs and toes, and on his face. I could feel the pull of his open smile.

He threw his head back in a thunderbolt of laughter.

I let myself go into him like a virus, inhaled, sucked into his lungs.

"Did you hear me?" he said. "Why did you mention the Athanatoi?"

I pulled myself back to full consciousness, as if from sleep, and withdrew from Christy's languid form. I turned my attention back to the monastery.

"Because I believe Yiayia was tortured. Father Stavros wouldn't torture anyone…it's unorthodox."

"We believe that the Athanatoi tortured Yiayia to get information," Auntie Georgie said. "But before she actually had any. So, go on with what you believe."

"I'm just conjecturing."

"Well, go on, anyhow," said Christy. "And keep your soul out of me while you do, or you won't be able to conjecture anything but my adenoids."

"Oh sure —Okay," I mumbled, startled and ashamed. Not really surprised Christy had been aware of my presence in his toes. I had to remember he was an angel. "I'll try to keep my soul out of you, cousin."

"Okay," he said.

Auntie Georgie smiled. "The ability to sense probes from other people is a family trait, too." She flipped a hand in the air as if releasing a dove. "But never mind all that. Tell us about Yiayia."

"Okay." I rubbed my eyes and softened their focus again, half-gazing at the fire, blinking. The smoke burned. I felt ridiculous, like Madame Blavatsky pulling visions out of a fireplace and donating to them various meanings. Still, I continued to play. "I see Yiayia getting out of an old-fashioned car, being greeted at the monastery by three lovely women. One is smiling, another is weeping and wringing her hands. The third, the most beautiful one, has a face of white stone. In a darkened chamber, she instructs Yiayia to strip and put on a black robe."

"Where are they?" Christy asked.

I squinted. "I don't know the country."

"I dunno either. Greece, maybe Bulgaria," Auntie Georgie admitted. "Or Croatia. Maybe Albania."

I squirmed on the sofa and cracked my toes. I pulled the chenille blanket up to my chin and settled into a down pillow. I decided not to resist, but instead to welcome the coming visions, the hazy sense of well-being that suffused my blood, my flesh, my consciousness. I took a deep breath and relaxed as the images rendered themselves before me in the flames, like a *panopticon*.

Chapter 29

Yiayia was weeping. The most beautiful one led her up a long flight of stone steps and down a corridor of crumbling arches that wound underground to the massive iron door of a secret chamber. She dragged the creaking door open, then let it slam shut behind them.

At first Yiayia squinted in the darkness, but then torches flared to life and illuminated the vaulted ceiling above. The stone walls, over a yard thick, would throw shrieks from wall to wall but never allow them to escape. She knew she was trapped.

A trapdoor in the floor housed a deep-water well to drown victims. Another covered a dry pit to store prisoners, like fall potatoes, waiting to be tortured. A third pit collected garbage and shit from distant chambers within the monastery. The three women pointed to each of the pits, but Yiayia refused to look. She stopped weeping and tried calling to her captors without words, imploring them with psychic messages for mercy.

A man in a black mask entered the chamber through a concealed door, bringing with him a scribe in a black robe who carried a large, leather-bound journal and flourished a quill pen made from the central tail feather of a crow.

The three women fell back behind a dusky veil of smoke. They pointed at the iron rings on the wall as if their fingers were swords. Then towards the rack, the wheel, the stocks, the pillory. The most beautiful one lifted an iron cat's paw from the wall and swept it through the air, sneering for a moment with mad cruelty, demonstrating how it could be used to rip human flesh. She put her own head into an iron crusher and with no expression on her stony face, reached up and mimed how its screws could be tightened.

The most beautiful one then showed Yiayia a hanging cage and threatened to put her in it. Tears rolled down Yiayia's hot cheeks, cooling them. The beautiful one explained the heretic's fork, an iron bar with prongs on each end. One set to be placed under a victim's chin, the other wrenched at the base of the throat so the head could be forced down… and there stood a row of stout stakes for burning, a rack, and a wheel… Yiayia felt pale as death as she cried into clenched fists. But the most beautiful one was relentless; showing and explaining.

In the shadows stood a hinged cast-iron case shaped like a bull. A man was already locked inside, his muffled screams barely audible.

"In the morning the bull will be placed in a coal fire," said the beautiful one, faintly smiling. "The man inside will be roasted alive."

Yiayia opened her mouth to protest, but couldn't form words, so great was her fear. She was so young… and the threat so horrible. It seemed unreal, a black storm cloud settling around her. She began to wheeze. Sweat beaded her temples and neck in dewdrops that fell and soaked her robe.

"Where is your Father Stavros now?" The beautiful one wanted to know, her voice sickeningly sweet. "Where does his organization meet? What is your purpose? Why do you know so many languages? What angels have you seen?" The questions were endless. Endless.

Yiayia would have told all, admitted all, but she had no answer to those questions. She had nothing to confess, knew nothing, and remembered nothing…at least not then. Maybe from a distance Father Stavros had washed away her memory like stains on cloth. Or maybe Yiayia had never known anything worth withholding.

Fire and curling smoke, images of torture flashed before my eyes, until a great boom interrupted the crackling of the fireplace, and jerked me back to the present. Out of that dark, bloody room....

Chapter 30

The sound had been a tree falling in the downpour. I blinked and looked at Auntie Georgie. I'd never before seen a look of terror on her face. She had witnessed plenty of creepy events, just being a member of our family. But Auntie Georgie had always seemed to maintain the calm of a jaded superhero.

She looked a little pale now. A pair of windows facing each other flew open. Her lips pressed together. Georgie leapt from her chair and ran to the west window. She held a balled fist to her chest and gazed across the water at the huge bulge of a seagull-covered rocky island blanketed by the coming night. A gust blew in, catching her hair in the breeze, and swept over the furniture, organizing into a dark cloud that threatened rain. A moist, salty wind fed the fire, now leaping wildly. In a few moments the windows slammed shut.

"Mom," Christy said, as the grey cloud hovering over the coffee table divided into black globs which separated into large flapping crows. "Open the window." He ducked as the birds fled outside, banking and soaring, cawing insults.

Auntie Georgie's eyebrows rose as she skated across the wet hardwood in her stocking feet, headed for the fireplace. She grabbed the poker and rolled the heavy top log onto the flame, squelching it.

"Auntie," I said. "No!"

"Sorry to interrupt your little TV drama, honey." Steam plumed towards her body. "But do you expect me to just sit here and watch the house burn down?"

I didn't have an answer for that.

Embers still glowed through the smoke, snapping and popping with moisture.

Christy folded his hands over his flat slab of a stomach and spun his Annapolis class ring around his finger with a thumb. "I think Persephone should try to continue."

"Of course I'm just making all this up." I folded my arms and glared between them. "You both understand that, right?"

"Anomalous cognition is a family specialty." Auntie Georgie pushed her glasses up on her head. "And you just…see it as you make it up?"

"Yes, I do," I admitted. I pulled at the damp, irritating cuffs of my blouse. My wrists were itchy, wet fabric sticking to them. I felt oversensitive, uncomfortable in my own skin.

Christy was watching with a pale soft gaze. "And does that scare you?"

I crossed my legs, then uncrossed them. "Well yes, I confess it does." I dragged the throw off my shoulders and folded it.

"Don't let it. Do you know what fear does to the mind?"

Of all facial expressions, which is the worst to have cast upon you by your guardian? Christy's eyes narrowed. I felt myself shrinking from an upcoming sneer, one that could have masked anger or fear. But I'd never known Christy to be afraid.

"Fear rusts the mind," he said, his lips soft again. "Causes corrosion."

Auntie Georgie coughed into a white napkin. "How true," she gasped, her eyes watery, waving away the lingering smoke.

A hum permeated the otherwise quiet house. The trace of port in the bottom of my glass vibrated with a faint rumbling that drew my attention back to the windows. Rain pounded the glass and pine branches slapped the house as the storm continued, drumming like hoof beats on a sodden road.

I saw him at the window—the golden bull. He pressed his muzzle up to the glass, head down and horns spiking the darkening sky. That same bull from the field behind the Newport Musical—Tavros.

His hoof beats had been replaced by the hammering of my own heart.

Auntie Georgie spun around to look at the fireplace that was snapping again, like a string of Fourth of July poppers. At the sight of her back, the bull thrust one horn at the glass. The window shattered, a glass matador pelted to bits.

I could see each long, flat eyelash, the fierce, crude beauty in his familiar clay-colored eyes. I got up and walked toward him, holding a hand out for him to sniff.

"No!" shouted Auntie Georgie, reaching for my shirt.

"It's okay," I said, sliding out of her grip.

I touched his pleated forehead and pulled a tiny fairy rose from his tangled forelock. He snorted, shook his head, then turned and loped off, taking the storm away with him.

Through all this Christy kept silent, eyes beaming. "That's my girl," he said.

## Chapter 31

I dropped onto the sofa. My mind went blank for at least five straight minutes, while my auntie and cousin waited for logic to pour out of me like syrup. The sweat of the bull had smelled like ammonia and salt. I looked down into my clenched fist at the tiny crushed pink rose.

The storm returned, less fierce, dropping slow, steady rain. The golden bull was miles away by now.

My mind drifted. The wall of icons. The bar in the shadows. The goose neck lamp. It finally settled on a rain-lashed windowpane across the room on which one red dot of light, as if from a laser pointer, meandered across the glass. Leaves behind it swirled in the frozen wind. A red dot, like a laser pointer, outlined the angles and curves of Yiayia's face and traced the rudimentary lines of her stone cell. Then paused, like an etch-a-sketch without knobs, as if awaiting instructions.

"Okay, do your stuff," I whispered to myself, and the red dot quickly sketched out Yiayia's naked body. And then, The Most Beautiful one, on her knees, inserting some strange device into

Yiayia's vagina. I gaped in disbelief. The bulb-shaped object was composed of iron sculpted into tulip petals. As she screwed it open inside Yiayia's body, it shredded her pink flesh. A flood of blood flowed between her legs.

"My God!" I screamed.

Auntie Georgie and Christy were sitting calmly, waiting for me to describe this new vision. I tried three times, but couldn't. Something held back my arms and restrained my tongue with its binding strength—a force that engulfed me in both horror and guilt. For in my vision, I had replaced the most beautiful one. Exactly how or why I'd commutated, I do not know. But now, I was the one crouched at Yiayia's bleeding vagina. Her screams were even louder than my own.

When I opened my eyes again, I was certain I'd slept for hours, for days. But I was still sitting there with Christy and Auntie Georgie by the marble hearth, my legs still stretched out over the huge eucalyptus coffee table, the fire still sputtering and smoking.

"Persephone." Christy tickled the bottom of my bare foot.

"I'm sorry." I blinked several times. "Just thinking. What was the question?"

"I was asking…." He tapped my foot with the toe of his own.

By reflex I jerked back.

"It's a great help," said Christy, "your senses being more acute now. Right?"

My head throbbed. I didn't want to see, hear, smell, or touch anything. I imagined a cave on Gaios where I could sit by myself, just me and turn out my lamp and see nothing. Hear nothing. Flee from this orgy of sights and sounds. I wanted my innocence back. "Maybe Father Stavros has sharpened my axe, or my senses are continuing to sharpen of their own accord. Or I'm experiencing Yiayia's life in pieces through my genes, or I'm psychotic—any of which might or might not be a gift. It feels more like a curse." I tucked a stray clump of hair behind my ear. "Take your pick."

Auntie Georgie walked to the broken window, reached between the edges of shattered glass, pulled in the shutters and locked them. "I like the rain. Cleans things up."

Christy stared at me, his torso tensed as if preparing to leap from his seat. He shook his head. "You're not cursed. No more than

Penelope, or Yiayia, or Medea. You're gifted. You ought to be used to the idea by now. If Father Stavros didn't expect you to transform, he wouldn't be so interested in you."

I squirmed in my seat, stifling a yawn, trying to stay awake.

"I agree with Christy." Auntie Georgie relaxed back into the squeaky leather chair. She took out a menthol cigarette, tapped the filtered end on the table, and put it in her mouth without lighting it. "We all knew you were gifted, not cursed, from the moment of your birth…that's why Christy must protect you, even at the cost of his own life."

The rain threw itself back against the house in small shining daggers. Christy walked to the broken window, bare feet trailing sparks across the beige Kurk wool carpet. Nests of sleeping owls had been woven into it by nomads. "It's what I was born to do," he said.

Flashes of lightning practiced tremolo bursts and filled the sky and stabbed into the room through the slats in the shutters. I flinched, almost shouted. Christy turned back toward us, a ghost made of light. Just then the tip of Auntie Georgie's cigarette glowed red. A rivulet of smoke spiraled from it toward the ceiling.

They both began to laugh.

Tears of mirth brimmed in Christy's eyes. Auntie Georgie smiled and looked at the tip of her lighted cigarette, then held it up so he could see.

"Thanks for the light," she said. "But I don't really need it. I'm trying to cut back." She went to the fireplace and tossed the cigarette in.

"What the hell do you think is so funny?" The muscles in my forehead ached. "A bolt of electricity nearly striking one of us is not a joke."

Christy's skin glowed as if he'd been dipped in gold dust. His eyes changed from deep-ocean to powder blue.

"And what's with the glow?" I snapped. "You look like a lightning bug." I shook my head and sighed. "See, what just happened meant something, but I don't know what. And both of you are trivializing it." I felt tears rising and collected them up for later shedding.

"Relax," said Christy, his skin fading back to only a hint of shimmer. "You dumped your fear into the sky, and it threw back light. What's so strange about that?"

I gaped at him. "I didn't dump anything."

"*Au contraire, mon amie,*" said Auntie Georgie. "Accept yourself. You have power."

Christy sat next to me on the sofa and enveloped me in his arms like enfolding wings. I felt the warmth of his skin through my shirt, and leaned into him.

"You have power to help the dying." He hugged me and patted my back. "You have a choice to make. The Orthodox Church needs you. The Athanatoi are heretics and murderers, well-meaning or not."

The words "Athanatoi" and "Orthodox Church" set off such anger in me the room turned a misty red. New blades of fire grew out to the smoldering fireplace, streaking from the logs and darting out beyond the andirons like lunatic tongues.

I looked at the shelves of flame piled in a stack that grew out of dormant embers. A new vision emerged out of the blaze between the rolling flames, as clear as a movie on a screen. Heat and smoke assaulted my eyes, causing them to store tears that escaped down my cheeks in tiny wet bundles.

"Yiayia was strung up on a strappado next," I said. "A heavy weight tied to her feet, her hands bound behind. Then the strappado was sprung and a rope tied to her hands jerked her six feet off the floor. There she dangled, arms yanked out of their sockets, while a man in a black mask whipped her naked body with thick leather straps. At a nearby table, a scribe with a crow-quill pen and open journal before him waited for disclosures that would never come, could never come."

"Yes, exactly," said Auntie Georgie, nodding. "Go on."

I swallowed the sickness gathering in my throat. "And then, in an instant, the scribe at the table fell over dead. The man in the black mask fell dead. And Father Stavros strode across the room to cut Yiayia down…to gently restore her arms to their sockets, to bathe her body, dress her warmly, and carry her from that haunted place."

My aunt and cousin nodded in rhythm like teenagers at a rock concert.

I shook my head to throw off the heaviness that had settled in my brain. "It doesn't matter," I said, sliding my legs from the coffee table. I felt far from defeated by them—by any of it. "I do not accept the role intended for me. I don't want to play. No, I think I'll go to college, then to medical school. I don't want knowledge to come leaking into me from my genes, or from the lives of others, or from some cracks in the curved universe. Or even from Yiayia. I want my own life."

"You'll have a total of seven," said Christy. "But Azrafel told me that you cannot escape your duty. You must obey. One way or another, accept what you're meant to be—or become something smaller. Strive for it or shrink from it, try to obtain it or fail. That's all."

"I think I'm a smoker, so I'd like a cigarette," I said. My nose stung. My fingers looked blue with cold, in spite of the fire.

Georgie and Christy locked eyes, then smiled at one another. They were so calm—so infuriating.

I covered my face and massaged my cramping forehead, tried to relax the contraction in my locked throat until I was finally able to swallow spit again. I counted to seven, then opened my eyes and turned them, unfocused, on the icon of Saint George above the mantle. "Anyhow, I don't know what you mean."

"We don't know either." Auntie Georgie's voice was firm and steady, closing the argument like an accountant closing her books.

I slumped back down on the sofa, momentarily giving up.

I'm not sure how long it all took, but I remembered later that no one said anything for at least a half hour. We sat in comfortable silence, and it was the first time I'd ever felt at peace with dead air time. Usually, I would feel compelled to say something sarcastic or shocking to fill the empty space. But this time I just sat there, perfectly content.

The hall clock finally chimed seven times and the red mist from the fireplace evaporated. I cracked a smile that brought nods from Christy and Aunt Georgie.

"Okay," he said, as if nothing at all had happened. "We'd better head off for bed. A lot to learn tomorrow."

"I'm sure you're right, cousin." I stood and stretched, kissed them both, and headed for bed.

Chapter 32

My floating bed in the quiet back room of Christy's house was supported by opposing magnetic slabs, one within the underside of the bed, the other bolted onto the floor. Draped with crisp white goose down comforters, it was a fluffy cumulus cloud suspended in the air. Reputedly the finest sleeping surface in the world. But still, I couldn't doze off.

The number seven formed and re-formed, cascading through my every thought, jumbling warring images of Christy's furniture, which featured an antique walnut Biedermeier armoire and childish Disney-character porcelain lamps he'd bought me for various holidays over the years. He had the house rigged so all the lights turned on and off by verbal instruction. I said nothing. I liked the look of the room with all my bedside princesses burning.

The "seven" principle glued my eyes open and kept my attention away from Christy's extravagance and humor. I got up from the levitating bed, and roamed to the sumptuous mosaic bathroom and back into my fluffy nest.

I counted all my past brushes with death: a rushing car was the first death at age four. My escape with Calliope from the golden bull was the second—I could still hear his bellowing, feel his fetid breath scorch my neck, and see again the wildness of his eyes, the sharpness of his horns, the thick trunk of his neck, his beautiful eyes and lashes. Number three was my tumble from my ingrate of a horse when he spied the star mare in the forest. I thought quickly thereafter of the night at the fair, when Yiayia had yanked my hair and thrown me off the Ferris wheel. Then, the explosion in the cigar store. And finally, the motorcycle bomb that had taken Guy Pappas, the only passionate love I'd ever known.

That made six. Five lives gone, already.

After a quick shower, I stepped out over the stone threshold onto the heated slate floor, wrote a huge number six in the fogged-over mirror above the sink and stared at it. The top loop dripped from its center, dividing my face in half.

One probable death for every three years of my life, I thought. At this rate, I'd be gone for good at twenty-one. Though how did I know I hadn't been killed already, five times over, and then arisen to live again each time?

On the other hand, the seven lives principle could apply to both my own existence and the six lives of my progenitors: Theodora, Hestia, Penelope, Yiayia Friday, Medea, and Auntie Georgie. Only Medea and Auntie Georgie weren't dead—and Georgie wasn't a direct ancestor.

To my foremother Theodora, the witch who'd died by hanging after refusing to burn and failing to sink, I attributed my ability to detect the scents of the earth, the faint fragrance of a dogwood sapling, and my youthful attempt to use magic with the fertile gift I'd given Ms. Block and Ms. Wick—which, I knew, had produced twins.

I brushed and rebrushed my teeth, minty foam pouring out of my mouth in whipped dollops of cream. No such thing as teeth that were too clean. Tears of laughter squeezed from my eyes at the thought of Ms. Wick and Ms. Block pushing a double stroller stuffed with twins clad in once-white onesies stained with applesauce. But then, the next image—of the same babies smearing zwieback drool on the couple's matching pastel suits and pill box hats—made me sob hysterically.

To Penelope I attributed a natural respect for sanctity and my capacity for feeling grief, which had been masked by the callowness of my years, at least until Guy's death. To Hestia I attributed nothing at all for sure, but guessed my lust for Sheriff Pappas had sprung from an unnatural source, so paramount it had become. And only cut short by murder, by a bomb that had been meant for me. And Medea? I shut my eyes tight and tried to imagine myself still playing the piano in her black box theatre, but couldn't. And I had vehemently, just two hours before, rejected any possible role in my church's fight against the Athanatoi. My rejection of these talents, or gifts, apparently, did more to confirm I had inherited them than did all my attempts to deny it.

I stared at my reflection and watched the comb slide through my wet hair. The bottom of the six I had written in the condensation on the mirror dripped like blood. Still, I cringed at the thought of taking anyone's life. Killing Athanatoi? Or even helping Christy hunt them down—the very idea sickened my stomach. I rushed for the bedroom and sleep. On the way, I told myself, "All these thoughts are nonsense, anyhow." My logic fell to pieces when I considered I did not share Auntie Georgie's common sense.

"Oh God," I said, asking for help.

The floating bed was waiting for me, suspended two-and-a-half feet above the floor. My legs felt heavy as I heaved myself up over the edge. The levitating mattress, glowing from the Snow White and Sleeping Beauty lamps at my bedside, seemed a strange island waiting in the semi-dark. An animated magic carpet. It hovered, ready to fly out the bedroom window to find its commanding genie. On the bureau next to the bed sat a Cinderella lamp, her mouse-drawn carriage frozen in moonlight.

But if I didn't have some element of Auntie Georgie in me, why was I up all night making lists of things like runaway cars, charging bulls, Ferris wheels, and explosions, and comparing myself to a roster of relatives—if not to find out all details Christy had to impart so I could make a final decision regarding things I already felt certain about? And why had I already made up my mind to go with Christy in the morning to see the new corpse he would undoubtedly show me?

I decided to get out of bed and write in my journal.

238

"Fire on," I commanded. Flames sprang to roaring life in the fireplace across the room. I found myself half-hoping Yiayia's face would be flickering there, and half-dreading the grand entrance of her frantic, sorrowing eyes. Would she talk to me? Tell me she was all right? In heaven, or suspended in an astral plane? Between one world and the other, like my bed?

I settled back in a leather chair, writing, growing warm in my light cotton bathrobe and rosy flannel nightgown. Theodora would've been muttering strange incantations and dancing naked in the firelight.

I closed my book and stuffed it between the cushion and an arm of the chair. Instead of sophisticated spells, I'd used simple materials like soured goats' milk and raspings of horses' hooves mixed with paste of horn to repel burglars at the Country Inn. But the thugs had still found my parents at the bank's night deposit vault. So was my inexperience at fault, or my ingredients?

Outside, rain flew at the house in an unexpected gust. Drops hard as stones pelted my window.

"Abracadabra," I muttered, ashamed of my childish simplicity. The rain paused, and did not resume until the nimbus cloud blew to a stand of huge juniper trees for a quiet drenching on the opposite side of Christy's house.

I was too far away from his hall clock to hear it, but imagined it chiming three times.

Unbidden, the golden bull of the pasture charged into my mind. The black horse with the star on her forehead loomed close enough to fog the window with a single derisive snort.

"Beware the golden bull and the horse with the star," Medea had warned. A streak of cold sweat ran from my neck to my spine and I reached behind my shoulder to pat it dry with my cotton robe. "Auntie Georgie," I cried.

But it was Yiayia in the room. I could smell her dank, olive-oily hair and old flesh, her skin saturated with lavendar. I sucked in my breath as fast as I could and held it, slamming shut the windows and door deep into their casings.

"Leave me alone, Yiayia," I muttered. "I did not call you from the dead."

The rain rustled leaves in the dark wood. The wind swept the blades of grass below. Water gurgled in the gutters. I restrained myself from calling out for Auntie Georgie again. As proof of her existence, Yiayia had smeared globs and tentacles of ectoplasm under my bed. She shook the floor. I wasn't very enthusiastic about her gift of cryptaesthetic goo which spread in puddles all over my room. But my neck cramped, so at last I slid out of the armless slipper chair and walked like a cat burglar toward the door, pausing before stepping over each gleaming strand of glop before descending with the lightness of a moth. The fire sputtered. Ringlets of arsenical smoke spiraled and blew up the chimney. An orange glow filled the room, then sank and carpeted the floor. I held my breath, trying to block out the rest of Yiayia.

The door wouldn't open. I had locked myself in.

A rusty mist slipped through the space under the door, and through the keyhole. Orange light lapped at the hem of my nightgown. I was unable to let my breath out, even when my brain commanded my lungs to let go. I pounded the door. Finally, I gasped and released it, but still the door wouldn't open. Pools of ectoplasm continued to expand—another present from the land of the dead. I was much too tired for all this weirdness.

A hard rain again battered the window. I imagined both Christy and Auntie Georgie lying in their beds, likewise warm, but sleeping, and felt foolish for my fears.

The door should've opened. I plunked down into the leather chair again and vowed to spend the night there, rather than in a comfy bed that was like sleeping with Prince Valium. I couldn't afford to be comatose.

Too late, I smelled the lavendar again—coming up behind me. Yiayia's spirit grabbed my wrists and jerked them over my head. I felt myself being lifted up, up toward the ceiling.

"No, Yiayia. Please don't," I said. "Please. I already understand your pain!"

But she was relentless. I heard the grinding and clanking of a strappado.

Then, she dropped me.

The floating bed caught me like the outstretched wings of an angel. Oiled Medusa locks grazed my neck as she kissed my shoulders, each small caress a dull narcotic that numbed my torn, burning arms.

"For only a moment you were strung up," she said, her blinking violet eyes lined with black kohl.

"You didn't have to hurt me to make me understand, Yiayia," I said, mesmerized by the translucency of her hands, her long gnarled fingers.

She stroked my neck; her breath felt cool on it. The stinging in my shoulder blades fell away like a silk shroud crumpling to the floor.

"The earth and sky of suffering is doubt," she said. "Now do you believe?"

"*Pistevo*," I whispered. Now, I believe.

Chapter 33

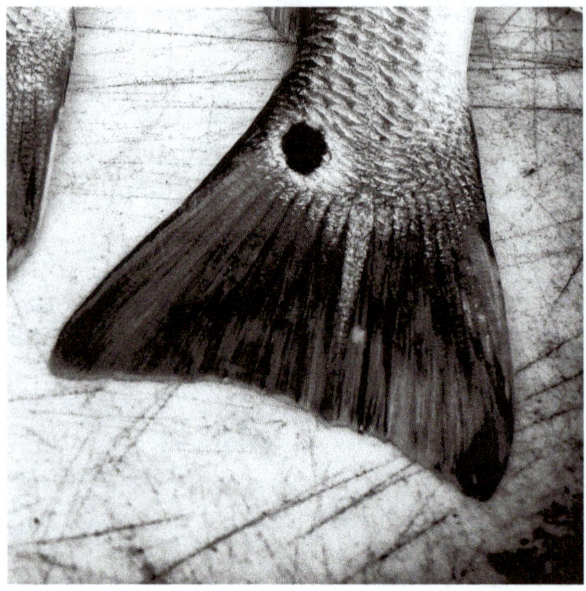

Christy gripped the leather steering wheel cover of one of his fleet of blood-orange Corvettes while I slumped in my seat, belted in, doomed to ride along. I dug into the book bag at my feet, and pulled out Robbins' *Textbook of Pathology* to look at the pretty pictures of skin biopsies in dyed hematoxylin pinks and eosin blues. We swerved through eucalyptus woods that lined the coast road to old downtown Monterrey. I dropped my book. It flipped open to the chapter on autopsy technique, the section on the disappearing non-forensic medical autopsy. I read that most autopsies of today are for medicolegal reasons, not for academic study. Ugh. I slammed it closed.

My stomach turned further when my thoughts rushed to imagine the sort of room to which Christy was probably taking me. When we reached The Devils Bend, the road looped to follow the crescent of Monterrey Bay. There, filigrees of tiny waves were ten-thousand feathers trimming a Komodo dragon's nest lined with trees and buildings, bridges and parking meters. The leaves of oaks hung still on their branches. I sunk into the neoprene-covered bucket seat, imagining a submarine's interior, thumbing through a flyer for a ghost tour of the old city.

Old Monterrey, former capitol of Mexican California, was the center of fiestas and balls, the glamour of dashing Spanish horseman, and the throb of guitars played by romantic suitors. It was also a town of intrigue with histories of lives full of lost treasures, found romance, and amazing adventures. Visit the sites of the Ghost in the Garden, ancient burial grounds, hauntings, hangings and frequent ghostly sightings.

"Hmph," I said. "Sounds like everyday life to me."

Christy patted my knee.

As we passed the San Carlos Cathedral, the winds became hellhounds crashing through underbrush without warning. Over the rectory, lights blinked with swarms of mosquitoes assaulting bug zappers. The air's decaying, clammy fingers reached through the spaces between the window casings of the Corvette and found their way under my shirt, caressing my nipples in the creepiest way ever. Then the fingers let go, pulled back out of the car and disappeared as we drove on.

"Weird," said Christy, crossing himself three times right over left.

"Did you kill those men?" I asked.

Christy glanced over at me, eyes narrowed. "Which men?" His fingertip glided over a fading pink whip mark Yiayia had left where my neck and shoulders connect, where she had flogged me with a birch.

"The men who kidnapped my mother and father." I yanked up my collar to cover the welt. I was used to Christy telling half-stories, just to tantalize and make me beg to hear the rest.

"Of course I did." He pushed his Serengeti shades up his nose. "They weren't Athanatoi assassins. But they were hired by Athanatoi. They stuffed your parents in the trunk of the T-bird. I killed both men, then opened the trunk and called the police."

"And disappeared."

"Yes," he said. "Well, I called an ambulance first. Medea and Angelo were unconscious. They had no idea I'd ever been there, and I wasn't about to tell the police."

"So who knows now?"

"Everyone in the family. Pappas too."

We stopped for a red light. A handsome middle-aged lady in a powder-blue pill hat pushed a baby carriage thorough the pedestrian crosswalk.

"Please don't mention Guy Pappas," I said, squarely facing him so he could see my eyes. We sat there, the car humming, looking at ourselves reflected in each other's pupils. I finally relented to curiosity. "What happened to the bodies of the men?"

"Their organs were donated to science for transplants," Christy said, his laughter thick and self-righteous.

"The butcher bird pads its nest with the bloody feathers of its prey," I said, rolling up my gum wrapper and pitching it at him. "The O'Malleys."

"I won't pretend not to know what you're talking about," Christy said, still laughing.

"Yiayia Friday's ghost came into my bedroom last night. She hoisted me on a strappado, but dropped me as soon as I was up. Then she whipped me once with leather strips and once with a switch of birch."

Christy took his eyes off the road to look at me. He was good at driving by feel.

The muscles in his forehead tightened until his face crumpled like a sheet of paper.

"I'm sorry," he said. "But only Father Stavros could've stopped her. She must've wanted to give you a taste of her suffering. Probably trying to show you something in her own very concrete way. Are you otherwise marked?"

"Only my neck. Only one second, but it lasted forever."

"Not much to do about it now," said Christy, elbows braced as the Corvette hugged the curb. "I'd like to help you relax, maybe take you to a hot springs. But I must do as instructed. Today. Right now."

"It's all right." I leaned back on the headrest. "I recovered from last night. After Yiayia left, my axe was sharpened."

Christy smacked down on the steering wheel and sped up to pass a semi with a silhouette of an Arabian horse in its back window, one side of its rump lifted as if it were lame.

"So, did you learn something from Yiayia?" He pulled in front of the semi and slowed down.

I rolled down the window. "I've had to accept the family knowledge. It's part of who I am. But I still don't want to be an angel of death."

He slowed down. Together we breathed the cool, moist bay air and the light aroma of fresh fried Portuguese sardines wafting from The Cannery. I had a momentary fancy for hot-buttered rum and creamy clam chowder as we passed the restaurants hugging the bay.

Christy glanced over at me through wire-rimmed Serengeti shades. "You're not ready to make that decision yet."

"There's been no progress toward my accepting anything, mortal or not." I leaned away, arms folded. "There never has been, and won't be, ever."

"Fine," he said, "Ah, here's our destination, just ahead."

"Fine?" I hate the word. "Christy, you say fine when you mean 'up yours'."

He stopped in front of a hotel that stood like a monolith on the sandy beach. Beyond it, sailboats were white kittens springing on draughts of light air, chasing one another's tails across the ruffling water. A boom box blared reggae for young men playing volleyball as young women watched, buttered in cocoa, adorning the sand on their blue and white striped towels.

Christy handed over car keys to the valet, who disappeared with the car into the parking garage, leaving us in front of the massive glass entrance of the lobby. The revolving doors spun, burdened with tourists in funny hats, necks strapped with cameras. In the lounge a waiter in a floral shirt and white pants and shoes offered chocolate and anise pizzelles piled high on a pewter platter. Girls in summer dresses carried plates of shrimp stuffed in edible rice paper, dusted with coconut shreds, and stabbed with toothpicks, all lined up like neat rows of coffins. The Tommy Bahama Room was crowded with figures in Hawaiian shirts and pastel coats and ties. The place was full of palm fronds and frozen drinks turned into peacocks by little umbrellas.

The Bamboo Bar was almost deserted. Christy and I found a quiet table in a corner under a banana tree away from the elevators and other customers. We lunched on fortified wine and wasabi peas. A lone patron at the bar had opened his wallet and was showing photographs to the idle bartender, who nodded, bored but feigning interest.

"I'd really like some shrimp," I said, drooling. "Can't you flag one of those girls over?"

A blonde waitress flashed a coral lipstick smile from across the dining room—first at Christy, then at me. She came over to our hidden table, carrying a pewter tray with the shrimp in their shrouds huddled together.

"Can I tempt you with an appetizer?" she said to Christy, grinning, her head cocked to one side.

"Oh, delicious," I said. "Thank you so much."

The waitress left the platter there on the table, smiled at me vaguely, and walked away.

I dug into my first succulent prawn, amazed at our incredible score. "How delicious."

"The bar is always empty at the end of the week. They're having their Friday Afternoon Club in the Tommy Bahama Room."

"Why did you bring me here?"

"I had to." He stabbed a shrimp with a toothpick. "And I think you know why."

My head sagged on my neck and an electric bolt shot down my spine. I tried to tune in to the chatter from the lobby instead of Christy's words.

"I'd rather listen to the pickup lines coming from the bar than to you right now." My fingers grew purplish and cold. "If you've killed someone else, tell me."

I stared at him, anger and sadness welling up in my heart.

He looked down at his plate, paused, then looked up again, as if mesmerized by the acrylic still-life of a pineapple on the wall behind my head.

I looked out the window at the beach, trying not to think about what he would say next. Christy continued to study the pineapple, squinting as if trying to make out the artist's signature.

God, it was a horrible painting. The colors were too pale, as if all the juice had been squeezed from the fruit. And the warped perspective was all wrong—distorted. The dead pineapple was sliced open and laid out on a dull platter that looked like a cheap, giant paper plate.

He laughed under his breath. But when he looked back at me his eyes were sad and apologetic. I put my hand over my face and shook my head. "Oh, Christy."

He took a drink of water. The ice cubes clinked against his teeth.

I dropped my hand and made the sign of the cross.

His face was still, neutral. "I had to do it, you know."

I said nothing. The room took a half-swirl and I stopped it by holding my breath, an exercise of will.

"I killed two men this afternoon and mortally wounded one," he said at last. "It required almost no preparation, just inspiration."

"Inspiration!" I said. "Well, that's just sick!" Another display of my angelic cousin's brutality and had no value to me whatsoever. I was sure of that.

"A death angel has to live with brutality," he said.

With great effort I held my voice down. "I'm not going to be a death angel," I whispered, through clenched teeth.

"This morning I had espresso at the wharf and saw a large sea bass displayed on a bed of ice. It was worth every penny."

"A sea bass…a frozen fish?" I rolled my eyes, folded my arms, and crossed one leg over the other.

"No, not frozen." Christy shook his head. "Fresh. Just iced. So I bought it."

I drummed my fingers on the table. "Why?"

"I had it wrapped up in newspaper and then took the elevator up to the Fourteenth floor."

By then my leg was vibrating, the table shaking.

"Why?" I said, leg still twitching with the kind of nervous tick kids at school find very annoying, like when you're trying to take an exam and your neighbor can't stop beating his leg up and down. I wanted to kick something.

"You already know why," he said.

"But I don't know." I chewed the inside of my lip. The table leg was in the way, so I kicked it.

"You're in denial. You do know."

"So, then drop it," I said, twirling a toothpick between my fingers. "If I don't know, then tell me. Quit talking in riddles."

"Fine."

"So up mine again, I guess." I folded my hands on the table in front of me so I wouldn't grab something and throw it at him.

"I knocked on the door of 14C." Christy put his elbows on the table and leaned in toward me. "And when a goombah answered, I represented myself as the hotel manager with a gift I'd like to have prepared for him in the hotel kitchen, because he was a V.I.P."

"The sea bass," I said.

"Yes. Then, I unwrapped the fish and showed it to him. He was, of course, delighted. The bass was enormous, with scales that shone like silver."

"You killed him with a frozen fish?" I felt suddenly itchy all over and scratched my elbows. "With the scales still on. Nice."

"He frowned. "I told you. It wasn't frozen. Only iced, plump, and promising to be delicious. The guy smiled, thumped the fish, and called out to his friends, both of whom emerged from different rooms to the suite with their jackets buttoned, the better to conceal their shoulder holsters."

"Did you kill him then?" I folded and refolded my white napkin.

"Well…" He took a deep breath and exhaled out of pursed lips.

A fruit fly hovered over his half-empty wine goblet. He covered the glass with one hand without looking away from me.

I decided I might as well listen. I plucked a flower from the vase and spun the stem between my fingers.

"One was grotesquely fat, the other cadaverously thin…like the Honeymooners."

"Who?"

"Forget it. It's beside the point. The three were Athanatoi, not ordinary gangsters. Maybe businessmen, sure—but still. I laughed when I picked up the fish by the tail and slapped the goombah with it across the chest. He flew backwards and landed in a chair. In fact, the other two were still laughing a second later, as if it were all a big joke, when I pulled out my silenced 1895 Nagant revolver and shot each in the head. When I left the room, the guy who answered the door was splayed over the chair, holding his chest and dying."

"And he's dying still?" I whispered, feeling sick all over.

"Yes, he is," said Christy. "By slapping him with the fish, I compressed his sternum enough to contuse his heart. Death takes hours."

"You're saving him for me?" I put my head in my hands. "Oh

my God."

Christy looked at his watch.

"He'll have about two more hours. Then, he'll die in one of three ways, either by leaking blood, cardiac arrhythmia, or cardiac tamponade. His vena cava is nicked within his pericardial sack, which is causing the sack to fill up with blood. Eventually, the pressure inside the pericardium will become so high the heart won't be able to fill again. He'll die from shock."

"Did you give him any anesthesia?" I spoke between clenched teeth. "At least—"

"Oh, I plan to give him anesthesia," Christy said, nodding. "That would be you."

Chapter 34

Except for the three prone bodies and blood pooling on the sealed cork tiles, room 14C appeared undisturbed. Christy closed the door behind us. Air-conditioning ducts tugged at the hems of the sheer curtains as if to mock the dying man's sluggish attempts to breathe. He lay draped over a chair, stuporous, looking up at the ceiling in amazement.

Otherwise, there was no movement or evidence of turmoil. The pastel abstract paintings on the wall, only faintly whispering of the wind and waters of Monterrey Bay, watched silently over the polished glass-covered rattan tabletops and overstuffed tropical print sofas and chairs. A hammered copper chandelier with amber shades hung suspended from a medallion surrounded by arabesques of plaster.

The tall thin man lay face down, brains dripping from a gaping exit wound. The short, fat man was crumpled beside him. Great gouts of blood and gobbets of brain had exploded out of his pierced skull and extended like a grisly oriental rug toward the suite's faux marble fireplace.

"Does this seem familiar to you?" Christy said, one hand rubbing my neck.

"Yes," I said slowly as if I'd been hypnotized. "I saw it when you described it earlier. You know that." My instinct was to shrink back. Instead, in my nervousness, I caressed the upholstery of a high-back chair. "So why bring me here?"

"As you know, I was told to do it." His voice was louder than it needed to be, his face pinked with blood.

"I'm sorry," I said.

"You're supposed to sense why you're here. And what to do. Haven't you figured that out?"

"I don't know," I said, quite honestly. But then I found an idea hidden in the light of thought. He was right. I was supposed to know. I did know. "I, um… need a few minutes."

I sat down on the floor between the two men who'd been shot. Both men wore the familiar tattoo behind their left ear. Both were Athanatoi.

I turned my back to the man draped across the chair near the door. I spun around at the gasp of his breath escaping. There was no ignoring him. His hands flopped open across the arms of the chair. His heart assumed the muffled beat of a dying seal on a spongy floe.

Tears burned my eyes but I held them captive in the jail of my eyelids. Just as I had floated into Christy to feel the warmth in his toes, my spirit flowed into the dying man's chest. I could feel the torn vena cava and his blood leaking into his pericardial sack, spurt by spurt, the pressure around his heart rising.

"What's the history of this man?" I asked Christy.

"He's a professional killer for the Athanatoi, but also a true believer," Christy said. "With no family. He's more or less sane and totally disciplined, the perfect assassin, despite his gangster's appearance and police record. From time to time, he let himself be nabbed for petty crimes. He was difficult to uncover."

I slipped into him via one of his infrequent stridorous gasps. I shot though the tunnels of apoptotic blood and lymphatic vessels.

"We were raised in a church orphanage," we said. The weak voice rattled with pooling blood and sputum—it was difficult for us to vocalize above a whisper. "Then we were selected and trained by the Athanatoi."

"Thought so," Christy said.

"Our intentions are good," we muttered from deep within the man's chest.

Then, with his next labored exhalation, I flew out of him.

"He still believes that he can end all dying by killing death itself." I wiped my forehead with the back of one hand, relieved to be back in my own body.

Christy shrugged. "All the intentions of the Athanatoi are good. That's the way it is, even with the worst of heresies—this one being one of the worst."

I got up from the floor and walked over to the dying man as Christy watched from a chair in the foyer. "Go ahead and touch him," he said.

I knelt and watched the man's convulsing chest rise and slightly fall. Unlike the two corpses, who were wearing expensive Brooks Brothers seersucker suits, gold Rolexes, and silk Italian ties, he wore a cheap grey-striped suit, a Timex and a clip-on tie decorated with flying ducks. I felt something like compassion. The Athanatoi paid well. He must've been tithing heavily somewhere.

The tissue under his ragged nails almost glowed cyanotic. Bloody saliva sputtered from his nose and mouth, his untrimmed brows catching droplets of mucous. His crooked teeth were yellowed, his shave uneven. I knew there were no family pictures in his wallet, no sheaf of high-limit credit cards. I didn't need to look.

"Are you in pain?"

"Help me," he gasped, unable to turn his head and see who was speaking.

I put a hand on his heart and felt the rhythmic flushing of his blood into his pericardium.

"You will die before death does," I whispered back, feeling a deep pain in my heart and a swelling in my chest that cut my own breathing short. "But I will bless your soul. Be comforted." I breathed the words into his ear. "You would not have sought me if you had not already found me."

I bowed my head and prayed for heaven to open. "Lord now lettest Thou Thy servant depart in peace, according to Thy word. For mine eyes have seen Thy salvation which Thou has prepared before the face of all people."

"He's in great pain and longs to die," Christy interrupted. "You should really let him go now."

"I'm trying," I said. "I don't know how, exactly."

"Yes, you do," said my cousin. "You've known all along."

I pushed gently down on his chest with my hand and the dying man's heart was stilled. In my other hand I felt a tiny spurtling of warmth. A lighted candleless wick, smoking. I closed my fist and felt heat surge through me, and then out every pore at the speed of light, filling my soul. The energy of a thousand windmills contained in that one small fire swarmed the room for an instant, fasciculating, then flew in a gust out through the ceiling.

Chapter 35

I was briefly taken aback when Auntie Georgie asked me to recount, detail by detail, the events of the day. It occurred to me that from that time onward there would be a gulf between us, even a gulf between Christy and me. I didn't have the capacity to fill the gaps between fragments of my memory of my time with Father Stavros at the Monastery of Saint John the Theologian. I held a submerged secret that kept trying to float up, but perhaps was so strange that some part of me kept it buried. The poached salmon and braised artichokes Auntie Georgie served on a steaming bed of lemon pilaf would've been comforting. But a quiet breeze had set spruce branches tapping against the dining room window like the fingers of an unfriendly Genie.

"I will never do anything like that again," I said.

The statement hung in the air, unaddressed for a moment.

"No one will ask you to," Christy said at last. Auntie Georgie raised an eyebrow.

I was still frightened by the whole thing: the deaths, the blood, the room, a theatre of mourning and the prolonged misery of that deeply flawed yet well-meaning man. "What if we're caught? The police have ways of…."

"Our Mormons are very efficient at clean-up. So is the waiter in the bar, the staff, and the hotelier. The only ones who'll ever realize what happened are the Athanatoi. They don't need evidence to know."

It seemed the whole of Monterrey was involved in Christy's business.

"Will the Athanatoi strike back?" I could feel my heart boxing my ribcage.

"Only if they can find us," said Christy. "They'll worry that you'll soon be part of the death angel saga if you're not stopped."

"They'll correctly interpret what happened today," Georgie said. "And suspect the cause was you." She squeezed the last bit of lemon on a salmon sliver, savored the final bite, and set her fork on her plate. "Tomorrow, you'll be somebody else and live in a different place. Your appearance will be slightly altered. You'll have a new birth certificate, faked degrees from high school and Peter's Rock Early College, and the door key to a room in a boarding house near a medical school."

"You can pass for a twenty year-old," said Christy, "but we need to get rid of that grey streak. It's gotten wider. Too easy to identify. My mother will buy a new wardrobe for you. And I'll be there—in the background. You'll begin a new life, one you may or may not enjoy—depending on your choices, as Father Stavros would say."

My heart was tired from throbbing, exhausted. I felt scared, but also excited, craving adventure. Yet angry at the audacity of my beloved auntie and cousin, who were supposed to be guiding me. "What? But I'm not prepared for medical school."

"Yes, you are," said Auntie Georgie, cutting a piece of Boston cream pie and handing me a spoon. "Your education has been excellent, considering your special tutors and your preparation by Father Stavros. Just as you've already acclimated to the traumas of today, you'll adjust nicely to advanced schooling. You'll absorb the whole texts of books and contents of lectures as if waking up to what you already know."

"But I don't want to," I said, pacing. I thought I might play along with them, then call Medea and have her come take me home. She might send me to an all-girls' school in Switzerland. Or to a finishing school for girls of noble birth. But did I want that either?

"I'm sorry," said my aunt. "But your natural abilities, once awakened, cannot be put back to sleep, except by injury or death. You can make all the usual choices, but cannot choose to unlearn. Not even Father Stavros can fundamentally alter the natural workings of your brain."

"I can choose to be my mother." I was pacing faster, talking louder now.

"You've already passed that possibility by," said Auntie Georgie. "Eat your pie."

"I'm not hungry." I crossed my arms, my fists buried at my sides.

Georgie was silent for a moment. "Fine," she said, shrugging. "Let's go look at the shrine. There's something to learn there."

They led me into the great hall that served as a foyer. Again, my eyes took in the icon of Agia Katarina, the patron saint of the Monastery of the Holy Myrrh bearers and the gold leaf icon of the Byzantine "Tender Mercy," Christos kai Maria. Agios Giorgos, Agia Paraskevi, and Agios Kostas were still waiting above the long lacewood table where burnt-out wicks floated in cups of gold and the daguerreotype of the black-eyed Penelope retained its prescience of impending death.

The hall was almost the same. This time the absence of images of Medea, Yiayia, Theodora, Auntie Georgie and Hestia ruffled my consciousness. As did the absence of any image of myself—as if I had never lived, or loved, or feared, or fretted, as I was doing now.

"What's the matter, Persephone—have you seen a ghost?" said Georgie. She stepped up to the iconostasis and crossed herself three times right over left, head bowed.

"No. Not yet. Not today, anyway. Not a ghost, exactly. Why are we here? What have you done with the rest of our family photos?"

"I told you I had to destroy them. We don't need them now," said Christy. "We're here to commune with ghosts. Primarily those represented by absences—those no longer living." He gestured toward the candles, the tiny flames floating in olive oil. "I am, first of all, asking you to think of Yiayia Friday and Theodora."

"I don't need to try to think of Yiayia," I said. "She's with me every minute of the day. I'd rather think of Theodora, the witch."

"What of her, then?"

"I can imagine Theodora," I said. "Since my time with Father Stavros, I seem to feel her spirit. When I close my eyes or am in the dark I feel myself slipping into her… into her shadow. I know something of Theodora and think I have, in some ways, since childhood. Now I see a cloaked figure penetrating a forest of dark-leaved trees, eyes and ears attuned to every murmur of wind or brook. I smell vines of honeysuckle and the earthy burrows of small animals, and can speak to them in voices they understand."

Auntie Georgie looked curious. "Do they have souls?"

"Yes," I said. "The animals all do, from smallest to largest, and their souls whisper to me, as do the souls of every rock or tree, or animate or inanimate thing. All have secrets. Some plants offer their medicines for my use and for the use of others. Some offer poisons to bring about relief and peace."

"Do you feel the burning of Theodora?" said Christy.

"No. There's no sense of burning, or of pain."

"The hanging, then."

"I can feel a noose around my neck. Yes. I can feel the hanging."

"Can you speak of Hestia now?" said Georgie.

At her question I forced my attention from Theodora to the forbidden name. Hestia. Hestia. Hestia.

"I'm sorry," I said. "Nothing comes."

"Unusual," said Christy. "But not unexpected."

"There's no family record of any kind about Hestia," said Auntie Georgie. "Except her name, passed down verbally from one generation of our family to the next, as the daughter of Theodora. No journals, no letters, no diaries. There are no images of her. But, unlike the others, there's no record or memories of their ever existing or ever having been destroyed."

"Do you know anything about this?" asked Christy.

"Nothing," I said, "Absolutely nothing."

"Not even from Father Stavros? Dig deep down."

"I'm trying," I said. "But I still get nothing."

"Do you know of the first angel of death?' said Christy, suddenly, his tone almost accusatory.

The question, coming as it did, brushed against my face, as if were the paw of some small creature from the woodlands, maybe. I backed up two steps and put a hand to one cheek as if to defend myself. "I know what everyone knows."

"No more?"

"I don't know any more about any angel of death than I know about Hestia."

Auntie Georgie switched her gaze from Christy to me. "The first angel of death was named 'Thanatos.' Does that bring any associations?"

"Thanatos means death. So? Of course the word, Athanatoi means 'those opposed to death' and the other usual associations."

"I see." Auntie Georgie slid her sunglasses down to peer at me, as if from a great height.

"So what does that mean?" I said.

"It means," said Christy, "that Father Stavros did not prepare you with the knowledge of Hestia or the angel of death."

I frowned. An omission? "Why not?"

"I don't know," said my aunt. "It might be that he didn't want to influence your attitude toward that subject, so we will have to educate you in the matter."

"Some things he leaves to chance," said Christy.

"If Father Stavros chose not to educate me in regard to the angel of death, why are you two doing it?"

"Because it just came up," said Auntie Georgie. "And because he didn't instruct us not to."

"But you two brought it up," I said, slapping my thighs. I always laughed at circuitous logic.

Christy chuckled. "Sit down." He indicated one of the massive armchairs in the hall. Its golden tapestry rose above carved cabriole legs with scrolled toes. It all but enclosed me. Auntie Georgie took the one across. For the first time since I'd entered Christy's house, we were about to have a family consultation without the company of food or a roaring fire, but still we were warm. I felt my heart and mind relax.

Christy wandered around the room, idly touching or gazing at pictures and icons as he spoke. "There are various names for the angel of death in the literature of many cultures. For instance, in Judaism, there's Samael, the archangel, who is thought of as evil, as well as Sariel, which is another name for Izriel. Izriel is thought of as a good angel and his name means 'whom God helps.' He has four faces and four thousand wings that spread over all mankind. His body is sometimes the body of a man. In pure angelic form, he is made up of eyes and tongues, one of each for every human on earth."

"What about the white angel with the white feathered train marked by a thousand eyes? He can't be the same." I wondered at my visit to the emergency department after I played the *Pathetique* for Medea and the chandelier had broken, imbedding its shards in my hands and face. "Who exactly is this Izriel? Do you know him?"

"We are not concerned with Izriel. He's mythical. Nor are we concerned with heavenly thrones, seraphims, and cherubims, whose identities as angels of death are one of many, such as the Archangel Gabriel, God's messenger. Or the Archangel Azrafel, whom we know as God's field commander in war."

"When we Greeks think of the first angel of death we think of a winged youth, Thanatos, a son of Nyx, the night, and Erebos, the darkness. Thanatos was the twin of Hypnos—sleep, whom the sun never looks upon, neither going up nor down from heaven. To our ancestors he was at once a cruel god, whose grip is inescapable, yet a kind god who brings ultimate peace."

"And you believe in such things?" I asked, tugging at a velvet tieback that draped the one huge window next to the door.

"Don't be silly," my aunt said, staring at the daguerreotype of Penelope and Capitan Matepas.

"Certainly not," said Christy," but we believe in the phenomena of our True God's creation behind the myth. Thanatos was a representation of an actual being."

"There have been angels of death throughout human history," said Auntie Georgie. "We've learned as much from the church and Father Stavros, and from history. Even from the Athanatoi, who believe they can defeat death by destroying death angels. The angels the Athanatoi are after don't come from heaven, like archangels, such as Gabriel and Azrafel. They issue from human stock."

"Oh, come on….I don't believe that," I said. But even as I spoke the words I knew I did believe. Still, I was convinced Father Stavros had never suggested to me the existence of any human-born angel. How could I not believe in angels, since the man in the black-billed hat, the Archangel Azrafel, had once caught me with his wings? And once accepting angels as real, how could I not imagine death angels?

And from there, how could I not conceive of the possibility some had been born human, with a human soul?

"I don't believe it," I heard myself say again. "No way." This time the words sounded hollow.

"We suspect a multiplicity of death angels," continued Auntie Georgie, "as well as a hierarchy of them. Also, many assistants from the astral plane perform needed functions. It's for sure, as well as we know there is a supreme death angel who serves God for seven hundred seventy-seven years before rising to heaven. Then a successor is named."

"Of course, the Athanatoi know all that too," cut in Christy. "Because the power of a supreme death angel is much too great for them to challenge, the Athanatoi focus on assassinating successors. And next, on destroying assistants. They try to kill anyone who manifests such talents, anyone they suspect of having a genetic link to a previous death angel."

"Like me?" I said, holding my breath, as if I could lock out the words sure to follow.

"Hestia was probably a death angel, dear," Auntie Georgie said.

Hestia, Hestia, Hestia. Repeating the name brought me no new information or sensation of any kind—only a sense of absence, as if the name itself caused my mind to go blank.

"I don't believe in death angels." I insisted on the lie because the truth was too confusing, too threatening. I considered the boundlessness of the universe and all that had happened to me so far in my life. I pondered what still might happen if I would ever become a death angel. "Archangels like Azrafel? Of course. I've played Go with him. But humans evolving into angelic beings? No way."

"You should know by now that I'm one of your guardian angels," said Christy, looking first at me, then at Aunt Georgie.

"I accept you as my guardian angel. Metaphorically," I added, sounding rather prim. "Let me see your wings. Up close. I want to touch them."

No one said anything. For a moment I thought I'd had the last word and was free to go back to my bedroom, which Yiayia was, no doubt, still haunting. But then Auntie Georgie's eyes went hard and determined, as if she'd made up her mind about something.

"Go ahead, Christy," she said, flapping one hand as if it were no big deal. She blew fog on her shades, rubbed the lenses with a napkin, then put them on again. "Show her."

Christy smiled slightly and backed up a few steps from my chair, as if to make room.

At first I felt a vibrant rippling of air. Then a radiance burst from his face that caused Auntie Georgie to cover her eyes in spite of her sunglasses.

Christy's wings unfurled downy white. From tip to tip, their span equaled the length of his body. They seemed to sprout and roll out from his back almost instantly, filling all the space around him in the foyer. He laughed once, then again, and turned around, displaying spotless, perfectly-manicured feathers that smelled like fresh snow.

He was head to toe naked, too, as if his clothing had evaporated and was being held in reserve by the air. But he seemed conscious of only the handsome wings as he turned before me.

Christy the angel was perfectly proportioned, with a hard upper body and muscular arms, his thighs built for thrusting.

It occurred to me then that Father Stavros had prepared me more for seeing an angel's wings than he had for seeing a fully-developed, naked man. The sight filled me with a sense of wonder and lust. And the naked man was my cousin Christy, for whom I'd spent most of my life in forbidden subconscious longing.

"Touch my wings if you don't think they're real," said Christy, moving closer. "Go on."

While his back was to me, I reached out and ran a hand over the soft feathers, the stiff flight feather, and then the hard, boney place where the spine of a central wing met his skin.

"Now do you believe in a man who is also an angel?"

"Um…yes."

"You don't think I'm some magician's trick?"

"No." I coughed. "I believe you're definitely an angel."

Christy turned around. And his magnificent, not so angelic genitals were less than an arm's length from my face. "And you can see I'm a man, not a ghost or a spirit?"

My face was burning, but I suppose no more than other parts of me. "Yes, I can plainly see you are a man."

"Good." Christy laughed again. "Then perhaps you'll soon choose to believe in death angels, too."

Chapter 36

"There will be a man or woman from the Athanatoi on this jet," said Christy.

"He or she will be the one who looks back at us once from the shiny surface of a cigarette box. Or perhaps from the mirror of a compact while powdering her face. This agent will then wait for us to pass his or her seat before leaving the plane. That person I must kill, I'm afraid. If I don't, he or she will follow us off the plane and learn our ultimate destination when we change our tickets."

We were flying over the Painted Desert of Arizona, looking down at the gray and red bands of the Badlands, streaked with purple and white fossil beds.

A phony driver's license sat nestled in my purse next to a roll of butterscotch Lifesavers. The name on the card was Stephanie Banes. Her birthdate was December 21, 1977. The card's owner was me.

"The Athanatoi are everywhere," said Christy. "Someone at your college will be one —the chancellor, a professor, a janitor, a student. There'll be someone from the Athanatoi taking tickets in Dulles when we make the switch. We'll have to avoid him, for sure. There'll be Athanatoi in Colorado—judges, congressmen, men and women on the street. Some will have your picture from the newspaper, caught by the man in the black-billed hat, the only picture of the old you left in the world that has your name attached to it—but a bad picture, taken from a distance when you were younger. Most won't bother with it. They'll know your appearance has changed."

"What about church?" I said, running a finger across my newly groomed starlet eyebrows.

"Don't go." He smiled. "Or become a Primitive Baptist."

"A Baptist?" I scoffed. "How primitive?" The night before, Christy's L.A. movie friends had paid a late-night visit and given me a makeover. Yiayia's critical ghost had looked on, paced the floor, then gotten so upset, she'd condensed into a fog and went to sleep in a perfume bottle. My own personal wild-haired genie. Who'd made her presence obvious only to me.

Once black and straight and streaked with white, my hair had emerged brown, full blown, and curly. My eyebrows had been bleached and sculpted into the thin, sophisticated arcs of a Twenties actress. My body, which for months had been fortified by daily weight lifting, surfing in a wet suit, exercise riding at Bay Meadows race track, and superb food, had also been artificially plumped using a made-to-measure, padded, push-up bra and derriere augmenting panties like those old World War II foundation garments. My height had been extended by lifts in my shoes.

"That's better," Christy had said, looking me up and down. "Quite different."

Auntie Georgie had assisted a plastic surgeon in making my lips poutier with collagen injections, suture implants, a wine-colored lip tattoo, and lusciously shiny with white tea extract. They dressed me in a long navy blue coat and a belted skirt-suit by Calvin Klein. I received permanent eyeliner and light brown contact lenses. I looked at least twenty-one now.

"It'll require a little maintenance," said Christy, patting my hand.

"Please don't kill anyone on this plane," I whispered. "We can lose him or her in the airport."

"If no one looks back, I won't have to," Christy said.

"What can I do to stop you?"

"You can't stop a guardian angel from protecting you," said Christy.

"Does everyone have a guardian angel?"

"Are you trying to be funny?"

"Do you know any other guardian angels?"

"No, I don't."

"Do you know of the existence of other guardian angels?"

"I'm as in the dark about that as you are. But it's scriptural, so it must be so."

"Don't you want to know?"

"No," said Christy, "I have very little interest in or knowledge of metaphysical things."

"Comes with the territory?"

"Comes with the territory," he agreed. "I'm interested only in my job, and the knowledge of how to do it well. Further, I have almost none of your talents. If you expect too much of me, you'll find me a very dull boy."

I laughed at that, and he did, too.

One of the flight attendants reached over to offer us truffles. The tattoo on his arm was three-looped, partially obscured by his cuff.

"Anything for you, Ma'am?" he asked. "May I offer you a cocktail?"

Ma'am, I thought. This disguise is working.

"I'd like a Perrier with lime." I tipped my head and smiled. Not being called 'Miss,' or 'Young Lady' encouraged me to continue the masquerade. "Oh! Could I see your tattoo? My father's a tattoo artist in Miami." Lying was easier, I found, when it was for the good of mankind.

"Sure," he said, rolling up his cuff to show me. "And for you, Sir?"

"Wall Street Journal is all," Christy said, keeping up the scribbling and list-making he was doing in his two-by-four inch notebook, the kind detectives use to jot down evidence at crime scenes. "I'm good."

To my relief, a long, blue serpent curled up the man's forearm, not a Mobius. "Nice." I smiled at him.

"Tell me." Christy turned to me. "Where does the truncus arteriosus of the primitive heart form?"

"In the cardiogenic plate located at the cranial end of the embryo."

"From what tissue?"

"Splanchnic mesoderm."

"And what do the endocardial tubes do?"

"After being forced into the thoracic region by cephalic and lateral foldings, they fuse to form a single endocardial tube."

"I see," said Christy, nodding in a professional way. "And what grows within the atrium, ventricle and bulbus cordis to separate the chambers?"

"The septa," I said.

"And how do you know all this?"

"Can you fly?" I said.

"I don't know," said Christy. "It's not my job to fly. Now answer my question."

"I don't know how I know all this," I said. "Independent reading, I guess. I've looked at my father's medical books from time to time. He started medical school but never finished."

"Look at the material about your new school," Christy said, engulfed by the first class seat. Despite his strength and alpha maleness, he was not a large man—perhaps five feet seven. "I need to take a nap. Wake me if anyone sneaks a look at us."

"How did you know enough about medicine to ask me those questions?"

"I was channeling Father Stavros," Christy said, yawning. "Actually, he told me what to say. I don't have the faintest idea what I actually asked you. Did you give me the right answers?"

"Yes."

"Okay," he said. "Well, good night."

Without my realizing it, night had fallen. Outside my little porthole the view was solid black. No moon, no stars.

"Curse you, darkness," I said, thinking of Father Bartholomew. "May your spleen rupture and your intestines flow with green springs of pestilence. May your own sperms devour you. I disown and abhor you. May God damn you as a theft of the light."

Christy was already snoring, softly. In vengeance I conjured up the remembered image of him standing naked before me, but this time frozen in place, not even an eye flickering. I moved my eyes, then hands, freely over his forbidden body. I made sure Auntie Georgie was frozen also, unable to notice anything.

"Get your hands off me," I heard him say. I startled, sat straight up, then giggled. The real Christy was still asleep though, and hadn't said a word.

"Okay." I turned on the overhead light and opened the manila envelope containing info about the pre-med program outside Denver, Colorado, to which I'd been promised. I would be starting as a junior with a transcript from Peter's Rock Early College that showed honors grades in chemistry, biology, and a host of other subjects that revealed me as a rising genius. I'd major in microbiology, enroll in a work-study program in anatomy and histology with a team of mammalian structural geeks. We would be dissecting out organs for photographers and medical artists and making slides out of tissues for a histology textbook. Thus I would take possession of my first cadaver, and get to wear a hall pass at Rose Hospital.

And so, seven weeks later, it happened exactly the way I had seen it while on the plane musing. And Christy hadn't needed to kill anyone at all.

#   #   #

The University seemed pleasant enough, in a neocolonial way. It sprawled around a placid, muddy lake, topped with overlapping lily pads. There was an occasional pink flower and plop of a frog. The walkway from the student center formed a bridge over which students could stroll from one side of the lake to the other. On one end of the campus sat a new rec center, field house, stadium, and a baseball diamond. On the other, classroom buildings and a library stood in a cluster. In the middle were the dorms, crowded together as if to confine the students in a controlled space, like lab rats.

My new home was on the third floor in a corner overlooking the lake. I had the room to myself, a necessity to hide my old identity and finish my training undetected by Athanatoi.

266

I slid through pre-med without any close calls.

Now I was Stephanie Banes, "Stephy," for short, an uncomplicated and dedicated medical student, Bahamian native, descended from British and Portuguese pirates. I had almost begun to believe in all this myself.

Chapter 37

The ground under my feet crunched with frozen crystals. Stars were beating overhead, the many hearts of heaven. I was a pilgrim crossing a snowy desert. Tall buildings of my Alma Mater, University of Denver Hospital, poked through the white blanket like laborers shaking angry fists at the sky.

I passed the Trident Bakery. A soft current of air carried butter croissants and coffee to my nose. A man in a full-length down coat, Canadian wool toque and ski gloves held the door for me. Only a small strip of his face and eyes was visible, the whites' redness making his irises appear an unnatural blue. I looked away, cheeks warming against my scarf.

I stopped at the counter, digging my hands into the pockets of my wool coat, and found a pair of wadded up one dollar bills. A pregnant waitress sagged at the cash register, her cheeks pink with beard burn.

"One plain croissant please," I said. "Oh! And a black coffee," almost forgetting.

She frowned at my wad of bills. I flattened out the crumpled money in a frenzy, her impatient hand hovering over the keys.

"Thank you," I said, almost bowing. Anything for caffeine.

While I walked, I inhaled the croissant at a speed that came from forgetting to eat for twelve hours.

The 1123 Ashe Street apartment building stood like a 1950s Bob Hope tribute to Palm Springs, its roof topped with architectural structures and a pool. I stood under the awning of the skyscraper, stalactites of ice hanging over the doorway.

I rang the buzzer and waited, applying lipstick in the dark by feel and sucking an Altoid, by then regretting my coffee breath and croissant and any food particles in my teeth. I wanted my toothbrush.

"Stephy?" hissed the man's voice from the intercom.

"Yes."

The elevator clunked and jerked its way up to the fourteenth floor. It was one of those antique coffins that had a sequence of buttons from basement to roof level, but not for a thirteenth floor.

The doors opened. Harry stood for a moment, motionless, staring at me. Then he reached for my wrist, and pulled me toward him.

"Ow," I murmured. "That hurts."

He swung me out of the elevator and twirled me to strains of big band swing that emanated from his open apartment door.

I rubbed my wrist, but the yank was not without its pleasures. He gripped my curls in his hand and bent my head back, planting a long wet kiss on my mouth.

"Mmmn," I said.

"That's my sweet baby girl," he said. "You're my angel food cake."

He pulled me to him again by the same sore wrist.

"I love you," said Harry. "You are a goddess. Do whatever you want with me, but for God's sake, don't leave me. Never forsake me."

Whatever he said to me, I put no trust in, nor had I any hope for it. Yet, I proceeded against trust and hope, eager for his kisses to find their way from my neck to my mouth.

He kissed me again, pressing his body into mine. The muscles of his shoulders were harder than I'd remembered; his mouth was sweet as licorice.

# # #

Ever since I'd first seen Harry Ripberger Nillsen IV in the rare books room at the grad school library, I'd wanted him, and was willing to pay for my desire. I'd often used that library on the weekends when the one at the med school closed early. I always sat in the same corner at a huge legal table next to the Victorian poetry section. I'd never looked through any of the books which rested within the glass cabinets. Sometimes, specialty grads or faculty came to examine them wearing cotton gloves, carrying delicate stacks into climate controlled-rooms with combination locks.

Harry would appear every Friday and Saturday night at ten after playing hockey. His face was always pink and cool from the ice. Even from where I sat he smelled like a quick shower after an aggressive manly work-out, testosterone and Irish Spring. He sat near me at the far end of the same table. He'd pull tomes from the map section, researching ancient maritime trade routes in the Mediterranean and Near East. As a hobby he studied a copy of the Pella curse tablet and researched relationships between the Macedonian and the Doric alphabet. He got all worked up over cuneiform tablets and hieroglyphics. Of course, he knew nothing of my telescopic vision— or why just sitting near me augmented his ability to memorize. He was superstitious and thought he'd found his lucky seat at the library. I found all this compelling.

After about five weeks of this solitary togetherness, he asked me for a pencil and eraser. He eased through a Venetian translation of the 'Iliad' by Casanova.

Then he came and sat down directly across my table. "Do I have to give you this pencil back?"

"No," I said, raising my head from a diagram of the electron transport chain.

"Is that interesting?"

"It's medicine. Of course it's interesting."

"Can I really keep the pencil? It's lucky."

"Sure. Keep it. I have a big box of them at home."

"Thanks."

"Welcome." My head dropped back down into my book.

He bounced the eraser side of the pencil against the table.

270

"Come skating with me tomorrow afternoon. I'll meet you here at three." He smiled. "Okay?"

I sweated and my heart raced. "Okay."

#   #   #

The rink was indoor and smelled like old popcorn.

"Bend those knees! March and move! Now pretend you're riding a scooter down the street," he'd said, skating backwards. "Lean on me!"

I'd clung to him, wobbly-kneed as a newborn filly.

"He's so dreamy," I'd thought then.

On the way back to the library from the skating rink, all the streetlights came on, so I made a wish.

The wish was the mother of the thought.

So now he was mine.

#   #   #

"I have something for you," he said, holding my hand and leading me down the hall through his apartment door in step to the music. A hiss of flame burned frankincense, like the kind that filled the Hall of Lights at the Monastery of Saint John the Theologian.

The walls were lined with bookshelves pressed against each other. Displayed like a statue on a ledge on the top shelf stood a crushed Sands beer can.

"I saved that can from the Maya Angelou poetry reading last week," he said, lifting the hair away from my ear. "That can is special because your lip print is on it. In 'Saucy Sangria.' It's sacred."

He opened my coat and pulled it off, then pushed me onto the sofa and put his hand under my shirt. He squeezed my nipples.

"Ow."

He lay on top of me and untied my scrubs.

"I need to take a shower," I said.

He pushed his tongue into my mouth again and peeled my clothes off.

We held hands and he lead me to the small square oak table just outside the kitchen. My wrist throbbed; it still had indentations in it.

271

A lighted beeswax candle eked out its faint perfume, casting shadows on an open leather-bound text of ancient Hebrew, a section of the Zohar. His translations glowed in indigo ink, the script loopy and slanted to the left.

What I liked most about Harry were his Waspy great looks and his Indiana Jones resume: archeologist, gentleman scholar, classicist, hockey player. His personality sucked. But it didn't really slow me down—the crappy persona. Men with bad personalities had become my chief hobby during the last few years, a diversion from medical studies, fueled by my blossoming lust.

"You sit here," said Harry. He offered me a chair and I sank into the squishy brocade upholstery, naked except for bra and panties. He placed a small sterling pail in front of me with a matching shovel.

"Dig," he said.

So I dug. Buried in the sand was a crystal hanging from a silver chain.

"Here," Harry said, snapping the clasp at my neck. "She comes from a giant mother crystal. She'll bring you luck."

I bristled. Mother crystal? The Ancient One? Was he onto me, but didn't want me to know it? But—then why would he mention it? He was like a saddle horse, the kind you can't tell is good or bad until you're ten miles from home.

I shivered, shaking off the thought.

He licked his lips and lifted me out of the chair. His body was thin, but his muscles hard. No, I didn't really trust him. He'd hurt me pulling me out of the elevator, but we both knew part of me liked it. How was it that I'd known Harry Ripberger Nillsen IV for a year, didn't trust him, but was still sleeping with him? What would he do next—tie me up? Tie me down?

The truth is I could've slipped into him if I'd wanted to and found out what he was after, but I didn't care to.

But why not?

Because I'd decided I could not escort souls into the next world—if that was to be my inescapable fate—without living all that's good in life and all that's depraved. Every bit of a well-rounded life I could get.

So I let him carry me to the kitchen counter. He pulled an 'amazing Ginsu knife' out of a cutlery block and came toward me,

272

throwing his undershirt over the back of a chair. "But wait, there's more!"

"Harry, are you going to slice and dice tomatoes with that knife? Or a tin can or radiator hose?"

He glimpsed his reflection in the shiny blade, admiring himself.

I recoiled. "Really, Harry. I don't think—"

"Don't be coy with me." He stood over me, naked except for his pin-striped boxers, holding his amazing Ginsu. "Now is not the time to be a little tart. You know you want this."

His pupils dilated. His pale irises faded into a lighter shade of baby leaf.

The knife was cold against my sternum. He pressed the handle against me like a lever and cut my bra between the cups, so that they fell away from my breasts like a severed chain.

The snow-lit moon extended its wide finger through the window and landed on us like a spotlight.

"What is the love that dare not speak its name?" he said.

I thought of Oscar Wilde, but I believed Harry was referring to his own sadomasochistic tendencies.

"We're just experimenting," I said. "Right?"

"Yeah, Dr. Stephanie Banes, we're only experimenting."

I squirmed whenever he called me by my alias. I wasn't much of a liar, so I simply had become Stephanie Banes, who put up with a lot more shit than Persephone Matepas-Vican ever would have.

He slid the blade next to my thigh and tore through the side seam of my panties, releasing one leg.

Amid the moonlight and the flicker cast by the candle, he released my hands, and stood. Then he walked back into the kitchen and replaced the knife in the block.

"I guess that wasn't a triumph," I said. "Was it?"

"I guess not," he said.

"You are definite on the subject, then."

"You're the most beautiful and wonderful thing in this world," he said. "It's what you are that's being lost in this kind of life."

I crossed my arms over my chest, hunching. What in the world was he talking about? How could he know what I am? He talked a lot about loving me, but didn't listen much. Conversations with him were always about his life.

He held my wrists together with one hand and tore the remaining leg of my panties with the other. The counter was stone cold. It burned my thigh.

Even so, a civet-like female musk, a perfume of sexual wanting emanated from me. I felt alive, full of blood. Sex was so confusing.

He threw me over his shoulder like a fireman and carried me down the hall to the unmade bed. The moon's dark shadow followed us and lit the four-poster and canopy.

"Turn over," he said. "Let me see your ass."

He was the type that could feed off a memory over and over.

"Would you want to look young and beautiful forever?" I said, rolling onto my stomach.

His breath tickled my neck. "If my soul was ugly, then yes."

He covered my shoulders with tiny hot breaths and cool licks. "Turn over," he said. "Show me your beautiful golden belly."

I rolled onto my back. He held his face next to my skin and caressed me with puffs of air. His was a face Da Vinci would've loved, the structure of his bones and features approximating divine proportion, *sectione devina.*

He held me on the edge of pain, my arms pinned over my head. Yet, in my captivity, he released me every moment I felt the urge to escape. In sex he set perfect boundaries, restricting my movement but yielding whenever I pushed against the imprisonment.

In technical horse language, I was a 'closed' horse. Harry restricted my forward movement. He kept me under him, but lightened his grip just before I'd decide to struggle free. He drove my haunches under, yet always within my natural rhythm, as if the bondage were my idea. How was he able to read my body? If he could read my mind, surely, I would've known it. He rowled me, but only with a faint touch of the spur. His reins organized me, and his mouth confirmed each surge of pleasure. His timing perfect, his cock drove, his hands reassured. The narrow corridor he drove me through was altogether pleasant.

"I've never seen such love in a pair of eyes," he said.

His lips parted and he kissed me, tearing my lip on his incisors, too large and sharp for his mouth. He pulled his strange cock out of me and put my hand on it. It pointed to the left and twisted widdershins.

He kissed my mouth and slurped the blood that was seeping from my torn lip, drawing it out sip by sip.

For a moment, in my mind, I matched the man to my dream of him. It had occurred to me Harry might've been a figure of terror, but I dismissed the idea.

Chapter 38

The next morning, I walked through the windowless corridor toward the morgue, the steady hum of the generator rising up beneath the floor, its seashell echo bouncing off the walls of my skull. Fluorescent tubes hanging in their inverted aluminum caskets illuminated the scuffed beige concrete-block walls with creamy unnatural light. The air enfolded me with a musty coat of sour vapors. Smears from rubber soles led the way to the great steel door. The hallway was empty except for dust, visible in light beams and lingering residue from unfiltered air that had seeped through long-neglected ducts. Housekeeping didn't like to go down to the basement of Denver General Hospital, affectionately known to its students and residents as "The Dog House." Yelps and cries of caged animals, and moans and rattles from the crematory's incinerator harrowed the soul of an average employee, so the industrial rooms below the hospital were squalid, dust-furred, their cleaning always deferred.

In the classroom lab down the rifle-barrel hall, new trauma personnel arranged themselves in teams around supine dogs strapped

to operating tables, their paws in the air like dead cartoon animals'.
Drains plugged every orifice, measuring bodily functions—urinary
output, cardiac output, gastric acid production—by catheters
attached to monitors. After chemicals and electric currents shocked
the dogs, all would be corrected, their electrolytes readjusted, their
kidney and heart function restored. They would be healthy as pups.
Then the team would crack their chests.

A scrawny Dali-mustached thoracic surgeon, Dr. Payne, taught
the new trauma team how to insert chest tubes, central lines, venous
cut-down catheters, tracheotomy tubes. Finally, before the dogs'
execution by lethal injection, the patent-winning surgeon would
teach open cardiac massage. Everyone around the table would get to
squeeze a beating heart. Yippee!

I'd resisted taking Advanced Trauma Life Support at the Dog
House because the dogs were always salvageable, the treatments
effective, the executions unnecessary. I'd flown to Loma Linda
Medical School to complete ATLS. Seventh Day Adventists were
vegetarian and committed to performing the animal sacrifices
with maximum anesthesia and minimum frequency. Determined
to stone the beasts out of their canine minds, I'd appointed myself
class anesthesiologist and injected the victims with mega-doses of
barbiturates—an effort to ease their passing into the next world. I'd
sung each of them 'A Song for the Dying,' praying Hail Marys until
flat lines drew on their monitors for five solid minutes. The class
indulged me this ritual because they knew I'd compensate them,
later, with well-timed, stress-relieving jokes.

I was twenty years old and knew that dogs had souls. I'd
channeled Yiayia on the issue and received a definitive answer in
the form of a postcard from The Palm Springs Bob Hope Golf and
Tennis Club, postmarked November 22,1963. The card showed a
newspaper ad reading, Wanted: coroner. The easiest job to do is
operate on dead people. What's the worst thing that could happen?
If everything went wrong it only means you got a pulse. On the back
of the card, in my Yiayia's own hand, she had written in purple ink,
"Yes Persephone, dogs do have souls. Any other questions? *S'agapo*,
Your Yiayia."

So I wasn't surprised by the wet dog and bug-spray odor
permeating every corner in the basement of The Dog House. I turned

my mind towards nicer things, like swimming with dolphins and making snow angels in the pink sand of Bermuda.

I typed my entry code into the key pad that screened all who entered the autopsy suite. I opened the steel door to the morgue, where corpses in stacked refrigerator drawers awaited funeral-home placement. The tables were strainers parked in larger tubs to rinse spare parts down the drain—pieces of fat, little flecks of human steak, clotted blood. The air reeked of bleach, caustic fumes parching my skin, singeing my eyes. My crying glands had already been exploited and exhausted by all the sadness that came with the job. Dog days in the basement of The Dog House.

"Hi Milton." I chomped my spearmint gum, the kind with the minty gel inside, so hard my jaw suffered with angina.

"Hi Stephy." Milton pointed to the gown and glove rack. "Only one size. Use the mask with the eye-guard. I think we're gonna have to take out the brain."

Milton was the department deiner, an anatomist who was also a medical illustrator. He had a thick Ricardo Montalban accent and always smelled like chili peppers and lime. Often his skin also exuded tequila, but he never drank during normal working hours.

Carabiners clinked together when he walked, swinging from his Levi 501 belt loops like Marley's ghost come to tell Scrooge to stop being such a selfish bastard and do something nice for the Cratchets. Keys to every creepy room at the Dog House were the bracelet charms Milton collected on his carabiners. One room held organs soaked in formaldehyde donated by patients who'd left their sick bodies to science. Plastic containers—resembling the kind that held the Neufchatel cheese my dad would purchase for his many sauces and salad dressings lined the shelves—catalogued by gender, age at death, date of death, and disease. Other rooms hid the treasured fascinomas of the department: strange tumors, infectious masses, developmental anomalies like horseshoe kidneys and hearts with all the tubes and valves in the wrong places. Behind another door were slide files of millions of surgical pathology cases, each slide containing a sliver of tissue with its own redundant pattern of cells and membranes stained with magentas and violets, sometimes silvers, saffrons, and Congo reds.

Milton's pressed jeans were accented by a massive shiny brass buckle he'd won in an international bull riding championship in Mexico City. A true work of sculpture, the buckle was a totem of the Aztec god of healing. Ixtlilton sat in the crotch of a tree, a cauldron resting on one upturned jaguar paw and a sword—balanced on its hilt—on the other paw. A god with two faces, he wore two masks, one light and one dark. His wings were raised and their tips met over a pair of crowns. Around his feathery waist he wore a girdle carved with magical plants: psilocybin, mescal, tobacco, and morning glories. That was some belt buckle.

Eyeing the gown and gloves Milton had pointed out, I swallowed. I'd assisted in many autopsies under Attending Pathologist supervision, but had never performed one with just a deiner to help. I'd mastered the Rokitansky incision, sprinted through bodies and held the record for emptying the thorax of organs at lightning speed. I had weighed organs, taken measurements, sliced, diced, and stained gross specimens before cutting crucial parts into tiny squares of flesh I then closed into little blue ventilated cassettes. I'd dropped the cases in toluene and they'd sloshed and sunk to the bottom, later to be processed by the central lab and returned as a finished work of microscopic art.

So, this was my first unsupervised autopsy as a pathology resident. I'd done it all before. What could be so hard? I was staring down at my feet in the morgue, thinking of bees, when the pager beeped. The swarm buzzed in swirls around my head.

"Yes, Dr. Sherba." Glancing at Milton, I slurped foamed milk, then guzzled my mocha.

"No, Dr. Sherba, I'm not eating anything." I unwrapped a ginger scone and caressed it for a moment. "Okay, Dr. Sherba. Milty and I will get started." I tossed the balled-up bag into the trash can labeled 'Hazardous Waste' and proffered the scone with my other hand.

"Want some, Milty?"

"Thanks, but no thanks, Stephy."

I ate the treat in big sticky bites and brushed the crumbs off the neckline of my scrub-shirt. A few pecan crumbles had found their way into my bra, so I turned around, reached into my shirt and rubbed the hard little lumps off my breasts.

"Red October will be up here any minute," I said. "Guess I'll gown and glove."

"Don't let her hear you call her that. She might challenge you to a sumo match."

"Wait." I bounded to the residents' call room. In sixty seconds flat I'd brushed my teeth and tongue with brown Listerine and was back in the lab.

"You're not scared, Stephy?" asked Milton, who, by the time I returned, was draped in a yellow paper gown and plastic facemask the size of a small motorcycle windshield.

"No, I'm okay." I checked my hair in the mirror, making sure I hadn't left any loose strands to trap flying pieces of dead flesh. I covered my face with the same sort of mask Milton wore, paper over the mouth and clear plastic past my eyeballs, steaming up when I exhaled.

"The body's in the fridge," said Milty. "Just got here before you came in. It's a boy. Story is he drowned. They found him in a six-foot drainage ditch behind his mother's house." His words slowed. "He'd been missing for two hours. The ED worked on him for three."

I put on a matching paper gown and double-gloved my hands, stopping my tremor though an exercise of will. I hated autopsies on kids. Premature death made me nervous. "What did they do for three hours?"

"Warmed him up, I guess," said Milty, shrugging. "You can't be sure a body's dead until it's warm and dead."

"So they say." My stomach made an embarrassing gurgling sound.

"Sure you're all right?" asked Milty. "If you need a few minutes...."

"No. I'm ready." I walked over to the table and loaded blades onto scapula handles with curved hemostats. I struggled with the tools, determined not to use my fingers.

Milty disappeared into the walk-in fridge and emerged pushing a steel gurney draped with a blood-stained sheet.

"The uncle found the boy's shoes. His mom had stepped out to the 7-Eleven for a newspaper and some smokes." Milty shook his head. "What a waste."

He wheeled the slab under a pair of Castle Surgical lamps and locked the wheels.

I crossed myself right over left three times, then bowed my head.

Milty pulled off the sheet and turned the bed scale on. "Eighty pounds."

"O Spirit of Truth who is everywhere and abides in all things, Cleanse us from Impurity and save our Souls," I prayed, quiet as a nun.

"Fifty-one inches," Milty said, ignoring my whispers. The tape measure whirred as it snapped back into its case.

I'd never seen a smaller thing than that boy lying on the gurney. He looked light enough to float on air. Leaves and sticks were caught in his golden brown halo of curls. I felt a gentle tug begin to pull me into him, heart first.

"Good afternoon, Dr. Sherba," said Milty. He stood at attention, ready to salute.

"Good Morning, Dr. Sherba," I gasped. She had an imposing figure. Fat, yes, but also powerfully built and taller than most men.

"Continue," she said, her Muscovian accent thick, her big carroty bouffant perfumed with L'Air Du Temps cologne and more than a spritz of Final Net. Her 'do was so crusty it looked ready to crack. "Don't just stand there!"

I sat down on the metal stool and turned on my Dictaphone.

Case number 723 (click).

I gazed up towards Milty, who checked the toe tag and the ID bracelet.

(click). Patient Jay Blair. The body is that of a well-developed well-nourished Caucasian male child who appears the stated age of seven. The body weighs 78 pounds and measures 51 inches from crown to sole. The hair on the scalp is brown. The irises are blue with the pupils fixed and dilated. The sclerae and conjunctivae are unremarkable, without evidence of petechial hemorrhage. Upper and lower teeth are natural, with seven retained deciduous teeth. There is no evidence of injury to the cheeks, lips or gums. There are no tattoos and there is a 2 by 3 cm Mongolian blue spot in the left axilla. There is fresh hemorrhage and bruising over his left patella. Neither rigor nor livor mortis is appreciated. The body is cool to the touch at the time of autopsy examination. The body is not embalmed. There is a 22 gauge IV lock in the left radial vein and a central line in the right femoral vein. The groin is unremarkable for age. Testes are descended. Rectal temperature is 92 degrees. (click).

"Good!" said Dr. Sherba, straightening the starched collar of her lab coat. "Carry on! And don't forget to run the bowels! And look for pills! Don't skip steps just because you assume he drowned!"

"Yes, Dr. Sherba," I said, my shirt already sticking to my armpits.

My fingers reached for his carotid. Somehow, he didn't appear dead to me.

"What are you doink?" she hollered, her coffee breath lingering in the air. "What do you think this is—emergency room? Dr. Banes, this is autopsy suite!" She squinted so the corner of her eyes crinkled. "Master Blair was declared dead over an hour ago! Now pull yourself together!"

Bitch, I thought, careful not to transmit.

"What dit you say?" She lifted the front of her coat off her hefty frame with her fingertips, then rested both hands on the shelf of her breasts.

"Nothing," I said, wondering if her coif might really be a wig. "I was planning how to proceed."

"Make your incisions here." Dr. Sherba drew an imaginary line between the tip of the boy's shoulder and the bottom of his sternum.

She trapped me in her glare. I held the number 9 scalpel in my limp hand over the boy. The room began to spin, slow at first, then faster. I looked over the body, feeling an immense pull toward his head. I leaned back to keep myself from falling. Then lost my balance and in an instant I was in his head, with him.

#   #   #

All that remained were his memories of laughter, a slip on a mossy rock, the murky green water, then silence.

Master Jay Blair's uncle had found the boy's empty shoes, toppled pigeon-toed by the edge of a swale. He'd pulled the boy out of the drainage ditch feet first behind his mother's Church Road house.

282

Jay Bird! Jay Bird! His uncle had swept algae and water out of his mouth. A brown duck dove into reeds and disappeared. Help! Uncle Bob's tears dripped onto the boy's face as he breathed into his mouth. The ambulance screeched across the lawn and Uncle Bob collapsed. Don't let him die! He's a ball of fire! A firecracker!

Images swirled before us: a tube down our throat, needle sticks, an oxygen bag pumping in slow rhythm, worried voices of people in scrubs working over us, a big plastic blanket hugging us like a bear, warm liquid running into our bladder through a tube in our penis. We aren't dead yet!

"No!" I cried, my voice foreign and childlike.

#   #   #

I opened my eyes, and saw my own body, cataleptic, stunned. The scowling face of Dr. Lena Sherba eased into slack gentleness, almost mournful. Her scalpel dropped to the floor with a clank.

"Code blue, autopsy suite, code blue, autopsy suite," said the metallic voice of the hospital operator over the PA system.

Then, with a short motion, like yielding to gravity, I shifted back homeward into my own body. I stared down again into the sky and fairy rose eyes of little Jay Blair, cool but still very much alive.

Chapter 39

That night, I slept for ten hours, luxurious for a resident. Daylight broke through a crack between heavy blackout curtains that covered the apartment's east-wall window, casting a spotlight on Harry as he sat at his rolltop desk, drawing on parchment with a quill pen, alternately dipping it in India ink and tapping it on a blotter.

"I'm mapping the Venetian Highway system, from the time of the Emperor Constantine," he said. The light caught his face, the blue veins meandering across his temples and forehead like rivers to the Holy Land. "I'll be presenting the paper in New York next month to the Classical Archeological Society," he said. "I want you to come with me."

I rubbed my eyes and stretched toward the light like some ancient Egyptian grateful to Ra the Sun God for bringing a new day. Perched in bed on a big pile of pillows, I opened DeGowan's Cardiovascular Pathology and started rereading the chapter about mucinous tumors of the heart.

He smiled a low, lopsided smile and walked toward me, offering a glass of crushed ice and water. "It's at Butler Library," he said, as if tempting me with a trip to Tahiti. "Please come." He reached out and tucked some hair behind my ear, then sat on the foot of the bed.

"I think we should go to Venice," I said, kicking the blankets off my feet and handing him a bottle of mentholated foot cream.

He held one foot in his hand, stroking the arch with the tips of his fingers, and dialed the black-kettle phone.

"Hey, it's Harry Nillsen," he said, pulling my toes until they cracked and I giggled. "Is the wind okay today for a jump?"

He smiled at me and nodded, nearly dropping the phone from the crook of his neck.

"Okay, 11 o'clock." He hung up, punctuating that action, like everything he did, with a pat on my shoulder.

From the kitchen, the drill of the coffee grinder rasped over the sound of the bells at St. Elizabeth's Cathedral. Harry emerged with a pair of dainty Dutch blue espresso cups, their rims rubbed with lemon peel.

It was a bit of a strain to watch him produce such rapturous displays of gallantry, almost ridiculous. He sang the Song to the Moon from *Rusalka* while I sipped black coffee. I soaked in the raven claw-footed bathtub, surrounded by floating pink rose candles and fluffy lavender bubbles. Sinking beneath the foam, I prayed for all my sins to be washed away. Heeding Christy's warning, I'd hidden my faith along with most of my opinions and all the details of my past. I felt irritated by this, wanting to tell someone. It was as if I owned a talking trunk that fought to open itself, but I'd forced shut, locked and covered. I hadn't seen my family in months, not even the shade of Yiayia Friday, who was mad I'd been "ashamed" of my roots.

"I'm not ashamed, Yiayia," I'd told her. "I'm following orders. I'm protecting our inheritance."

"From whom?" she'd said.

"From everyone, anyone who could be Athanatoi," I'd told her. "But mostly from Harry."

"Get rid of that," she had commanded, then evaporated again into the perfume bottle.

There was something putrid about Harry, as Yiayia insisted before hibernating for months in her Waterford six-ounce crystal home. But what was it that was so foul?

He'd been born in Philadelphia, to luxurious and sweet circumstances, the stars in his sky always rising higher and higher. He'd grown up with a lot of staff, and had been spared many of the stresses one experiences when we just don't have enough help. He'd had a driver when his car wouldn't start, access to planes and tutors. Up until he left home for college, he'd had an attractive Dutch nanny named "Anky." His personal assistant, Giles VanderCleef, was dapper and efficient, chummy, yet discreet.

Harry loved all things Greek, including me, it seemed—though he didn't know my heritage. I'd told everyone who asked I was Bahamian, descended from Lord Craven on my mother's side, and Edward Teach, better known as Blackbeard, on my dad's. Harry had PhD's in Greek and Roman Archeology and in Hebrew from Ivy League universities. He summered in Newport with his family, sailing aboard their schooner, My Only Virtue.

We'd gone back to Newport in the late summer for a long-weekend to help his father prepare the boat for a race. The docent from Rosecliff, a childhood friend, had called him in a panic after an employee had unscrewed a massive Murano chandelier and left it mixed in one heap on the dining room floor, then stormed out of the house, tantrumming, vowing never to return. Somehow, Harry had mastered the secret of putting the lamp parts back together. I'd joined a tour of the mansion while he and the docent spent hours reassembling the parts. Later, he'd told me he'd decided to finish a post-doc in Maritime Archeology in Denver.

"Why Denver?" I'd said. "Not many boats."

"Because you're there."

Now it was April, a year later, but Denver was still blanketed by a crust of snow. The driver offered us a New York Times and we headed down I-25 toward Boulder. Ahead, the flatirons were shaded by clouds, their granite faces grey and worn.

At the end of a cul-de-sac at the Boulder Airport, a group of three male students were playing Frisbee with the parachuting instructor, a burly, middle-aged guy with a mop of golden hair and a deep tan, a cross between a surfer and a biker. He owned an operation called "Flax Footer's Skydiving Academy."

"Okay, dudes," said Mr. Footer, twirling the Frisbee. "And
dudette." He nodded in my general direction. "Today is your third
jump. Providing all goes well, next time y'all can free-fall." He
squinted and looked into the horizon. "Nothin' in the world like a free-
fall."

We mimed a succession of movements: step out, hold the brace
under the wing, arch back and look up, then jump, pull faux cord on
left shoulder, check parachute, pull emergency release. Of course, the
chute had an automatic release, and from my two prior jumps I knew
I would only get to hang onto the bar for a moment before gravity and
the wind would pluck me from the plane.

"And don't forget to steer clear of those oil pumps," yelled Flax,
over the washing-machine battering of the tiny plane's engine. "Ya
wouldn't want to land on one of them. Heh. Heh. Heh." He lifted his
chin and looked out the open door to the pasture below. "Who wants to
go first? Hey, dudette. You look ready. Show the dudes how it's done."

I fell, until the cord attaching me to the plane, so much like
an umbilicus, stretched taut. I checked the chute above me. It had
expanded—a great sail carrying me on the waters of the wind. My
only job was to steer clear of roads and oil pumps. The vista was both
a cultivated and wild landscape, a rolling world in harmony with itself,
the vast fields of snow like lines in a poem punctuated by the periods
of round hay bales, the commas of aspen trees lining the perimeter.
Horses and cows faced away from the wind that had lifted and set me
down.

I landed, bent my knees and absorbed the shock of the earth
meeting my boots, dropped to the ground, then rolled, cracking the
thin frosting of snow. I lay there looking up into the invisible breeze
that carried the dander of horses until my heart slowed to a normal
pace. The top of my head and the bottom of my feet began to tingle. I
touched my hair and felt it springing up, electrified with static, waging
war with itself.

I squinted against the glare from a sun hole-punched out of the
sky. A thin layer of snow melted under me, so I made an angel.

I smelled her before I felt her—the star horse Agrippa had bolted
after, the day of the eclipse. I doubted my eyes. Could this really be the
same black mare? I felt weak all over, as if my body were melting.

"Hey, girl," I said, reaching out for her. She exhaled into my nose, sharing her breath with mine. Then she nudged me with her muzzle, tickling my neck with her whiskers, tiny quills against my skin. I felt pure joy, like an orphan reunited with lost family, the sheer impossibility of it delicious. She blinked, black eyelashes rimming her snapping brown eyes, alive yet forgiving. She nuzzled again, urging me to move.

"What is it you want?" I laughed on the ground letting her tickle me with that meddlesome lips. Her whiskers were like a seal's. Her legs stood long and slender, leaving plenty of air under her belly, accentuating her tallness. The metallic bloom of her coat flashed in the sunlight as she knelt next to me, her great neck arched and bulging. I pulled off my gloves with my teeth and rubbed her velvety nose. After sneezing onto my face, she shifted her weight to her haunches and sat down on the snow like a Labrador retriever.

"Okay, okay," I said, sitting up to face her. "Hold on while I detach my parachute."

She sat and watched while I folded the orange fabric into triangles like a flag. I turned and rubbed her back, her neck, her face, her legs.

"Hey girl, why're you sitting here like that?"

She sneezed seven times.

"Hair balls?" I asked, unable to stifle my joy. I pressed my face against hers to feel her radiant coat.

She sneezed again, still sitting like a coal-black sphinx.

Unable to resist the invitation, I climbed onto her back, careful to keep my weight towards her withers as she rose to four feet. I asked for nothing, just sat there and waited for her to take me wherever it was she wanted to go. She stood still for a moment, then spotted another parachute about four hundred yards away. She cantered, her tempo slow, lowering her haunches as if I'd asked her, offering the highest degree of collection. The canter became four beat, changing leads in perfect balance, gaining only six inches of ground each stride.

Harry was waving his folded sail at me, but the mare was taking her time. He'd landed about six feet in front of a round hay bale, and crows were beginning to circle around him, cawing in disapproval. The more Harry called and waved, the slower my mare went, with no aids from me, till it seemed she was cantering in place.

288

"Can't you make that thing run?" he hollered, his voice raspy in the cold.

I'm not making her do anything, I thought. I know this horse. Harry could never understand I was in the midst of one of the most magical experiences of my life.

The snow was softening, melting in the mid-afternoon sun; tiny spots of clover and old brown grass poked through holes in the thin, white cover.

"Stephy!" His voice went higher and tighter than usual. The crows clustered and hovered in a dark cloud over him.

Coming into his presence was like stepping up to a gas heater, a row of blue fire tongues burning high in a convection of heat that pushed us away; we were careful to keep a safe distance. The star horse halted square, facing him, and squealed, sending the crows rioting off into the nearby woods.

"What're you doing on that stinky dirty horse?" Harry said, one hand raised, poised to commence with his dreadful finger wagging. "I liked those birds!"

"Don't talk that way about the horse. She's fabulous," I said, patting her neck. I slid off her back. She stood for a moment, ears turning, wall-eyed. Then she pressed her star to my chest as I stroked her shoulder.

He had stuffed the folded triangle of fabric like a large wedge of *spanikopita* under his arm and walked toward us. The star horse turned on her haunches and bolted from a standstill to a flat-out gallop.

"You certainly don't have trouble making horses run away," I said.

It was as if the parting birds had exposed him, letting the sunbeams filter through his skin, exposing blood vessels and shadows of bone. I don't think I'd ever seen him in natural full light before, never in the outdoors at noon. His complexion took on an almost yellowish cast, as if he had no melanin of his own, except in the dark brown of his hair—like Andy Warhol with a Jackie O dye-job, his grasshopper irises taking on a slight pink hue. I supposed these were capillaries arching above the faint pigment of iris, but....

He stepped toward me to deliver a preternatural kiss, which I evaded by turning my head to look after the mare stampeding away in the distance.

"Harry, you've bitten yourself." I rubbed the corner of his mouth with my thumb. The crystal around my neck warmed. I looked at my bloody thumb and instinct brought it toward my lips. I hesitated, then rubbed the blood off on my jeans. He grabbed my wrist, pulled me to him, and forced a bloody kiss on me, pushing the taste of rust down my throat. I hiccupped. Impulse guided my hand to yank the burning crystal from my neck and stow it in my coat pocket.

"Harry!" I pulled my face away. "Yuck! Don't you realize you've bitten yourself?"

A thick drop fell to the frozen snow and seeped in, staining it to raspberry sorbet. I thought of the heart of Snow White, and of the boar, murdered by the woodcutter. "Begone, woodcutter! And bring me the heart of Snow White."

He who had at times seemed so dashing had somehow transformed into a vampirish form of Lord Byron. The year we'd spent together cast tall shadows in my memory. I shoved them out of my head.

The crystal fired up again in my pocket. I had to get away. I could've gone into him and heard his thoughts, but didn't want to. I felt as though he was harboring something leprous, something nettling inside him. Perhaps dangerous, only waiting to lash out.

"You think love is pure and limitless," he said, his nose reddening. "This is a hateful time in the world. There is no perfect love."

I wanted to grab him and shake him. "Words can't describe how wrong you are."

I turned and stomped off ahead of him to Flax Footer's Skydiving Academy's pick-up point—in the middle of the field by the largest and the most vigorous of the oil rigs.

"Good jump," said the burly blonde jump master who'd collected us into the van to carry us back to our cars.

I sat in the back of Harry's Jag, plastered to the door, my legs crossed, arms folded.

"Little bastards!" said Harry, trying to power lock the doors.

I held my breath until he gave up.

"Where to?" said the driver.

"Home," I said.

"No," said Harry.

"Yes," I said. "We need to get a few things straight."

#   #   #

It had been a long day and it was only half over.

I'd nudged the door to his apartment open with the toe of my boot, trying to be gentle, but the Sands beer can fell off its pedestal anyhow and lay there on the floor like a dead soldier.

Harry stepped on the can, crushing it, then threw it in the trash.

I'd been collecting clothes, books, and cosmetics when Giles returned with Harry's lunch.

"Have some lunch, Giles."

"Thanks, Harry," he said, holding up a bottle of Chateauneuf-du-pape for Harry's approval. While I packed, they drank and dined like a pair of English lords in the Palace of Westminster, discussing how the cold war was finally over and whether or not East and West Germany would merge currencies.

"Delicate," Harry said, biting into a lump of meat. The sweet perfume of braised rabbit had expanded and filled his apartment. The half-eaten bunny on the platter was sickening. Skinned and garnished with rosemary like some Christian martyr roasted in oil, it tainted the asparagus logs that had rolled into it.

"The only thing better than this is sweetbreads," said Giles. Harry and Giles were made for each other.

"You know how I get away with screwing around?" whispered Harry, as if he were telling Giles some great secret wisdom. "I always fuck them up the ass and that way they don't tell anyone."

"Nice," I thought, rummaging through a bedside table for my stethoscope and pager.

He and Giles had finished in the dining room. I realized we were alone again, so I hurried.

"You're leaving?" he said, following me to his bedroom. "This doesn't mean I'll never see you again. Does it? He exhaled through his nose, the gusty way a horse does.

"It's alright, Harry." I kept my voice nice and low, using the same tone I'd used when I'd go out into the pasture at night to catch Agrippa the Ingrate.

"Well, then." He went to his closet and pulled down a cigar box. He mumbled to himself all the way to his desk, from which he retrieved a pair of scissors.

I said nothing and proceeded to the opposite bedside table where I collected several bottles of pearly nail polish I'd squirreled away behind a bunch of junk. Lately, when I'd stopped talking to him, he'd burn out like candlelight under a snuffer.

"Relax," he said, scissors in hand. Little did he know I was not afraid of him, or of death, or really, of violence. He laid a warm hand on my neck and gave me a soft push onto the bed. He looked unconcerned with the reality of my disgust.

With great calmness, he pulled an endless rope of pearls from out of the box, cut it in thirds, and handed me one string.

"There you are, Stephy," he said. "I want you to have these."

I figured I could donate them to charity after I got out of there. "Thank you," I said, stuffing them in my jeans pocket.

"You have forsaken me," he said, sniffling, rubbing his forehead.

He lit a clove cigarette, took a few drags, then pressed it out in a blue glass ashtray that looked like it was lined with fish eyes and held together by glue. Still somewhat confounded by his physical beauty, I did not recoil when he took off my socks and kissed my ankles. I sat stunned as he worked his way up to my belly, lifted my shirt, and kissed my waist.

"Harry?" I said. "Are you all right?"

He lifted me up and pulled me by the hand through a low, hidden door at the back of his walk-in closet to a sofa in a secret room. I was a sucker for little cubbies and secret hatches. Intrigued, I felt trapped on a platform between two trains traveling in opposite directions, not knowing whether I did or didn't want him one last time. Harry took advantage of my indecision, pulling me closer.

I heard a ticking sound.

"Harry, what're you doing?" I said, pushing him away. The ticking grew faster. "That's a Geiger counter."

I jumped up and turned on the overhead lights, revealing a steel laboratory hood covering a ladder of viscometer tubes, a decanter, and a row of beakers, some empty, some containing powders and crystals. Others contained liquids, all covered. A breadbox-sized green lock box sat on a wheeled tray in the middle of the tiny room.

"I'm analyzing a piece of wood from an old barge I found at a dig in Croatia."

"Harry!" I tucked my shirt back in. "There's a mass spec at the lab. What about the radiation?"

"Come back here!"

I ran out of his freakish Dr. Frankenstein lab and stuffed my stack of clothes into a black garbage bag like an eighteen year -old foster child. I was sliding into my coat when he knocked me over and pinned me under his weight. I closed my eyes as his breath puffed on my eyelashes.

"Being with you is like being strapped to a bomb," I said.

"I'm leaving you," he said, anger leaking out of his skin in the beads of sweat on his cheeks.

"OK, Harry. I think that's a good idea."

"You're just not beautiful enough for me, Stephy."

"Then get off me."

"I don't want to hurt your feelings. Your looks are coarse, and you're a little plump, like my mother." He released me and cleared his throat. "I mean, you're pretty in a street Arab sort of way."

"OK. Then I'd better go." I put the stack of books in a plastic milk crate and slipped my bare feet back into my boots.

"I mean, I could marry you," he said. "We might not be completely happy. But it might be tolerable."

"No…umm…. That's okay. Really Harry, I think you should find someone else. You deserve better."

"Do you want help with that stuff? I could call Giles."

"No thanks." I was unharnessed, and would peel myself from him later, object by object. "Bye."

I laced up my shoes in a hurry, slung the purse strap over my shoulder and exited down the hall, balancing the garbage bag on the milk crate.

What I really wanted to do next was spray paint "Piss off, Harry Ripberger Nillsen, IV," on the west wall of Denver General Hospital in big balloon letters.

Maybe he was dangerous, but I wasn't scared. His character was blackened like a Cajun catfish and I wasn't going to stick around anymore. That was all between him and the Holy Ghost.

Chapter 40

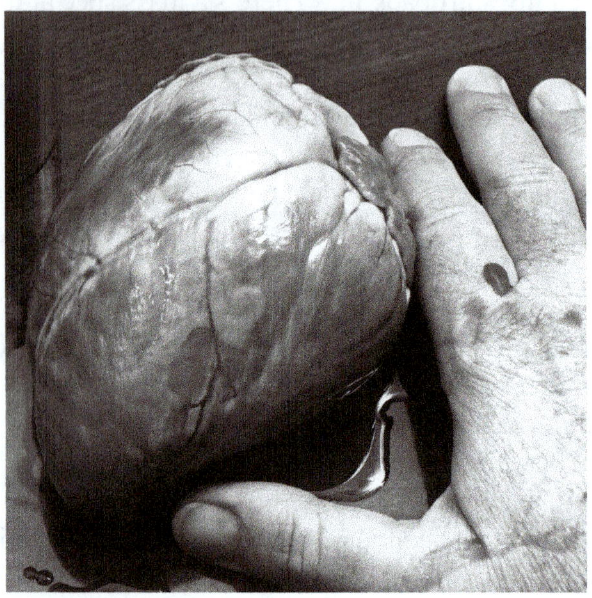

For two solid days after I left Harry, I felt numb. But despite my disgust at my own dissipation during that relationship, no matter where I was, an image of him formed then locked in my brain. I shook my head to clear it.

Now, I was on autopsy call for the Office of the Chief Medical Examiner. I was in my final rotation as a pathology resident, Forensics. I had been paged to the central morgue, deep in the heart of Denver's Forensic Sciences lab. The good news was Milty moonlighted there on the weekends, so we would get through the case without too much aggravation.

I stared down at the corpse of an elderly woman, a shopkeeper who'd sold Italian culinary imports from her grocery store in Cherry Creek. The police record showed her unknown assailant had taken $22.50 from her cash register and left her with a gaping bullet wound through the neck as a thank-you.

Her hair was iron grey with a blue wash, a typical style for Cherry Creek Bridge players. The folds in her face and neck were so deep they looked like well-healed slash marks.

Everyone's naked on the autopsy table. But in spite of her age and her nudity Mrs. Rosso wore her dignity. The hands resting alongside her hips on the steel tray showed a freshly sculpted French manicure. A platinum band encircled the ring finger of her right hand and a pale tan line showed on the left. Both feet were sanded free of calluses, the toenails alabaster and perfect.

"Are you Okay, Stephy?" asked the deiner, Milty, adjusting his bull-riding prize belt buckle. "You're turning green. Don't throw up. OK?"

True, I was nauseated. Not because old Mrs. Rosso was on the table about to be sliced by my scalpel, but because I could still smell Harry's hidden laboratory, reeking of ink, dust, and mucilage. I could still see him fixing diagrams of old Venetian boats onto maps of a pre-Claudian system of canals and waterways.

The pictures of Harry in my mind turned my stomach, so I hyper-focused, pinning my gaze to the body to make it through the autopsy.

The torn borders of the wound were stippled with gunpowder, Mrs. Rosso's windpipe exposed, the edges of her sternocleidomastoid and trapezius muscles macerated by the bullet that had exited her neck and was still imbedded in the wall of the crime scene, behind the counter of Italian pastries and English cigarettes. I'd confirmed what I already knew when I opened her chest cavity: blood had saturated her lungs, her heart had overfilled and ruptured. It dumped a whole liter of blood when I cut it from the aorta. Even the dark congealed fluid that filled her pericardium reminded me of Harry.

I considered Harry's elongated incisors. He would like all of this. Despite the fact that he was a vile, bloodsucking pig, I had imprinted on him during a critical period of my development, disregarding all consequences.

After returning her organs to her thoracic cavity in no special order and sewing her chest wall closed, I covered Mrs. Rosso with a clean, white sheet and stood over the body until Milty slid her back into the cooler. I pulled off my gown and gloves in one sweeping motion, and, after scrubbing my hands, took off my mask, soaked with perspiration.

I ran to the showers, stripped off my scrubs, and threw them
in the laundry bin lined with red plastic stamped with the universal
warning for infectious materials.

Covered with soapsuds, I dry heaved, then finally vomited bile
into the drain. I opened my mouth toward the shower head, savoring
its coolness, and stayed there until the water ran cold and I finally felt
empty.

#   #   #

I climbed the stone stairs of Saint Elizabeth's cathedral
muttering small prayers of exorcism in an effort to drive out whatever
piece of him was lodged in me. Magenta DaVinci roses in concrete
vases on plinths stood guard as I struggled up step after step, their
sweet balm promising the healing waters of the Holy Mother. Two
huge mahogany doors opened outward to let in the soft midmorning
light. Inside the vestibule, a squirrel sat, holy bread grasped between
his furry paws. Spilling crumbs onto the ruby carpet, he nibbled like a
careless epicure under smoldering candles erected in sand beneath the
icons of Saint Elizabeth and the Jesus and Mary Tender Mercy.

A priest emerged from the transepts carrying a felt cloth and
an olive branch. He bowed his head and with the branch sprinkled
holy water, then made the sign of the cross over the fabric, praying,
"Heavenly Father, open our eyes to see all things willed by thee."

He turned toward the altar and dusted an icon of the stoning of
St. Stephen the Protomartyr, who had been painted in deacon's robes,
holding a censer.

I walked half-way up the aisle.

The priest, whom I'd never seen before, turned to look at me,
his robes rustling like leaves of an old book. His eyes were pale
green, the corneas opaque, as though they had been burned by fire.
"I'm Father Tiresias," he said. "Can I help you?"

'I'm looking for Father Andrew."

"Well, my dear, when was the last time you've been to church?"

"Umm…not since the First Sunday of Lent…last year," I
confessed. I couldn't tell him I'd been concealing my identity and
therefore not attending church. My eyes focused on the hem of the
priest's robe.

"I see," said Father Tiresias, whom I now realized could not see me. "Father Andrew has gone to a conclave with the Metropolitan of Chicago. He left six months ago. I've been here since last summer. My last Parish was in Jackson Hole." He stroked the gold leaf around the icon with his felt cloth, then scrubbed back and forth over the top of the frame several times. "Can't I help you?"

Why not, I thought. Almost bursting with the story I was dying to tell, I restrained myself.

"You're scowling," he said.

"How could you possibly tell?" I blurted out, then felt embarrassed.

"Come, sit next to me." He patted the pew. I sat down next to him, holding all my tension in balled-up fists.

"The devil wants you to accuse yourself." He rubbed one sightless eye. "Evil wins when you think you're beaten."

I hunched over my knees, pulling my skirt down. He scooted closer to me on the pew, his breath releasing a faint odor of cigarette smoke. Relieved that the monk beside me was not without vices either, I inched closer and relaxed my hands.

"Your value is not tied up in your mistakes," he said. "For instance, I smoke. My lungs crave nicotine, yet I'm not turned to tar. I'm beyond what I do, just as you are. I've defiled my temple, yes." He reached over and cradled my palm with both hands. "Have you defiled your temple, Persephone?"

"How do you know my name?"

I tried to pull away but his grasp was tight. I tried to slip into him to read his intentions but got no further than the tips of his fingers. Father Tiresias was no ordinary monk.

"I'm no ordinary monk, Persephone," he said, and I flinched.

"I'm not scared of you. I can tell you're good."

He squeezed my hand until it hurt. "Do you still think I'm good, Persephone?"

"Yes. I know you are. You're just trying to teach me a lesson."

A bolt of pain shot up from my wrist into my head.

"My grip is like sin," he whispered.

The worst part of the squeeze came from a thick ring he wore that bore a seal of the Nativity of the John the Baptist Monastery, a warm block of metal relentlessly denting my hand.

"Your instinct is to pull away." His shoulders tensed, as if he wasn't stating the obvious.

"Of course, I want to slip out of your grip." I squirmed on the warm pew. "It hurts."

"Think of a Chinese finger trap." He stared into me with his thickened corneas. "Try pushing your hand as hard as you can into mine."

When I did, I felt my fingernails bend in an unnatural direction. But I did what he said and pushed anyway.

"Your nails are raking my hand." He let go and rubbed his palm.

"Well, what should I do then?" I squinted at the icon of St. Stephen, the three rocks in his hands seemed to glow.

Father Tiresias lay his stole across my shoulders, carefully, as if he were trying to calm a skittish horse. "Push, don't pull."

I almost collapsed out of the pew onto my knees. The ends of his stole felt like the hands of God reaching down from heaven to cover me.

I opened my eyes. Under the stole he wore partial vestments of red which marked a feast day dedicated to the Holy Spirit. The space defined by the fabric was overcast in garnet like the inside of the shell of an unborn condor.

I crossed myself three times right over left and wondered how I could ever confess everything. It could take a week to hatch out of this thick-shelled egg.

I sat back on the pew, the stole still on my shoulders. "I have plenty to say."

"Go ahead," said Father Tiresias. "God already forgives you."

"I've just left a man who defiles me. Last fall on a trip to New York he blindfolded me, put me in a limo and took me to a hotel where he kept me for days, feeding me, bathing me like a child. There was a gentle lady who wore a bell on her ankle and waited on me. She would sometimes lick me like a cat. I never saw her. He kept my hands cuffed and my eyes covered, then chained me to a post and had sex with me every way he wanted. He kept me masked this way for a week. Then, like a thief, he laid me back in the limo. This time the ride was bumpy, as if the axles had been misaligned by a wreck, or as if he were carrying a too heavy load in the trunk. He took me to a bawdy house in New York. In each room, a different form of debauchery was taking place."

I felt my voice rising to a shriek. I swallowed and relaxed my throat.

"There was a room for orgies catering to every sexual preference. A room for Ecstasy, for heroin, for cocaine. When Harry offered my favors to a Saudi diplomat, I decided I'd had enough and headed for the safe room, where no one could touch anyone. I was alone in there with a beautiful girl from Russia, a mail-order bride. I promised myself then I'd leave this dreadful boyfriend for good. Yet I let him convince me to take him back."

My forehead felt fevered, my vision was blurred. I can't go on, I thought. I can't keep telling him all this, priest or not. But then, I wasn't telling God anything he didn't already know.

"He promised to be normal after that. He was a professional at acting normal, what with his Philadelphia socialite parties and his Ivy League academics, his Greek, Latin, and Hebrew translations, his devotion to the classics. He is also an archeologist."

I lowered my voice, refusing to rush on with the words. I wanted to seem measured, controlled, not a loose cannon like Yiayia.

"Why he'd taken me to that whorehouse I can't even imagine." I waited for a reply. Ten seconds went by, and the priest said nothing.

"Yet he wanted me blindfolded. He liked to watch." I wrung my wrists, feeling for scars. I felt like a sunflower poking my seedling head up through muddy gnarled roots of poison ivy and thorn trees and broken machinery. "I could have gone into him, to find out why. But I knew there was a badness in there I didn't want to feel. He's an addiction. I've wanted to do everything and see everything because I always felt my life would be short. Anyway that's it. I've left all of it. I'm a fugitive. I'm moving to another state to do another residency. And if I see him again I'll confront him with a push so *he* will run away, not me."

I bit my lip and stared past the iconostasis into the sanctuary beyond, painted with light that flowed through stained glass. The icon of Jesus stood to the left of the Icon of St. Stephen the Protomartyr. I slipped down again onto my knees in front of the icon of Jesus.

"O God, I confess I have sinned against you in thought, word, and deed, more than the number of grains of sand in the sea. I've omitted to do what your holy law requires of me. But now with repentance and contrition I turn to your love and mercy."

Father Tiresias stroked my hair and drew the stole up to my head. He delivered the prayer of repentance. "Separate the blood and bitterness that the foe has sent your servant Persephone and grant her Thy grace and renew in her the lineaments of Thy image. Nourish her with them on the grass of Thy Holy Mysteries by the prayers of Thy most pure Mother and all Thy saints. Amen."

I stood up and hugged Father Tiresias. "Thank you."

"Go in peace, and remember to say the Jesus Prayer."

Chapter 41

I paid a driver who looked like a preacher and hummed like a blues singer to load, haul, and unload my chief belongings into a mini-storage unit in Metairie, outside New Orleans.

I flew to Boston to take my pathology board exam, and then took the number 7 train to Commonwealth Avenue to sit for boards at the Adams Medical College. When the train had passed the stop for the Tobin Bridge, for an instant I thought I'd caught a glimpse of Harry on the platform putting out a cigarette with the toe of one wing tip, a briefcase tucked under his arm. I slumped in my seat, borrowed a newspaper from the man next to me and held it up in front of my face.

At Logan Airport, I'd spotted Harry slipping in and out of a crowd that expanded around a crate containing the smuggled remains of a collection of mummified pets from the temple of Ramses. The first cat, wrapped in linen, was discovered by airport security beagles.

I turned on my heel and walked fast, but not too fast, blending into the crowd of over-caffeinated commuters checking their watches. Every moment I imagined Harry might be following me.

I stopped in front of a florist's window. Every flower-shop I'd ever seen had clean, polished glass so onlookers would be coaxed in by blooms of mums and birds of paradise. But I stayed outside the reflective window, making a show of checking my lipstick. Then I looked for reflected images of Harry in the crowd behind me. Not there. I sighed, letting a breath slip from me as I said a quiet prayer. Breath to me had become a holy force, a gift from the Holy Spirit surrounding me like an impenetrable bubble.

The pale-skinned, rosy-cheeked clerk moved to the cash register behind the counter of the flower shop. He smoothed back his hair, pushing against its natural cowlick. He fingered his chest hairs and slipped his hand into his pants pocket, jingling change. For an instant I almost thought he too was Harry, so similar were their mannerisms. Thank God for the bubble around me. Without looking up, the clerk studied a sales slip and began laying red tulips and blue irises atop each other on wax paper.

I inhaled and clenched my fists. My fear of Harry was transforming to anger. I saw myself in the window, a woman driven by mere shadows of a vile person who had no respect for my God or me. I was an object, a blow-up Venus, and so reduced by rage it brought to mind the words of Father Tiresias: "push, don't pull."

I burst into the room of lavish freesias, portly hyacinths, and stands of gladiolas surrounded by small fragrant stock. A gilded frame with a poem written in gold embossed Victorian capital letters, which I knew from my time in the rare book room to be the Royal Font by Altus, hung behind the clerk.

> *If of thy mortal goods thou art bereft,*
> *And from thy slender store*
> *Two loaves alone to thee are left*
> *Sell one, and with the dole*
> *Buy Hyacinths to feed thy Soul.*

How sad, I thought.
And magnificent. Cut flowers, life and death.
My fingernails twitched like the claws of a panther as if preparing, of their own accord, to tear out Harry's eyes. I blinked

hard. But the clerk was a teenage boy, a younger doppelganger—not Harry.

"I'm sorry for slamming your door," I said. "I thought you were someone else."

"It's okay, lady." He nodded. "No problem. Would you like an arrangement?"

"I would." I checked my watch and blew a stray lock of hair out of my face. "But I'm in a hurry."

#   #   #

I wanted to find Harry, to tell him off, to push him away, to invite him in, to dare him to cross a line I'd drawn in quick-set concrete. None of these desires seemed healthy.

So I called my cousin Calliope, who lived now in Casadega, Florida. She was a journalist waiting to matriculate at Stetson Law School. She'd been writing a long, involved series of articles for Provincetown Arts Magazine on the veracity of paranormal practitioners who held séances, channeled spirits, and conducted moon watches at the spiritualist conclave of Casadega.

I called Calliope and told her what time to pick me up at Orlando International Airport. We didn't arrange a meeting place, so I used the metal box to find her.

I kept my eyes peeled for Harry, expecting him to follow, half hoping he would, so I could let him have it. But the box was no help.

Casadega is a rural town in central Florida founded by a Lily Dale spiritualist, George Colby, who followed his spirit guide, Seneca, to this hidden spot, which would become the most active religious community in the southeast.

Calliope and I parked near the corner of Casadega and Stevens close to the Spanish Mission style Casadega Hotel in front of the main spiritualist camp. Tucked away in a setting of Cypress trees and Spanish moss, quaint little Victorian houses dotted the streets. Slow-motion butterflies and dragonflies swam through the moist air. Cats, foxes, songbirds, and squirrels roamed the streets and sidewalks—familiars without worries.

"Let's take off our shoes," said Calliope. "We're in a holy place. We can put them back on when we get past the spiritualist

303

camp." We walked down Stevens and waved at smiling locals on
roller skates and old bicycles with bells.

We stopped at the Bending Spoon Tea Leaf Café and found
a table in the back under a spun-glass dreamcatcher that stared
down at us like a great blue eye. On the Moveable Feast day of the
Ascension, thirty-nine days after Easter, we celebrated with loose-
leaf Typhoo and fresh crumpets. We resisted all offers for psychic
readings.

Calliope was unlike other journalists in that the local
spiritualists trusted her. She'd lived in Casadega for three months
and knew them all by name, and, unlike most journalists, she was
looking for authentic psychics to believe in, not mountebanks to
expose.

Calliope took my teacup, flipped it over, and offered it to me.

I turned it three times counterclockwise to access the past.

Calliope's deep brown eyes were shaded by a fountain of dark
brown curls that seemed to flow out of her head like a river eddied
by wind. Her lips were extra full, soft with moist flesh and kindness.
She was slight, tall—not as tall as me—and she had no grey hair.
I already had one white streak, which I had been coloring, despite
having lived only twenty-four short years.

Calliope squinted at the bottom of the cup. "Hmmm…
interesting. You've been up to a lot." She shook her head.
"Appalling, really." She rubbed her forehead, shut her eyes, and
waved one hand, as if to push away all the pain and darkness that
had frontloaded her brain. "Well, I don't see any reason to spin
a long yarn about what you've been doing. What matters is what
you're going to do now."

She turned the cup over and pushed it toward me. "Let's look
toward the future."

Outside the windows of the teashop, gulls in slanting flight
soared up toward the scant clouds in the eastern afternoon sky.

"Turn it the other way," she said.

I crossed myself three times right over left, guided the handle
thrice clockwise toward the future with my index finger, and pushed
the cup and saucer towards her.

Calliope looked inside lifting it to the level of her chin instead
of slumping over it. She sat upright, tilting her head to peer inside.

She gazed as though it were an endless cave spiked with stalactites and stalagmites of tea stems, carpeted by water moving in and out of shadow.

She gave a sour little smile, and sighed.

"Oh Calliope, don't think I'm going to ask you for any answers that would make you feel uncomfortable." I shrugged. "You don't have to tell me what it says."

She bit her lip. "No, it's all OK. I've trained myself. I'm not embarrassed by what I find."

She touched her cheek to brush away a stray eyelash. She closed her eyes and made a wish, and blew to send it flitting through the spring light.

Calliope took a deep breath and unfocused her eyes. "There is a dark form spreading its cloak over you like the wings of a bat. A crusader driven by half-truths who means to destroy you. He's lost you in Casadega. Strong energies here swirl from every house and church. The psychic noise has buffeted his wings, which are luffing like slack sails. You only have one connection to him, and must find and destroy it. It's not with you now."

"Is it a thing? A thought? Magic? An emotion?"

She stared into the spun glass eye. "I'm not sure. But he could use it to find you."

I closed my eyes, then opened them to see Calliope poised and leaning forward, still waiting for my response.

"Well, it couldn't be the box," I said. "Because I have that with me." I shuffled a deck of tarot cards that'd been stuffed into little silk bags nestled next to candle centerpieces at each table. "I used the box to find you."

"But Persephone, I see you are after him. You want to exact revenge, force explanations. To yell and carry on like Medea after a failed musical production. He's not going to let you go if you find him. So drop it."

Calliope folded her hands on the table and surrounded the cup. "The leaves are clear on this. They say drop it and forget him. Take your name back. And just be yourself."

Chapter 42

I took a post as a forensic pathologist while completing my final
year of internal medicine residency at Louisiana Medical University
in New Orleans. I had given up disguising myself. So, to protect
myself from Harry Ripberger Nillsen IV and the Athanatoi, I cast an
impenetrable white light around my aura to keep my enemies from
finding me.

My apartment intercom buzzed, knocking me fully awake with the
loud sound of a familiar voice.

"Persephone, dear." Medea's shrill tones disturbed the waters of my
brain.

At first I thought it must be the tail end of a nightmare, but the
voice grew louder.

"Persephone, your father and I are standing outside your apartment,
and your doorman won't let us in." She snapped her gum straight into my
ear. "Ring Victor, darling. Tell him who I am! We're famished and tired
from the flight. First class isn't what it used to be! There were the most
dreadful people onboard. A child of about sixteen playing his drumsticks
on a book called me a bitch! Can you imagine that?"

I rubbed the sight back into my eyes. "Is Daddy with you?"

"Not in spirit, but his carcass is parking our hideous rental. The damn thing looks like an unmarked police car. It's American-made. Oh Lord. Really Persephone, this whole city looks like post-war rubble. The ragtag people—*yeeftee* with their accordions and empty Maxwell house cans on street corners. *Touristas* everywhere you look with cameras slung around their necks in bunches as if they're trying to sell them. They probably are, Dear. *Hellia*! And women who look like human traffic! Ha! Hurry and tell Victor to open this door, will you?" She snapped her gum again. "I need a shower! Oh, here comes Angelo. Can you get Victor over here to help us with the suitcases?"

I opened my door, leaving it ajar. The familiar click of Medea's heels echoed down the corridor between the elevator and my apartment. My mother's lavender-gloved hand attached to a can of Lysol crossed the doorway first. The button of the can pressed and deployed.

"What are you doing, Medea?" I coughed and lunged for the can, grabbing it from her before she pushed her way into my living room wreathed in a cloud of disinfectant. "This stuff's poison!" I set it next to a magnolia bud on the polished oak mission-style coffee table.

"No it's not!" said Medea, stance firm and wide in my entry, hands on hips. My father stood gripping two suitcases three steps behind her.

While Medea listed all the airborne pathogens endemic to New Orleans, Angelo stacked the suitcases in a corner and raised the windows.

"I don't believe in Lysol either," Dad said, chuckling, "or Windex."

"I'm offended." I shook my head at my mother. "Are you saying your own daughter is dirty? Infectious?"

My apartment wasn't half bad, really. I had cleaned and straightened, arranged the pillows on the chenille sofa and matching chairs, dusted the fireplace mantle, scraped bugs from the windowsills and peeled cobwebs from the chandeliers.

"What a dump!" she said, channeling Bette Davis. Ignoring my collection of signed prints by Maxfield Parish, Aubrey Beardsley and Edward Gorey, she totally missed a watercolor I'd found at a garage sale in the French Quarter of a peacock under a waterfall, painted by a teenaged Tennessee Williams.

"Medea," I said. "You can hardly cast a stone. You're one of the baddest, trashiest, most warped of all femme fatales!"

"Come give your mother a big hug!" She smiled and her arms spread wide. She wore a monochromatic Jackie O. number, handbag and stacked heels, all matching her lavender gloves. "That's the nicest thing anyone's said to me all day!"

I squeezed out of my mother's World Wide Federation of Wrestling embrace and parked myself with my father on the sofa. He patted one knee and kissed my cheek.

"I love you, Daddy," I whispered into his ear.

He kissed me again.

Medea checked her one-eyed forties' moviestar hairdo and corrected a wayward lock in my Chippendale mirror, also scored at the same garage sale. It stood over the mantle, the frame exhibiting a subtle, patched crack. She cleared her throat and ran one index finger over the blemish. She spat her gum into a tissue pulled from her pocket, tossed the wad into the fireplace, took the customary deep breath to make herself an inch taller, and advanced to the sofa like a tugboat steaming into harbor.

I inched closer to my dad. His eyes followed Medea, lips compressing into a smile.

"Persephone!" she said, arms folded. "I want you to get off that sofa and start packing right now. This minute! You're coming back home with us!"

"No, I'm not," I said.

She reached for the aerosol can on the coffee table and gave the apartment a big arcing spray.

"Stop it, Medea!" I said. "Give me that can right now."

"I won't!"

"You're poisoning us!"

"I'm saving you!" she said, spraying everything in sight.

"You'll ruin the finishes! Give me that damned can!"

"No!"

"Have you been talking to Calliope?" I leaned forward, eyes watering from the airborne chemical droplets.

"Hmmph!"

"Then why bother to come here?"

"Because I knew you wouldn't listen unless I came in the flesh and dragged you onto that plane myself."

"You did talk to Calliope."

"I don't need to talk to Calliope. Séance nonsense! I don't need to talk to anyone. I can find out whatever I want. I can walk on the dark side too, Persephone, maybe better than anyone else. I can do more tricks than all of you little Greek witches put together!" She wagged a finger at me nonstop like only Medea could. "Who's Theodora anyway? Do you think I'm afraid of Penelope or your Yiayia?" Medea wrinkled up her nose. "Or your beloved Auntie Georgie?"

"Well, what about Hestia?"

"I went further than any of them," Medea said, lips tight, as if she'd just taken a sip of bad ouzo. "No one mentions Hestia."

"I mentioned her. Did you hear me, Mom? Did you go further up the astral plane than Hestia?"

"I told you not to speak of her," Medea whispered. "Never say her name out loud. Just get your bags and let's go."

"I'm not going anywhere. I'm going to stay here and finish my internal medicine residency."

"I don't want you to be a doctor!"

"Why not? I'm already a doctor. I became a pathologist and look—the stock market didn't crash!"

"Yet!" said Medea, eyes narrowing. "But you mark my words, little lady. The stock market will crash along with the real estate market! You're coming with me."

"No, I'm not."

"Doctors are only doctors!" Medea's eye muscles drew a horizontal line across her nasal bridge. "They're not kings of Persia or defenders of the bloody faith! All you'll be dealing with is death and dying, bad smells and pain control."

"What's wrong with that? The train's left the station. I already am a doctor. Pain control is a good thing. Wait 'til you need it someday."

"Death angels relieve the ultimate pain," said Medea. "But if you became a death angel you'd have seven hundred years of it. Seven hundred seventy seven years, to be exact. Think about what it would be like. Taking souls from dying bodies for seven centuries."

"How do you know everything a death angel does?"

"I came closer to it than Theodora or Yiayia. My natural gifts were stronger than all of them put together."

I smiled. "What about Hestia?"

"Maybe not her."

"I'll never be a death angel, Medea. But I don't mind being something very close to it."

"Bitch!" she screamed, throwing her fists in the air like Scarlet O'Hara. My mother stepped up onto my coffee table, straddled the bud vase with the magnolia in it, and shook the Lysol can in a fury.

"That's it, Medea," said Dad, voice low as if he were trying to cajole a stray dog into his car. "Get off the table. Now."

My eyes went wide with shock. In all the years I'd lived with my parents, I had never witnessed my father pick a fight with Medea. I'd heard tales of his rebellions against her rule, his interventions during her hysterical fits—like when she went bonkers over the straps and harnesses that held the drunken cattle in our barn that was eventually converted into the black box café. But I'd never seen anything like what I was witnessing now.

My father's face turned red. In an instant, he was on his feet, white knuckled, neck veins dilated like hoses, the blood vessel that crossed his forehead pulsating under his glistening skin. Still, he had control of his voice. He spoke with a measured hiss, forced into a low register—the voice of a military officer accustomed to commanding obedience. And I remembered that, before he'd met Medea, he had been a spy for the Greek royalists during Nazi occupation. It was built into his character to hold his hand close to his chest when he and his brother, the chief of secret police in Athens, were card sharks for Niarchos.

For the first time ever I was looking at the man as he had been, before Medea had ever met him.

She lowered her arm and narrowed her eyes in contemplation of his request.

Seeing her aegis down, I grabbed the spray away from her and ran toward the kitchen, intending to throw it in the trash.

"No you don't, you little tramp," Medea lunged at me like one of those panicked grannies who lift cars off squashed children. She knocked me to the floor and grabbed the can, then pointed it at my crotch.

"Let's stop beating around the bush, young lady. You need to clean up your act."

Dad pulled her off me like Hercules toppling the Nemean lion. "No, you don't, Medea." Angelo squeezed her wrist until she dropped the can. "*Stasi.*"

She resisted for a moment, then collapsed like a wilted lily in his arms.

"Angelo, I'm just so scared for her," she said, sniffling.

Within seconds she was drooped in his embrace and purring like a kitten, wetting his collar with her crocodile tears.

"I just don't want anyone after her," she pleaded. "Make her come back with us." Her face slackened and for an instant lost shape, all its handsome planes. The first time I could remember, he finally looked his age.

"Be civilized," he said, after a few moments. Then he turned to me, holding my sobbing mother in his lap in the middle of the living room floor, the bud vase toppled on the table, the magnolia tipped on its side, the center of its cup hidden. "Persephone, you can come with us, or stay here. But you must have someone to keep an eye on you, to protect you. You won't even know he's around."

"Christy?" I could see myself reflected in the shiny surface of the tabletop, looking like I had just woken up from a bad dream.

"No, someone more powerful," he said. "The chauffeur."

I studied my father's words, his posture, his close-cropped shadow of a beard that had begun to gray. Stubble filled his pores. It occurred to me now that he knew the chauffeur was Azrafel. "But I don't need him. Do I?"

"Yes you do, and he's already here. He's been here since before you even left Casadega."

"But I haven't seen him."

"You don't need to see him."

"That's not good enough," said Medea, tears glazing her eyes, purple mascara smeared on her cheeks.. "My daughter's in danger."

My heart, which had been locked shut against my mother's intrusions, swung open. A second first. Not only had I seen my dad in a new light, but now Medea appeared to be less operatic ogre than panicked mumsy.

"Persephone," she said, sobbing. "I can't go on fighting you like this."

"Don't fight me then," I said, wishing I could just bolt for the door. But I lived here.

My parents' concern for my wellbeing had an element of strange attraction. If the man in the black-billed hat was really watching over me, what danger could I possibly be in? He wouldn't let me die. After all, he'd caught me falling from the sky when Yiayia had yanked me out of the Ferris wheel.

"I love you, Persephone," Medea said. Her eyes turned toward mine, casting the same purplish hue that Yiayia's did. "I've always loved you. There! I've said it. I don't say that sort of thing often, but I'm saying it now. I'm trying to protect you. Become a death angel, and you'd be giving up all the joys of this world. At least in part."

I rolled my eyes. "How would you know?"

"You'd live with death for seven hundred seventy seven years, every waking and sleeping moment haunted by the deaths of those you've served."

"We all live with death every moment, anyway," I said. "We just pretend otherwise. Death is not the enemy. It's a new beginning." I picked up the magnolia, then put it back in its vase. I stuck my nose in it for a moment, inhaling lemon and sugar.

"But think of all you'd miss in life," she cried.

My eyes shifted to Dad. He seemed a preferable focus for my attention.

Wild ascending notes poured through the open window. A jazz funeral was making its way to Liberty Cemetery. Tubas, trombones and trumpets blew an emphatic statement to the triumphant air, crying out, "Just a closer walk with thee."

Medea went to the window to look, me following. Down the shotgun road, the brass band was swaying, parasols twirling with the music. A team of dancing pallbearers in white tuxedos rhythmically raised and lowered a casket draped in white lilies. One last dance with the dead.

"You'll miss normal relationships. And children," Medea said. "Who will take care of your soul when you're taking care of others?"

"I've already said I'm not going to be a death angel, Mother."

"In spite of all I've done, all the attempts I've made to try to distract and discourage you. The music lessons, the theatre, horseback riding, your education. Still you're only a step away from a seven-century career commitment, and I fear you're going to take that final step."

"I love you, Mother," I said, reaching around and patting her shoulder. "Auntie Georgie was right. You've tried to shield me. I've misunderstood your purpose my whole life, I know that now. But you don't have to worry."

"I couldn't tell you why when you were little," she said, reaching up her sleeve for another wadded Kleenex. "I thought you were too young to understand. I didn't ever guess you'd find out about all your potentials and possibilities. I should've known better. Of course you found out eventually. We all find out."

The funeral marched right under my window. After a dirge, the brass band broke into "N'awlins' Dizz Dat or Dudda." The crowd swung under my wrought-iron balcony towards the massive scrolled gates of the cemetery down the road. The odor of each sweating body commingled with tea roses and levitated through the window.

"Let's not worry about the past, Mom," I said, wiping a tear off her cheek with one finger.

Medea stiffened. "I suppose you are worried. That's why your hair turned white at your age. Pack your bags!" She stuffed the tissue back up her sleeve. "Please, Persephone."

"Sit down," I said. "I want to tell you both something."

They returned to the sofa, Dad stroking the lemony petals of the magnolia blossom. I served Typhoo in a Famille coral ground porcelain teapot painted with a blue-green landscape. A collector from Sotheby's had once offered to purchase the Qing Dynasty masterpiece for two-hundred-and-fifty-thousand dollars. But the handle on the top had been knocked off by Medea during one of her fits about a mis-sung aria. She'd glued it back on, but though still exquisite it was imperfect, and therefore worthless. So she'd given it to me.

I stood in front of both of them, looming like a factory foreman as they huddled over their tea.

"I want to tell you both together, once and for all. I am not going back with you. I'm going to stay here and be a doctor. And I will never, ever be a death angel."

Chapter 43

I eluded the usual prolonged, high-tension dialogue with Medea, and we three got along for two straight days. We went on a pirate ghost tour and visited Marie LaVeaux's House of Voodoo so Medea could satisfy her shopping impulses for Santeria memorabilia. We searched records at Saint Louis Cathedral to find Marie's marriage certificate to Jacques Paris and found out their address, now a museum. Medea went to the door, all charm and honeyed words, and introduced herself to Marie LaVeaux the Seventh, garnering us an invitation for tea with the old Creole healer, who'd been a nun at the Ursuline convent.

We took in the jazz and blues that saturated the air of the Crescent City at Dropkick Murphy's, Preservation Hall, and the Funky Pirate. Medea insisted we take Angelo to Commander's Palace and Antoine's so my dad could puzzle out the ingredients of their secret recipes, like wild burgundy escargot from the Commander and crab ravigote in a pastry dome from Antoine.

My parents were right. My ethics had eroded; my behavior had been dissipated. I trusted Calliope, Medea, and Angelo now.

Calliope had seen danger in the tea leaves. It was true Harry had vacillated between obsession and hatred. Though she'd only seen him once at the America's Cup Race in Newport, my mother had probed into Harry's mind and recognized the profile of a stalker, dangerous and delusional. His mind had been so dark for so long she hadn't dared filter through all the twisted images scrambling around his deep gray matter. But she'd seen chaos and felt his brewing hysteria. Now it struck me as odd that I'd wanted to hunt him down, confront him, make him confess the truth of why he'd been following me. I could've read his thoughts if I'd wanted to, but why bother? Also, he was scary. He'd been so self-centered, so irregular in his attachments, so untruthful. Now I knew he was insane. And slipping into an insane mind was the last thing I needed. If a person was too unstable for me to float into, then why would I want to confront such a person? After all, there had been madness in my own family.

And then I made a second connection. Harry had developed a mechanism for finding me, like my parents' internal radar, something like the box I'd found in the fairy ring and learned to use as a compass. But, the box wasn't a homing device for Harry. Wait a minute. The necklace!

Its pendant had been chipped from the mother crystal at Saint John the Theologian Monastery, where I'd been indoctrinated by Father Stavros.

But how did Harry ever get his milky white hands on it? I could imagine him staking out the monastery in cat burglar clothes, slipping by the sentries on a moonless night, chipping off chunks of the Ancient One, one piece to set in the necklace he later gave me to dig out of the silver sand pail, another chunk for him to keep. Perhaps the crystal he kept was the homing device for my crystal necklace?

Yet I wasn't sure. Nor did I know how Harry had learned about the crystal in the first place, or if he'd really found his way into the hive-mind of the monks who used it as a meditation object. Perhaps I would never know, for sure. But what difference did it make? I was through with Harry Nillsen IV for good.

My cell phone rang over the shrill din of hawkers from the street below selling postcards, pleine air paintings, customized perfumes to attract the opposite sex, tropical drinks in Styrofoam cups, and steaming cheesy muffeletas.

"Dr. Vican?" Her voice was hoarse, like that of a woman who smoked and drank straight whiskey.

"Speaking."

"This is Helen, medical death investigator from the Office of the Chief Medical Examiner."

"Hi, Helen."

"Got an MVC with one fatality. Young kid."

"How young?"

"I dunno," she said. "Looks about twenty-five. Face was in good shape. On his way back from a fishing trip. Car's been impounded. It was filled with red and speckled trout. One hundred fifty, maybe two hundred of them. Poor dude was covered in fish. Those boys had a great day up until the accident. The other guys were wearing seat belts. They walked away."

"Do you need an autopsy?"

"The body's at Estelle Evangeline Funeral Home," Helen said. "We just need you to view it and take samples of blood and vitreous."

"OK. I know where that is," I said, sighing.

I'd planned to drive over Lake Ponchartrain to the Tattersall Stable and go for a ride on my old horse, Agrippa the Ingrate. I threw scrubs over my breeches and flipped open my jewelry box, digging for the crystal necklace, that sinister gift from Harry. I held it up to the light, looking for flaws that might reflect the shadows of his face. But the crystal was clear, telling me nothing. I put it in my purse, along with a hand-hammered silver spoon etched with the letter M to bury it with.

My hand settled on the knob of the door and I started to turn it, but something clawed at my hair and yanked me back. I felt a fluttering, then a tightening as steel fingers took hold of the long strands twisted back into a pony tail.

Yiayia! Again! I knew it! So she'd decided to leave the peace and quiet of the perfume bottle.

Her cold fingers tightened into a fist. She hung onto my pony tail as if it were a bell rope, and the bell had pealed once but then locked in a second mid-ring.

"Yiayia," I pleaded. "Not my hair again." My head slammed back and a lancinating pain ripped through my neck and shoulders. My scalp was alive with needle and pins as my follicles seemed to loosen and crawl over the top of my skull. My hands and arms flew backwards to strike at her. But she melted into vapor each time I swung.

The grip on my hair tightened further, pulling downward. My eyes watered. My breath exploded from between my teeth. "Yiayia, don't. Please!"

Two hands came from behind me and slapped both my cheeks at the same time, while another continued to tear at my ponytail.

"I know your tricks, Yiayia Friday," I gasped. "I feel three hands."

A catch in my brain released with a click like a door lock picked open by a bent paper clip. I saw stretching before my dazed eyes a scene of the astral plane that Yiayia had once showed me in a textbook on ancient cosmology. Only this time I looked upon a rolling expanse of translucent sky, heavy with moisture.

Aurora borealis rose out of the blue fog of blinding pain that wrenched my scalp. Like all fog, it smelled like spring. Yiayia showed me the rainbow bands of the eight astral spheres that rotated between Earth and Heaven. They were jewels set in orbs and the final sphere far off in the distance was swimming with lights, speeding tiny blazes of shooting stars. Their motion decelerated until they appeared first as fireflies flashing, and then as winged angels. Within the farthest ring a prismatic flower exploded like a dandelion seed pod drifting upon the wind.

I was gazing at a vision of Heaven.

Three rings away from the angelic sphere, the amethyst light of Yiayia's soul gleamed with the same violet radiance as her eyes.

"That's you, Yiayia," I said. "I understand that's you."

The feeling returned to my scalp. She had unveiled a sacred truth, at least up to my capacity to perceive it.

Yiayia's hands remained entwined in my hair, but now reached down and rubbed the ache out of my forehead.

"Show me where my mother dwells," I said.

I saw Medea and Theodora embedded in the outermost ring, emeralds set in platinum ether.

"And Christy?" Toward Heaven the glimmering opal of Christy's soul burst into iridescent view, begging to be seen and admired.

"And—Hestia?

Past Christy, one just step from Heaven set in bold relief, floated Hestia, like a pre-Raphaelite angel. Each slow motion flap of her silver-spotted grey wings cast off a dust of metallic luster, like platinum dust.

"You must get to that ring where Hestia dwells," Yiayia said, "and be a Death Angel."

My grandmother had drawn together a yawning chasm that stretched between two worlds. I understood that my own velvet black light still glowed outside these spheres, next to Georgie in an earthly realm.

I like it here on Earth, I thought.

"Yet, in the minds of the living, death in his black-cloaked skeletal form casts a fearsome shadow," Yiayia said. "So the duty of a psycho-pomp is to ease the passing of souls from beneath the shadow into the next life. People cry for a solution to the riddle of life—and the answer can be found in the riddle of death."

Yiayia evaporated again, and my hand finished turning the doorknob. Warm wind blew an oak leaf across the threshold. I climbed into my beige Volvo and drove west down I-10 towards Baton Rouge. The car rattled as I pulled off the road into a ditch by the Whiskey River Bridge over the Atchafalaya Swamp. The trench was hollow, an enclosure beneath the swathe. I skidded on wet leaves and climbed over crumbling tree trunks, then squatted in the deep soft carpet of pine needles soaked with swamp-water and dug a hole with my silver spoon. M for Matepas. A susurrant rhythm of distant hooves vibrated through the soft earth. I held up the crystal by its chain and inspected it one last time. Then I dropped it into the hole and covered it with loam and decaying leaves.

Chapter 44

All nine beds in the Intensive Care Unit at Centenary, a small private hospital affiliated with Louisiana Medical University, were filled. The drugged patients were laid out on ice-white sheets, like fresh ocean perch, visible within glass rooms that circumscribed the nurses' station. Tubes attached to beeping drips pierced their limbs and orifices amid a fracas of beeping alarms and blinking monitors. A team of general surgery residents and scut-monkey medical students surrounded the chief resident and also the professor emeritus for "Chief's Rounds."

The disciples looked on with straight, stern faces, clipboards in hand. Professor Cornwell wore a long, white lab coat reaching to his knees. It would protect his tweed suit—the kind with the suede elbow patches—from the most virulent, resistant, and persistent pathogens grown in infection control laboratories. He could've been the President, or an investment banker, or a museum curator, or a CEO of a life insurance company. His large, square jaw and straight, well-proportioned nose were angled down in a bronze study. His black pupils scanned his two dozen minions like a periscope searching out ships on the surface of the sea.

Professor Cornwell cleared his throat. His gaze flitted across the semicircular ICU from one post-op bed to the next, eyes quick as a pair of hummingbirds.

"Pimp time," whispered one straggler to another in the back of the crowd. They both stifled yawns, heads down.

Professor Cornwell's well-bred features tensed. "Take bed six," he said to the assemblage.

I strained my ears. My patient, Noelle Thibidaux, had been fighting for her life for three weeks.

"She's in shock after a ruptured appendix, peritonitis, and antibiotic anaphylaxis." His eyes landed on a baggy-eyed medical student who held up a pharmaceutical manual to cover his stiff-jawed yawn. "What are the three main causes of shock?" The professor rocked his weight back and forth in his polished Italian shoes. "Mr. Stone, what is your answer?"

"Uhh….Anaphylaxis?"

"Wrong! Tomorrow you will give me a fifteen-hundred word exposition on the etiology and pathophysiology of shock. If you expect to graduate. Eventually."

Cornwell's sharp gaze landed on another student. "Dr. Wing?"

The nervous intern sucked a bloody cuticle and looked up from his shoes. "Sir. I believe the three main forms of shock are cardiogenic, hypovolemic, and septic."

The chief resident, Dr. Skip Kelly, a curly-black-haired young man with a diamond earring, grinned like a wildcat, pearly teeth exposed.

"Dr. Wing, is that your final answer?" Cornwell's eyes were x-ray probes that appeared to see through Wing's skull, straight into his brain.

"Yes sir. It is."

"You are correct."

Some of the members of the team sighed in relief. Others rolled their eyes.

They roamed through the ICU from patient to patient, like bees exhausting the nectar of peach trees along an orchard row.

The students gathered around bed six behind the professor emeritus and the catlike chief resident. Skip stood beside the intern, Wing, who was bent over the sedated patient, unstapling her abdominal incision. I'd seen him that morning trying to parallel park by braille. The license plate on his little square car proudly read, "MD2B."

"That femoral line needs to come out," said Skip. "It's been four days. Could cause bacteremia. Close to her …" He met the eyes of each member of his audience, then in a snide whisper said, "genitalia."

Professor Cornwell resumed rocking in his shoes.

Wing resumed biting his cuticles. "Yes, sir," said the anxious young Asian, seeming more youth than man.

"Tell the internist," said the chief res, who now reminded me of an older, sober version of Lou Reed from The Velvet Underground.

"That's me," I said, hands in pockets, rattling my calipers and penlight. "But if you take out the femoral, she'll still need a central line." I lowered my voice, trying not to sound excitable. "Can you put in a subclavian?" I said, using the sweetest tone possible.

"Not in here," said the dark-haired rocker. His diamond stud sparkled. He walked over to me and lowered his voice. "This place is a cesspool. I'd need to take her to the OR. Besides, our team was on-call last night. We're trying to finish rounds and get outa here. Buzz the operator for the on-call surgeon."

Wing looked away and fiddled with heavy manuals sagging in his pockets.

"Fine," I said, trying not to look offended. Female physicians were often sneered at for being too empathetic, too emotional, or too excitable. I was a hot-blood in sea of cool-blooded creatures teeming with testosterone. I chose to contain my excitement and retain credibility among them.

"Operator," I said, in my bossiest Judi Dench voice. "I need the on-call surgeon."

"I'll page," she said. "Hold on." I answered my beeper and held both phones to my ears, one in each hand, on hold.

"This is Dr. Sharp!" His voice was loud, course, amplified like the booming bass of the Wizard of Oz. Or maybe James Earl Jones, or God. But not the God of the New Testament.

"Hello, this is Dr. Vican," I said. "Could you have one of your residents put in a subclavian central line for me?"

A handsome young cop walked by and winked, holding a cup of steaming coffee in each hand. He was headed for bed seven, which held a slight Cajun male from Angola Prison who was suffering from blood poisoning and a heart valve infection due to shooting up Mexican black-tar heroin. The patient was tucked in tight as a letter in an envelope. Police officers and black-tie agents of the law hovered over him. He was doing ten years for heading up a child slavery ring that'd been busted in the attic of an Opelousas plantation, where small nimble fingers cut emeralds imported from Venezuela.

A groan echoed from the receiver into my left ear, then a sigh.

"Aren't you listening? This is Dr. Dante Sharp!" he yelled.

I pressed the speaker button so the entire ICU could hear him.

"Do you know to whom you are speaking? I am the chief of trauma. I am the director of the American Thoracic Society!"

I dialed up the speaker volume.

"I have dined with the President and have lectured in Geneva! Don't you know who I am?"

"I'm so pleased to make your acquaintance," I purred. "I hope we get to meet soon, in person."

I let my gaze rest for a few extra moments on the young policeman. Even under fluorescent lights, his dark auburn hair was fiery, tinged with gold, like my dad's. He smiled at me as I spoke.

"I'm Dr. Persephone Vican. I've made tissue diagnoses on many of your biopsies. So now you have a voice to go with my name. I'm the assistant chief of pathology. And I'm finishing my Internal Medicine Residency. Isn't that something?"

I turned the speaker volume to maximum and sat down at the desk in front of the nurses' station outside of bed seven. A maternal-looking nurse with a short bleached-blond bob offered me a Boston Crème donut on a paper towel. It didn't look infectious, so I ate it. I could smell the soap on the cute cop, ultra-pure, like Dreft or Ivory Flakes wafting out of the open door. I could hear him conversing with the other cops around bed seven and couldn't help but feel anxious. Or maybe I was labeling the feeling wrong. Maybe it was really longing.

"I have a septic patient in bed six who needs a central line," I told Dr. Sharp, who now was breathing like a winded horse on the other end of the line. And your chief resident said I need to speak with the on-call attending. So would you be so kind as to either insert the line yourself or call one of your residents?"

Jaws went slack around bed six. The cute cop by bed seven smiled, dimples pressed into his cheeks. Professor Cornwell stifled a laugh in the caduceus pinned on his tie.

"I don't call residents," said the enraged voice of Darth Vader. "And no one of your station calls me!"

"I can't see why not," I said. "You're really charming."

The intern removing staples from the bloated abdomen of my patient in bed six dropped his scalpel. The Professor Emeritus released a short belly laugh, then coughed. The cute cop sipped his coffee. The inmate watched, arms folded across his barrel chest, tattoos of snakes writhing up his arms. A male nurse slipped me a below-the-waist high-five.

The rock-star surgeon rolled his eyes. OK, I'll do it, he mimed, pointing at himself. Of course, I could also hear his thoughts. You're a tough bitch, babe. I'd fix your plumbing any day.

"Well, thank you," I said. "I have a qualified surgeon here who just offered to help the patient. Have a happy day!"

The nervous intern knocked the surgical tray off its stand, scattering bloody staples and instruments on the patient's sheets.

"You made my day," said Dr. Cornwell.

"Way to go!" said the nursing supervisor.

"That was wonderful," said the cute cop, sipping his coffee. "I've got a commissioner I'd like to do that to." His name plate read "Det. Breard."

Agrippa the Ingrate had a brass nameplate too, on his boxstall. Only bigger.

"Hi, Detective Breard," I said.

I noticed a shadow of baby powder under his collar. He had the swelled physique of a horseman, all brawn and biceps and bulging hamstrings. He rubbed his thick neck with his free hand and held out his coffee cup.

"Can I buy you a coffee?"

"No thanks, Detective Breard."

His teeth were straight except for a charming gap between the two front ones, which were big and white like Chiclets.

"I've already had a lot." I rubbed my face with the back of one hand to wipe off any residue of Boston crème donut.

"Name's John. What about lunch?" His grin was steady, almost brazen, and he spoke as if he enjoyed the sound of his own voice.

"I'm not done. Besides, lunch is for wimps." A flush heated up the hollows of my cheeks. "Are you a horseman?"

"Yeah." He tipped his head back and laughed. "You're observant. I guess that's why you're a doctor. I grew up on a ranch. Family farm's in Covington. The horse trade—a shitty business all around. You know horses?"

"Love them. Have an old horse, Agrippa the Ingrate, at the Tattersall Stable."

"Well, I'd love to go riding sometime," he said, his face pinked by sun and wind, smile steady, voice musical. His N'awlins' accent was thick and galvanized as the man himself. "Hey, you like cartoons?"

"Well," I cocked my head one way, then the other. "Yeah," I said, almost like a question.

The erratic clapping of clogs, preferred footwear of surgeons everywhere, echoed through the circular hall of the ICU. The surgical team, heads down, followed the distinguished professor out the double doors, leaving only the rock star resident with the rockabilly lid and the pale nervous intern with rounded shoulders at the bedside of my patient.

"Which subclavian should we thread?" asked the Chief Resident.

"The right."

"Correct again, Wing. Tell me why."

"The large lymphatic duct is on the left and the right lung is lower in the chest."

"Excellent, Wing."

They unfolded a sterile surgical blue fenestrated cloth over the sleeping patient's right neck and shoulder and half her face in order to place the line.

Noelle was a wasted-looking woman of twenty-eight with sunken temples and thinning brown hair tied in a loose bun. Her skin was sallow from resolving liver failure. She was somnolent, though arousable by shaking and loud talking.

"You OK, ma'am?" the chief asked the patient beneath the rag in calm, quiet voice.

No response; still sleeping.

"Okay, Wing. I'm going to insert the introducer needle aiming toward the contralateral nipple. You pass the guidewire."

A bedpan odor wafted by, then dissipated. The unnatural light couldn't help but reflect the beauty and good health of Detective Breard.

I felt a queasiness I interpreted as embarrassment—both for the patient in bed six as well as for myself—ashamed that such aromas could even exist in my presence. Like when you're driving past a septic field and say preemptively, "Well, that certainly was not me." Irrational. There were lots of smells in the ICU I had no control over.

John Breard gave me a remote, but kind nudge, like one horse to another.

"I have a cartoon art show at the 'Lil' Red Tricycle Gallery on Bourbon Street," he said, rotating his watch around his wrist. "What about tonight? There's a reception afterward. Soul Food meets Chinese take-out, catered by Miss Francoise."

An elderly black lady with a hairnet knotted in the middle of her forehead pushed a wobbly cart by. It was stacked with steaming lunch trays offering conservative portions of chopped chicken with gravy and peas, heavy on the rosemary.

"Hospital cuisine," I said, scrunching up my nose.

The conscious patients sat forward, mouths watering as if they were being served a power lunch of Shrimp Roumalade, Stuffed Eggplant and Café Brulot from Galatoire's.

"Okay," I said, the heat rising to my face again. "What time?"

"Seven?" said Breard, brushing his hands together as if to get rid of the sweaty smell of the place.

"Good then." I shifted my weight from foot to foot, trying not to appear too eager. "I can meet you there."

"Are you sure I can't offer you a police escort?"

"No thanks. I mean no—but thank you." I saw clarity in his dark brown eyes, no broken capillaries, no shifty eye movements. Just the steady gaze of a person who didn't seem to be hiding anything.

"Good." He leaned forward and whispered, "I'm done questioning my jailbird over there. Got to get back to the station." He had one big dimple and one small one.

Back in room seven the other cop shook his head, gave me a fleeting smile, then sat down in a chair and opened up the sports page. The convict pouted, dark sunglasses pushed up his nasal bridge, arms crossed. He leaned his head back on a stack of pillows. A stone statue of a sick, angry mobster.

"Get me a chest tube tray and a stat x-ray!" called Skip, the rock star resident, just then. "We've popped her lung!"

Within seconds nurses were milling like ants on a sugar cube.

I poked my head into room six. "You need anything?"

"No, thanks. We've got it under control."

"Hey, Skip," I said. "I'll write for your x-ray and order you a Diprovan drip and a flutter valve."

"Thanks," said the chief res, flipping curls out of his eyes. "We can handle it after that."

Noelle Thibidaux was an unfortunate young woman whose multiple organ failure had required hemodialysis. She was finally off pressors and peeing on her own. The skin on her lips sloughed with Stevens Johnson's Syndrome and her face and torso flaked with toxic epidermal necrolysis. Just like it sounds, TEN is an allergic condition in which the deep cells in the skin die and the surface peels off in sheets.

Now the perpetual worried look on the face of the intern contracted into a deeper scrunch, halfway between a lament and a scowl, as the chief resident put in a chest tube to expand the collapsed lung. Wobbly wheels of a portable x-ray machine rattled down the hall to take a picture of the reinflated lung.

I thought I'd leave the surgeons to fix their mistake, pump the lung back up, and save face. I was hot and sweaty. Trying to butt out of my patient's chest tube drama, I took the stairs instead of the elevator. I'd decided to get some fresh Cajun air in the bougainvillea garden. I longed to sit for a few moments beside the fountain of the beautiful moon goddess Phoebe, who had a dolphin at her knee spewing oracular waters.

Chapter 45

In the breezy garden, I took off my lab coat. Unlike those of the other residents, its pockets carried no manuals. Not that I practiced medicine with hubris. I had faith. Faith helped.

I folded my coat and laid it beside me on a stone bench in front of the marble fountain. Quarters and pennies rolled out of the pockets onto the flagstone footers. I picked them up and threw them in one by one, watching the water ruffle as the wind picked up and carried each ripple further out towards the low wells of the granite pool that surrounded the fountain.

I'd never wished at a well before, but prayed instead. Not that wishing wasn't valid. But prayers were like wishes with bulging chest muscles, the kind you could tap with a reflex hammer, then watch contract.

I sat on the stone bench and looked up at Phoebe, a Delphinic precarnation of the Holy Virgin. I bent my head and whispered, my hair draping my face like a veil.

"O Lord Almighty, the Healer of our souls and bodies, You Who put down and raise up, Who chastise and heal also; do You now, in Your great mercy, visit our sister Noelle Thibidaux, who is sick. Stretch forth Your hand that is full of healing and health, and raise her up from her bed, and cure her of illness. Put away from her the spirit of disease and of every malady, pain and fever to which she is bound; and if she has sins and transgressions, grant to her remission and forgiveness, in that You love mankind; Lord God, pity Your creation, through the compassions of Your Only-Begotten Son, together with Your All-Holy, Good and Life-Creating Spirit, with Whom You are blessed, both now and ever, and to the ages of ages. Amen."

And in the garden of the Delphinian statue, the live oaks whispered back. I struggled to hear the murmurs as their leaves rubbed together and fluttered. New leaves opened in cries of birth while mature leaves shook in under-breaths carried by the spirits surrounding me. Yes I believe in all things seen and unseen.

"We are what is left of an ancient forest," whispered one.

"I am six hundred years old," said another.

"You, you, you," said the leaves, sighing.

"Yes, I hear you," I said. "I'm listening."

The garden was a courtyard banked by cherry-bark oaks and bald cypress that refreshed the exhausted air from Liberty Street. Scents of the city—cars, garbage, and cooking grease—breezed by to be consumed by the leaves of the band of trees that stood guard behind the towering stone walls. Branches bowed and swept the ground, their exalted limbs twice as long as their trunks. A pair of dueling oaks stood in the corners of the great courtyard, fifty feet apart, where many men had thrown down a glove for honor. A suicide oak stood in another corner. Under it, hopeless TB patients had taken their own lives by heavy ingestion of angelica and opium tinctures.

"Where you stand is an ancient tributary of the Mississippi River," murmured the still, small voice of a massive tree. "A whole family is buried beneath me: mother, father, two children. Their bones are my roots. This is a holy place."

"Yes," I said, listening for the fluttering of wings.

"Jacques Iberville's wedding band was tossed beneath me in a lover's quarrel. Now the ring encircles one of my delicate tendrils below the ground."

The wind was awake in the leaves, lisping, ruffling the water. I looked for koi, but only the coins at the bottom of the fountain shone silver and copper.

A hot wind swatted down, a gust animating my white coat, as if it was trying to stand up from the bench. The fountain water began to bubble. Not Jacuzzi-sized bubbles, more like soda bubbles, which rose to the top and drifted together to form legible words in an otherwise quiet pool.

Angelikes, aoratos, doree pheroomenon non taxeseen. Invisibly attended by the angelic hosts.

The words lingered long enough for me to read them in Greek. I mumbled them many times, then looked up at "golden-wreathed Phoebe," sister to Zeus, one of the original children of the Titans. Her consort was her brother Coeus. They had two daughters: Leto, who bore Artemis and Apollo; and Asteria, the mother of Hecate.

I sat on the bench staring at words embossed in water that was unlike water. The words did not move, the message appeared solid as ice. Marble Phoebe towered above me, a dolphin to her right spewing from his blow hole, a sprig of laurel in her left hand. In her right hand she cupped a bowl, water spilling over its edge into the fountain pool. She sat on a tripod chair, over a fissure carved out of the rock base through which fountain water was in continuous flow as though from an underground stream. *Invisibly attended by the angelic hosts.* I reached into the pool to dispel the words, but they reformed around my finger. I agitated the sentence, but it rewrote itself. Images of darkness, a moon shrouded by clouds passed through my mind. Still the words persisted in the fountain pool.

"Listen to my breath," whispered the largest bent oak, leaves fluttering.

"Tell me," I said.

Two eagles passed overhead, silent except for the rippling patter of soaring wings. A murder of crows descended, flooding the branches of the suicide oak, oddly flocking before dusk.

The hushed whisperings of the great tree carried the rustic aroma of a crushed leaf of bay laurel. Cloudy memories of my days at the bedside of Noelle Thibidaux burned my eyes like pepper. Then, something wonderful happened. The bracing scent of laurel darkened and joined something in the Cajun air to produce the smell

of my favorite flower, the lily. This time I submerged both hands to
the wrists, stirring up the letters into Greek alphabet soup. The water
seemed to bubble harder, faintly sulfurous, as though it were coming
from some subterranean source through a fault in the Earth that lay
beneath the fountain. Yet the letters reformed. *Invisibly attended by
the angelic hosts.* Then, below them, a name: *Noelle Thibidaux.*

Chapter 46

I took the stairs two at time. I was panting by the time I reached bed six in the ICU.

"I'm calling it," the anesthesiologist was saying, tiny sweat droplets coating his upper lip.

The ER doc, Skip, the rock-star chief resident, and a team of nurses and techs stood back away from the bed.

"Time of death, 3:58 p.m.," said the anesthesiologist.

The chief resident peeled off his gloves. "I'm sorry," he said, meeting my eyes and locking his gaze. "She arrested five minutes after we got the chest tube in. Maybe an embolus." He hung his head. "I'll fill out the death certificate and do the death note. Then I gotta get some sleep." He slipped out of Noelle's room, found a phone in the arc of the nurses' station, and started dictating a death summary.

The nervous intern sat hunched over Noelle's chart, reading, chewing a pencil, yellow paint flecking his teeth.

"No," I said to myself. Then, "Why?" I whispered, now standing alone next to the body.

Noelle Thibidaux lay still and white on the bed, the sheet pulled up to her neck. I lifted the sheet and pressed my hand under her left breast—no apical pulse. Still, I felt she somehow remained in that body. Perhaps not securely, maybe half in, half out.

Her bun had come undone, and her hair fell back from her face in loose brown twists of light. As I opened her eyelids I began to feel a pull, as if I were the Earth torn from my orbit, wanting to fling myself into her. I wondered if there was anything I could do.

Fine, I thought. I'm supposed to be a potent being. They say I'm a death angel in the making. I could do something about Noelle, right? It can't be too late. She's not completely gone. I can feel her soul, see her memories, her twin boys at home sharing comic books, her husband weeding the hydrangeas.

The smell of lilies hovered in a violet cloud above the head of the bed. A small, weak, flickering green light floated next to Noelle. Then a gleaming sword slowly pierced the cloud. I rubbed my eyes, and watched as Noelle's mouth opened, as if to let out a small breath. From the tip of the sword hung a drop of gall, brown—dark, but with a hint of metal, like oxidized copper.

"No!" I said. I probably shouldn't have been surprised to find Hestia right there in the ICU, but I was. "Please!" I reached over, grasped Noelle's small chin, and closed her mouth.

The gall waited, like a bit of roasted lamb on the end of a stripped green stick. I shoved the bed frame, forcing my weight against it. It wouldn't budge. I reached under the mattress, took hold of the bottom sheet and yanked, pulling, sliding the weight of Noelle's body a few inches toward me.

"I know you're here!" I pleaded, but softly. "Stop. Please."

I held my breath to lock the door to room six and sucked in another deep breath on top of the last to draw the privacy curtain. My stomach and lungs heaved as if I were watching a murder take place—and I was. I had to stop it.

The gall hung closer to her mouth now. Her soul light sputtered.

"Please don't take her," I begged, dragging the sheet, struggling to slide her body toward me a few more inches and away from Noelle's hovering death angel. But no one turns a bed on Hestia.

A ball of blue fire encased in a smoldering crust buzzed across the ceiling. It followed the course of a metal beam, floating down like a pin-holed helium balloon. It hovered for a moment, and then, spinning like Jupiter, slammed me against the wall with such force I saw stars. I slid to the floor between wall and bed.

Essence of lilies blanketed the room. The ball of lightning seemed to stare hard into my eyes. It reinflated and levitated, even slower than it had descended, spinning in place like a fragment of a torn-off star in furious rotation. The sphere fizzled across the metal-beam construction of the room, a giant luminous bowling ball rolling along a pinless lane. It whizzed through an air vent, then disappeared.

A multitude of white birds gathered in the air above the bed.

I heard the voice, soft, familiar, maternal. "Persephone," it said.

I slouched deeper onto the floor.

"I am taking her soul to heaven," said the voice.

The hair on my arms stood straight up. "Why can't you reveal yourself? You're scaring me," I said, my face heating up as I admitted the truth, which I was certain she already knew.

"I *am* revealing myself," she said. "Do not for a second confuse a death angel with a villain. Demons lie and make people believe there is no order in the universe, only pain and doubt. Have faith."

"But I can't see you." I tried to relax my eyes, to see with my soul the way Yiayia Friday had taught me when we'd read the coffee grounds.

"You don't see me because I'm not your death angel. I have not come to birth you to your next incarnation. I belong to Noelle Thibidaux."

"Please, don't take her now," I said. My stomach tumbled and groaned. "It's not...."

"No one escapes fate." Her voice expanded to fill the room. "Stay back, watch and learn. Or I will show you a force more fierce than any golden bull or starred horse of the Apocalypse, or even of a ghost on a strappado. I can show you seven fiery heads of dragons, fourteen faces of flaming fire, a three–headed asp engulfing a mingled cup of aromatic poisons—melanite, cordite, and villainous saltpeter. Stay back, and let her be born!"

I shivered, my ears ringing from the boom of the voice. "How do I know you're real?"

"Angels see all things at once." Her voice came feminine again, melodic, rich and ringing. "And angels don't need logic, memory, or faculties of reason."

Cold sweat erupted on the back of my neck. "But I'm not...."

"So grow," she said. "Become one."

The gall fell into Noelle's mouth. Her tiny light flickered and went out with a lazy sibilance of smoke.

"No." I clenched my fists. "I'll never become one."

Noelle exhaled the final collection of air trapped in her lungs—the death rattle.

"Cup your hands," said the voice. A flapping that came from above startled me. A grey wing, speckled white, like that of an enormous guinea hen, stretched down once through the ceiling, brushed my forehead, then vanished. I looked into my palms. A flaky substance like thin honey-cakes fell as dew, landing soft as poinsettia petals.

"Manna," Hestia said. "Eat it. You're of a certain purity. It will give you physical and spiritual nourishment."

"Thank you," I said, nibbling one of the crisp sweet puffs. I wrapped the rest in a paper towel for later.

A shimmering column of pixilated light rose before me. Hestia held the soul of a sleeping child in her arms. Then the two, like fractals, floated through the ceiling in a shower of prismatic rays. And were gone.

Chapter 47

I returned to the garden of wind-music and rustling oaks, to Phoebe and the Dolphin. The water was liquid glass now. The faint breeze carried only a morsel of bay laurel, not a whole feast like before.

I dipped a hand into the fountain pool, surprised by its coolness. I churned it back and forth, in circles and figure eights. If I listened hard enough I might be able to hear gas beginning to bubble up in the water to form another message. Maybe it would sound like a soda can being opened, or the hissing of the volcano in the Caldara of Santorini. Maybe it would sound like me finding myself in a paddle boat in a giant glass of champagne.

I drooped like a willow for Noelle Thibidaux, for her bereaved husband and young twin sons. The stone bench felt warmed by the churnings of the Earth herself. I looked up at marble Phoebe and water the color of clear eyes erupting from the dolphin.

The wind stirred, like sleeping oaks awakening. The smells of rotting leaves that had fallen onto the grass carpet mixed with decomposing bark under a mist of rain. Lucent vapors rose up and swaddled me in a sticky embrace, heavy as a robe of buffalo skin or a wet saddle blanket.

Phoebe's pale marble lips began to redden and twitch. They parted and she breathed, nostrils flaring. A fleshy tone broke through fissures on her stone face, like a baby chicken cracking open its shell. She raised the curtains of her eyelids, onyx pupils indistinguishable from irises.

My heart pounded in agitation, with extra beats and pauses, anticipating the next crisis.

Then Phoebe spoke. "Do you believe in God, Persephone?"

"I—yes. I do."

She smiled. "And can you prove it, Doctor?"

"To myself. Yes."

"How?"

"Because I see God just as I see you here, only more intensely." I answered with great formality, as if at once I had become solemn and old.

The afternoon sunlight slanted through spaces between the ancient oaks, not quite reaching the dolphin. Phoebe gazed at me steadily through a beam of light. Then she closed her eyes, becoming marble once more. The narrow sky over the courtyard began to drop clear pellets of water, so I put on my white coat and walked home, cooled by the large, occasional raindrop.

Chapter 48

The Greek revival building my French Quarter apartment was carved out of what had once been a local magistrate's getaway cottage, where he partied on weekends with his Haitian mistress and second family. Seventy years later the building had been repurposed into a quadroon whore house. My rooms had once been the salon where beautiful consorts would sing and dance, recite poetry, and serve absinthe and laudanum to Confederate soldiers, whose bones ached with fatigue and deep cold, prior to lovemaking.

But my home had received many house blessings thanks to my Beloved Father Seraphim, a monk from the local skete. The Spirit in the air had been restored.

I opened the windows and fastened back the shutters, inviting the cascading waves of jasmine, like the hair of a wood nymph, to visit as I recuperated from my sparring bout with my patient's death angel. And not just any death angel—the one with the grey-spotted wings. And when my ancestor Hestia, her ministering interrupted, had flung ball lightening at me, I had given up.

It had been a big day already. But I was passion's slave, and I had a date.

I stripped off my scrubs, *PROPERTY OF ANGELICA HEALTHCARE SYSTEM* stamped all over the pockets, and tossed them into the Rattan clothes basket already filled to the brim with wrinkled greens. I slipped into a steaming orange blossom bubble bath. The foam peaked like perfect meringue.

My favorite place to dine was in the tub, so I feasted on croissants smeared with cream cheese and transparent violet jelly a friend had sent me from France.

I submerged ten times, for the ten nodes of the Tree of Life, praying "*Hypnee meta angeles, Noelle Thibidaux, sto kalo.* Sleep with the angels, Noelle Thibidaux. You have gone to the good."

I dressed in a black sateen silver-belted sheath Auntie Georgie had bought me when we'd gone to see "The Wraith's Progress" at New Orleans Opera Company on opening night, not long ago.

An hour later, the buzzer rang and I ran to the window. Mine was the right front apartment facing Decatur, so I always had to stick my head way out and crane it to the left like an owl to see who was at the door.

"Hi Pete!" It was the sweet UPS man from church, whose wife owned the best Greek pastry shop in town.

"Got something for ya!" he hollered.

"Baklava?" I asked, my voice full of hope.

He stepped away from the iron-scrolled gate and craned his neck back to see me. "No. Next time, though. But you got something here from Greece."

"Do I need to sign?"

"Yeah." He was still holding the box, shoulders pulled down like a monkey's.

I held my breath.

The iron gate to the courtyard unlocked and Pete came up to my front door. His belly drooped over his belt from a combination of his wife's honey-seeped pastries and weekend afternoons playing cards and consuming café au lait and beignets with his buddies from church. So he had a mobile shelf he could balance the box on to give his arms a little rest.

"Got a date?" he said, offering me a signature pad that sat on top of the unwieldy package like food on a waiter's tray.

"Yep," I said, in a bland tone. I didn't want to let on how excited I was, and I'd had a lot of practice using my Valium voice at work with all those cocky alpha-male doctors and their epidemic testosterone poisoning.

"Is he a Greek boy?" said Pete over one shoulder as he carried the box in for me and set it on the cluttered black countertop, knocking over an orchid.

"No." I shrugged, with one hand scraping the soil off the counter and back into the planter. "I used to date a Greek man. Well, half Greek. Long time ago."

"What was the other half?"

"Viking, I think." I could imagine every detail of Guy Pappas, create a visual life-like vision, but it wasn't Guy anymore, not now. He had gone somewhere else.

"No other Greek boys around?"

"Nope. He was the only one. I think I scare them off. They're homebodies. Not that that's bad, but I'm too busy."

"You need to find yourself a nice Greek husband and settle down. What about that Georgiou boy? His parents got a good business, and he'd treat you right."

I laughed. "I think I need to marry a priest."

"Yeah, that's good too," he said, nodding. "The kid's a nice boy… but…." He leaned close to my ear and whispered, "I think he's got the gambling bug." His motorized eyebrows went up and down. "And ya didn't hear that from me."

"Nope." I shook my head. "I'm good at keeping secrets."

"Hope ta see ya Sunday," he said, letting himself out. A chain of many keys hung from his belt loop, jingling like Santa's sleigh.

The gift package had come from Christy, from Hagios Odos, Holy Mount Athos, Monastic State of the Holy Mountain, Haldiki, Greece.

Just in time. Christy, you've read my mind again. Whatever's in there, I'm sure I really need it.

Despite the fact that my cousin often sent frivolous gifts when he went to a monastery, he usually sent something very special, a holy relic—a bone or piece of robe—an icon, or an ancient text of the writings of the desert mothers and fathers.

I grabbed a paring knife out of the oak block and ripped through the tape labeled "Fragile, Product of Greece" encasing the box in its tight plastic cocoon. Inside, a magnum-sized bottle stood like a captive soldier, surrounded by bubble wrap, fluted cardboard, wadded up newspapers, and packing peanuts.

The green bottle was corked and topped with a Muselet wire cage covered by a strip of white paper tape with blue Greek crosses stamped on it. The packing released a musty smell of sage, probably incense or some holy unction so popular with the monks it had blanketed Athos. I was surprised anything with such a strong odor had gotten by the beagles in customs. But, after all, the sender was Christy. Like Hermes, my cousin could sneak a soul past Cerberus himself without waking the dog.

Translated, the label read:

Holy Water from the Holiest Fountain
In the Garden of the Blessed Virgin
Under the Jurisdiction of the Ecumenical Patriarch of
    Constantinople
Drink and Be Free
And underneath, *best to drink chilled.*

Christy must have pelfed a diamontorion, a special visa to stay with monks at one of the sketes. Something I'd like to do too, but women weren't allowed on Mount Athos. The lore claimed we were banished, not due to a belief in male superiority, but because the ascetic monks doubted their own powers to resist sexual temptation.

Perhaps I ought to visit sometime through my astral body. Yiayia was an expert at traveling through astral planes, but her last visit had given me a neck ache, not to mention a near shoulder dislocation.

The Holy Mountain of Athos is a slice of unlikely history, and still running on the Julian calendar. The tiny peninsula protruding into the Aegean had been an island of tranquility, a spiritual sanctuary in the turbulent sea of everyday life. A trip down the astral plane to Athos with Yiayia might be counterproductive. Maybe some other time, when life wasn't so hectic.

I put the holy water in the fridge, lying on its side, and called for a taxi to pick me up out front.

## Chapter 49

Bent-metal blue notes rocketed out the open door of the "Lil' Red Tricycle." Squirrel and the Loose Screws jammed out hot electric blues, inspiring little black dresses to shinny on up to summer linen suits in the center of the studio. It was fun to watch from a distance, but mainly I liked doing that with someone I knew well.

Stir-fried chicken livers served with a wasabi Roumalade over jasmine rice drifted by in Chinese blue and white bamboo-patterned cups, balanced on trays by Creole waitresses wearing black cat suits.

"I promised you Gumbo Ya-Ya-Mein," said John Breard, tapping me on the shoulder.

I took a deep breath, charmed all over again by his uneven dimples and broad open smile.

"Hard day?" He pushed back a reddish wave that had fallen onto his forehead.

"Yeah," I said, pulling the hem of my tight knit black dress down. "Hard."

"How 'bout I help you forget all about it,'lil sister?" he said, smiling so hard he started to laugh.

A kitty-cat waitress offered a tray of putty-colored bowls filled with cellophane noodles, shrimp, and a red sauce that smelled like sassafras, each topped with half a hard-boiled egg.

"That's Gumbo Ya-Ya Mein," said the cat. "Served with a daily allowance of attitude and soul."

"It looks delicious!" I Cheshired back. "But I just ate something."

True. I had eaten the croissant with cream cheese and violet jelly in my bubble bath, and a flake of manna in the taxi before it had dropped me off at the corner of Dumont and Chartres. I'd nomadized the length of Bourbon Street, breaking in my new high-rubber-wedge-heeled patent-leather pumps.

"Four of these walls are mine," John said, offering a hand to lead me there.

Cartoon art hung from the walls MoMA style, by steel filaments, stacked.

I scanned the first wall. My eyes first settled on a "Faith" poster, famous in New Orleans, a black and white image of Dr. John with oversized wings, his face wearing a visionary look of amused concentration as he surveyed the future.

"Well, your nameplate at the hospital didn't say 'Lil Big Man,'" I said.

"It's my tag," he said innocently. "Strictly professional."

We stood half a person's distance apart. He offered me a hand again, so I took it. The fingers were short and flexible, palm thick and pink, a "fire palm." I felt its creases while I read his framed "Portrait of the Artist" bio.

A "Faith" poster hangs alongside about fifty slick and for the most part irresistible works by 'Lil Big Man'—most of them surrealistic, if not distorted and bloated. The New Orleans-based street artist and city cop was born and raised in Covington, Louisiana, where his father is a doctor and the family raises thoroughbred horses. At fourteen, 'Lil Big Man,' a budding rascal, started decorating skateboards and mailboxes. His antics eventually led to his interest in the law, the distinction between art and vandalism being permission. He graduated from Tulane with a

*criminal justice degree and a minor in studio art, in 1997. He began
doing posters and acrylic paintings because, face it, altering public
and private property is vandalism, and that's just plain illegal. Still,
'Lil Big Man's' street work has helped popularize a going fashion for
academic agnosticism, with pretensions to exposing the malignant
machinations of mass culture. Plus, he's a city cop.*

"Do you have any other secret identities?" I said, scanning the
wall of graffiti paintings.

"No, it's only me," he said, shrugging. John was from one
of those ancient bloodlines where heft of bone balanced in perfect
DaVincian symmetry with mass of flesh. Some Balkan Galacian
ancestor bred back into his Gaelic and Gaulic blood.

"Do you?" He slipped two buttons free of the holes of his sport
coat.

"That's a secret," I said. "I'm really good at keeping those."

"Then you're a rare creature."

"Intriguing." I blinked and opened my eyes again to unfamiliar
distortions trapped in acrylic paintings. "The paint's so thick in some
places it really does look like I'm at IMAX wearing three-D glasses.
Cool."

A four-foot-tall blue tea cup, its handle a serpent curved into
an 'S,' with a pocket watch the size of a penny hung from its rim, set
at noon or midnight. Next to it hung a six by eight painting of men
in drab military attire with large gold halos like crowns. Saints, the
graffiti lettering spelled in a rising angle from the bottom left corner.

"Saints," he said, as if he wanted to read to me. He was like
a horse. Really a wild animal, but domesticated enough by his
upbringing and willingness to adapt to rules in order to insure his
own survival. He chose goodness, but out of a sense of freedom and
independence. He displayed an aristocratic pride that far exceeded
his social standing, but was preserved in his absolute projection
of complete sincerity—all by choice. But deep inside, he was
untamable. All this I just knew.

"*Pousse café?*" he suggested, tipping forward in a gentleman's
bow.

"I've always wanted to try one." My lips felt dry so I licked
them. "I'm from Denver, land of Coors."

I caught him watching my tongue and felt like a lizard—not an image I was trying to stir in his mind.

I stepped back and took in the whole of him from head to foot, surprised by his overall softness in spite of that muscular, athletic body. I half expected him to bellow like a bull.

"You remind me of a unicorn," I said.

Again, a throaty chuckle. "I think you'll like the wall in back. You can go sit on the sofa then, and I'll bring you a drink."

He patted my elbow to guide me through the gallery as if I were a large horse negotiating a narrow aisle. He gave my ribs small tender pokes like the ones I'd often delivered myself to Agrippa the Ingrate. In the back room my ankle collapsed and I fell off one clunky heel, but a sofa saved me. I acted nonchalant and sank into the nest-like down cushions, opposite a wall of graffiti paintings of mythological subjects: Bellepheron with an enormous swirling tail tangled in his hooves, a midget Apollo trampling an oversized Galatian shield, Aphrodite taking a bubble bath, the bubbles floating like balloons the size of her breasts.

I kept my eye on his ochre cotton summer suit as he chatted his way past art dealers and tourists off the street, shaking hands and smiling, in rhythm with the low-amped second set of easy metal blues by Squirrel and the Loose Screws. He disappeared between the walls of the gallery that divided the space into a maze. I could still hear him explaining his work, and again imagined him as a horse, powerful in a field full of weaker, less equipped stallions. Nickering, head low, blinking, and relaxed.

I studied the paintings and the people. I could hear them all at once, but the separate conversations divided with ease into scripts. Maybe it was a boost from that tiny flake of manna.

John Breard returned with a lovely, layered, liquid work of art in a tall straight glass, the famous *Pousse café*. He sat next to me, careful not to jostle it, which would have loosened the strata and mixed them into unappealing brown sludge.

He opened his coat and pulled out a pair of silver straws.

"Take off your shoes," he said.

"I love to be barefoot." I leaned forward and looked at the Route 66 blue neon clock that hung over the sofa. "But I don't want to get too comfortable because I can't stay long." Still, I kicked them

off, crossed one leg under an ankle, and pulled my dress down to
partially cover my knees.

His lower eyelids hung like pails on horse stalls, looking blood-
houndish. "I understand."

"I wish I could stay out all night, but I have to take call in the
morning."

"Here," he said, lowering the straw into the drink with care,
then handing me the concoction. "Have a sip."

"Should I try the top, or the bottom first?" I asked.

"Your choice."

"I think we should start at the bottom."

A maraschino cherry lay at the bottom of the glass. I slurped
half the red syrup and passed it back to him. "Well, that's grenadine,"
I said.

He nodded, took a sip, then held out the glass for me again.

I sipped. "Mmmm…yellow chartreuse. I love that."

This was like one of those fun tasting games in home
economics in middle school, where the teacher blindfolds you and
you get to eat and smell things like Nilla wafers and parsley and
guess what they are.

"Hey," he said. "Do you know why the yellow chartreuse is
lighter?"

"Because green chartreuse has slightly more alcohol content
and more chlorophyll, and therefore a higher specific gravity."

"I always wondered," he said. "Thanks." He dabbed
condensation off the bottom of the straight-edged glass with a
cocktail napkin bearing his tag.

We went back and forth with the glass. He was very careful to
keep track of his own silver straw and I didn't taste any backwash.
Crème de cassis… crème de cocoa… green chartreuse…then
Benedictine and brandy floating in a little puddle on the top.

"We're like a couple of Indians in a teepee passing a peace
pipe," I said. Or Dead Heads at a concert sharing a bong. But that
was illegal, and he would never do anything against the law …
anymore. I giggled.

"Which do you like best?" he asked. "Assuming you like any
of them at all."

"Well, of the liqueurs, I love the yellow chartreuse. Carthusian monks pick upwards of one hundred and thirty herbs and do the distilling themselves. Since chartreuse is handcrafted by monks it comes out of the barrels blessed. It's been sought for its medicinal properties since the early 1600s. It's got a beautiful history. And the monastery is beautiful, too."

John Breard sat straight, shoulders relaxed.

"You know a lot," he said, smiling. "I don't mean to be forward, but there's nothing more attractive than a woman of intelligence."

"Thanks." I didn't know how to answer that, so I went on about the art.

"As for your paintings, I especially love the tiny banjo." I looked across the gallery at a four by six inch painting. It hung five degrees cocked off center. A fingerprint smudged the matte steel frame. "It's surreal. The instrument is so small and the broken string seems so thick and huge, like curled ribbon."

He followed my gaze and squinted. Then he tipped the glass back and waited for the last drop of *Pousse café* to roll between his lips.

"I love it," I said. "I love small things like doll houses and miniature books." I cocked my head five degrees to the left to match the painting. "It's a little bit catawampus up there."

"No one can see that far." He looked back at my eyes, then at the tiny painting, then back to me. "You can see that? Who are you, Wonder Woman?"

"Well I can see it sort of. Your paintings aren't what I expected."

"What were you expecting?" He unbuttoned his collar. A small triangle of dark hair peeked out. I caught a drisk of Ivory soap.

"A subway door," I said. "And lots of spray paint." That was the truth serum talking. I told the truth anyway, but not always the whole truth.

"Ironic," he said.

"You're ironic," I countered.

"No, you." He threw his head back and laughed with a beautiful singing voice which I had not yet heard but knew was there.

"I want to give you something," he said, standing. "Come with me."

I reached under the sofa and grabbed my shoes, then followed him through the crowd to the back of the gallery. He lifted two glasses of red wine off a cat-waitress tray on our way toward the rear of the gallery, back behind a hanging display of luminous neon sculptures of jellyfish. I ducked under a lime green and magenta Portuguese man of war.

Behind charcoal velvet drapery stood a tiny kitchen where the furniture and appliances tilted on a heart pine floor sloping with age.

"Sit here," he said, gesturing to the repurposed church pew along one wall.

I watched him mix green-brown powder from the refrigerator with two brown ice cubes he first melted in the microwave.

"Henna soup," John said. "I use lime, pomegranate, and instant coffee. Tea tree oil darkens the henna." He mixed the paste like a beautician stirs hair dye. "And a few drops of frankincense or whatever else is in the cupboard."

"Sounds delicious," I said.

"It's not really soup, so don't eat it." He pulled open a drawer and grabbed a handful of hog bristle brushes of various sizes.

He scooped out some paste with a wooden spoon and dropped it into another ceramic bowl. He placed both bowls on a pine card table. Hunched over his witches' brew, John added a few drops of an essential oil that smelled like camphorated roses to the smaller bowl and turned the paste over with a wide brush. "I'm mixing Ravensara to deepen the pigment." His voice was easy, soothing. "The Choctaw used Ravensara to prevent scurvy and stuffed it in mattresses to repel lice and fleas."

"You're not putting that in my hair," I said, pulling back.

He shook his head. "I want to give you a bracelet," he said, dribbling wine into the darker, smaller mix. "I'm thinning it." He took a sip of wine and handed the glass to me. "1989 Opus One, a very good year." He raised the second glass to toast.

I sat on the pew and held my glass up, not moving, waiting for him to clink. "Mmm," I said, my nose in the glass, inhaling the intoxicating aroma of vanilla and wood.

"Mmm," John said. He sat next to me, spinning the dark paste into a texture similar to goose liver pate. At last he put the pigment down. "Needs to rest a minute." He picked up his glass of wine and tasted it. "Earthy. Wears a cloak of leathery tannins." John put down his glass, resumed his concocting, then spooned both bowls of paste into the toes of a pair of trouser stockings. He squashed the henna through the hose "to get the lumps out."

"Yummy wine." I swirled my glass, inhaled the bouquet, and took another tiny sip, cupping the wine on my tongue, then pressed it to the roof of my mouth, the way Medea would have me sit and choose wine for her dinner theater when I was little. "It's got a sweaty, saddle-like character. Builds nicely on the attack and mid-palate." I held the ruby-purple glass up to the pendant light. "Do you think it finishes short?"

"It does finish short, so you can just drink it faster."

"I think it's a really good pressing, but a victim of wine snobbery," I said.

"Paint's ready." John's face loosened and a flush crept up his neck. "Put your arm on the table and lie down." He opened a packed cabinet, and two moss-colored velveteen bolster pillows toppled out, along with a ragged cardboard box with *1988 taxes* scrawled on all sides. He stuffed the box back behind the door. The pillows lolled like old fallen logs. He tucked one under my knees, then lifted my head, setting the other pillow beneath it. He spread my hair over the mossy fabric in tendrils like vines. Next, he unfolded an ancient patchwork quilt, torn and musty. Horseshoes were piling, boots fraying, and portraits of horses galloping across fields were re-patched in denim and corduroy. "My grandma made this for me in junior high. Now don't move, and just let me paint."

I lay still on the pew and surrendered my arm.

He began just above my right wrist. The soft paintbrush drew tiny lines in cool paste that crusted as it dried. I closed my eyes, lulled by the hypnotic quality of the slow caress of the brush. It felt something like when Calliope and I fingered messages onto each other's backs on the beach in Gaios, or when Guy drew on my skin under the table at Vendetto's while a car bomb deployed around us.

I imagined what shape was manifesting on my forearm as John painted thin loops.

"I'm making a ring of foofies," he said.

"Oh? What in the world—"

"Foofies are just a series of perfect looptyloops. We'll go around twice and then I'll use the dark Mehani to make wibbleleaves."

"What's a wibbleleaf?"

"I'm glad you asked," he said, his face closer. I peered up with one eye. The top of his cheeks and nose were pink from wind and sun. "Ravensara oxidizes the henna. Makes it almost black. I use the next-size brush and wiggle the tip as I make the leaf. At the end I pull the brush away. I've mixed it to the consistency of tempera or a gouache. It's thick enough so it makes a nice tail."

He anointed me with more paste, the smell somewhat medicinal, reminiscent of eucalyptus with undertones of roses.

"I can make rings of looptyloops, then fill them in with darker, more oxidized henna. Or alternate the wibbleleaves on a winding stem. Or draw parallel lines, and attach wibbleleaves, then surround the whole thing with humps. There's no end to what I can do."

"Somehow, John," I said. "I know that's true." I looked into his eyes, which were so deep they seemed like passages to somewhere else. I closed my own and imagined where his might lead. I was sung to sleep by the touch of the bristles, the cooling of the paste, the feeling of aromas evaporating off my skin as the mehani dried into a thin plaster coat. I began to dream of sandy beaches made black by ancient volcanoes and the still-lingering scent of sulfur.

"Persephone, wake up." A ring of light circled his face. "We're done. You fell asleep. "Look."

I wiped my eyes. "Oh, I love it."

Four parallel bands of swirls, colored in brick red and indigo, wrapped my arm in foofies, humps, and wibbleleaves. He had fitted seven colorless crystals on the seven curves of the winding stems.

"Seven," I said.

"Yeah. Swarovski crystals. I used eyelash glue." He pawed though bottles and cans of art supplies that cluttered the counter of what once was someone's kitchen, retrieved a plastic squirt bottle, and pointed it at my arm.

"No! Don't!" I cried, now fully awake. "That's not Lysol. Is it?"

He gaped at me. "Or course not. It's hairspray. We need to coat the bracelet with a sealer or it won't last."

"Oh. Well, Okay. It's just the way you came at me with that bottle. It reminded me of my mother."

"Don't worry. We only need a light spray." He pointed the bottle at my forearm. "Hold your breath."

He deployed a fine mist, and I flinched. I just couldn't help it.

"Don't wash it until tomorrow. Should last six weeks."

I touched it. My arm felt as tight with glaze as a lemon-drenched poppy-seed cake. "Thank you."

"It's a kind of blessing on the skin. Like a talisman."

"I need to get home," I said. "It's three AM. Gotta round tomorrow. I'd better call a taxi." I considered leaving something like a purse or a scarf to begin to build a lair, so I could lay my scent. Or at least have a reason to come back. But I hadn't brought any accessories—no purse or scarf. Only my shoes.

"I'll take you," he said. "You're a little unsteady." He tipped his head in a small Edwardian bow, so I curtsied. "Which is my fault and therefore it's my duty to see you safely home."

Really it wasn't his fault at all, but I'd let him go on thinking it was. Liqueurs and wine were swirling in my head on top of the manna.

My legs felt rubbery, but my powers of concentration were great, so I fixed all my coordination and intelligence toward the goal of acting sober and somewhat lady-like. I gathered my shoes and arranged them parallel so I could step into them without tripping. I stood up and loosened my clingy dress from my staticky stockings, having forgotten to wear a slip.

"Okay, then," I said, balancing on the tall rubber heels. "It was a lovely evening, all of it. Delicious, colorful, and indigenous."

Laughter came easy to him. "I can take you now." We glanced at each other with renewed wonder. Even going home felt like an adventure.

He pressed me with more of those tiny horseman-like pokes through the catacombs of wall art, neon jellyfish sculptures, paintings, collages, photos, slowing as we passed the four walls that held his own creations.

His taps were precise, sufficient to guide me, and I let him do it. I liked it. He was directive yet gentle. I could tell by his touches he was a sensitive rider.

We took a taxi driven by a middle-aged guy with copious ear hair and thick eyebrows that popped over the tops of his tortoise shell frames. He spoke with a Turkish accent, so I answered his question of "Where to?" in his native language.

"Yakin Liberty Cemetery. *Adil yol boyunca.*" Just across the road from Liberty Cemetery.

"How did you learn Turkish?" asked the driver.

"I took an immersion course," I said, suppressing a thought at my time at the monastery.

"Your accent is good."

"*Cok mersi!*" I said, thanking him for the complement.

"*Buyrun!*" He inspected us in the mirror. Eyebrows jumping up and down, he shook his head a couple of times. He closed the window between the front and back seat of the taxi. There was nothing dishonorable about us except for my rumpled clothing; the general presentation of a tipsy girl in a little black dress. We didn't kiss or hold hands. We were quiet. What the driver didn't realize was the static cling between my dress and my stockings was acquiring more and more electrical charge, sending off sparks that were now singeing holes in my nylons, sending up little green curls of smoke. John Breard jumped, his knee close enough to receive a shock that lit up between us like a firefly. He patted my thigh, holding himself together out of sure politeness, I'm sure. My restraint was an artifice. I could've thrown myself at him then and there.

"You must have had a good mother," I said.

"I still do," he said.

"That's what I meant." I stretched my neck to one side and then the other until it made a popping sound. I leaned my head back against the bank seat of the taxi. A disc of pink schmutz was stuck to the grey stained ceiling, the size of a quarter, probably bubblegum. I closed my eyes, letting the small bumps and loose turns lull me to sleep.

"We're here." John poked between two ribs, just enough to wake me. I found my head was resting on his shoulder. "I'll be right back," he said to the driver, who was working on a bag of jelly beans.

I took off my shoes and ran across the small wet lawn, the grass cool on my sweaty feet. I unlocked the door to the courtyard with a released breath, then the door to the entry of the apartment building. A green lizard scuttled across the threshold and through a tiny vent under a column.

"Do you always leave your place unlocked?" He frowned, holding the door open for me.

"No," I said, scratching my shin with my other foot. He didn't need to know all the details—my remote control breathing, Yiayia's spirit, the angels. No one did.

"You need to be more careful. A girl was killed over on Esplanade by a rapist. No sign of forced entry."

"Oh, I have a security system. I always have it on."

"Wait," he said, lowering his face to mine. My lips unlocked, loose like the rest of me. I closed my eyes and felt the lingering vegetal essence of chartreuse on his mouth, loose warm lips that brushed my face, ran down my neck, and planted that same softness on my hand. "When can I see you again?"

I backed up a step and let him cross into the entry. If I'd closed the door, we'd have been alone in a small enclosed space.

"Sunday, Church of the Annunciation," I said. "I'll be in the back pew on the right-hand side under the icon of Saint Theodore, the warrior. Seven-thirty for Orthros, nine thirty for Divine Liturgy."

"Till then," he said, bowing and smiling with the friendliness of purest innocence, his dark auburn locks loosening into swoops of curls from the bit of pomade that had earlier organized them.

Chapter 50

By the time the front door closed behind me, I'd begun to despair my choice to wait until Sunday for my next date. Assuming John could drag himself out of bed for Divine Orthros, matins, psalms and litanies, and Byzantine chanting in eight tones. I wanted to see him sooner.

My burnt stockings were lacey with tiny holes and runs. I threw them in the trash, then checked the freezer. Behind the spinach, for the manna in waxed paper surrounded by foil. Still there. I considered taking one flake out to examine, maybe taking it to a chemist at the med school for mass spec analysis, or electron microscopy. Or even to Father Seraphim. I started to unfold the paper, then remembered the beautiful, lonely bottle of holy water chilling on the rack in my refrigerator. The most luscious of kisses had made my lips and tongue insatiably thirsty. So I stuffed the food of angels back between a bag of frozen spinach and box of filo dough, and pulled out the water instead, unscrewed the cage and finally found my corkscrew stuffed into a square space in the knife block.

I poured some into a Champagne glass and took a sip, then crossed myself three times, right over left. "For this whole day, may it be perfect. And for an angel of peace, a faithful guide, a guardian of our souls and bodies, I entreat the Lord."

I grabbed a handful of macadamia nuts, munching as I peeled off my clothes on the way to the bedroom. I freed myself from my underwire bra, the kind that rounds up one's breasts and points them in the right direction, and threw open my camisole drawer to find something loose to wear to bed.

I put jeans and a shirt on, then sniffed, frowned, pinched a piece of the fabric and held it to my nose. The stretchy cotton smelled like I'd worn it lake swimming and left it in a duffle for days, similar to the sulfury smell of the box the bottle of water had been delivered in. Stacks of lingerie in the drawer looked foreign now, somehow different from the usual disarray. In fact, as if a housekeeper had done a quick tidy. I'd never been meticulous about folding things, and didn't have a maid. The camisoles seemed too neat, as if little housework elves had snuck in while I was out on my date. In each drawer of the dresser, my bras and panties were also folded, something not even Medea, the controlling matrix of the universe, could bring herself to do. I bent and smelled my things, detecting a musty odor, grassy and foreign. Again, sulfury, like the forest floor.

I flipped on all the lights, checked the doors and windows—all tight in their frames. Opened the cabinets in the kitchen. They'd been wiped down. Did the white glove test on top of my refrigerator. Even my kitchen had been dusted. I took out some saltines, opened the wrapper. The sweaty, musty, smell permeated the box. My apartment had been incensed by someone within the last few hours. The intruder had been through my possessions while I was with John.

I checked my purse, money and cards—still there.

The intruder must be after something else. Something personal. So who'd sent him?

My world was covered with this strange musky man-scent. My jewelry had been handled, the necklace chains neatly untangled. Nothing missing, except for the silver spoon used to bury the crystal. I checked behind my socks in the lowest drawer of the highboy for the box found in the hollow tree in the fairy circle. It was closed, but no longer had the surprising heft it'd once held, for so small a thing. No pull or warmth came from it now. The widget inside—which I'd never examined because I couldn't get the lid open—had been removed. And the box closed back up? Scratches scored the rim, as if it had been jimmied with a pocket knife.

I struggled to open it, but the jaws remained clenched. Masculine pheromones rose from it. Sweat respired from every object in the apartment and engulfed me in a pungent embrace. Even my dirty laundry was masked now with an odor no longer altogether unfamiliar. It covered me like a moss covers rock, and felt just as cold and clammy.

I went to the kitchen and gulped half the perspiring Champagne glass. The compass-box had been forced open, and the mechanism inside—the brain—had been snatched. I decided then not to waste healing waters from the Fountain of Mary on simple rehydration after a night of fun. I prayed instead.

"May the end of our lives be without torment, blameless and peaceful and for a good account at the seat of Christ, I entreat the Lord."

I went to the refrigerator for manna, figuring a bite of it would give me some extra magical awareness. Then I grabbed my phone, and sat on the bed. Who to call first?

I could always summon Yiayia. No phone needed for that. But she was always so moody and might only give me a riddle. Medea would have a nervous breakdown and shriek at me to come home this second. Auntie Georgie would make me go to a nice hotel, and come out herself to investigate, bringing staff with her. Or there was Christy.

Of course, I would call Christy.

When I lifted the receiver, the line was dead. I checked the jack, then all the plugs. Still dead. And where was Azrafel? My so-called protector.

Bile rose in my throat. I covered my mouth with one hand and swallowed the pooling spit. Staggered to the bathroom, leaned on a wall for balance, then grabbed my purse from the vanity and dropped it in the middle of the sink. That way I could rummage and still turn to the toilet to throw up if need be. I pulled out my cell, then held it against my chest, with both hands, tight. I leaned against the wall,

still standing, but only barely, and punched in Christy's European
cell number. No answer. Could it be there was no cell phone satellite
for Mount Athos? No, the monks all had cell phones. Mount Athos
had its own security department. Mount Athos was its own country.
I dialed Christy's U.S. cell number, but fumbled the phone and
dropped it in the toilet. It belched one last dying bubble and sank to
the bottom of the bowl. I left it there.

All right, then. I would have to summon Christy, the expert at
cryptic evidence left by fugitives.

Alarmed by the pallor of my reflection over the sink, confused
by double images of everything, I staggered out of the bathroom
and into the parlor. Leaning on the back of the sofa, I looked out the
bay window, covering one eye with an unsteady hand. No sign of
an intruder. I tried the casement latches—locked from inside. The
balcony looked unchanged, crammed with pots of geraniums still
in bloom, though winter in New Orleans had already whispered
its sentinel breath. Arching branches of bougainvillea spilled out
of larger pots—undisturbed—white papery bracts veined in green.
Their trunks twisted together, then separated, the sprays of flowers
crawling up and over the Juliet balcony. They competed with
tumbles of jasmine that yearned to throw themselves passionately
over the cast-iron edge. I clenched the back of the window seat,
wobbly, fighting to stay upright. The window, the walls, the
surrounding trees, the balcony revealed no sign of forced access.

Dawn was approaching. A streetlight bled through the fog and
illuminated a ghostly image on an interior pane. A greasy outline.
I stepped closer to peer at it. The profile of a face besmirched the
otherwise spotless glass.

I'd looked out that same window earlier today. Leaned out
over the window seat to find Pete, the sweet UPS man from church,
at the courtyard gate holding the package from Greece. The man
who'd left the print on this window had been trying to view the
entry too, and had pressed his face against the glass, leaving this
silhouette, a clue to his identity.

Christy would figure out the source of the odor, decipher the
print fragment and the bizarre intentions behind it.

I grappled to a chair in the kitchen and slumped at the table.
I ate a flake of manna, willing my physical strength to return. The

taste was honey-sweet, but frozen. It required chewing and left a dry sensation on my tongue. I took another bite, then a sip of water, surprised by its bitter taste. A powdery substance had precipitated on the surface, like talc, but glistening. I trapped a few pieces on my fingertip and examined them in the light. Definitely precipitants. I put the glass down and tied a knot of worry out of my forehead.

I lay down on the floor, too exhausted to stay awake much longer. Strange to think theologians and angelologists had spent so much time sorting out the rank and place of angels. Angels live in no one place, as God lives in no one place. They are everywhere and within each other and sometimes in our hearts. We serve as channels for angels and they can channel us.

I pictured Christy in my mind, in an oversized brown leather upholstered chair in an oak-paneled office in a government building. Across sat a middle-aged man with salt-and-pepper hair and a right-to-left comb-over, thinning at the temples. The official wore a blue suit and cranberry tie with slanted blue stripes, pinned by a cross and crown tie tack. The man smiled, blue eyes sparkling, left hand crossed over right. He held horn-rimmed glasses, forearms leaning on his right leg which was crossed over the left, as if posing for a portrait. His mahogany desk was Alice-in-Wonderland large, stacked with legal books. A name plate read WILLEM WOOSTER.

"Yes, Christy," he was saying. "We have data supporting our hypothesis. Iraq is now undoubtedly the largest producer of chemical weapons in the world."

Christy's mouth opened as he exhaled. With his next inhalation, my narcoleptic ions flew into him and assisted by his wicked gravity, was sucked through his one hundred-thousand miles of blood vessels —all the way to the tips of his nails, the ends of his hair—deep into his cells.

Then…we blinked. We looked down at his cell phone with my number on the tiny screen. Missed call. That'd been me.

We stood up.

Mr. Wooster set his folded glasses on top of a tome called Complete Index of Poisons—CIA 2000 Reference, and sprang to his feet. Eager, hyper-alert, vigilant.

"I apologize, Willem," we said. "The call was a family emergency. I'll take care of it and be back in DC by next week.

Whatever day works best." We looked down at the poison guide and tapped the cover. "I advise, sir, that you get a nonpolitical dust jacket for that text. Maybe a Sherlock Holmes library issue with plastic cover. And spine label."

"Will do." Wooster chuckled. "I'll have Francesca call you Monday. Best of luck. Do you need a plane?"

"Yes. A flight to Louis Armstrong. N'awlins."

"Done."

We nodded. "Thanks again, Willem. It really is very serious. Otherwise…." We shrugged.

Wooster pressed a button on his phone. "Francesca, please order a limo, and a plane to New Orleans out of Dulles." He examined us with narrowed eyes, leaning forward. "Christy, you look tired. Feeling all right?"

We nodded. "I'm fine."

We shook hands again, his grip looser than expected. He patted us once on the shoulder and held the door.

"Your car's waiting at the OHB entrance."

We jogged through acres of hallways, past twenty-nine elemental paintings—post-modern—depicting the simplest shapes and hues. Past the Memorial Wall, the Book of Honor, a bas relief of Allen Dulles and a bust of George Bush the First, former director of the CIA. We crossed the sixteen-foot granite seal—an eagle clutching a compass in his talons. Over the exit projected a stone engraving. *And Ye Shall Know the Truth and the Truth Shall Make You Free.*

We exited CIA headquarters into the snowy air, eyes dilated from the drugs, making everything blurry. We buttoned up Christy's herringbone sport coat, tucked in his scarf, put the Serengeti shades back on his nose, tipped his Fedora forward, and ducked into the black limo.

Get back into your own body, Persephone, and go home! Christy thought.

We yawned.

No, Persephone, I haven't been to Mount Athos. You've been drugged. Athanatoi. I'll dust the face print, but first I'll call an ambulance, tell them you need Romazicon. You drank tap water in a fancy bottle. Poisoned with Rohypnol. Roofies. The forget-me-pill.

The date-rape drug.

When I slipped back into my body, the ends of my digits had gone fuzzy, as if I were a stuffed doll leaking cotton. My physical weakness and disorientation were much worse than when I'd left. My limbs might has well have relocated like sand bars carried off by surf to form a new false cape.

But now, I wasn't alone. The stench of musk and alluvial mud filled my head; He was here, with me, next to me… ugh…touching me!

Flumazenil, Romazecon, Reversed… The antidote would be here soon, and I would be carried away by ambulance. Just one shot of Romazecon and normal tone would return to my now-slack muscles. My mind could switch back on.

Harry Ripberger Nillsen IV leaned down to look into my face. "Hello Persephone." After unbuttoning my white cotton shirt and unzipping my jeans, he pulled them off still puffy, then pounded the air out of them, made a neat pile, after which he marched down the hall to my Rattan laundry basket whistling Reveille. He seemed to have all the time in the world. But when he returned from his casual trip to my bathroom, he got right back to business. I couldn't have opened my legs if I 'd wanted to, or closed them. Within seconds, he was in me, seeking, pushing, seeking more, and I tried to force him out, but my spaghetti limbs disobeyed my frantic, commanding mind.

"What're you looking for, Harry?" I slurred, dragging my eyelids up. I imagined them popped open by metal grates.

They fell back down, but I jerked them up again in a thrash of will. Harry turned his face to the left. Hanging over me now was the same profile as the one on my window collecting dust. And I saw it. A pale Mobius tattoo deepening in color on his neck, intensifying to a vibrant royal blue, edges red and raised. Harry cocked his neck to better display the entire mark. I felt the pressure of his mind then, and fought back against my fear of his evil. I entered just far enough to know him as he was: Harry Ripberger Nillsen IV, Angel Hunter. I almost laughed at how ridiculous it sounded, like "Father Donald Frank Duck, Vampire Slayer" or "Professor Abraham Von Helsing," inviting Dracula to "bare his fangs in the immortal night."

Harry gazed out the window and smiled at the murder of crows gathering on my balcony, origami ravens devouring confederate jasmine flowers. They peered in through the glass with depthless black eyes. He waved as if to shoo them away but they reclustered, flapping and cawing.

I'd left on the day of our last skydive—he'd sat in his windowless laboratory, Geiger counter ticking, radiolabelling scrapings from an old boat and other Croatian detritus dragged home from the University. I'd gotten rid of him—forever, I'd thought, in Casadega. Calliope had said he'd been confounded by the swirling energies in the spiritualist haven where we'd visited. But now the crows framed a smudged silhouette of his face with a flutter of wings, their pneumatic bodies floating like hellish black hummingbirds.

He thrust harder, paused, then thrust again. As if I were a blow-up sheep purchased at some sleazy French Quarter sex store, like Chickie Darlin's Garden of the Lewd and Luscious.

I fell comatose, then was awakened by a last brutal thrust. Otherwise, I felt nothing. Harry seemed to melt away inside me, to nothingness. Like a dick, only smaller, I thought. I wasn't sure of the exact duration of the rape, but it seemed like I'd been back in my body for about five minutes.

He collapsed on me. His smell was earthy as the forest floor, crushed grass mixed with the salty sweat of a bull.

# # #

Harry wrapped me in an orange Bellini prayer rug, the kind with a keyhole at one end and a pair of woven hands on the other to show where a supplicant should kneel during prayer. He lifted me out a picture window to the landing of the fire escape behind an ancient maple. Kicking over the flower pots, he lowered me over the wrought-iron railing, cursing under his breath. He slung me—now wrapped loose as a cabbage roll – over one shoulder and descended the fire escape. My bare feet ached and burned. His shoulder poked my belly as he swung a hinged ladder from the lowest platform to the ground. He hurried down a series of claustrophobic alleys buttressed by narrow brick apartments, then shoved me, still enveloped by the prayer rug, into the sticky vinyl back seat of a pick-up. The truck swung around speed bumps as we left my neighborhood. Ambulance sirens blasted by—surely meant for me—then waned behind us.

I didn't know how long we'd been on the road when I woke up again. I'd hoped for an ambulance. But this was no engine of mercy. There would not be paramedics, or an antidote. Plump drops of rain tapped the windshield. A saucer of sun high in the sky told me it was noon, but stratus clouds shrouded its direct light.

The truck turned off a smooth surface I figured must've been I-10, and onto an unpaved road. I bounced with each rut and pothole. My consciousness had been waxing and waning, so we could in fact be in a nearby bayou, or as far as Arkansas by now. I rolled against the back of the seat to keep from falling on the floor with each jamming jolt and thump. Harry slammed his brakes and skidded into a rut, the top of his head slamming the roof. His wheels spun fruitlessly in the intractable earth. I felt us sinking. He hurled a fist into the dashboard, then shook it out and hissed, groaning in pain.

He opened the door next to my head, looked in and poked me. "Death is the enemy," he said. Then slammed the door shut, missing my scalp by millimeters.

He climbed into the truck bed and retrieved two boards and jumped out, mumbling something about a typhoon in southern China. He crawled back into the driver's seat, feet and hands smeared with mud, then rolled the car back and forth with tiny careful accelerations until he'd backed the wheels over the boards and out of the furrow. I could smell the resin of crushed pine needles stuck to his shoes.

"Well, you weren't any help." He looked back and grinned.

I shrank away under the prayer carpet. I'm practically paralyzed, you asshole.

He pulled under a dark canopy of trees, the sun now sunk midway across the arc of the sky, still softened by fog.

The sulfuric stink of rotting pinecones, dead fish, swamp water, and decaying Spanish moss, which together smelled something like working oil wells, told me we were near the Atchafalaya Basin. Bullfrogs and crickets sang eulogy for the swamp so dismal. And, I suppose, for me.

Harry deposited my carpet-wrapped self under moss-draped trees and left for a while. A cool breeze cooled my face. Though able to move my limbs, when I tried to sit up, I collapsed and lay back exhausted, holding my eyes open until they dried out and burned. The henna bracelet on my right forearm had darkened. The seven tiny gems reflected the green-coated alluvial banks of a river.

The sun's rays lowered in the overcast sky. The final drops of rain dissipated into mist, and the seven crystals on my arm caught specks of daylight amid darkness. Turning my wrist to reflect the scintillations upward into the forest, I sent a sign into the sky. I'm here, on a musty bank next to a levee, by a bridge in the Atchafalaya Swamp.

I considered the Seven Principle again. Circe, Theodora, Hestia, Penelope, Friday, Medea, and me. And today would be my seventh brush with death. The car at the beach house, the golden bull in the field with Calliope, the burglars searching while I hid in the cedar closet at 140 Red Chimney, my fall from Agrippa the Ingrate and my teleportation to the Mexican Eclipse, the bomb at Vendetto's, the explosion that had taken Guy's life. And now this trickery, this poisoning, this violation and whatever else would happen before I got away—for I was certain I would—heralded the commencement of the seventh and final of my lives.

My head was clearer, but the strange fancies adrift in it brought an elation all their own. Again I looked at the painted vines on my forearm, a visible blessing, reliving each stroke of John's paintbrush, cool and light.

Only the wind in the trees spoke. A red mangrove rooted in the levee curved toward me, bearing a cluster of seed pods. The shoot lengthened before my eyes, growing greener and fuller, then dropped into the brackish water. It floated a few inches toward the bank, then rooted in the black muck. A seedling unfurled from the mud as soon as it had planted itself, like a time-lapse film. An exaggerated fertility caused by a sudden and full infusion of the God's light, a holy woodland rite. The magic beans had planted themselves. And the giant….

"Sorry, Persephone." Harry interrupted the fairy-tale pleasure of my discovery. "Don't take this personally." His tone was measured, the words sounded rehearsed. "It's not because I never loved you. When I found out what you were, I tried to stop you, but couldn't. You are the enemy of all mankind. It's you or me. I choose life." God. He sounded like a bumper sticker.

He patted my face to rouse me. The Rohypnol having reached peak concentrations in my blood, I would be conscious now for only about ten seconds at a time.

"Are you cold?"

"I don't know, Harry," I mumbled. "Don't see why it would matter to you."

I rolled my head to look at the baby mangrove, now three feet tall. The magic beans were growing and would soon penetrate the clouds.

I was like a floppy baby, still relaxed to the point of paralysis. The half-life of Rohypnol, roofies, the date-rape drug, was eighteen to twenty-four hours. Perhaps twelve or thirteen had passed since I'd first sipped the tainted unholy water.

Harry unrolled the carpet from me, flattening the corners to cover that piece of decaying, yet living earth as if it were the corner of a room. He positioned me like Thumbelina atop a bed of pumpkin pie. Over my camisole he wrapped a blue-warp cambric sheath, the same fabric used to make prison blues.

"Ha!" he laughed. "What's that on your arm, Ephesian letters? A Hindu charm?"

From inside his coat he pulled a surgical skin pen he must've stolen from a hospital. Lifting up my arm again, he examined the painted bracelet. "Is Anath adorning herself with henna to celebrate a victory over the enemies of Baal?" He snickered. "Well, now I'm gonna give you a very special amulet."

At first I expected a black-ink swastika. But no—of course he would mark me with the Athanatoi brand, the fascinating Mobius.

Okay with me. Whatever buys me some time.

First he drew on my feet, then on my hands. He started with a figure eight on the sole of one foot, moved to the other, then repeated this work on my palms. He went back to the feet and drew sides, shading a band on each picture, making it appear three-dimensional. He tilted his head like a cocker spaniel, then backed away as if he were M.C. Escher himself, admiring each loop that had no beginning, no end.

The color of his tattoo deepened to a blacker blue against his drained white skin.

"You must die so others will live. The Athanatoi cannot allow a single death angel to come to maturity. As you know." His hands paused, the fingers long and thin, spider-like. The skin was scrubbed, but black rimmed the neatly-trimmed nails.

A murder of crows descended from the darkening sky, landed in the woven, crooked branches of the lowering young mangrove.

Harry flinched and turned his head toward the birds, but did not appear to notice anything unusual about the new tree, now fifty feet tall. He squinted at me, then at the crows. "As far as death angels go, I feared you were destined to be my own," he said. "Hmph!"

The ravings of a religious fanatic, a cultist spewing heresies that to my ears were insane. If today hadn't been such a rough one in the earthly school of suffering, I would've found such rantings boring, redundant, ridiculous. But with my neuromuscular system still blocked, I would not be able to move for at least four more hours, at least not physically. Unless someone in an ambulance could find me and inject the antidote soon.

"Guess I'm…captive audience," I mumbled. Why not engage him in dialogue the way special agents converse with hijackers, kidnappers, terrorists, in films?

I looked over to the young mangrove, hyperkinetic, now the tallest tree in the forest. The crows lifted, like pennies thrown up to the sky.

"No one's going to save you." His face was smooth and empty. "You're not the only ones with power, you know, you Goddamn offspring of Lilith."

"Lilith?" Oh, here we go again with the creepy Garden mythology.

"On the fifth day, Lilith came out of the sea to tempt Adam. She rested by the flaming sword at the gate of Heaven until the fall, waiting. First she seduced Adam, then Cain. Their offspring leashed death onto the world."

I refused to address the obvious corollary: Before Lilith there was no death, thus all death angels must be the so-called "Daughters of Lilith." First, he ought to have checked the historical record.

Second, his failure to form logical conclusions was not his greatest of crimes, so I let it go.

"Correlation does not… prove causation," I muttered, unable to totally contain myself.

"What?" he said, frowning.

"Nothing."

He hovered over me, glaring. The red mangrove behind him sprouted rubbery yellow buds from a tangle of branches.

"They're not coming," he said.

"Who?"

"The cavalry. We have our tricks too." His voice was dry and raspy. "Time."

"What is that?" He was pathetically eager to blab all about what great and superior magic the Athanatoi could dispense.

"The continuity of time." His eyebrows rose, as if he was telling me some new fact of physics. "The past has already occurred but is also still occurring. And what seems like hours may only be moments."

I was quite familiar with borrowing time. Yiayia had shown me horrific tortures and the order of the universe in moments that'd seemed like hours. I wasn't scared. And I was beginning to wake up. Not just physically, but metaphysically. I'd remained plugged in to all souls. My spirit would always be free. But I still liked the gift of my body and meant to keep it as long as possible.

"You misuse your free will, Harry," I said. "It's a foolish choice to bury yourself alive. To wall yourself off."

"Solitude is as full of secrets as the swamp," he said in a heavy, portentous tone.

"Then how do I know you're real?"

He lifted one pant leg and removed a folded knife from a sheath strapped to his calf. The sun was slipping beneath the horizon like a raw red egg sliding across a frying pan. Its low lights penetrated a dense thicket of vine. A gut hook and the serrated and polished edges of the blade glinted in the darkening daylight, shining brief as lightning. Harry nicked the tip of his index finger, watched the blood coalesce into a pearl, then sucked it.

He knelt and began to carve thin lines of flesh out of the sketches he'd drawn on me. Addressing one limb at a time: first feet, then hands. He removed thin slivers like chipped beef and stacked them in a tiny mound near the edge of the rug. What little pain I felt, I didn't care. My brain was flooded with endorphins.

He held my feet in different positions while he traced and sliced, pausing to adjust the angle of his blade. My blood dripped as tears do when silent weeping goes on for days. Blood trickled between my toes, over the tops of my feet, down my ankles, and puddled at my heels, congealing.

"We don't have long to live," he said. "The sun is setting on all of us because of you." He pared meat from my right palm, whittling out the familiar shape of a Mobius. He took his time, meticulous as always. Pausing only once to slap his neck, to smash a feeding mosquito, smearing blood into the collar of his pristine white shirt.

I let out a tiny chuckle, thinking of how he'd spent the time to fold all my socks and underwear.

The red mangrove completely shaded us now. New shoots heavy with waxy leaves sprang from its trunk and spread like raised Spartan shields. A stand of mangroves leaned against one another behind the mother tree that still sprouted new limbs and pale yellow flowers. Aerial, partially submerged prop roots embedded in the muck sheltered nesting snowy egrets and wading spoonbills. Knobby knees of old cypress trees appeared to walk on water, advancing down the river's edge. The croak of frogs, the grunts and chirps of feeding birds mixed with the bubble and splash of hundreds of jumping fish. This organic music lulled me to sleep again.

#   #   #

There I was, in my most horrible extremity, ever. When I awakened, I found myself no longer on the ground but hanging. Suspended from a trestle on 10-E by a sign that read Whiskey River Bridge. Of course he brought me here. Of course, because he knew I'd buried the pendant in the swale under me.

A grey-green canopy of trees hooded the murky waters. Swaying black walnuts and slayed cypresses studded the bayou. In the warm breeze, they waved, revealing glimpses of a strip of land between levee and swamp.

Beneath the bridge, I swung from the steel trestle like the pendulum from a grandfather clock. He'd square-knotted two ropes around my torso, one binding my waist, passing under the other which encircled the ribs just below my breasts. The pooling blood from my carved-up wrists soaked though my dress, dribbling down my legs, and rippled the water as though fishes were nibbling the surface. I reached up and grabbed the braided nylon line to relieve the squeeze on my ribs.

As I spun I glanced up and caught a glimpse of the anchor snubber he'd slung over a bracing. Now, in my vertigo, I understood the arrangement. He had passed the cord hugging my belly under the nylon boa constrictor around my ribs, then looped it on the trestle by a huge steel hook. The knot dug like a fist into the small of my back. He'd hoisted me like some great sail on a Venetian ship.

I looked up again, scanning though the deck's spaces. He stood high above, balanced on a beam, embracing a safety rail. Harry was no stranger to the secret human passion of torture. It'd always burned in him. His silhouette drooped, tired from his labors, slumped in indignation that his endless battle with mortality seemed impossible to win.

I slowed my breathing and waited. True, the angels hadn't protected me any of the six times before—not until the last possible moment. Azrafel had caught me just before I hit the ground when I'd fallen from the Ferris wheel. I'd barely missed getting blown up twice. I'd been one breath away from being gored by the golden bull. In order to earn my wings, I knew I must be challenged to the limit in my earthly life. "Earn your Wings" had been hard wired into my brain, into my DNA. It was meant to be difficult. I needed to face the task not with hope, but with certainty. So I tried to remain patient, but felt somewhat disheartened by this continued, edgy brinksmanship of the angels.

I hung tethered to a girder like a figurehead on the bowsprit of a ship. My breaths were shallow, diaphragm constricted by the taut rope that looped through the anchor snubber and latched to the brace. Harry handled the remaining line like the expert sailor he was, coiling it like a snake that lay curled, asleep on one wooden slat of the bridge. Behind him, gray Spanish moss billowed like a rapid current over a rocky riverbed.

I slipped into his mind for a moment, but flew out immediately in horror, my numb but pain-racked body still a better place than inside there. He'd planned to kill me out of a righteous delusion justified by his twisted religion. He'd practiced my death by hunting, by finding game and cutting hundreds of throats. Dried blood infused his hands, caked under his nails. I could smell it. The greatest secret in a man's life is a passion for killing. Harry intended to relish each bloody step with the wide eyes of a tired, but committed, predator.

Below us a pair of orange globes glowed like dim flashlights, down in the vagabond mist that hung low over the bayou. Golden orange reflective orbs circled beneath the blood-scented water. Two large reptilian bodies slithered across the levee. They heaved with a splash into the swamp at my feet, releasing a sulfurous belch of marsh gas mingled with the stench of decaying offal caught between their teeth. The pair lunged up out of the water, snapping at my ankles, then they fell back in the dark, tea-stained bayou. Muddy water splashed and bathed my legs as the gators leapt and tumbled beneath me. A chorus of bull-gator bellows and grunts, a whole congregation, echoed through the alluvial swamp.

Something had awakened in Harry, too. Maybe mere blood-hunger, like the alligators' unapologetic appetite. Or perhaps once a ritual was set in motion, Harry, like a crazed rabbi, must mutilate his lamb in reverence to God—whom he so misunderstood.

But when Abraham had held the sacrificial knife over Isaac bound to a rock on Mount Moriah, prepared to kill, Azrafel had stopped him.

Where the hell was Azrafel? Christy? Or even Hestia?

The bloody sun squashed against the horizon. Waxy leaves of the red mangrove turned their palms upward and fluttered in crowns of greenery. My three angels appeared then, descending from the darkening sky, shimmering in the falling light, and landed on the highest branches, bearing mute witness to my ordeal.

Harry's eyes glistened. He'd discovered an atavistic passion that totally suited him: ritual mutilation. Pursing his lips, he grinned in a kind of ecstasy and drew up the rope as seven sets of orange eyes now circled below me. Jaws snapped in a water-ballet sequence.

"Why not let me go. Just drop me in the water and let them have me?" I said. "Waiting for more alligators? Seven's not enough?"

Ignoring me, he climbed up the cable and onto the tree that held me, still carrying the rope.

My breathing slowed. Grew shallow, inadequate. The rope burned and scraped the skin over my ribs. My clothes were impregnated with the carrion rot trapped in the alligator's teeth, the blooming trees, the swamp cabbage, the decaying leaves, the tannin-brown water, the decomposing pine needles on the mossy floor, all tainted by the iron of my dripping blood.

I felt a creeping chill like hoarfrost—almost a miracle in a southern bayou. But not the kind I had hoped for.

Oh, hush. Do something. Bring your faith healer up. Rise like Lazarus. Death has been a common visitor. Just survive. Get through this.

I wiggled in the harness, relieving the pressure on my ribs. Pulled my knees up to my chest just as an alligator lunged upward. The swamp breathing all around me. Nocturnal hunters emerged— bats, cats, snakes, moths. Their shining eyes stalked sleeping creatures nestled up in hideaways. The swamp was a place of great routine, a well-organized but sometimes violent boarding house.

"Death sucks," said Harry. "Wouldn't you agree now?"

"We're meant to lose people we love," I said, my chest wall now able to move, my tingling shoulders rubbed raw from the scraping of the rough fabric of my dress. "How else would we know how important they are to us?"

He was balanced on a massive buttressed trunk, securing a constrictor knot around the huge branch that leashed the ropey serpent gripping me.

My host of angels glimmered motionless deep within the hollows of the new red mangrove, witnessing my struggle without interference. As I looked upon the faces of the angels, it occurred to me my soul-light had remained deeply hidden, the diffusion of particles of the dynamically disordered lattice of my still-living body of no immediate interest to them. No one waited to carry my child-soul off into its next life.

I was in my next life.

From the depths of the mangrove, a powerful gust, like a thousand sheets blowing in the wind, swept across the swamp. Christy's swan feathers spread, stood luminous in a crotch of the

tree. He released the nock of his crossbow. The arrow sliced the rope
that hung me swaying from the bridge, the wooden slap of the bolt's
action silencing the crickets and frogs. I was dropping, dropping.
The severed rope slapped the surface and descended into the mire
like an eel stalking crayfish.

The croaking and chirping resumed, louder. The water was
only a few inches away and approaching, yet in slow motion.

A draft of air circulated counterclockwise, whipping up dust
and fog. The wind buzzed like bees, then escalated to the roar of a
train. A funnel cloud wrapped, then hoisted me skyward.

The warm swirling dust and dew sucked me up, yanking my
hair. The rotating wind on my cheeks bitch-slapped me awake.
It seemed I had no say-so about it at all, nor even any time to
think. The seven pairs of orange eyes dispersed, no doubt in great
disappointment.

And then, then—I was rising.

I stretched my sore neck and arched my cramped back, looking
up at the Milky Way. Massive black iridescent wings sprouted
and unfurled from the nubs on my buzzing shoulder blades. I tried
flapping them without holding back, the way you'd drive a hot
sports car for the first time, pushing down on the gas to see how
fast you can go in an instant. I flapped harder, straining my chest,
and galloped through air as if upon a flying horse. I beat those vast,
wieldy wings to rise from the water's surface as fast as possible.

I'd become something new and strange, caught between a
skylark and a condor. I flew away from the fertile stench of bayou
until I found a thermal plume and could soar without effort. In my
peripheral vision, my dark vibrating wings shone blue. Their feathers
curved upward at the tips. I leaned in and caught a current of warmer
air. I flew over asphalt and discovered boundary layer thermals. The
hot column of air filled and lifted my great wings, which spread
twelve feet across. And I discovered I was built for soaring, not
having much of a sternum—unlike my cousin, the swan.

Illuminating my flight, the persimmon moon tipped its crescent
toward the Pleiades, the seven sisters—companions to Artemis and
teachers of Bacchus—sailing the waters of the heavens. I circled
the Whiskey River Bridge over the Margouin Basin in a widening
gyre, looking down on the tops of bald cypresses like pins stabbing

upward into starlight. A gust of raindrops rattled my wings.

"Yes," I said. A moment lapsed before I knew what I was saying yes to. To being, in particular, a death angel of the Lord. Occasionally I teetered, then held my wings in a tighter V-shape that kept me steady. And what I loved best was the sound of my own flapping, rhythmic whooshes as I beat my wings to build the current of air that carried me.

Looking down on the banks of the Whiskey River, I saw Christy still standing in the tree, his swan-white feathers quivering as he fitted another arrow into the crossbow. He released the bolt with a thwack. It pierced Harry's left wrist and pinned it to the truss.

He slipped and, with a hoarse cry, fell over the rail, suspended by one arm over the tannic waters. Seven pairs of round reptilian eyes blinked up again from the Atchafalaya Swamp. The arrow's head and shaft had crucifixed his hand to the bridge. Yet gravity tore the wound wider as he dangled and kicked, screaming as his blood rained on the water in wine-dark drops.

It was then I saw the second angel weave through a maze of branches within the enchanted mangrove. Her plumage spread to lift her from the tree. Her eyes widened, then darkened. She floated down through an avenue of sky—great, grey wings tipped with dense, white dots like a guinea fowl's.

Hestia!

And there too was Azrafel, following her, his indigo-eyed peacock train flowing behind. In one hand, he carried the glowing sword tipped with dark gall. He brushed the rustling tops of scrub palmettos, passed the stand of mangroves, and ducked under the great spread canopies of ancient umbrella oaks.

Azrafel folded his wings and landed on the Whiskey River Bridge just above Harry. Hestia fluttered and descended to hover by Harry's side. Azrafel dripped gall onto his lips while Hestia embraced his drained body with furled wings, shrouded by sprays of wisteria. Her sorrow was veiled with a sympathetic smile. And then, from the palm of Harry's arrow-hammered hand, she cupped the sputtering wick of his soul.

Chapter 51

Irene's garden is lined with Roses of Sharon that have been sheared to form a neat corridor past the fountain statuette of Ruth pouring water from her amphora. Crunching through a crust of snow blanketed with chimney ash, I pass a Corinthian porte-cochere leading to a great door carved with acanthus leaves, lit by a bronze lantern. I stand staring at the crumbling mansion, reviewing my instructions, given by the Archangel Azrafel.

The knocker in the lion's mouth is heavy in my hand. I lift the ring, then ease it down without making a sound. Wind whistles through dormant willows, chilling my neck. At last I turn the knob, pushing one shoulder against the aged wood. The dead bolt strains in its strike, but does not yield. I let go and press an ear to the chilly panel.

"Je vais avoir un biftek 'vec frites ou je te battrais comme un cochon!"

"Va-t'en! Jamais me touche à nouveau."

I've heard Henri and Irene shout like this before—in the dark, in my dreams, or when I'm about my rounds at the hospital. I've seen her in the emergency room—lips bruised, blood swelling her brain—mumbling nonsense. Once Henri beat her with his *cavaquinho*, an old Creole mandolin. I've heard Irene moaning in the CT scanner, a splintered rib shredding a nerve. That time, he'd struck her with a rolling pin for burning his eggs. I've smelled her warm, metallic blood as it pooled on the floor, the time he straddled her and sliced her wrist with a straight razor. Later, in the examination room, he'd said, "she cut herself."

But no more. Enough. I bow my head. *Agios o Theos. Agios ischiros. Agios athanatos, eleison eimas.*

The locked door is solid oak a full two inches thick, but feels like heavy smoke as I close my eyes and step through. I grow instantly faint, for each time I take angelic form, my mortal body grows weaker.

I open my eyes to the faded ochre light of a filthy leaded-glass electrolier. Henri hulks in the shadow of the foyer, blood-soaked briefs stained with urine. The air's scented by well-cooked beef, bay leaf, and the sweat of rage. Weeping, he limps from darkness into anemic light, waving a cast-iron frying pan like a signalman flagging a train.

"You're broken," I say.

Tears pool in jaundiced pockets below his eyes and drip from the long gray hairs poking from his nose. His ears are stuffed with wet, sour fur, each eyebrow a woven mass of curling strands like briars.

"Your mind and body are spent, Henri. We can do nothing more."

He totters, convulses, and falls backward, striking his head against the amber varnished banister. "Help me," he whispers.

A woman's voice twitters down the stairs. "I'm hurt."

"I'm coming, Irene," I say, walking toward Henri's half-naked, sallow body, slumped on the terrazzo.

"Forgive me," he says, eyes focused on the onyx clock perched on the mantle, its hands welded by rust.

"Forgiving is not my job. But this is." I open my left hand. A freezing white flame sputters to life in my palm.

"Time to rest, Henri," I say. My hand becomes fog and sinks into his chest. I grip his heart and squeeze, then whisper an *aitesis* for peace, pardon, and forgiveness. *Kirie eleison.*

My left hand closes. The light goes out. Henri smiles; a fat tear rolls out of one eye as he expels a last agonal breath.

May God have mercy on your soul.

Chapter 52

My bedroom draws itself around me in a perfect cube, each wall streaked with long shadows. Yellow tulips nod on the dresser, shy heads drooping over the milk glass vase.

I slip back into John Breard's arms, the sleigh bed catching my weight, its crisp cotton pillows gardenia scented.

The phone rings. Jesus. Five seconds of comfort. That was nice.

John gropes for the receiver and cradles it between chin and shoulder, his other hand gripping the brass base. "Hello?" He yawns silently. "Address? Oh. I'm sorry." He sighs. "Well, bound to happen, right? Fifteen minutes."

"Irene and Henri," I murmur into the pillow.

He's already pouring himself into black jeans pre-assembled with belt, keys, badge, and wallet. He straps on a shoulder holster, checks the magazine of the Glock .45 pistol, then re-seats it with a click. He pulls on a black bomber jacket, Det. Breard stitched in gray letters on the chest pocket.

I slide into green scrubs and scuffed black clogs. My equipment—badge, toe tags, needles, syringes, vials, death certificates for the state of Louisiana, and the safety-sealed bags labeled *toxic materials/universal precautions*—are always stored in a tackle box in the trunk of my car, along with a fluorescent-orange medical examiner's vest.

John grabs me by the hair. Candles flicker in his irises. As he kisses me he tongues a peppermint Lifesaver into my mouth.

I cross myself three times, right over left, climb into the car and call, "See you there."

#   #   #

At 623 Saint Charles, the EMS and Forensic trucks have already pulled into the porte-cochere, lights strobing blue onto windows and stone walls. I park on a patch of frozen grass next to John's white Vespa, careful not to nudge Ruth's marble pedestal with my bumper.

Snow falls in goose down clumps. Neighbors huddle on the lawn, rolled up in blankets, whispers and sobs muffled by wool.

The icy crunch beneath my heels echoes into the swale below. Irene's stone house stands in a grove of walnut trees, its colonnaded silhouette softened by layers of snow. Rime slicks the copper gutters; icicles hang from every eave.

I reach for the cold knob again and startle at my distorted reflection. I look older in the leaded glass inset panel. I hesitate, then turn the knob like any reasonable person. John steps up behind me, his familiar musky sleep-smell arriving first.

"One's under the stairs, the other's in the upstairs bedroom. Looks rough," says a tall paramedic. "T.O.D. less than two hours ago. Still warm."

Inside, I set my tackle box next to Henri. His corpse lays supine, limbs shriveled and discolored. Doughy and cool, but not cold. What's left of his energy flows without resistance through my latex gloves, sending his current deep into my bones, like a drum roll.

"Huh. Peaceful," says the paramedic, shrugging.

Henri's belly is taut with fluid, pushing a small hernia through his torn umbilicus. Retracting his eyelids, I look into one pupil and then the other. Surrounding the black discs, his corneas are yellow as buttercups. I tap his abdomen, then open his mouth. Six missing teeth in the lower jaw, as though he'd once been kicked by a horse. No canines.

"Sad. He was my teacher at the French school when I was a kid,"
says the paramedic. "You thinking liver disease?"

"For sure. But what killed him, we'll figure out at autopsy."

"Persephone," calls my tough blonde assistant from the foyer.
Helen enters in jump boots and a vest like mine, her glistening badge
stamped Office of the Chief Medical Examiner.

"In here. Two D.B.s.," I yell back. "The other's upstairs." My
hands shake. Sweat plasters the scrubs to my skin. My shoulder blades
feel heavy where my wings were. It's not quite fear, but that haunting
awareness that every time I take angelic form, death comes closer.
"Have the guys help you bag the hands and feet. Turn him over. Take
pictures. Meet me in the bedroom."

I close Henri's eyelids, then reach into my tackle box and retrieve
a lighted magnifier, noticing the frying pan has skidded beneath a
marble-topped table. "John. That's evidence. Bag it."

I search Henri's chest wall, looking for marks. As suspected,
none. Only sick, yellow skin and tiny capillaries from years of
drinking grogue and cognac and chain-smoking Turkish cigarettes.

"Helen." I offer the dermatoscope. "See any marks on his chest?"

"What?" She frowns, looking down. "Nah. Just lots of hair and
age spots. Old bruises. What're you thinking? Why should there be
marks? Persephone, you don't look so good."

"Just tired. Maybe I'm getting a cold."

When I open my jacket, I nearly collapse from the sudden loss of
body heat as I fumble in a pocket for a tissue. I fingertip my wrist and
count beats, then press both palms against my eyes and cough. I inhale
as deep as the drawstring ties of my scrubs allow, then rub my neck in
the groove where a pulse bounds, until the pounding in my head slows.

"Persephone," John whispers.

"Hey," calls the paramedic from upstairs. "Better check out this
one up here. You ain't seen nothin' yet."

Oh, yes I have. "John, come with me, please," I say. "Carry my
box."

I trudge the stairs with a hand on the rail. Under the Venetian
pendant lamp suspended from a cciling medallion of art nouveau lilies,
John ascends like Apollo leaping the marble steps of Olympus, two at
a time, ice-blown hair flowing behind him.

"I got your back. I got your front. I got your side," he says. "And I got your box," he whispers into my ear. "Dead or alive."

Refusing to pant, I hold my breath and run up the last risers, ignoring the cramp in my side.

Heavy burgundy draperies tied back with tassels shroud the edges of the window opposite the fireplace. The sconces have been dimmed, crystal fobs jaundiced with cigarette tar. The rusted hands of the marble clock on the stained mantle point to eleven, as they have for years.

I check my watch. Five twenty-three.

The bed is neatly made, covered with a lone star quilt. A chinoise dinner tray lies overturned, beef and fries scattered across the Afghan carpet. Bay leaves are glued to the wall by splatterings of gravy.

"Look here," says the paramedic, hovering over Irene LeBas, whose small frail body lies stretched out on a loveseat, eyelids closed, hands cupped, right over left, ready to receive last rites. "Ever seen anything like this?" He whistles. "Holy Mother. Whoa."

A foot-long ice dagger teeters upright from Irene's chest. As we watch, it slowly arcs from her body, as if spat out, hits the floor, and shatters into melting crystals. Dark water rises from the dead woman's vacated depths, gurgles, then pools at the mouth of her wound.

"God," said the paramedic. "Did you see that?"

"Yes," I say. And more.

All of my life has led to this moment. To these broken shards, these gleaming portents, the susurrus whispers of my name: Persephone. Persephone. Like the subtle hum of waves on a beach, when I was only a child. Even then, I could feel the air thick as honey with the souls of the discarnate....

Chapter 53

John kisses me, and lingers as if to murmur a secret. His breath warms my cheek.

"What is it?" I say.

"I hear a tuning fork that has been struck upon a star," he whispers, and kisses me again.

Two weeks since I first sprouted wings, I lean against a Doric column outside LeBas House and scratch my shoulder blades against its cold fluted surface. Those wings are itching to unfurl.

John dashes across the slate path carrying my tackle box, his black duffle, and camera. The street lights of Carondolet fade as dawn creeps toward the porte-cochere.

A copper hummingbird feeder hangs from the blue painted ceiling of the portico. A lone viridian bird hovers, wings humming as he sips. His delicate sides are washed with cinnamon, his throat marked by rose-red iridescent feathers.

John leaps across the footstones and takes my hand, then presses it to his flushed cheek, coarse with stubble. "I'm going to take you home and feed you. Then put you to bed."

"Let's walk a little first." I lean against him, shivering. The hot lead in the pit of my stomach cools to warmth and runs up my spine. He embraces, then leads me across the garden, past the fountain of Ruth pouring water from an amphora, through the stand of roses of Sharon.

Across the street, the man in the black-billed hat glides back and forth on the porch swing, studying constellations. He meets my gaze, nods. Touches the brim of his hat and smiles. Azrafel is smoking his favorite cigar, a Cohiba Especiale. My gaze meets his and locks for a moment. It's been two weeks since I've seen him last. He knows I want to fly.

John and I thread our way through the boxwood maze, a thin crust of snow crisp beneath our soles. The garden, at first black as a catacomb, is beginning to wake. The velvet sky is dusty with mist. The chatters of swallows and calls of robins sing farewell to the copper moon.

We find ourselves in an outdoor room deep in the maze's green confusion. The walls are ancient camellias, and in the corners, grandmother magnolias loom like chaperones of the garden. His beaming eyes are moist as he says, "I need to keep you alive."

He smooths my hair and kisses my cheek. Our breaths make smoky circles that coil together into the disappearing darkness.

He cups my face in his hands. The persimmon moon hangs low behind him. "Let me show you something." He reaches into his breast pocket and takes out a condor feather. Carefully holds it up to the moonlight, rotating the quill. The edges bristle with blue light.

"Sometimes I find your feathers by the window. Sometimes on your pillow," he whispers in a woman-soft tone. "They seem to help me find misplaced things. I've been collecting them. I'm going to make a coat of feathers. Like Tehuelche medicine men, who make serapes to find lost treasures."

He lifts my chin again and runs the feather across my cheek and lips. I swallow, melting each time he caresses me with my own shed feather.

I think of cresting the highest peaks of places while he slept—ignorant, I'd assumed of my travels.

On Carondolet, someone is burning apple wood in a stove, engendering a mouth-watering smell of fresh sweet blossoms after a rain.

"You believe in me, then," I say. "Well, I want to hang onto life for as long as possible. You're my anchor to this earthly existence, John."

"I know," he says. "So show me, please."

To reveal then what I most fully am, I step backward five paces into a bower of holly vapor lit by moon glow, lifting a hand to freeze him where he stands. I crouch and dig my fingers into the melting snow and the wet grass under it. My chest heaves. On my shoulder blades, nubs sprout through my clothes. He gasps as I rise and spread my wings, like an accordion opening, each feather fluttering and luminous in the pre-dawn breeze. He steps forward, reaches out and strokes one extended wing. His hand against its glossy black is like a five-pointed star fallen out of the sky.

He wants to go on this journey with me. It is a fearful thing to love what death can touch.

About the Author

Aphrodite Anagnost is a first-generation Greek-American Maniot, descended from the ancient Dorian tribe of Spartans who hail from Areopolis. Her first employer was her horse riding teacher; and her second, her parents, who entertained Vegas acts in their barn-turned-cosmopolitan-restaurant next to the once-famous Warwick Musical Summer Theatre. It was at the Country Inn Restaurant where Aphrodite learned to cook a lobster, mix a martini, serve celebrities, mingle with the Rhode Island mafia, wash dishes, and swab the deck. Later, her mother, Panagiota, gave her the American name "Frances" to make growing up easier.

She has studied world religions, including the ancient Pagan practices of her ancestral clan of Maniates, and is a devout Orthodox Church member, though she believes all religions seek the truth. Later Dr. Frances Aphrodite Anagnost Willams worked as a laboratory assistant, chemistry tutor, dressage horse trainer, family physician, obesity specialist, hospitalist, medical examiner, and hospice director. She lives on a horse farm in rural Virginia with her horse-listener husband and extraordinary sons.

Acknowledgements

I wish to thank my Eastern Shore's Own writers' group, led by Lenore Hart and Dave Poyer; my poetry teacher, Robert P Arthur; the Right Reverend Mihael Montagnus Plettner, for his wonderful and offbeat contribution to my Orthodox education; and all persons who left a warm imprint on my youth, whose personalities permeate this story. Thank you to the Virginia Center for the Creative Arts and to LifeScience visiting artist programs for their fellowship support.

And thank you to Richard, Jack, and Max for putting up with me.

About the Photographer

Richard Hatch purchased his first camera in 1972 at the age of 15 and has made images ever since. With an immersion into the digital realm of photography beginning in 1998, Hatch recently brought the world of film back into his life.

He feels photography is a tool which allows us to look deeper into the world. We think; we see.

> "Through our eyes we may only see a small portion of what passes before us. An image captures a moment in time and
> allows us to process detail and experience emotions not always available by other means."

Richard and his wife Karen live, work, and play on the Eastern Shore of Virginia.